A STEP IN THE DARK

Judith Lennox

headline

First published in 2006 by Headline Review
An imprint of HEADLINE PUBLISHING GROUP

First published in paperback in 2007
by Headline Review

12

ISBN 978 0 7553 3547 3 (A format)
ISBN 978 0 7553 3132 1 (B format)

Typeset in Joanna by Palimpsest Book Production Limited,
Grangemouth, Stirlingshire
Printed and bound in Great Britain by
CPI Group (UK) Ltd, Croydon, CR0 4YY

Headline's policy is to use papers that are natural, renewable and
recyclable products and made from wood grown in
sustainable forests. The logging and manufacturing processes
are expected to conform to the environmental
regulations of the country of origin.

HEADLINE PUBLISHING GROUP
A division of Hachette Livre UK Ltd
338 Euston Road
London NW1 3BH

www.reviewbooks.co.uk
www.hodderheadline.com

To my daughter-in-law, Lizzie.

Part One

Bess Ravenhart

1914–1919

Chapter One

On the boat, sailing from India, Bess Ravenhart thought about her child.

His white-gold hair, his gap-toothed smile, his plump hands clutching a leaf, a nut, to place on her lap. His bubble of laughter when the nut rolled to the floor, and she caught him up in her arms and covered him with kisses.

Gazing out over the intense blue of the Indian Ocean, it occurred to her that her marriage had begun and ended with laughter. 'I heard you laugh. That was what made me look at you,' Jack Ravenhart had once told her. 'And when I saw you, I knew that I would marry you.'

They had met on an ink-black evening, when the Mall in Simla was brightly lit and busy and the night air was heavy with the scent of woodsmoke and spices. Bess had been staying in Simla with friends while her widowed father was away on business. All Simla society paraded on the Mall. Assignations were made, quarrels picked and mended, love affairs begun with the flash of an eye.

Bess could never afterwards recall why she had been laughing. But for the rest of her life she remembered her first sight of tall, handsome Jack Ravenhart. He was on the far side of the Mall, mounted on a restless black horse. There was the glint of spurs and tunic buttons, and his eyes following her as she walked past, her laughter dying a little in the heat of his gaze. On his face she recognized the expression that soon became familiar to her, that characteristic mixture of greed and delight and recklessness.

They married three months later. Jack swept aside all objections. He wanted her, and he was in the habit of having whatever he wanted. At eighteen years old, Bess found herself Jack Ravenhart's wife and the daughter-in-law of Fenton and Cora Ravenhart. She and Jack lived in a bungalow in Simla with a staff of a dozen servants and a stable full of polo ponies and hunters.

A year later their son, Frazer, was born. Once Bess had recovered from the birth, their life seemed to go on much as before. Frazer's ayah looked after him while Bess and Jack went to fancy-dress balls and picnics and hunted and attended the races. But Bess knew that something had changed, though she kept it to herself. Dressing for the evening, she would steal a few moments to watch her baby as he slept in his crib, absorbed by the plump curve of his cheek and the fat star shapes of his hands, until Jack, coming to look for her, hurried her out of the house, still buttoning her gloves or pinning up her hair.

To be with Jack Ravenhart was an adventure, and she enjoyed every minute of it. He never refused a dare; he

4

sought out excitement and danger. They laughed and they danced, heedless and exhilarated, throughout the two years of their marriage. They spurred each other on; in Jack, she found someone whose appetite for life matched her own. They were two of a kind, living for the moment, careless of the future.

The laughter stopped only on the day he died. It was dawn, and they were riding in the hills above Simla. He challenged her to a race, and her sudden fear, her premonition – the unfamiliar stony path, the mist that swirled round the pines – made her cry out to him: *No, Jack!*

Her words hung ragged in the air as he spurred his horse to a gallop along the narrow track. Before the horse threw him, the last sounds she heard were the drum of hooves and, from a distance, his laughter.

A broken branch across the path, they told her, and the mist disguising the edge of a steep escarpment. The fall had broken Jack Ravenhart's neck. And with his fall, the long, intoxicating party that had been their life in Simla came to a sudden, shocking end.

His absence rubbed the colour from her life. At night, alone in bed, she still seemed to hear his laughter.

'What do you intend to do now?' Cora Ravenhart, Jack's mother, asked Bess, on the day after the funeral.

Cora had called at the bungalow that Bess and Jack had shared. Cora was tall and imposing, her bosom one great, undivided mass sloping into a tightly corseted waist. Her black clothing showed up her pallor and deepened the furrows that grief had carved into her face.

'I thought . . .' began Bess, but the sentence trailed off as she glimpsed traps, pitfalls.

Mrs Ravenhart did not sit, but moved round the room, her fingertips brushing against a vase, a length of curtain, a carved wooden screen. 'I'm afraid it isn't possible for you to remain here, Elizabeth. Jack's affairs were not left in good order. There are a great many debts. Your house-keeping bills . . . his mess bills . . .' Cora's blue eyes rested fleetingly, disdainfully, on Bess as she added, 'The life you led . . . you were living beyond your means.'

Bess murmured, 'I hadn't realized.'

'Hadn't you? A cavalry officer's pay is not generous. You could not have lived as you did without our help – our *considerable* help. This bungalow . . .'

'Our bungalow?'

'It is Fenton's, of course.' Fenton Ravenhart, Jack's father, was a man as cold and distant as Jack had been warm and generous.

Cora paused, her gaze caught by the photograph of Jack on top of the piano. When she spoke again, her voice was harder. 'Everything belongs to Fenton. You own nothing. And we really can't be expected to keep up two house-holds in Simla now. The expense . . .'

Bess blurted out, 'Have you come here to tell me that Frazer and I must live with you?'

A trill of laughter. 'I don't think that would do, do you, Elizabeth? I must be frank. I don't think that would suit either of us.'

The dislike in Cora Ravenhart's eyes, carefully veiled in Jack's lifetime, was naked now. 'I assumed,' said Cora softly, 'that you would go back to your father. He would take you in, presumably?'

'Yes . . . I don't know . . .' It was now almost two years since she had last seen her father, Joe Cadogan. Joe was a wanderer and a dreamer, always searching for the new venture that would make his fortune. He had returned to the country of his birth shortly after Bess had married.

She said, 'My father's living in England now.'

Her mother-in-law was looking out of the window, her silhouette black against the blurred blue-greens of the garden. 'Please don't think me ungenerous, Elizabeth. Whatever our differences, you were Jack's wife. I am here to offer you help. I will pay your passage to England, and I will take care of Frazer until you are able to send for him.'

I will take care of Frazer. Swallowing her first angry retort, Bess managed to say coolly, 'Thank you, but I'll take Frazer to England with me.'

Mrs Ravenhart sat down. 'Do you know where your father is living?'

'Naturally.' But Bess was aware of a sudden uncertainty; it had been months – as many as six months, perhaps – since she had heard from her father. Though she had written to the hotel in which he was living to tell him of Jack's death, so far she had received nothing, neither a note nor a telegram, in return.

'Do you know whether his residence is suitable for a child? No? I suspected not.' Cora gave a small, tight smile. 'After all, I hear that he left India under something of a . . . a cloud, shall we say.' Mrs Ravenhart's voice dropped to a murmur. 'There were gambling debts, I believe.'

7

Bess had to dig her nails into her palms to suppress her rising temper.

Cora Ravenhart went on, 'I only want what's best for Jack's son. As you do too, I trust. Which is why I am suggesting that Frazer remains here while you travel to England to make arrangements. We have been intending for some time to visit Fenton's elder brother, Sheldon, in Scotland. Everything is arranged – we will sail next April and we plan to stay with Sheldon for the summer. We can bring Frazer with us. By then you should have set up a suitable establishment in which to bring up a child. In the meantime, I shall write and send you news of him, of course. I'm sure it will all work very well.'

Bess cried out, 'But I can't just *leave* him! He's all I have left!'

'Frazer is a delicate child,' said Mrs Ravenhart. Now, her voice was cold and hard, like steel. 'To take him from India to damp, chilly rooms in England might ruin his health. And your separation will only be a matter of months, after all. You mustn't think of yourself, Elizabeth. You must think of Frazer, of what's best for him. He is all that matters now.'

India had almost vanished, but Bess remained sitting on the deck of the P&O liner, her gaze fixed on the compressed charcoal band of the coast. It was the first time she had left India, where she had been born and brought up, and she found herself thinking of race meetings at Annandale, with the horses' breath clouding the air and the tall pines and deodars black against a pearl-white sky. She thought of parties at the bungalow – the thrill of a seance and the shrieking silliness of games of truth, kiss and dare. And the card games in the early hours of the morning, in a blue haze of cigarette smoke, a crumpled pyramid of fifty-rupee notes in the centre of the green baize-covered table. And she remembered the pinks and yellows of the girls' silk dresses, the purples and oranges of hibiscus and bougainvillaea, and the gold of the sun on the white peaks of the Himalayas. And she thought of Frazer, of the first time she had held him in her arms and looked down at his tiny, crumpled face and his unfocused, knowing, dark blue eyes.

Seeing her black dress, and that she was alone, a couple called Mr and Mrs Williamson had taken her under their wing. Mrs Williamson was kind and vague and untidy, her conversation a succession of breathy, unfinished phrases. 'This war . . . so awful . . . those poor boys . . .' she said, and shook her head, and Bess recalled that, on the other side of the world, a war had broken out. Not that it mattered to her. Everyone said it would be over by Christmas.

Mrs Williamson spoke to her of her son, in an army training camp in England, and of her two married daughters, one in India, the other living in the Williamsons' home town of Edinburgh. She showed Bess photographs of solemn-faced grandchildren, festooned in lace frocks or clad in sailor suits. In the evenings, Bess and the Williamsons played games of whist and piquet for pennies – except on Sundays, of course. On board ship no one played cards on a Sunday. Or danced or read a novel or even smiled, Bess thought desperately. Sundays passed slowly, in a state of scratchy, furious boredom, nothing to be found to relieve the tedium in the wide blue of the Indian Ocean or the intense heat of the Red Sea.

Soldiers joined them at Port Said, where the ship stopped to re-coal. The bolder ones came to speak to Bess as she sat on deck, sheltered from the fierce sun by an awning. Their uniform buttons and epaulettes flashed gold; talking to them, she had to put up her hand to shelter her gaze from their brightness, and the flash of light on the sea. Their fingertips twirled the ends of their moustaches and their eyes feasted on her, an oasis in a desert. If she put her mind to it, she thought, she could find herself another husband before the ship reached Southampton.

At night, in her cabin, she took out her most precious possessions and placed them on the narrow bed. Her cashmere shawls, with their rich swirling patterns of blues and ochres and rusts, the heady colours of India; the necklaces and bracelets and brooches that Jack had given her on birthdays and anniversaries; photographs of Jack and Frazer, and a jacket that she had knitted for her baby son. Pressing the jacket against her face, closing her eyes, she breathed in the powdery scent of him, still woven into the stitches.

Sitting on the bed, looking at the photographs, she acknowledged that her mother-in-law had only forced her to face the reality of her situation. She must endure this temporary separation for Frazer's sake. In a week's time she would be in England. She would go to the hotel where her father was staying and her father would help her to rent a house. Then she would write to Mrs Ravenhart and ask her to bring Frazer to England without further delay. Or perhaps her father would pay her return passage to India and she would go back and fetch her baby herself.

Yet the sense of unease she had felt ever since she had accepted Cora Ravenhart's offer to look after Frazer remained undiminished. She remembered how deeply Cora had loved Jack, her only child. How, when they were together, her gaze had followed him round the room. How Cora had patted the sofa for Jack to sit beside her, how she had softened when he was there, and how she had smiled for Jack, only Jack.

The ship docked at Southampton. Steam billowed from funnels and porters rushed from ship to train, pushing mountains of luggage. It was November, and the sky was an iron-grey mass of cloud. Bess shivered. As she left the ship, reaching the end of the gangway, she found herself suddenly hesitant to put her foot on dry land. A step in the dark, she thought; her first step into a new country, a new life.

She parted from the Williamsons at Waterloo station, their shipboard acquaintance ending in hugs and cries of good wishes and promises to write. In the cab, she stared out of the window at the London streets, her gaze darting this way and that, trying to take it all in. So many motor cars and trams, so many people. Though it was only mid-afternoon, the skies were already darkening. The bare branches of the trees loomed through an orange-grey fog and all sorts of unfamiliar smells hung in the thick, soupy air. As the cab turned the corner of a street, the fog thinned for a moment and Bess glimpsed the black slick of the Thames. She could hear the hooting of foghorns, the cries of street sellers. And it was cold, so much colder than a summer's evening in Simla. The icy damp seeped through her thin coat and her fingers chilled inside her cotton gloves. I am in London, she thought, with a thrill of excitement. I am in London, city of wealth and power and plenty, the greatest city in the Empire.

Outside her father's hotel, she fumbled with the unfamiliar coins to pay the cab driver. The foyer of the hotel was marbled and cavernous. Palms in brass pots drooped over polished floors, and gilt mirrors reflected the flickering light of the chandeliers. Ladies in beaded and ostrich-feathered evening gowns descended the stairs; through an open doorway, Bess glimpsed gentlemen lounging in leather chairs. They smoked and read their newspapers and summoned the waiter with a snap of their fingers.

She asked for the number of her father's room at the reception desk. The clerk studied a large, leather-bound book. Then he looked up at her.

'I'm afraid we have no one of that name staying in the hotel, madam.'

Bess insisted he check again. He ran his fingertip down the column of names. 'No. There is no Mr Cadogan here.'

'But there must be!'

'No, madam. I'm sorry, madam.' The book closed with a smack.

She stood in the foyer beside her luggage. What now? She tried to think; then a voice interrupted her thoughts.

'Perhaps I may be able to help, my dear.'

The man who had addressed her was tall, white-haired and florid, much the same age as her father, she guessed. 'Harris is the name,' he said, bowing to her. 'Dempster

Harris. I reside at this hotel. And what may I call you, my dear?'

Bess told him her name. '*Mrs Ravenhart*,' he repeated, luxuriating over the syllables. '*Enchanté.*' He kissed her hand. 'You must excuse my impertinence, my dear Mrs Ravenhart, but I couldn't help overhearing you asking for Joe Cadogan.'

'Do you know him?'

'I most certainly do. Dear old Joe.' Mr Harris smiled. 'Always such good company.'

'He's my father,' she explained.

His eyes widened slightly. 'You haven't the look of him.'

'I'm told I take after my mother. I thought my father was staying here. Do you know where I might find him, Mr Harris?'

'Rather lost touch, I'm afraid.' He looked regretful. 'Joe left here after his accident.'

'Accident?'

'Knocked down by a tram, poor chap. London is quite impossible these days. You take your life in your hands whenever you cross the road. And poor old Joe, coming here from the tropics . . . well, he wasn't used to it, was he?' He shook his head. 'There, there, you mustn't be alarmed, my dear. Walking wounded by the time he left the hotel. Perhaps he took himself off for a spot of sun. Recuperative, don't you know.'

'I have to find him.' Her father would help her make a home in this dark, cold city. And she must have a home for Frazer.

He glanced at her luggage. 'Have you travelled far, Mrs Ravenhart?'

'From India,' she said.

'*India*.' He beamed. 'You must tell me all about it. I know, we'll have a spot of supper. No, I insist. And then I'll rack my brains and try and think where dear old Joe might have gone. One thinks so much better over a spot of supper, don't you agree?'

In the hotel dining room, Bess's natural optimism returned, and she felt intoxicated: by the champagne Dempster Harris ordered, and by the opulence of her surroundings. The silks and satins of the ladies' gowns – rich crimsons, sapphire blues and violets – contrasted with the khaki of their army officer escorts. These women had a polish and elegance that made the ladies of Simla seem in retrospect old-fashioned and provincial.

Mr Harris sat back in his chair. 'And what do you think of London, Mrs Ravenhart? Are you enjoying yourself?'

'Oh, *enormously*!' She smiled at him. 'And thank you so much for supper, Mr Harris. It's splendid.'

'The pleasure's all mine.' He gave a little cough. 'Your husband . . . ?' he enquired tactfully, glancing at her black dress. 'He has passed on, I fear.'

'Jack died in a riding accident.'

'How frightful . . .' There was a gleam of interest in his eyes. 'Leaving you to soldier on on your own, you poor little thing, alone and unprotected.' He squeezed her hand. 'Tell you what, how about a spot of dancing when we're finished here? That'd cheer you up. I know a smashing little place.'

She reclaimed her hand, murmuring polite expressions of regret.

By the time they parted, Bess had the names of her

father's friends and tradesmen and the addresses of his favourite clubs and pubs. In the room she had taken in the hotel, she studied the handful of letters her father had written to her since he had left for England – he had been only a fitful correspondent – for clues to his whereabouts.

Then she stood for a long time at the window. Passers-by were still drifting along the pavements below: a soldier, his arm round his girl's waist; a couple in evening dress, stepping out of a cab. Her gaze moved from the street lamps that glowed through the fog to the buildings, so massive and numerous, that jutted above the skyline. And she wished that she could soar like a bird over those houses and shops and offices, swooping from one London street to another, peering through windows and down chimney pots until she found him.

The next few days reminded Bess of the treasure hunts she and Jack had liked to devise in Simla. Tracking her quarry took her from cafes with private booths lined with crimson plush banquettes to dining rooms where white-aproned waiters rushed to and fro with plates of chops and tankards of ale. She called at red-brick villas in sedate streets, where she spoke to widows and grass widows of fading pretti-ness. The widows talked fondly of Joe Cadogan before shaking their heads and saying, no, they couldn't tell her where Joe was living now, but when she found him, would she kindly remind him about the ten shillings he had borrowed.

She visited pubs and betting shops, where the only women in the establishment served behind the counters, and the men eyed her and called out to her. She answered back smartly and did not pull down her veil. She would not see the world through a mesh of black. She travelled in cabs and buses and underground trains; she walked for miles and miles. She was always cold, no matter how many coats and stockings and gloves she heaped on, and she grew increasingly troubled when, as her search continued, she found herself walking down ever meaner, narrower streets.

In a street market in Spitalfields, barefoot children gathered fallen apples and cabbage leaves from beneath the stalls, and a tramp slept in a doorway, a bundle of tattered rags.

Bess knocked at the door of a lodging house. To one side of it was a furrier and to the other was a herbalist. Musky scents from the herbalist cut through the sourer stench of the streets, reminding her briefly, painfully, of India.

The landlady showed Bess to an upstairs room. An old man was sitting in a chair by the fire; she did not at first recognize him. Then he looked up and smiled.

'Bess,' he said. 'My Bess. What on earth are you doing here, dear girl?'

The accident had knocked him back a bit, her father told her, but he was as fit as a fiddle now. She did not believe him. His skin was yellowish, a legacy of the malaria he had contracted in India a long time ago. When he coughed, his handkerchief was flecked with blood. His years in England had diminished him, as if the dark and the cold had drained him of vigour. He was pleased to see her, he said; times had been hard, and most of his old friends in England were dead or had forgotten him, and the doctor's bills had left him rather short, so if she could lend him a guinea or two . . .

Her letter telling him of Jack's death had not reached him. When she explained to her father that she had recently been widowed, his eyes filled with shock and bewilderment. 'That poor boy . . . so young . . . my dear Bess.'

When, later, she left the lodging house, she had to bite back the feeling of panic that had come over her, finding her father old and ill in that small, comfortless room.

Back at the hotel she took a star sapphire pendant and a gold bracelet from her jewellery case. She found Dempster Harris in the smoking room. 'Forgive me for troubling you, Mr Harris,' she said, 'but I wondered whether you could tell me where I might sell these.' She showed him the jewels.

He took out a leather billfold; she heard the rustle of banknotes. 'There's no need for that, my dear Mrs Ravenhart. Always happy to help a lady as lovely as you.' His long, yellowing teeth showed beneath the fringes of his moustache as he held out the notes to her. 'And you needn't worry about paying back my little loan. It would give me great pleasure if you were to accept my offer of . . .' he searched for the word, 'of *protection*.'

She thought of Frazer. Frazer in her arms, reaching up to pull the silver combs from her hair. Frazer in the bungalow garden, wide-eyed with wonder at every bird and flower. Take the money Dempster Harris held out to her and she could send for Frazer tomorrow.

Yet she murmured her refusal. She could manage; she would find a way. She need not make *that* sort of bargain.

Dempster Harris sighed. 'A pity. We could have had such

17

fun.' His eyes softened. 'You remind me of a girl I once knew. Black hair and blue eyes, just like you.'

With the money she received from the sale of her jewellery, Bess rented a furnished terraced house in Ealing. She engaged a maid-of-all-work to do the housework and washing and placed an order at the grocer's.

She wrote to Cora Ravenhart, in India, asking for news of Frazer. Wrapped up in an eiderdown because of the cold, her thoughts wandered. She thought of her childhood in the cantonments of Madras during her father's army days. She remembered the years after her mother had died: they had travelled to the hill country after Joe Cadogan decided to earn his fortune planting indigo. After the plantation failed, they had returned to the searing heat of the plains, where her father had tried his hand as a merchant, selling teak and mahogany and Indian cottons and silks. During those years, a succession of aunties had come to stay at their various bungalows. If she had become Dempster Harris's mistress, she would have ended up much like one of the aunties, a transient creature, only of value so long as her looks lasted and she could amuse and entertain.

Bess had never known a settled home; all too often, her comfort and well-being had been dependent on the turn of a card or the swift run of a horse. It had been a change-able, rackety sort of life. Sometimes she had had a wardrobe full of silk dresses, at other times she had sweated over her needle to let out frocks long grown out of. She had had a freedom that few other Anglo-Indian girls of her age were permitted. No one had stopped her roaming through the bazaars or bathing in the stream with the native children, clad only in her drawers and camisole. No one had taught her that she must not roar with laughter at her father's friends' ribald jokes, and no one had explained to her that when she was in company she must sit, hands clasped, ankles crossed, and not speak until she was spoken to.

She had been staying in Simla with friends of her father's when she had met Jack. It had been in Simla, that tight little capital of Anglo-India in the hills, that she had first become aware of the power she possessed. Dressed up in borrowed finery, introduced to society, she had noticed how men's eyes followed her as she danced round a ballroom or rode down the Mall. All their desire had been distilled in Jack Ravenhart's hungry gaze. She had married him because how else could she get on in life? How else might she survive?

Had she loved Jack? She had never been sure. She had liked him enormously. And she had desired him. She hadn't known about desire until she had met Jack. Did liking and desire add up to love? She did not know. She knew only that she would have given a great deal to have Jack in bed beside her now, to roll over and find him looking at her with that greedy, devouring expression. She remembered how he had liked to run his fingertips the length of her body, tracing its contours, as though he was making a map of her. She remembered how his touch had drawn delight from her, and how, when he was away, she had longed for that delight.

She dashed away her tears. Tears were futile, looking back was a waste of time. She caught sight of the envelope on the dressing table. There were things she had left out of her letter to Cora Ravenhart. That her father was ill. That he was penniless. That England was not as she had assumed it to be, that it was too cold, that it rained too much, and that she had not expected those barefoot children, those heaps of rags huddled in doorways.

When there was no reply to her letter, she wrote again. The letter had got lost, she reasoned; it was a long way from London to India. Throughout the winter, as the war on the Western Front settled into a murderous stalemate, she wrote to Cora Ravenhart again and again. Cora never wrote back. The darkening of the city, as the street lamps were dimmed for fear of air raids, echoed the darkening of Bess's heart. Questions haunted her. Why did Mrs Ravenhart not write? Was Frazer pining for her? He had been thirteen months old when she had left India – how could he possibly understand why she had had to leave him? Worse, what if he was ill? Had Mrs Ravenhart not written because she could not bear to impart bad news? Something seemed to grip like a tightly wound spring inside her. Frazer's absence gnawed at her heart, shredding its surface, leaving it raw and bleeding.

Her rings and bracelets paid for her father's doctor's bills, rent and food. Each piece of jewellery contained a memory, trapped in a moonstone or frozen in the cold flare of a diamond. The winter passed slowly, marked off by the chapters of the book she read aloud to her father and by the hands of cards they played. The fog and rain seemed to surround the city like a palisade, cutting her off from the

20

life she had once known. In the coldest months, she dreamed of the monkeys at Hanuman's shrine on the hill of Jakko. The children of Simla had fed them biscuits; in her dream the monkeys rushed endlessly through pine and honey-suckle, their chatter and the patter of their feet filling the air. Running with them, she shook off the mixture of grief and frustration that was with her throughout the winter.

More and more often she dreamed of Frazer. Sometimes he did not know her and turned away from her; some-times he was oddly altered and she did not recognize him. Once she dreamed that she was going home. When she reached Simla, she found the bungalow empty; outside, looking down the Mall, she caught sight of a tall, golden-haired young man, who turned and smiled and waved a farewell to her before he walked away.

In this cold country, all the front doors remained shut, and people did not gather in the street as they had in India, talking long after the sun went down. She sensed her neighbours' disapproval of her in their tight, frosty smiles, and in the lack of any social invitations. When she was lonely, she spoke to the man who swept the streets or the woman behind the counter in the sweet shop. On the tram, she chatted to the soldiers who, their arms in slings or band-ages round their heads, were in London convalescing from their wounds.

Sometime in the spring of 1915, she accepted that her father was dying. It was around the time of the second battle of Ypres, when German troops used chlorine gas for the first time. Like the gassed soldiers, her father now fought for every breath. Sitting at his bedside, holding his hand, she heard his ragged lungs search for air, and she witnessed the slow, relentless stripping away of the spirit and optimism that had always been a part of him. Far better to die from a fall like Jack, Bess thought: the rush of cold air, the clean end.

Her father died on the first day of May. There was blossom on the trees, and, for the first time since Bess had set foot in England, a flicker of warmth in the air. After the funeral, she sorted through her father's belongings: a teak elephant; a brass lantern; a jewelled dagger, which he claimed had been given to him by an Indian prince.

Because her father had died of tuberculosis, his clothes and bedding were burned. Bess sold his small library to a second-hand bookshop, the teak elephant and the jewelled dagger to an antique shop in Belgravia. She sold several of her lighter summer frocks and grander evening gowns to a dealer in second-hand clothes – what need would she have of them, all alone in this cold country? She packed her remaining belongings in a small suitcase.

While she tidied the house, readying it to return the keys to the landlord, she thought about Cora Ravenhart. *Fenton and I have been intending for some time to visit Fenton's elder brother, Sheldon, in Scotland,* Cora had told her. *Everything is arranged – we will sail next April and we plan to stay with Sheldon for the summer.*

Bess remembered the photograph on the sideboard in her mother-in-law's bungalow, the photograph of Ravenhart House, vast and grey, set against a dark backdrop of mountains. 'Uncle Sheldon's place,' Jack had told her. 'Hideous, isn't it?'

In the library, she looked up Ravenhart on a map of the

22

British Isles. She traced the journey she must take, to Perthshire in Scotland, from one end of the island to the other. She would not write, she decided; she would not forewarn Cora Ravenhart of her intention to visit. Over the long, cold winter her unease had hardened into distrust. Into her mind came a picture of Cora's lace-gloved fingers stroking Jack's blond hair. This time she would not let herself be swayed by Cora. This time, she would take her son, and afterwards, when they were together again, she would never let him go.

Bess changed trains in Edinburgh before continuing north to Perth, through countryside rucked up into mountains and valleys, as though someone had pushed their hand along a length of cloth. She arrived in Pitlochry that evening and stayed overnight in a guest house. After supper, she walked round the small town. It was hard to contain her excitement. Tomorrow she would surely see Frazer. Tomorrow she should be reunited with her son.

She set out in a hired pony and trap the next morning. There was a sharpness in the air, an edge to the wind. The narrow road wound over hills and between woods and outcrops of rock. The camber of the road tilted this way and that; she had to grip the back of the seat for support. Beyond the flat plain of the river valley, the mountains rose up, lit up every now and then whenever the sun came out from behind the clouds. It took Bess by surprise that the nearer she got to Ravenhart House, the more it felt like going home. The pine trees and the twists of honeysuckle in the hedgerows reminded her of Simla.

At last, a gatehouse signalled the track to the Ravenharts' estate where it branched off from the road, curving over a humpbacked bridge and threading through the glen. Now the mountains soared to either side of the track, swelling high into the sky and casting a dark shadow over the far side of the valley. A shallow river meandered through a stony bed, its banks edged with silver birches that shivered in the breeze. All that she could see belonged to the Ravenharts, the driver told her − and, for the briefest of moments, Bess forgot why she was there and was awed by the beauty and majesty of the scenery. In this vast open space, she felt as though, for the first time in months, she could breathe properly. London had crushed her, had squeezed something vital from her, but now she felt free, as if she had been unexpectedly released from captivity.

Then the fir trees thinned, and she saw Ravenhart House for the first time. She thought, Jack was wrong, it isn't hideous at all. It's glorious.

Crow-stepped gables rose above small-paned windows, and turrets, their conical roofs borrowed from a fairy tale, clung to the corners of the wings. A grey-blue slate roof topped the stone and rendered walls. Box and rhododendron walled the garden, and tall pines provided a dark, dramatic backdrop to the house.

As the pony and trap halted on the gravel courtyard, Bess's gaze darted to the windows, searching for a glimpse of Frazer. But there was nothing, not a shimmer of movement, as if the house were inhabited only by its ghosts. She climbed out of the trap, and looked up. Ravenhart House seemed to her a place of mysteries and of secrets. Hidden by the trees, guarded by mountains, what old shades and shadows might drift along those dark corridors and tall staircases?

She pulled the doorbell. Waiting, she recalled with almost physical pain the softness of Frazer's plump hand in hers, and the warmth and weight of him in her arms. She felt a rush of elation; perhaps, when she entered the house, she might see him, hear him. Perhaps she would call out to him and he would run to her. She knew that he would have altered in her absence — he would be taller, less of a baby, more a little boy. He would walk confidently and would have begun to talk. Yet it seemed to her that some memory of her must linger, that the sound of her voice and the scent of her skin must stir some recollection.

The maid took her name and showed her indoors. The walls of the reception room were panelled in dark wood; logs burned in the vast carved stone fireplace. She couldn't stand still; she found herself pacing the room, her gaze flickering from the hunting trophies on the walls to the furniture, dark like the panelling and so massive and weighty it might have belonged to a giant's house. A thin felting of dust had settled on the surfaces of sideboard and table; spiders had slung their cobweb ropes between the branched antlers of a stag. Photographs were arranged on the sideboard and mantelpiece, snapshots of girls in white summer dresses and straw hats and stern-faced women encased in crinolines and bonnets. Groups of tweed-clad men, guns slung over their shoulders, stood triumphant and masterful behind the body of a dead stag. There was a portrait of a young man in an army officer's uniform; Bess thought that he had a melancholy look.

Her heart was racing; she felt warm, almost feverish. Peeling off her gloves, she went to the window. Perhaps Frazer was playing in the garden. Perhaps she would catch sight of him, a flicker of white, running between the rhododendrons.

She heard footsteps; she spun round. 'Mr Ravenhart?'

Sheldon Ravenhart was short and stout. Like the house, he seemed down at heel, his sparse grey hair uncombed, his waistcoat missing a button. 'Fool of a maid told me Mrs Ravenhart had called,' he said irritably, glancing at Bess. 'Nonsense, I said, you've got the name wrong.'

'I'm Jack Ravenhart's widow,' Bess explained. 'I ask your pardon for coming here unannounced, sir, but I must speak to Mrs Ravenhart.'

A bark of laughter. 'Then I'm afraid you're five years too late. My wife died in nineteen ten.'

Reddening, she apologized. 'I meant that I'd like to speak to Mrs Cora Ravenhart.'

'Cora? Cora's not here. She's in India.'

Her heart jolted. 'India?'

'Of course.' He crossed the room to her. He smelt of pipe tobacco and of something damp and musty that reminded her of old furnishings and fabrics after the monsoon. 'If you're Jack's widow,' he said, peering at her suspiciously, 'surely you must know that Cora and Fenton have lived in India for years?'

Disappointment washed over her. 'I've come too early, they must still be travelling—'

'I wouldn't know,' he muttered. In the light, she noticed the stains on Sheldon Ravenhart's waistcoat, and his frayed cuffs. 'Fenton never was much of a letter-writer.' He glanced at his watch. 'The maid will offer you some refreshment, Mrs Ravenhart, but I'm afraid I cannot extend an invitation to luncheon. I live simply these days, now that I'm on my own.'

She began to feel frightened. 'But Cora has written to you, hasn't she, Mr Ravenhart?'

A flicker of irritation crossed his face. 'Cora informed me of the death of her boy, of course. Your husband.'

'Mr Ravenhart, Jack's parents are visiting you this summer, aren't they?'

'I don't believe so. Now, you really must excuse me.'

Her alarm intensified; her heart was hammering against her ribs. She grasped his arm, staying him. 'The Ravenharts are coming here – in a month or two, perhaps?'

His impatience showed in his taut, cold smile. 'You appear to be under a misapprehension, Mrs Ravenhart. No, I am not anticipating the pleasure of receiving my brother and his wife.'

There must be some mistake, she thought. There must be. Now, the figures in the photographs, and the eyes of the stuffed birds and animals mounted on the walls, took on a haunted, anguished look.

She said desperately, 'But Cora told me – she told me it was arranged!'

'Perhaps there was some talk of a visit. I cannot recall.' He went to the door. 'Forgive me, Mrs Ravenhart, but I have business to attend to.'

Though she tried to control it, her voice shook. 'So my son isn't here? There is no plan to bring him here?'

His hand on the doorknob, Sheldon Ravenhart glanced back at her. 'Your son?'

'My baby. Frazer.'

He was looking at her as though she was a madwoman. 'There is no baby in this house, I assure you. I'm sorry, Mrs Ravenhart, but I really can't help you.'

As she was driven away from the house, Bess stared back at its grey facade, her gaze jumping from window to window as though, if she only looked hard enough, she might yet see him. Then a cloud covered the sun, veiling the house in shadow; the fairy-tale beauty was gone, and the black windows stared blankly from the grey stone, dark and malevolent.

The trap took a sharp corner, the fir trees closed their green curtain, and the house was gone. She was cold now; she buttoned up her coat. Looking round, she saw that it wasn't like Simla at all; in that, too, she had been mistaken. This was another country entirely, and she was separated from her child by half the world.

She felt dazed, unable to think clearly. She forced herself to concentrate; she must try to work out what had happened. Perhaps, shocked and confused in the aftermath of Jack's death, she had misunderstood what Cora Ravenhart had told her. Or perhaps the Ravenharts' plans had gone awry. What had Sheldon Ravenhart said? *Perhaps there was some talk of a visit, I cannot recall.* She had wanted to shake him, to force him to remember.

Perhaps the Ravenharts had changed their minds about travelling to Great Britain because of the war. Perhaps they had not wanted to risk the long sea voyage. Yes, that must be it, she thought, and felt a flicker of relief. Newspaper headlines told of merchant shipping torpedoed off the coast of Britain. The *Lusitania*, a passenger liner, had been sunk off Ireland earlier that month with the loss of more than a thousand lives. Perhaps she had been mistaken in her belief that the war would not touch her. While she had been nursing her father and waiting to reclaim her son, war had spread across the world like a plague, affecting everyone.

Of course, there was another possibility. She shivered. Perhaps Cora's plans had not gone wrong. Perhaps everything had happened exactly as Cora had intended.

Perhaps Cora Ravenhart meant to keep Frazer for herself.

Was it possible? Yes, she saw now that it was all too possible. Cora had always disliked her; Cora had tried to stop Jack marrying her. Bess Cadogan, daughter of a rootless merchant, had hardly been a suitable bride for the Ravenharts' only son. But Jack, used to having his own way from the earliest age, brought up like a little prince in the Ravenharts' bungalow, indulged by the servants and adored by his mother, had refused to comply with Cora's wishes. Like Cora herself, Jack had had an iron will.

He had been handsome, brave and devil-may-care, but he had had his faults, too. He had demanded attention and expected adoration. He had hated to be thwarted; whatever Jack wanted, Jack had, and if he was denied his prize, he sulked and raged. In the two years of their marriage, they had laughed, yes, but they had quarrelled, too, angry, door-slamming, plate-hurling quarrels that had made the servants run for cover. Jack had been capable of great kindness, but he had had his darker side – a carelessness, when it suited him, of other people's feelings, and an inability to accept criticism. Those faults had been bred in him by his mother, who had spoiled him, never checked him, never admonished him.

All the affection of which Cora Ravenhart had been capable had been lavished on her only son. Not once had Bess seen Cora Ravenhart betray liking, let alone love, for her husband. How did you survive the loss of the only person you loved? Did you mourn for the rest of your days? Or did you, in your grief and hatred, search for a substitute? Did you grasp for the lost love's closest replacement, whatever the consequences, whatever the damage you caused?

On the train from Perth to Edinburgh, a young couple came to sit in Bess's carriage. The man's arm crept round his girl's waist; giggling, she pushed him away. 'No, no, Ken, behave yourself.'

'Aw, c'mon . . .'

'*Kenny*.'

'You don't mind, do you, missis?' Ken grinned at Bess. 'We've just got married,' he confided.

'Congratulations.'

'Me and Annie, we only met each other a month ago.'

'Goodness,' she said politely.

'There's no point hanging about, is there? Two days' honeymoon and then I'm off to France.' He was wearing khaki. 'Never know what might happen, do you?'

'Ken.'

'Don't you worry, sweetheart. I'll be back. Two nights aren't going to be enough for *me*.'

The train rattled along the line. The newlyweds shared a cigarette, whispering to each other. Bess turned away, huddled up against the window, staring out and seeing, instead of hills and woodland, Frazer, with his white-gold hair and blue eyes, waving to her as she walked away from the Ravenharts' bungalow for the last time.

She would go back to India, she thought wildly, and she would fetch him herself. Cora should not have him; she would not let Cora take him from her. But to sail to India would cost money. And once she had reclaimed Frazer she must have, as Cora Ravenhart had pointed out, a home for him. Furtively, she looked in her purse: five pounds and twelve shillings. Not enough, nowhere near enough. Money, she thought bitterly, it always came down to money. You could do nothing without money.

She must find work, then. But what could she do? Her education had been sketchy. She could ride a horse as well as most men; she could curse in three different languages. She could swim and dive fearlessly, and she had always been lucky at cards. What use were such talents here? Objectively, she considered the sort of work that would be open to her – a bar or a hotel, a ladies' dress shop or, God forbid, domestic service. Office work, if she learned to type-write. Would such employment enable her to earn enough to support herself, Frazer, and the nursemaid who would be needed to care for him while she was at work? She felt unsure.

The cold had spread through her body, chilling her to the core. Fear took away from her all clarity of thought. Fear that Cora Ravenhart, whose only son had died, had decided to keep her grandson in recompense. That she had lied, inventing an intention to travel to Scotland that had never existed, so that she might keep Frazer. Fear that she, Bess Ravenhart, had made a terrible and irretrievable mistake, and had stepped blindly into the trap that Cora had set for her.

In Edinburgh, Bess took a room in the first cheap lodging house she found. She was too exhausted to travel further, and besides, where would she go? Why return to London, which she disliked, where she had no home and where no one was waiting for her?

Her room was on the fourth floor of a tenement in the Old Town. It was small and damp and the bedding had not been laundered often enough; her window looked down over a narrow close, walled on the opposite side by another tenement block. She slept fitfully, cocooned in scratchy woollen blankets, and eked out her remaining money in cheap cafes and buns bought from bakers' shops. She hid the diamond earrings that Jack had bought her for their first wedding anniversary, blue Ceylonese diamonds that she loved with a fierce, possessive passion, behind a loose piece of skirting board in her room. It was that sort of lodging house.

The city, with its great rocky peaks and its confusion of levels, seemed, as she roamed through it, to spit her out at random, so that sometimes she found herself teetering high above the rooftops, and at other times she was submerged in a low maze of dark wynds and closes. She felt bewildered, unable to see what she should do next. She had never been so alone before. She had always had *someone*, her father, Jack, the acquaintances with whom she had stayed in Simla; there had always been friends, always company. Loneliness gnawed at her; once or twice, when she was sitting in a cafe, making a cup of tea last an hour, a man caught her eye, and she found herself tempted to smile back. She remembered the offer Dempster Harris had made her: *protection*, he had called it. It would probably pay better than working in a shop. She knew that she was treading along a precipice, she knew that it was all too possible that she might slip and fall, down to the depths.

Then, one morning, she woke from a deep, dreamless sleep. As she dressed and combed out her long black hair, she found herself thinking of the P&O steamship that had taken her from Bombay to Southampton. She remembered the Williamsons, who had been kind to her, and the soldiers who had flirted with her as she had sat beneath the awning. The beginnings of an idea fluttered at the back of her mind. She tried to seize it, to bring it into the light. Another memory: the honeymoon couple on the train from Perth to Edinburgh. *We only met each other a month ago.* She paused, looking at her reflection in the mirror.

Her eyes, narrowed now as she ruthlessly appraised her image, were long slits of dark sapphire blue. Her endless worries about the price of food had meant that her face had become thinner, emphasizing her bone structure – her high cheekbones, her thin, straight nose. Her full mouth, that Jack had so loved to kiss, was now set in a determined line. Of course she had a talent: a *saleable* talent. Everything that Cora Ravenhart had despised her for she must now use to her advantage. Mrs Ravenhart had seen through the veneer of good breeding that she, Bess, had adopted to make herself acceptable to Simla society; Mrs Ravenhart had thought her fast, flirtatious, wanton.

She *had* to get Frazer back; she *had* to. She went to the window, flung it open and breathed in the sharp, fresh air. Then she put on her hat and gloves and went outside.

As she walked up Castlehill, she made her plans carefully. First, she would find the Williamsons and remind them of their shipboard friendship. She would dress well, she would remember her best manners and she would hide from them the disasters that had overtaken her. Bess Ravenhart, widow of Jack Ravenhart, nephew to the owner of the Ravenharts' vast Scottish estates, would be welcomed; a penniless exile from a backstreet boarding house might not.

She looked out over the city, first to where sunlight glinted on the roofs of the elegant Georgian houses of the New Town, and then beyond, to the distant silver tongue of the Firth of Forth. She must use the Williamsons to find an entrée to Edinburgh society. She must coax invitations to soirées, at homes and parties. And as soon as she could, she must embark on a wartime romance. She must discover the richest, most eligible man in Edinburgh, and she must marry him.

Chapter Two

Bess sold one last piece of jewellery, a pearl brooch. Now, only her wedding and engagement rings and the diamond earrings remained. She sold a fur cape, a velvet evening coat and a silk frock to a dealer in second-hand clothes, and moved to a small but respectable hotel in the New Town. Her wardrobe was pared down; as she walked to the hotel her possessions rattled emptily in her suitcase. How much longer would her money last? A few weeks, she guessed – perhaps, if she didn't eat much, a couple of months. She was always hungry, always watchful that something might give her away – the darns on her gloves, the holes in her stockings. The effort of hiding her poverty wearied her; the need to maintain the appearance of demure and respectable widowhood irked her. But all that was nothing compared to the dread that came to her in the early hours of the morning that her plan would fail, and she would be left with nothing.

When she had decided to look for a husband, she hadn't

anticipated that there would be such a great scarcity of young men. This wretched war, she thought furiously, which seemed to have a way of disrupting so many of her plans. Through the Williamsons, she met young women, married and unmarried, who showed her photographs of their brothers, fiancés and husbands, who were fighting on the Front. She met older women, who struggled to hide their constant anxiety for their sons. She met married men, lawyers and doctors and factory owners in their forties and fifties, who murmured compliments to her when their wives were out of earshot. She met ageing bachelors, whose threadbare cuffs and greyish collars betrayed the decades that had passed since a woman had cared for them. And she met boys of sixteen and seventeen years old, who had patchy moustaches and blemished complexions, and who gazed at her with undisguised admiration while confiding to her their impatience at not yet being old enough to join up.

Then, just as she was beginning to despair of ever meeting a suitable man, she was introduced to Ralph Fearnley. Ralph was a bachelor in his late twenties. Though not exactly rich, a few discreet enquiries to Sarah Williamson reassured Bess that he was very comfortably off. Ralph was a senior partner in the accountancy firm established by his late father; he lived in a village a few miles south of Edinburgh. Just now, he was waiting to be called up to his regiment.

Ralph had reddish-blond hair, a smooth, pink, plump face, and blue-grey eyes fringed with light-coloured lashes. Persuading Ralph Fearnley to fall in love with her was like reeling in a hooked fish. A plump, gleaming fish that hardly wriggled the smallest protest. She didn't have to chase him, he chased her. Except that *chased* was hardly the right word to describe Ralph's dogged, plodding pursuit. Drop a hint that she might attend a recital, and Ralph would be there, waiting in the foyer of her hotel to escort her, his admiration naked in his eyes as she descended the staircase in a cloud of L'Heure Bleu, diamonds glittering in her ears. Whenever she looked round, Ralph was beside her, ready to spring into action to fetch her a drink, or to open a door for her, or to help her into her coat. He reminded her of a dog she had once owned in India, a keen, faithful, lugubrious labrador.

When she touched him – her hand threading through his arm as they walked along the pavement, or their fingers brushing as he handed her a glass of wine – he started, as though he had made contact with a live wire. Often, an expression of bewilderment mixed with the adoration in his eyes, as though he found himself all at sea, floundering in uncharted waters. He spoke to her about his work and about his favourite pastimes: walking in the Pentland Hills, fishing, and studying military history. Once he had fixed on a subject that interested him, his awkwardness fell away, and he could talk, it seemed to Bess, endlessly. He might fail to notice that she had not said a word for at least ten minutes – had not had the chance to say a word. All over the world, Bess thought, with a touch of irritation, men liked to lecture women, from Simla to Scotland. Even poor Jack had had a habit of talking about polo for hours. Sometimes, conversing with Ralph, she had to stifle a yawn; once, after a sleepless night, she actually found herself dozing off as he spoke of trenches and defiles and enfilades, things she had not the least interest in.

There had been rather a lot of sleepless nights recently. At night, her resolve faltered, and she found herself questioning whether she could marry a man she did not love, a man she cared little for. Ralph Fearnley seemed a good man, an honest man, and his faults – a mild pomposity and a nit-picking attention to detail – were not grave. He did not deserve a loveless marriage.

But, oh, what would she do if she did not marry Ralph? She might never become accustomed to the solitariness that had been her lot since her father's death. She had never liked to be alone. She needed people, she needed company, needed chatter and laughter and someone with whom to share the small events of the day. Most of all, she needed Frazer. If she did not marry Ralph, she might never return to India. And then Frazer would forget her. He would not love her. As he grew up, he might even believe that she had willingly abandoned him. Brought up by Cora Ravenhart, what would happen to him, her only and beloved son? She feared what Cora would make of him.

She had written one last time to Cora Ravenhart, asking why she had not come to Scotland and pleading for news of Frazer. In her heart, she knew that Cora would never answer her letters. The events of the past year had robbed her of illusions, hardening her. She pushed her doubts aside and pursued her goal ruthlessly, letting nothing get in her way, neither the doubts that came to her at night, nor her own intermittent awful realization of the tedium that marriage to Ralph Fearnley would entail.

Ralph introduced Bess to a friend of his, Pamela Crawford. Pamela was a neighbour of Ralph's, and they had known each other since early childhood. Bess dismissed her as a possible threat. Large-boned and sturdy, Miss Crawford wore her hair in plaited earphones, and her heavy fringe touched her thick, dark eyebrows. Her clothing was chosen for its practicality and warmth rather than for its seductive appeal, and she smelt of Imperial Leather soap instead of L'Heure Bleue. If Pamela Crawford was in love with Ralph – and Bess, with a feeling of guilt that she quickly suppressed, suspected that she was – then she wasn't going the right way about ensnaring him.

One thing she had noticed about Ralph: his parsimony over small matters. In spite of his prosperity, he had a habit of walking to save the cost of a cab fare, a reluctance to pay for the best seats in the theatre when the second-best might do just as well. He had seemed shocked when she had chosen lobster from a restaurant's à la carte selection instead of choosing, as he always did, the set menu. She had been careful not to make the same mistake again. Ralph's penny-pinching was, she guessed, a habit brought on by years of bachelorhood, years in which his natural tendency to financial prudence had been allowed to run unchecked.

Over dinner one evening, she asked Ralph's advice on financial matters, hinting that Jack had lacked the foresight to provide properly for his widow in the event of his death. She restricted herself to the sort of genteel dilemmas that a lady on a reduced income might encounter, carefully avoiding any intimations of poverty, knowing how it repelled and how people shied away from it, as though it was catching.

Ralph was sawing through a tough slice of beef – the restaurant was second-rate, and he believed in leaving his plate perfectly clean. 'Too many men,' he said, 'make the mistake of not keeping their affairs in order.'

'I suppose Jack thought he would live for ever. You do, don't you?'

'Do you? I've made provision. One must guard against all eventualities.'

She thought of Jack, laughing as he rode to his death along a misty precipice, and she said sadly, 'Jack never thought of the future. He never thought that anything bad would happen to him.'

Ralph paused before speaking, chewing determinedly. 'I see that time and again in my business – this past year, especially. Off they go to France, the married men, the men with children, and then the worst happens and their families are left in a frightful mess.'

She shivered. 'Please don't speak of such things, Ralph. It makes me afraid.'

'Afraid?'

She gave him a melting look. 'Afraid for you. You've been so kind to me, so sweet. I've felt so alone since Jack died. I don't know how I could have managed without you, Ralph.'

He went scarlet, made a succession of incoherent noises and choked on a piece of gristle so that she had to pat him on the back. When he was recovered, she turned to light-hearted topics of conversation, nothing that might scare him off. There were subjects she knew she must not yet broach. It was far too soon, for instance, to bring up the tricky question of Frazer. That must wait until she had, at least, an engagement ring on her finger. Once or twice recently Ralph had seemed on the verge of making his declaration, but then the smallest thing – a waiter coming to clear away their plates, a car hooting its horn in the street – would distract him. *Oh, for heaven's sake, get on with it*, she had found herself wanting to hiss impatiently at him, but had managed to stop herself.

Ralph escorted her to the Corstophines' party. The Corstophines were close friends of the Williamsons; Jane Corstophine shared Mrs Williamson's love of music. Earlier that day, Bess had rinsed her hair in lemon juice so that it gleamed, black and heavy, in loops and curls at the nape of her neck. A touch of lipstick, a whisk of powder, a spray of L'Heure Bleu. She wore a black silk dress and her diamond earrings sparkled, drawing the gaze.

She had taken extra care over her appearance because Ralph must propose to her tonight. She simply could not wait any longer. She had hardly eaten that day. Her financial situation had become critical; her need to save money meant that she must reduce her spending on food to a minimum. While she talked to Ralph, and while they danced, she was aware of a hollow in her belly, an urge to rush into the adjacent room where the buffet was spread out, and eat as much as she could. But that would never do; the appearance of fragile widowhood, which she knew appealed to Ralph, must at all costs be maintained.

Throughout the evening, Ralph hovered at her elbow, fetching her drinks, darting out of the room to gather her

41

unsatisfying little morsels of food. It must be hunger, she thought, that was making her so irritable. Once or twice, she was on the verge of speaking sharply to him, to tell him to stop fussing – she never could bear fussing – and to beg him to try not to tread on her toes while they danced, risking laddering stockings she could not possibly afford to replace. Alarmed by her own touchiness, she compensated by being particularly nice to him, smiling into his eyes and stroking back a lock of hair from his brow in a way that reduced him to reddened speechlessness. She knew that anyone seeing them together must assume that they were already engaged. Well, all to the good, she said defiantly to herself, and drank another glass of wine to calm her brittle nerves.

Ralph pointed out to her some of the other guests. 'You know Stewart and Jane, of course. They're talking to the Murrays and the Irvines. John Murray is a lawyer and Gilbert Irvine is a publisher. In fact, I have a hand in Irvine's auditing. The girl in pink is the Irvines' daughter, Louise. She's engaged to the Murrays' son. The elderly couple to Louise's right are Lewis and Jean Kincardine. Lewis is a rum fellow – interested in bugs and beetles, that sort of thing.'

'And the man in the crumpled jacket talking to Mr Kincardine? Who's he?'

'Oh, that's Dr Jago. Rather an odd character. Never seems to have two pennies to rub together. And there was some sort of scandal, I believe, but I can't recall exactly . . .'

There now, she thought exasperatedly, the first very slightly interesting thing you have mentioned tonight, and you can't even remember it properly.

An old friend hailed Ralph, and Bess took the opportunity to excuse herself. The dining room was almost empty and servants were starting to clear away the plates. With a quick glance over her shoulder, she swept up what food remained. Then she wandered through the house, looking for sanctuary.

Eventually she found herself pleasingly surrounded by hoya and plumbago, in a glass and metal conservatory. She sat down, the plate on her lap, pulled off her gloves, kicked off her shoes, and gave a sigh of relief. Just for a moment, before she began to eat, she closed her eyes, breathing in the scents of the flowers, letting the sounds of the party fall away, letting herself, for the first time that night, relax. Then she set to work. Sandwiches, savouries, vol-au-vents, she devoured them all.

There was a sound, and she looked up, a piece of cake clutched in her hand. She was no longer alone; the man in the rumpled jacket had come into the conservatory. Quickly, she tried to hide the plate behind a pot plant, but as he made his way to her through ficus and palm, stumbling over an outthrust branch, she heard him say, 'I was rather hoping you could spare me something. I forgot to have supper and everything's gone.'

She thrust the plate at him. 'Here. Have it. Please. I'm not really hungry.'

He sat down beside her, saying, 'I've always thought the convention that obliges women to eat like mice in company as a sign of refinement is utterly nonsensical. Most men like to see a woman eat well. It makes them feel less clumsy, less gross.' He offered her his hand. 'I'm Martin Jago.'

43

'Bess Ravenhart.'

'Tell you what,' he suggested. 'We'll share it.'

As they ate, she studied him covertly. He had short, fine dark hair and a pale, bony face. He was quite tall and rather thin. She found it hard to tell how old he was – somewhere between twenty-five and thirty-five, she could estimate no closer than that. He was very badly dressed – there were ink stains on his cuffs and his black jacket was greenish with age. He was odd-looking, she decided, and not handsome at all. The only remarkable thing about his appearance was his eyes, which were a piercing dark greyish blue, the colour of slate.

She finished the cake and began to lick the crumbs from her fingers. Suddenly realizing what she was doing, she said, 'Oh Lord. My father always told me I had the manners of a guttersnipe.'

He smiled at her. 'Perhaps you'd prefer me to leave. Perhaps you came here to escape.'

'Is that why you're here? To escape?' She touched the pink papery flower of a bougainvillaea. 'I'm here because I like it here. It makes me think of home.'

'Home?'

'India. I was born and brought up there. The flowers remind me of India.' She felt a stab of homesickness. 'I tell people that I'm English. But my father was a mixture of English and Irish and my mother had a little Scots, I believe – I don't know for certain, she died when I was very young and my father didn't keep in touch with her family, or with his own. But all the time I was in England I felt as though I was in exile.'

'You're a mongrel, then, like myself. How long have you lived in Edinburgh, Mrs Ravenhart?'

'Six weeks. Just six weeks.'

'How do you find it?'

'Cold,' she said, and shivered. 'Always so cold. And you?'

'I come from France, originally. I went to school in England before studying medicine here, in Edinburgh. And since then I've travelled a bit.'

'Have you been to India?' She longed to hear of it, even at second hand.

'I'm afraid not. Though I should like to, one day.'

She said angrily, 'I have to go back to India. But this war!' She thought of Frazer, thousands of miles away, battle-fields and navies dividing them. 'Oh, why must men have their wretched wars?'

'It's in our nature, I suppose.'

'If only it would hurry up and finish!'

'I'm afraid you're going to have to wait quite a while for that.'

'How long?'

'Oh, years.'

She did not believe him. 'Surely not! It can't possibly go on so long!'

'Neither side makes any progress, you see. Both armies move back and forth over a few feet of muddy ground. There are no victories and no advances. There can't be, because modern weapons counter any attack before it has time to gather momentum. And Kitchener would hardly be training numerous battalions of volunteers if he thought there was an end in sight.'

She said, 'When we win—'

'If we win,' he interrupted.

She stared at him. That they might not win the war was not a possibility she had even considered. She thought of Jack, in his glorious scarlet uniform, at the head of his troop of horse. 'We'll win,' she said firmly. 'Of course we'll win. We always do.'

'We're an island, which is both our strength and our weakness. The sea's a natural barricade, of course, but we're heavily dependent on imports from the Empire for food. And yes, we may well win the war. But at such a cost, such a great loss, that it may feel more like a defeat.'

She gave a hiss of exasperation and despair; she heard him say, 'Do you have someone in France? A brother, or a cousin . . .'

'No, no one.'

He took a flask from his pocket and offered it to her. 'Would you care for some whisky, Mrs Ravenhart?'

She drank a few mouthfuls. It warmed her. 'Tell me about your travels, please, Dr Jago. Which countries have you visited?'

'Italy – and Greece and Spain, and, more recently, Egypt. I've been fortunate enough to visit the Valley of the Kings. A couple of years ago, the Earl of Carnarvon, Howard Carter's patron, managed to get permission to excavate there, but of course last summer the war broke out and all that came to an end. Medicine is my trade, you see, but archaeology is my passion.'

'Two careers!' she said sharply. 'How fortunate men are to have such choices.'

46

His cool blue-grey gaze settled on her. 'There are always choices, surely.'

'Not for women like myself,' she said bitterly. 'Our choices are very limited.'

'The professions are starting to open up to women. Women can nurse – a few have trained to become doctors. Think of Sophia Jex Blake—'

'How much does it cost to train to become a doctor?' she interrupted him.

He admitted, 'A rather large sum of money.'

'And how many years does it take?'

'Six, seven years.'

'I can't possibly wait that long. No, there's only one career open to me.'

'And what's that?'

'Marriage, of course.'

'Is that how you see it? As a career?'

'Carefully chosen, marriage secures both status and an income. In much the same way as a profession would, I should think.'

'That sounds . . . calculating.'

'Does it?' She looked at him coldly. 'Then let me assure you, Dr Jago, that innocent young debutantes calculate their marriages just as carefully as experienced adventuresses do. Men are fools if they think we do not.'

There was a silence; her words echoed in the room. Then he said smoothly, 'No doubt. But Ralph Fearnley may not see it in quite the same way.'

She flushed. He had been watching her, she realized. 'That's Ralph's business.'

'And yours, Mrs Ravenhart? He's pleasant enough, Ralph Fearnley, but I should have thought he would bore you to tears.'

She began to interrupt angrily, but he put up a hand, silencing her. 'I only mean to point out that men and women don't always see things in quite the same way, and that they have an inconvenient habit of falling in love with each other. Doesn't that upset all sorts of calculations?'

'I'm not sure that I believe in love.'

'Is it a matter of belief?'

'Perhaps we tell ourselves that we're in love to make ourselves feel better, to make our calculations more acceptable.' She knew that she sounded hard.

'Perhaps. I've little experience of such matters.'

'You're not married, Dr Jago?'

He shook his head. 'And have no expectation of being so.'

'Why not? Is your character so flawed?'

'It's hugely flawed, I'm afraid.' He made a vague attempt at brushing the cake crumbs from his jacket. 'I'm forgetful and I'm untidy and I dislike staying in the same place for too long. And I've been told that I'm awkward and unsociable, and when I'm preoccupied, I neglect to speak to people.'

She thought, and when you do speak, you say things that you shouldn't. As she rose from the bench, she smiled. 'Oh, I don't doubt some woman will take pity on you, Dr Jago, and will be only too happy to look after you.'

As she threaded her way between fig and passion flower, she heard him murmur, 'Pity. How unendurable, to marry out of pity.'

*   *   *

She had drunk too much and her head ached and there was a sour taste in her mouth. She was unsure whether the bad taste was because of the wine and the whisky, or the memory of Martin Jago's words. *He's pleasant enough, Ralph Fearnley, but I should have thought he would bore you to tears.* How dare he, a man who had only just met her, who knew nothing of her circumstances, who, by his own admission, was destined to remain a bachelor, presume to judge her?

Later, there was music. Careful sonatas and polite little duets for piano and violin to begin with, but then some of the guests came forward to sing, and the evening, which had until then seemed flat and slow, began to lift. Dr Jago accompanied the singers on the piano as they sang selections from operettas and popular songs.

An aria from *The Merry Widow* ended. When Martin Jago asked her to sing, it seemed to Bess more of a challenge than a request. So she stepped into the centre of the room and sang a ballad she had learned from her father. She was not a strong singer, but she had always been able to hit the notes true. The song she sang told of love and death and betrayal, all those timeless things. *'Where have you been, my long lost love, these seven long years and more?'* she sang, and she thought of Frazer, and felt a shiver run the length of her spine.

She could feel the gaze of her audience, and she saw that Ralph was watching her, unable to drag his eyes away from her. And when, after the end of the song, he murmured to her, under cover of the applause, 'Bess, I must speak to you, there's something I must say to you,' she felt a flare of triumph.

They had left the house and were walking back to her

hotel when Ralph told her that he had received orders to join his regiment in a fortnight's time. And that he loved her, adored her, couldn't live without her. When they kissed, she saw how, as she drew away from him, he remained motionless, as though the touch of her lips had turned him to stone.

And if the promise she had just made to him was little different to the transactions of the whores in the street, then so be it, she thought defiantly. She had made her choice.

They were married two weeks later. Telling Ralph about Frazer proved less difficult than Bess had feared. He registered the fact that he was now the stepfather of a little boy with much the same dazed expression she had seen on his face throughout their brief courtship. But persuading him to give her the money to pay her passage to India so that she could bring Frazer to England proved far harder than she had hoped.

She chose her time carefully. They were in bed, his arms were around her and they had just made love, a rushed, awkward joining of two bodies that didn't seem to fit together properly, and that gave her none of the pleasure she had experienced with Jack.

Ralph seemed happy enough, though. He nuzzled the top of her head. She said, 'Darling, I must talk to you about Frazer.'

'Frazer?' He sounded vague.

'You remember, my son. I must go and get him. So if you could just let me have enough money for my fare . . .'

'Your fare?'

'My passage to India.'

He gave a little laugh. 'You can't possibly go to India, sweetheart.'

'I have to.' She slid out of his arms and turned to face him. 'I don't suppose Frazer remembers me at all now. The longer I leave him there, the worse it'll be.'

'It's out of the question, I'm afraid, my darling. For one thing, there's the cost, which would be considerable. There would be not only your own passage to pay for, but the additional expense of your train fare to Simla, as well as the hotels you would have to stay in and the servants you would have to engage. And there would be numerous other expenses, I daresay. Prices have gone up so. And while I'm away, the partnership's takings will inevitably decline.'

'I'll travel steerage, I don't care—'

'Quite apart from the cost, it would be far too dangerous. The enemy won't baulk at sinking passenger liners, they've made that perfectly clear.'

'But I *have* to go, Ralph!'

He patted her hand. 'How could I bear it if something were to happen to you? Remember the *Lusitania*. All those poor people drowned. I'm afraid you'll have to wait until the war is over before you can fetch your little boy. And besides,' he kissed her cheek, 'I wouldn't dream of letting you go so far away from me, my little darling, so soon after our wedding.'

She had not expected that he would be so unbending. She pointed out sulkily, 'But *you're* going away.'

'I'll be back as soon as I can. You mustn't worry. I won't leave my precious little wife any longer than I have to.'

Ralph left Scotland the following morning for a training camp in northern England. When, in September, the newspapers reported the sinking of the liner *Hesperian*, with the loss of thirty-two passengers, Bess was forced reluctantly to acknowledge that Ralph had been right. Though she herself would not have hesitated to take a chance – would have sailed for India tomorrow with the greatest joy – how could she put Frazer at risk? As Ralph had said, she must wait for the war to end. And surely it must end soon! It had already gone on far longer than everyone had expected.

She knew that she must be patient, and that she must make the best of what she had. Ralph's house, Hollins Lodge, was big and cold and ugly, built of grey stone. An air of shabby Victorian gloom pervaded the cavernous rooms. It was always dark, always cold, no matter how many sweaters and shawls she wore. And it seemed to Bess that there was not one single thing of beauty to be found in the entire house. All the ornaments and pictures were ugly, and the furnishings had been bought for serviceability rather than elegance.

At first she tried to make the house brighter, helping Mrs Brake, the housekeeper, give it a thorough spring clean, and consigning some of the most hideous items of furniture to an outhouse. She arranged her Indian shawls over the heavy leather sofas and chairs and, from a street market in Edinburgh, bought yards of brightly coloured fabric to replace the dingiest curtains. Yet after a while she gave up. Dust seemed to settle overnight on every window sill and mantelpiece, and the red and blue cotton curtains she had made looked out of place, tawdry even, in the high-ceilinged, darkly-distempered parlour. She couldn't *like* Ralph's house – she was grateful for the shelter it provided, but she couldn't *like* it.

Apart from Mrs Brake, Hollins Lodge employed a maid, Pearl, and a very old and rheumaticky gardener. In India, Bess had had a dozen servants to maintain a smaller house and garden. In the autumn, after women began to fill the gaps left by male workers who had gone to the Front, Pearl left Hollins Lodge. The wages were better in munitions, she explained to Bess.

Before he had left for training camp, Ralph had shown Bess the account book in which the household's expenditure was noted, from the servants' wages down to the cost of a box of matches or a bottle of ink. The sums were itemized to the last farthing. She would receive from his bank a monthly allowance, Ralph had told her, to cover her house-keeping expenses, plus a sum for her own personal needs. She was to keep note in the account book of all her expenses. Poring over the book, forcing herself to concentrate on additions and subtractions, Bess discovered that there was hardly a penny to spare from the housekeeping, and certainly not the pounds she would have needed to persuade Pearl to remain at Hollins Lodge.

Ralph came home at Christmas. Waiting for him at Waverley station as the train disgorged a seething crowd of men in khaki, Bess had to check two, three times that the figure striding down the platform towards her was really Ralph. How dreadful, not to remember clearly what your husband looked like. All around her, soldiers embraced their wives and sweethearts, catching them up in their arms, the women squealing with delight. Kissing Ralph was like kissing a stranger.

At Hollins Lodge, she waited expectantly for Ralph to comment on the decorations she had spent days putting up in an attempt to make the old house seem welcoming. She had wound wreaths of holly and ivy around pictures and banisters, and had coaxed the gardener to dig out and pot up a fir tree. But after a vague, 'Very nice, darling,' Ralph ate the supper Mrs Brake had prepared, then spent an hour in his study, checking the household bills, before going early to bed. As she undressed, he watched her avidly. As soon as she had put on her nightgown and climbed into bed, he flung himself on top of her. It was all over in a minute or two; then he lay back on the pillows, gasping, and fell asleep immediately.

For Christmas, Ralph bought her bath salts and a pair of silver earrings. Bess bought him a cashmere scarf, a pair of leather gloves and a small valise containing horn-backed brushes and shoe-cleaning things. 'They're lovely, darling,' he said, but he looked worried. 'Weren't they terribly expensive?'

'I saved up my allowance.'

'How sweet of you.' He kissed her. 'But you must be careful. Times are hard, you know.'

She had sent a Christmas present to Frazer in Simla, a toy train. She wondered whether he had received it, whether it had survived the long, perilous journey to India. And if so, whether Cora Ravenhart had given it to him. Did Frazer like trains, or might he have preferred something else? She wondered, with a rising panic that she seemed to feel more and more often these days, whether she would recognize him if she saw him now. Would she know her own son?

Ralph went back to his regiment after New Year, leaving Bess alone in Hollins Lodge. The village was a small community of two dozen houses, a church, a school, and several outlying farmhouses. Bess quickly learned that her appearance, background and amusements were not those of her neighbours. The conversation at genteel tea parties consisted of gossip about people she neither knew nor cared about. Bridge bored her; she preferred poker. Lecture evenings – 'A Visit to the Norfolk Broads', 'How to Plan a Perennial Border' – reduced her to a state of near-tearful tedium. And however hard she tried, she always seemed to transgress unspoken social rules. She wore the wrong hat to church; invited to supper, she laughed too loudly or too long, and she told jokes that made the men chortle while the women sat stony-faced. After a while, the invitations tailed off.

As often as she could, she escaped to Edinburgh, and to the company of the Williamsons' pleasant, lively, artistic circle of friends. When she was there, she felt alive again, released from a sort of imprisonment. As she returned to the village, her spirits fell.

Pamela Crawford's family farmed land outside the village; Pamela offered Bess the loan of one of the farm ponies whenever she wanted to ride. The pony was old and slow – all the best horses had gone to the Front to pull guns and transports – but riding through the hills allowed Bess to work off some of her frustrations. Throughout the spring and early summer, she spent as much time outdoors as she could, riding or working in the kitchen garden. The German blockade had begun to bite; U-boats regularly sank merchant shipping in the seas around Britain. The food shortages in the shops were worsening, so keeping slugs and snails off the beans and lettuces meant that there was more to eat. Each day, she read the newspapers diligently, searching for a sign that the tide had turned, that they were winning the war at last.

In May, the papers began to speak of a 'great push' on the Western Front. Ralph, who had come home for a week's leave in April, before his regiment was sent to France, had hinted at the possibility of a renewed offensive. There were rumours that a bombardment was about to begin, a bombardment so great it would break through the German lines and put an end to the deadlock on the Front.

The artillery barrage began on 24 June. The newspapers reported that the thunder of the great guns was such that the sound crossed the Channel and could be heard in the south of England. The bombardment was a precursor to the offensive which was launched along the River Somme on 1 July. Bess traced with her fingertip the course of the river in an atlas. There was a sense of anticipation in the air, and a hopeful expectation that the dreadful events of the year so far – the retreat from the Gallipoli peninsula, the loss of the battlecruisers *Indefatigable*, *Queen Mary* and *Invincible* at the battle of Jutland – were about to be reversed. Now the newspaper headlines breathed optimism and excitement as they told of the success of the initial infantry assault on the German lines. Bess's spirits, dampened by the long, grey, lonely winter months, began to rise at last. At night, she lay awake, imagining the ending of the war, Ralph's homecoming, her voyage to India. Once she had Frazer back, she would feel whole again; once she held Frazer in her arms, her decision to marry Ralph and immure herself in the bleak Scottish countryside would be vindicated.

But all too soon, the newspaper reports changed. Confidence in the speedy success of the assault faltered; heavy losses and a slow war of attrition were hinted at. When the lists of casualties began to be reported, they were greeted with universal horror and disbelief. A battalion of local men had been involved in the fighting at the Somme; when the village shop pasted up in its front window lists of the dead and wounded, Bess found herself at first too appalled and stupefied by their length to search for Ralph's name. Behind her, a woman began to sob. The sound broke the spell; Bess ran her eyes quickly down the Fs. He was not there.

Her horror increased as the days went on and the full cost of the Great Push began to be realized. Those long, long lists, those weeping women. This was not victory, she thought, as grief and sorrow laid a pall of silence over the village. One of Pamela Crawford's brothers was wounded, and the Williamsons' only son was killed on the first day of the battle. When she returned from Edinburgh after visiting the Williamsons to offer her condolences, Bess saw that another list had gone up in the shop window. A quick glance to check for Ralph's name, and then she had to push through the crowd that had gathered round the shop before being sick at the side of the road.

Someone touched her shoulder, a voice asked hesitantly whether her man had been hurt. Bess straightened and shook her head. No, that wasn't why she was sick. She walked home, her eyes blurred with tears, and she put her hand to her belly in an instinctive gesture, as if to protect the child that, these past few weeks, she had known with increasing certainty was growing there.

When she had been expecting Frazer, she had felt perfectly well, had played tennis and ridden a horse long into her pregnancy, to the disapproval of Simla's matrons.

This time, she was vilely ill long before the baby began to show. She was sick in the morning and in the evening – she seemed to spend a great deal of the day enclosed in Hollins Lodge's dark, clanking bathroom, either being sick, recovering from being sick, or wondering whether she was going to be sick again. She couldn't think how the baby managed to grow, she kept down so little, but grow it did, far quicker than Frazer had, so that by the end of July she could no longer do up the buttons on her blouses and had to tie her skirts together with tapes.

And then there were all the aches and pains, and all the horrible, sordid complaints, none of which she had suffered with Frazer: the backache and the aching legs and the indigestion and insomnia. The restrictions that this pregnancy imposed further constrained a day-to-day existence that already seemed almost unendurably narrow. In the hottest part of the summer, Bess sat in a deckchair in the orchard, sheltering from the sun, counting off the time till the baby would be born. Months and months to go – how would she bear it?

Yet she longed for this baby. She longed to hold a child in her arms again. She longed for someone to love. Her greatest worry was that, if the war ended tomorrow, she would be unable to travel to India to fetch Frazer. Pregnant, lumbering, her stomach turned by the slightest whiff of anything unpleasant, how could she possibly tolerate a long sea journey, or the heat and crowds of Bombay, or the precipitous, vertigo-inducing train journey to Simla?

But the war showed no signs of ending. Men continued to die on the Western Front as well as in the other theatres of war, and though the Allied troops had advanced and the German army had retreated some miles behind their original line, even the most optimistic of newspaper reporters was forced to acknowledge that the great loss of life — twenty thousand British dead on the first day of the Somme alone — had not achieved the decisive breakthrough that the military leaders had hoped for.

When the sickness finally passed, she began to feel breathless, tired even by the short walk to the local shop, exhausted by the two miles to the Crawfords' farm. This must be what it feels like to be old, she thought, as she puffed and panted up the stairs, or struggled to weed the garden, the hard curve of her belly making bending difficult. On a trip to Edinburgh, she had to endure the humiliation of feeling faint in a department store, anxious shop assistants fanning her while black dots swam before her eyes. After that, she did not dare venture out of the village again.

In her seventh month, after examining the great dome of her belly and murmuring about the possibility of twins, the doctor ordered her to rest, to take only gentle exercise.

Deprived of her usual distractions, the days, now darkening early because of the deepening winter, seemed very long and very dull. There were only so many tiny nightgowns one could smock, only so many khaki mittens and balaclavas one could knit.

She would have gone mad that winter, she often thought, shut up in the great, draughty house, had it not been for Pamela Crawford. Pamela now worked part-time in a hospital in Edinburgh; she spent the rest of her time helping out on her parents' farm in her brothers' absence. Yet she gave up her few remaining spare hours to play cards with Bess, or just to sit and chat.

One afternoon, Pamela asked hesitantly, 'Have you heard from Ralph?'

'I had a letter this morning.'

'How is he? Is he well?'

Ralph's letters were lists of what he and his men had had to eat, descriptions of the chilblains and stomach upsets he suffered from, and reminders to Bess about Hollins Lodge's household bills. Bess had a tendency to doze off halfway through reading them. 'He's perfectly well,' she said vaguely. 'Here.' She handed Pamela a couple of sheets of paper. 'You can read it, if you like.'

'Oh, I couldn't possibly—'

'I don't mind, really, I don't.' She had only skimmed through the letter – it was always a struggle to decipher Ralph's cramped penmanship, and the content of his letters, which was unrevealing, varied little.

Pamela's eyes were shining. She read eagerly, every now and then exclaiming, 'Rabbit stew for three nights running!

The poor dear! He never liked rabbit!' or, 'And he has had a bad cold! Poor Ralph, he does suffer so miserably from colds in the head!' Bess was aware of a feeling of discomfort. She, Ralph's wife, had had no idea that Ralph disliked rabbit stew, or that he was a martyr to head colds. Her initial scorn for Pamela – those beetling eyebrows, that wind-weathered complexion – had vanished a long time ago. Pamela's cheerful, guileless generosity would have moved the hardest heart. Pamela was incapable of being manipulative, incapable of deviousness. It would never have occurred to Pamela, for instance, to make a man fall in love with her.

Bess spent the Christmas of 1916 with the Crawfords. One of Pamela's brothers came to fetch her in the pony and trap. She had sent picture books to Frazer in India; to Ralph, in France, she had posted chocolates and cigarettes, as well as a 'Soldiers' Half Guinea Box' from Harrods, containing cocoa and nuts and Christmas pudding. Ordering the presents, wrapping and posting them, she felt as though she was sending them into a void. She found it hard to imagine what Ralph endured – hard, if she was honest with herself, to picture him at all in her mind's eye. And Christmas, along with birthdays, only served to emphasize her separation from Frazer. Her third Christmas apart from him, she thought at intervals throughout the day, and there it was again, that sense of panic, the fear she dare not voice even to herself, that she might never see him again.

Nineteen seventeen must be a better year, they all said, it must. Bess toasted the New Year alone with a glass of port

61

from Ralph's cellar, wrapped up in blankets, sitting in front of the fire. When she woke the next morning, her labour pains had begun. It was snowing, great white clotted flakes that floated down from a sky of grey steel. Mrs Brake sent one of the village boys for the doctor; Bess passed the time until his arrival sitting on a window seat, watching the snow as it settled on walls and branches.

Her son, Michael, was born first, at half past eleven that night. Twenty minutes later, just before midnight, her daughter, Kate, entered the world. When she held her babies, curled in the crooks of her arms, her gaze drifting from one pair of navy-blue eyes to another, all the frustration and difficulties of the past months fell away, and she was aware of a moment of pure joy. 'I'll never leave you,' she whispered. 'I'll never let you out of my sight.'

Chapter Three

Nineteen seventeen was a year of hunger, a year of grief. It was the year in which Bess watched from an upstairs window as children climbed over the wall into her kitchen garden on their way home from school. Crouching down, they pulled turnips from the ground, hardly bothering to dust off the soil before eating them raw.

It was the year in which she daily collected any leftover vegetables and uneaten crusts of bread to give to Pamela, who took them to a soup kitchen in Edinburgh, where penny breakfasts and lunches were served to the hungry. The year in which, following the introduction of coal rationing, and in the most bitter weather, Bess fed the nursery fire with wood hacked from wardrobe, armoire and sideboard.

It was the year in which troops fought the battles of Arras and Passchendaele in the acres of muddy wasteland that the war had made of the Flanders countryside, battles which took Mrs Brake's nephew and Pamela Crawford's eldest brother, Archie, and deprived Bess's Edinburgh friends of husbands, brothers and sons.

But it was also the year in which she felt that, with the birth of the twins, her life had turned back onto the right track at last. The world was falling apart, yet she found a great measure of happiness. Watching Michael and Kate grow from tiny, squirming newborn babies to twelve-month-olds who crawled from room to room, leaving a trail of destruction in their wake, entranced her.

Two halves of the one whole, they were devoted to each other. They were beautiful babies, everyone said so, with large blue eyes and pink and white complexions. There their resemblance to each other ended. Michael was dark; Kate's hair was a pale gold. Michael was bigger, stronger, and more robust than his sister; Kate was prone to colds and coughs and just that little bit behind Michael in crawling, walking and talking, as though she preferred her brother to try out things first. Kate had a way of surveying the world with a cautious, considering air, pausing for a fraction of a second before plunging into each new venture.

Only to herself did Bess admit her particular tenderness for Michael. He was her boy, of course. Though he could not fill the gap caused by Frazer's absence – no one could do that – Michael's babyhood reminded her, in a way that was both painful and consoling, of Frazer's. Every milestone Michael passed recalled to Bess her pride in Frazer's first smile, first tooth, first step, first word.

It seemed to Bess that with the twins she had been given a second chance. This time, she promised herself, she would not make the mistakes she had made with Frazer. This time, her babies would not be handed over to the care of a servant. She carried out most of the day-to-day work herself, although a young girl from the village came in to help in the early months. Sometimes Bess wondered whether her contentment lay in no longer having time to think, to brood. From the moment the twins' cries woke her at dawn to the moment she fell exhausted into bed at midnight, she was busy. Breakfasts and suppers were snatched, a few broken hours of sleep taken between feeding, changing, bathing and playing with the twins. Hollins Lodge revolved round their needs. Mrs Brake worshipped them; Pamela adored them.

Ralph saw his children for the first time when they were six weeks old, when he came home on leave. Kate was asleep; Michael had started to cry. Bess lifted him out of the cot.

'Come and see your son, Ralph.'

Ralph peered at the baby anxiously. 'Is he all right? His face, it looks so red.'

'He's just hungry. He's perfect, aren't you, Michael? Would you like to hold him?'

'I couldn't. I might drop him.' Ralph took a step back.

Yet, later that day, when she returned from the village shop, Bess found Ralph sitting in an armchair, a baby cradled in his arms, with Pamela crouching on the floor beside him. They did not see her at first, and for an odd, unsettling moment, watching the three of them from the doorway, Bess felt as though she was the intruder, the outsider.

Increasingly often, as the war went on into 1918, she

acknowledged, with a flutter of guilt, that when he was away, Ralph drifted far, far from her thoughts. The babies occupied so much of her time and energy. The struggle to keep house and family fed and warm during food and fuel shortages took up what little remained. When Ralph came home on leave, she felt, on first seeing him, an immense pity for him. His deep distress was visible in the facial and verbal tics he had acquired; she could hear his anguish when he cried out in his sleep, stricken by nightmares. An undemanding man, war did not suit him. He had never craved adventure or danger, would have been happy left with his fishing and his lists.

Yet all too quickly, pity changed to irritation. Bess felt ashamed of herself; Ralph's leaves were so fleeting, so rare, that she should have been able to tolerate his penny-pinching, his pernicketiness, his questioning of every rise in price, his checking of the household accounts to the nearest halfpenny. If a bill or receipt was missing, every drawer and shelf must be searched until it was found. She was used to running her own household – she had done so since she was ten years old, when her mother had died – and it infuriated her to be treated like a silly schoolgirl, her every expense questioned. It had seemed more important, she found herself yelling furiously at a bewildered Ralph, to look after the babies than to worry about a few old bills.

Never close, the war pushed them further apart. She had no real picture of what Ralph endured in the trenches, and he, in turn, expected everything at home to remain just as it had always been. He would have liked a cheerful, sweet, submissive wife to be waiting to welcome him when he returned from France, rather than a tired, harassed harridan, whose hands were worn with housework and childcare. He was another mouth to feed, at a time when their food supplies were more and more dependent on Hollins Lodge's kitchen garden. Yet to Ralph, gardening was her hobby, her pastime, rather than a means of survival.

They were both exhausted, she supposed, they had both lived on their nerves for far too long. They rubbed each other up the wrong way, and failed to answer each other's needs. She could not help but notice that when Pamela called, she seemed to know instinctively how to soothe Ralph's edginess. In Pamela's company, Ralph twitched and stammered less.

A mild man, he did not quarrel with her, but the expression of adoration that Bess had seen in his eyes during their courtship was replaced by a mixture of disappointment and hurt. Sex was rushed and joyless, an attempt to obliterate the present. When they talked, it was mostly of the children.

Increasingly, she suspected that *she* had begun to irritate him. What had entranced him during their courtship – her difference, her spontaneity – now confused or even embarrassed him. Looking at her reflection in the mirror, she could understand why Ralph's adoration was these days reserved mostly for his son and daughter. She hadn't had a new frock since before the twins were born and she couldn't remember when she had last worn her diamond earrings. Her flask of L'Heure Bleu was empty, though she still kept it, every now and then lifting the stopper to breathe in the ghost of the scent imprisoned in the glass. Ralph had fallen in love with one woman, she thought unhappily, and now he found himself married to another.

In the spring of 1918, Germany launched a major offensive on the Western Front. The British fell back around the Somme, up to almost forty miles in some places, their lines broken through. Amiens was threatened, and the British military hospital at Étaples came under fire. The French army retreated also, towards the Marne, only fifty miles from Paris. Now, German guns were able once more to reach the French capital, terrifying the inhabitants, just as in 1914. Bess recalled that peculiar man at the Corstophines' party – what had been his name? She could not remember – saying, if we win. For the first time, she shared his uncertainty.

She rarely read the newspapers now, no longer tried to trace the ebb and flow of battles in the atlas. Her visits to Edinburgh were infrequent, especially after the influenza epidemic broke out in June. Schools closed and church attendances dropped because of the fear of infection. On trains and in cities, people wore gauze facemasks, and the authorities sprayed the streets with disinfectant in an attempt to stem the spread of the epidemic. The disease was indiscriminate, taking the young and strong as well as the old and frail. Death came quickly, sometimes after only a few hours' sickness.

Bess's days revolved around Michael and Kate. Her thoughts flew to them when she opened her eyes in the morning and their image remained with her as she fell asleep at night. All she wanted, all she strove for, was to protect them, to keep them safe. Even if the war went on for ever; even if she never saw Frazer again. When she thought of Frazer, and of her life in India, it was as though she was remembering a dream. Her memories had the bright colours, the insubstantiality of a dream.

As the war continued into its fifth year, she became unable to imagine it ever coming to an end. She thought of it as some gigantic, sharp-toothed machine, a juggernaut that swept up men into its iron jaws, and spat them out, mangled, blinded or mad. By late summer, boys of eighteen and men in their early fifties were being conscripted into the army after only six months' training. At harvest time, the fields were busy with women and children, carrying out work that had previously been done by their fathers and brothers. But there was, at last, better news from the front. The German advance had been halted, and the Allies, now with American help, were pushing back the enemy and freeing much of occupied France and Belgium.

With the coming of autumn the influenza epidemic, which had seemed to be on the wane, returned with increased virulence. In London, hundreds of people died each week. Halfway through October, Bess received word that Ralph was coming home. He had been diagnosed as suffering from a stomach ulcer, and had been given a medical discharge from the army. Waiting for him at the railway station, she was aware of a feeling of apprehension. She should have being longing for this day, longing for her husband to come home from the war. Yet her emotions were a mixture of relief at Ralph's survival and unease about what the future would bring. She was no longer used to married life. She was used to organizing her own day, to controlling her purse strings, to going where she wanted and seeing whom she chose. How would she manage, sharing her life with someone she hardly knew?

The engine drew into the platform with a squealing of brakes and a hiss of steam. Carriage doors were flung open and she struggled to pick Ralph out of the crowd. Catching sight of him, she took a deep breath, put a smile on her face, and began to head towards him. They'd get along; she'd manage. They'd be fine. They just needed time, she told herself, time to get to know each other.

Of course, she was mistaken. It wasn't a failure to know each other that was the difficulty. Quite the opposite. The war had stripped away disguises. And the trouble was that, knowing each other, they disliked each other.

Disliked was perhaps too strong a word. She intimidated him – her strong will, her capacity to turn her hand to anything, the apparent ease with which she ran the large old house and tended the garden. The seedlings, he found himself thinking, would not have dared fail to grow tall.

He couldn't see where he fitted in any more. Hollins Lodge had changed since he had left it three years earlier. It was arranged for women and children; he had no place. There were hairpins and nappy pins in the bathroom. Furniture was in odd places, ornaments and books had been put on high shelves, out of reach of small hands. He stumbled around his old home, taking wrong turns, losing things, ill at ease.

The country, too, had altered, its mood irritable, rather aggressive. Girls drove trams, or streamed out of machine works at the end of the day; their voices, as they called out to each other, were loud and demanding. Along with the extra money in their pockets, working men had acquired a measure of confidence. In the cities, Ralph noticed, they seemed to take up the pavement more. They had a cocksure bravado; beside them he felt old, old and damaged and overburdened with memories, ashamed that he had survived when others, better men than he, had not.

There was no sense in anything now, only a muddied chaos that frightened him, that seemed to pervade everything he had once believed constant. Often he thought how wrong he had got it all, before the war. He had not known himself, his needs, his limitations. He was not brash enough to fit into this new world, hadn't the backbone to learn everything all over again. He pictured himself as a fish, floundering on a bank after it has been reeled in. It flapped and gasped pointlessly, and then you battered it on the head. He was like that, flapping, gasping and battered. The ulcer was only a focus for his loss of belief, gnawing away at him from the inside.

Against doctor's orders, he went back to work. He needed his office in Queen Street, with the big dark oak desk and the oil painting of his father over the mantelpiece. He needed to fill his head with figures; figures had a blankness that might soothe him. But, sitting in his office, he found himself unable to concentrate; every rumble of traffic, every closing door made him jump.

The next day, he woke with a headache and aching limbs.

He thought it was the ulcer, some new complication to torment him. He lay back on the pillows, his eyes closed, and tried to think of columns of figures, neatly printed, running up and down a page.

Pamela called that afternoon. The twins were playing in the garden; Bess went back outside to keep an eye on them while Pamela sat with Ralph. It was a fine, crisp day. Later, Bess always remembered that. The sharp beauty of the day, the distant hills grey with frost, and how every leaf was fringed with ice; the twins crouching on their haunches, searching for conkers beneath the horse chestnut tree. The cold: she should have put on her coat instead of a cardigan.

The sun was in her eyes as she looked round and saw Pamela crossing the lawn to her. And then Pamela was saying, 'I don't want to alarm you, Bess, and the doctor will have a much better idea, of course, but I think it's possible that Ralph may have influenza.'

There were layers of hope – she had always been an optimist. The hope that Pamela was mistaken, that it wasn't flu, but the ulcer; the hope that if it proved to be influenza, then the children wouldn't catch it.

In the space of a day, her hopes were peeled away. The doctor confirmed that Ralph was suffering from influenza; Kate was unwell by the following evening. They separated the twins, putting their cots in different rooms. By midnight, Kate's temperature had soared. Bess sponged her with tepid water, coaxed her into drinking a little warm milk, and comforted her when she cried. She had a secret conviction that she could make Kate pull through by the strength of her own will. If she never left her, if she concentrated all the time, then Kate would get better, Kate would survive.

She lost track of time. The days muddled into each other, their usual divisions — mealtimes, bathtime, bedtime — torn away. Late one evening, she rocked Kate in her arms and sang to her, and Kate's eyelids drooped and closed. After a while, it seemed to Bess that, for the first time since she had fallen ill, Kate was sleeping soundly. Careful not to wake her, she tucked her baby into the cot.

She had meant to stay awake, to keep watch over Kate, but instead she fell asleep almost immediately. She dreamed that she was in India, in a bazaar, confused by the multitude of alleyways and entrances. She was running through dark, narrow passageways, searching for a way out.

Waking was like pulling herself out of something viscous and clinging. In the pale dawn light, Kate looked bluish-white. She heard herself sob then felt weak with relief as she saw the pulse fluttering at her daughter's throat.

She rose and left the room. Her eyes were gritty and her limbs ached and her lungs felt tight. A possibility occurred to her that she had not previously considered: that she herself might fall ill. She had to put her hand against the wall to support herself as she walked. On the landing, the corridor rolled out unsteadily ahead of her. She was aware of the raised pattern on the wallpaper beneath the palm of her hand, the swirls and loops like the designs on an Indian shawl. Very slowly, very carefully, she set about putting one foot in front of the other. She couldn't possibly be ill; Kate needed her.

There was a sound. She looked up and saw Pamela, at

the far end of the corridor. 'Bess?' said Pamela. Her voice echoed. She tried to answer, but nothing came out, and Pamela seemed to blur, to blacken. Bess could no longer stand; she slid to the floor.

She was in that grey, pinnacled house in the Highlands, running from room to room. She was calling out someone's name, but the words mutated in her mouth to a scream.

Once, when she woke, Pamela was there. Another time, Mrs Brake was sitting beside the bed. 'I must write the grocer's order,' Bess murmured, and tried to sit up. A cool cloth was laid on her burning forehead, water held to her mouth as she coughed and coughed.

The next time she woke, the house was dark and silent. She was alone, but she thought there was an echo in the room, as though someone had called out to her. She shivered as she climbed out of bed and shuffled down the corridor to Michael's room. Gripping the bars of the cot, she looked down. Michael lay motionless under the blankets. His eyes were half open, strips of dull dark blue. His skin was dappled, light and dark, as though he was lying under a branch and the sun was shining down between the leaves. As she reached out to touch him, she heard herself begin to moan, a strange sound, like a rising wind.

A voice said, 'How is she today?' and a different voice answered, 'A little better, I think.' Sometime later, when it was dark outside, she heard bells ringing. She whispered, 'Why are the bells ringing?' and Pamela said, 'It's because the war has ended.'

Something was troubling her; she tried to remember. '*Kate*,' she whispered, and Pamela told her that Kate was sleeping soundly, that she was making a good recovery. Ralph was getting better too – he had been able to come down to the sitting room for an hour that afternoon. She mustn't worry, she must rest, she must go back to sleep.

But when she closed her eyes, there was still an absence. Frazer? No, not Frazer, this time. And she remembered the cot, and the dark blotches on Michael's face, and she heard herself say his name, over and over again, louder and louder.

And then Pamela was telling her that Michael, her Michael, whose hair had stuck up in little dark tufts when he was born, and who had been the first to crawl, the first to walk, the first to talk, and who had once brought her from the garden a present of a slug, which he had put in her apron pocket, and who had thought that conker shells looked like hedgehogs, and who had loved bread and honey but had hated peas, was dead, gone, buried already, erased from existence, as though he had never been.

They parted three months later. By then, they had rubbed themselves raw with grief and anger. At first, her anger was with Ralph, for bringing the disease into the house. 'You brought it home! You killed him!' she screamed at him, and then clamped her hands over her mouth, appalled.

Then she was angry with herself, for leaving Michael, when she had promised not to. She had promised to keep him safe, but she had failed him, just as she had failed Frazer. Mixed with her anger was guilt, and a conviction that she was being punished – for her carelessness in losing

Frazer, and for marrying Ralph when she had not loved him at all.

At last the anger seemed to seep away, leaving her exhausted and drained. She could not bear the house, where reminders of Michael were printed on every room – ghostly coloured trails where he had once scribbled with his wax crayons on the walls, a pale seam between the scullery tiles where he had upturned a bag of flour. She found his favourite toy, a white rabbit that she had knitted for him, hidden beneath the sofa cushions. It hurt her beyond endurance that they had not discovered it, that they had not known what it meant to him, that they had put him into his grave alone.

Weeks passed, weeks in which she stayed in her room while Pamela took care of the household. Sounds filtered through to her – someone playing the piano, and the canary, which she had bought for Michael and Kate on their first birthday, singing in its cage. Each morning, Pamela brought Kate to play in Bess's bedroom. When Kate searched for Michael – under the bed, in the wardrobe – Bess felt as though her heart was being scored with a knife. When Kate stopped looking for her brother, it was worse.

Once, looking out of her bedroom window, Bess caught sight of Pamela hugging Ralph, giving him the comfort he needed, comfort that she herself was not able to give. It helped her make up her mind. If they stayed together, she knew that they would destroy each other. She couldn't patch over her marriage, any more than she had been able to patch over the ugliness of Hollins Lodge. Now, she could not bear Ralph to touch her. What she had once been able to endure she could endure no longer. Her reaction was instinctive, visceral, and she knew that it would never change.

When she told Ralph that she was leaving him, he wept, though it seemed to her that he was also relieved. She would live in Edinburgh, she said; she had liked Edinburgh. She would take Kate with her, but he must visit his daughter as often as he wanted. She would leave it to him to choose whether he wished to divorce her; for herself, she would not marry again. She thought, but did not say to him, that marriage did not suit her. It seemed to wear away at the edges of her, like a length of fabric that has begun to fray.

Ralph insisted on renting a small apartment for her. She argued with him – For Kate, he said, with a rare forcefulness, and she abandoned her protest. He also told her that he intended to put some money by each month so that when Kate came of age, or when she married, whichever came first, there would be a lump sum for her. He showed her the documents he had drawn up in his neat small handwriting, which would make sure that Kate was always secure. When Bess looked down at it, the words blurred with tears. And when, the following day, she left the house, she kissed Ralph's cheek, wished him luck, and then walked away, Kate's hand in hers.

She had always imagined that as soon as the war was over, she would set sail for India. She had pictured herself steaming away from Southampton, travelling across oceans to be with her son at last.

Yet she did not buy her ticket or book her passage. For one thing, there was Kate. Bess found it hard to leave her daughter with anyone for any length of time at all. Leaving her in the care of a friend while she visited the shops, Bess would find herself standing at a department store counter, suddenly stricken, her heart pounding, afraid that in her absence something bad had happened to Kate. After all, she knew what happened to babies when you let them out of your sight: they died, or they disappeared.

She could not take Kate with her to India. Now, she saw danger in everything: the sea voyage, with its risk of storms and sinkings; the Indian climate, so conducive to fevers; railway accidents, landslips, flooding, riot, all the violences of man and nature that tropical countries were subject to.

Instead, she wrote to Cora Ravenhart once more, making it clear that if, this time, she received no reply, she would travel to India as soon as possible to reclaim her son. In a few months, she told herself as she posted the letter, she would be stronger; in a few months, she would have thought of what to do with Kate.

In the aftermath of the war and the influenza epidemic, Bess was surrounded by loss. By spring, the men had begun to come home from France. She saw them on the street corners, the blinded and the crippled, begging for change. She saw them in the shops, the shell-shocked and the mad, muttering to themselves, their limbs jerking, their hands repetitively brushing away some invisible stain from their clothing. More than seven hundred thousand British soldiers had died in the war. The influenza epidemic, which finally petered out in 1919, had taken the lives of almost another quarter of a million. Shortages and rationing continued, long after the Armistice.

Cora's letter arrived towards the end of April. Bess's hands at first shook too much to open it. She sat down, took a deep breath, then she ripped open the envelope. Cora's brief letter told her that she, Fenton and Frazer were shortly to travel to Scotland. They would be staying at the North British Hotel in Edinburgh during the first week of June. That was all, nothing else, no description of Frazer's progress, no acknowledgement from Cora that she must return her grandson to his mother.

But Frazer was alive and well and he would soon (if, this time, Cora could be trusted) be in Scotland. For the first time since Michael's death, Bess's heart lifted. Towards the end of May, she found herself walking frequently to the North British Hotel, near the station, gazing through the front door and windows, as if her longing could conjure up her son.

On the last day of the month, walking home with Kate, her gaze was drawn once more towards the hotel, and she caught sight of a familiar figure leaving the front entrance. Bess stopped suddenly, frozen, her heart pounding. Then she swept Kate up in her arms and ran, keeping her eyes fixed on where, in the sea of people, an ostrich-feathered hat bobbed.

She called out, 'Mrs Ravenhart! Cora!' and Cora turned to face her.

'Elizabeth,' said Cora Ravenhart calmly.

Cora was wearing black, a sheened, shimmering black that looked, thought Bess, like a sheet of metal, beaten thin. Her hat was heaped with feathers and crowned with a veil. Little black knots, sewn into the veil, mottled her face.

Bess struggled for breath – the run, the shock. 'Frazer – where is Frazer?'

'He is with his nursemaid, naturally.'

'I must see him.'

A small, cold smile. 'I don't think that would be desirable.'

'I desire it! I need to see my son!'

Beneath the veil, the blue eyes snapped. 'Not in the street, Elizabeth. We are not washerwomen.' Her gaze slid to Kate. 'Is she yours?'

'Yes.' Bess held the child closely, as if to guard her. 'This is my daughter, Kate.'

'So you have married again? I assumed that you would. Tell me, how long did you mourn my son before you remarried? A year? As much as that?' A shake of the head. 'What you need is of no interest to me, Elizabeth. It never was.' A pause, and then, as she turned to go, Cora added, 'But you may call on me this afternoon, if you wish. At four o'clock.'

Bess left Kate with Mrs Williamson and walked to the hotel. A bellboy showed her upstairs; her nerveless fingers fumbled to find a coin for him.

The sitting room glittered with giltwork and mirrors, and there was the scent of lilies. Cora Ravenhart was standing at the window. Stripped of the veil, her face was pale and smooth, mask-like. She said, 'I won't offer you tea. I doubt if either of us wishes to be in each other's company for any longer than necessary.'

'I'm here to collect Frazer. Then I'll go.'

'*Collect* him?' Cora's brows rose. 'I'm afraid that won't be possible.'

'I won't leave here until I have him.'

A thin smile. 'Then you'll have to wait rather a long time, Elizabeth.'

'You mean to keep him?'

'Certainly I intend to keep him. You don't think there's the smallest chance that I would give him to you, surely. Never. Frazer is my grandson. He is Jack's heir.'

'He is *my* son.' It was hard to contain her fury, hard not to send the vase of lilies and the cut-glass sweet dish crashing to the floor with a sweep of her arm. She said, her voice low and accusing, 'When I came to England four years ago – when you told me you would be travelling to Scotland – you lied to me, didn't you? You deliberately lied to me!'

'I wouldn't put it quite like that.' A quick, vague gesture. 'There was some intention to visit Scotland, but it did not come to fruition. The war . . .'

Liar, she thought. She shook her head slowly. 'I won't let you steal my son from me.'

'Why?' For the first time, Cora's stony blue gaze focused on Bess. 'You stole mine.' The words were cold and unyielding.

'I didn't *steal* Jack. He *wanted* to marry me.'

'You *enticed* him into marrying you.' The mask had slipped and now Cora's eyes were dark with hatred. 'Women like you know how to do that.'

'It wasn't like that.'

'Wasn't it?' A dry laugh. 'Do you expect me to believe that you married Jack for love? And your second husband, did you marry him for love, too? How soft-hearted you are, Elizabeth, how susceptible!'

Bess felt herself pale. She whispered, 'Jack loved me. I didn't entice him. I didn't have to. He loved me.'

'Jack desired you.' Cora had drawn nearer, so that now Bess felt the heat of her breath. 'That isn't love, it's lust. And even the meanest, lowest animal is capable of lust.' The harsh, contemptuous voice went on mercilessly. 'You were nothing before you married my Jack, nothing but the penniless daughter of a scoundrel. You were not worthy of Jack – you were not worthy of a Ravenhart. But you seduced him, you made him want you. How I hated to see what you did to him! How I hated to see you encourage my poor Jack to all kinds of wildness!'

'No—'

'You – you are to blame. If it wasn't for you, he would be alive today!'

Bess saw in her mind's eye a path through the mist, deodars and pines growing to either side of it, and she heard Jack shout to her, Come on, Bess! I dare you!

She said coldly, 'If Jack was wild, if he was reckless, then it was because of you. Because you spoiled him.'

Cora Ravenhart gasped, and raised her hand. For a short, obscene moment Bess thought that she might strike her.

But then Cora's hand fell to her side, and she muttered, her voice low and tormented, 'I loved Jack so much. Since he died, I have felt only half alive. You are incapable of such love. Now go. Please go. I never want to see you again.'

Bess stood her ground. 'I won't go till I've seen my son.'

A silence. Then, unexpectedly, Cora smiled. She said crisply, 'Then you're a fool.'

She opened a door and spoke a few words to someone

in the adjoining room. The air seemed to still; Bess thought she could hear her own heart beating. Then she heard footsteps.

A nursemaid came into the room. She was holding a little boy by the hand. He had white-gold curls and blue eyes and a child's version of Jack's thin, Roman nose.

Bess whispered, 'Frazer?' and the boy looked up at her.

'Frazer, don't you know me? I'm your mama.' The old nursery name slipped out unconsciously.

His eyes darted uncertainly from his nursemaid to his grandmother. Cora drawled, 'Frazer, my darling, this woman wishes to take you away from me. She wants you to go and live with her.' He looked alarmed; he put his thumb in his mouth. 'Do you want to go away with this woman, Frazer? If you do, you will never see me again.'

Frazer shook his head. Cora smiled once more. 'You see? He doesn't want you, Elizabeth. He's frightened of you.'

Bess knelt in front of him. 'Frazer, don't be afraid.' Very gently, she stroked his cheek. 'Please, my dear, don't be afraid, there's no need for that.'

But he was crying now, great tears overflowing and trailing down his face. When she tried to comfort him, he pulled away from her, running to Cora and burying his face in her skirts.

'You've upset him enough, don't you think?' As Cora sat down on the sofa, her eyes were triumphant. 'You see, he doesn't know you any more. And he doesn't love you at all.'

'Frazer . . .' but he did not even turn to look at her as he scrambled onto Cora's lap, and hid his face in the folds of her gown.

Now there were tears in her own eyes. She heard herself beg, 'Please, please, Mrs Ravenhart—'

'Would you take him away from the only mother he knows? Would you take him from the home and the country that he loves? Would you put your wishes before his happiness?'

'I implore you—'

'Go. Go now. You know that it's the right thing to do.' Cora's voice had softened; it coaxed and cajoled. 'You know it's the right thing for Frazer.'

Bess could not speak; she could only shake her head mutely.

'Go, Elizabeth, and leave us in peace.'

And she ran out of the hotel. She ran down the street, across a bridge, along cobbled roads. Smoke billowed from the railway station, passers-by stared, and her tears choked and blinded her.

She reached the end of a narrow alleyway; she saw that she was standing outside a garden. There was a gate; though she tried the lock and shook the railings, it would not open. The round balls of the box trees and the dark spikes of the cypresses inside the garden blurred, and the neat gravel paths and stone benches misted over as she rested her forehead against the iron railings, and wept.

Part Two

Martin Jago

1925–1935

Chapter Four

'Are you ready?' asked Davey Kirkpatrick. Martin Jago looked from his friend, who was standing in the doorway, back into his rooms, his gaze washing over the stacks of books and papers, the scattering of stones and potsherds, as if they might provide a clue.

'The concert,' Davey reminded him, as he followed Martin into the room. 'Had you forgotten?'

'Certainly not.'

'Liar,' said Davey amiably. 'How's the paper going?'

'The introduction isn't quite right.' He put on his spectacles, made to pick up his pen.

'No time,' Davey pointed out. 'And you can't turn up dressed like that.'

Martin quickly exchanged his corduroy trousers and frayed tweed jacket for black tie and dinner jacket, and five minutes later they were walking from his lodgings in the Old Town to the Assembly Rooms on George Street. He and Davey were old friends. They had attended Edinburgh

University together, Martin reading medicine and Davey reading law. They shared the same interests in music and archaeology. In character and appearance, though, they were opposites. Davey was handsome and athletic, a perfect specimen if you discounted the limp that was the legacy of a war injury, and he had a cheerful, open character. Apart from his physical deficiencies – he was short-sighted and rather thin – Martin knew himself to have an habitual reserve, a tendency to be solitary and sometimes gloomy. He and Davey got on well, he supposed, because they were so unalike.

It was midsummer, and this far north the light lingered late into the evening. There was a clarity in the air and, in the gardens, the roses and lilies seemed almost luminescent. In the branches of a tree a thrush sang. Martin had returned to Edinburgh after spending a number of years abroad partly because the city had always been a centre of excellence for medicine, but also because, living there before the war, he had come to love the place. He loved it for its fertile mixture of culture and raffishness and decay. He loved it because the dark underbelly that lay not far beneath the surface grandeur fascinated him – and so did the way that you could almost see the history, all the layers of it, like strata in rock.

Martin asked, 'How's Elspeth?' Elspeth was Davey's younger sister.

'Blooming. But fed up, to tell the truth. You know she likes to be on her feet, up and busy.'

'When's the baby due?'

'A month. And Primrose was spot on. We Kirkpatricks

believe in being punctual.' Davey smiled. 'I hope this one's a boy. I'd like to have a nephew.'

'You should marry, Davey. You should have sons.'

Davey made a dismissive sound. 'Who'd have an old crock like me?'

'How's the leg?'

'Oh, the same. Just fine.'

'Perhaps women don't care as much about that sort of thing as men do.'

'Most of them like you to be able to get round a dance floor without making too much of an ass of yourself.' They had reached the Assembly Rooms. 'And besides, advice on marriage is a bit rich, coming from you. There you are, hale and hearty, with all four limbs untouched, and not a wife in sight. You're a cold devil, Jago, and that's the truth of it.'

They were late; the concert was about to begin. As the conductor came on stage, Davey muttered, under cover of the applause, 'And besides, I, at least, am madly in love.' He gave a self-satisfied smile. 'And she is – *perfection*.'

Davey's face had taken on an ecstatic, and slightly stupid, expression. He regularly fell in love with shop girls, chorus girls and dancers, as well as the sisters, wives and daughters of his own class. Martin assumed that the true reason Davey had not married was because Davey could not bear to confine his attentions to only one woman. He had a particular fondness for girlish blondes, all curls and lisps and giggles.

'How long have you known her?'

'Almost a fortnight. She's an angel, the most beautiful creature. The most elegant, the most ravishing, the most—'

The conductor raised his baton, silencing Davey's search for another superlative. The first piece was Vaughan Williams's *Fantasia on a Theme by Thomas Tallis*. Such English music, thought Martin, and pictured in his mind's eye Stonehenge and Avebury and Silbury Hill, all those ancient, enigmatic structures that littered the chalk plains of south-west England.

He had visited England only briefly since the war. There it was again, the division, like a great, jagged mountain range that cut through the lives of all of his generation: the war. *There you are, hale and hearty, with all four limbs untouched*, Davey had said, but he wasn't untouched, any more than the shattered bones of Davey's leg would ever be *just fine*. They all had their demons, and his were the insomnia and nightmares that he had spent the last few years trying to escape.

He had returned to Edinburgh three months ago, to work as a GP in the practice of an old friend, Charlie Campbell, who had been his commanding officer in the RAMC. 'You won't make your fortune,' Campbell had said as he poured Martin a whisky in the sitting room of his comfortable house in Canongate, 'but there's enough going on to stop you getting bored. How was Egypt, by the way? See any mummies?'

After the concert ended, they left the building. Davey Kirkpatrick said, 'There's a party at Izzy Lockhead's tonight. It's her birthday. Shall we go?'

'I haven't seen Izzy in years. How is she?'

'Oh, bonny, very bonny.'

'I remember her as a plump little girl of fifteen.'

'Well, she isn't plump any more. In fact, she's rather a corker. She's gone a bit arty and crafty – peasant smocks and sandals and keeping chickens – in Moray Place, for heaven's sake.' Davey raised a hand to hail a taxi. 'Izzy's a poppet,' he added, once they were heading off towards Moray Place. 'Now, Hester—'

'The eldest sister.'

'That's right. There's three Lockhead girls, remember – Rosemary's the youngest.' Davey frowned. 'Poor old Het married Alex Findlay. Regular soldier, friend of Johnnie Murray, nice chap. He took a bad crack on the head at Arras. Never been quite right since.'

'A severe head injury can change the personality.'

'I believe the marriage is pretty hellish. Hester has a bit of a sharp tongue, these days. I don't think Alex can work much, so Het does up people's houses – tells them what colour to paint their walls, finds them knick-knacks and whatever.' In the dark interior of the cab, Davey's eyes gleamed. 'Anyway, I'm hoping that Izzy may have invited a certain friend of hers tonight.'

'Ah. The angel.'

'You're so right, my friend, the angel.'

'What's Izzy doing now? Is she married?'

Davey shook his head. 'Plenty of admirers, of course. She runs an agency, a domestic service agency. She finds the rich and idle their cooks and maids.' The cab drew to a halt; Davey paid the driver. 'You could do with a maid, Jago. Perhaps you should ask Izzy to find you one.'

At Isabel Lockhead's house, light blazed from the cracks between the curtains, and music seeped through an open window. Inside, guests gathered in little clumps in the high-ceilinged rooms, or danced in a swirl of silk and beading to the crash of brass and timpani.

Isabel was in the kitchen, sitting on the draining board beside her sister, Rosemary. Hester was standing nearby, smoking. Hester was tall and slim, and her smooth dark hair was cut short and close to her head. Her younger sisters' brown curls flared out in haloes round their faces. All three women had coal-black, expressive eyes, but Hester's were longer and narrower than her sisters', and she had lined them with kohl, which gave her, thought Martin, the look of an Egyptian queen.

Seeing them, Isabel slid to the floor, and squealed, 'Davey! How sweet of you to come! And Martin! Darling! It's been such an age – I thought you were dead!' She flung her arms round them. Hester gave both men a cool kiss on the cheek. Davey ruffled Rosemary's hair.

After he had wished Isabel a happy birthday, and after she had extracted a promise from him to come to supper, Martin left the kitchen and wandered from room to room. Many of the guests were known to him. They were the younger, less conventional segment of Edinburgh society, which had always been small, enclosed and exclusive. He himself existed only on its periphery.

In an adjacent room, he caught sight of Davey Kirkpatrick, standing by the window. 'Captivating, isn't she?' Davey murmured.

'Who?'

'You must have noticed her. *There.*'

He glanced across the room. Her back was to him. She

92

wasn't the insipid blonde of his imagination: her hair, which was coiled at the nape of her neck and kept in place with silver combs, was very dark, a foil for her pale skin. She wore a gown of shimmering black stuff. It crossed his mind how strange it was that the colour of mourning had such other associations: the forbidden, the erotic. Though she was not dancing, her foot tapped to the jazz music, as if she could not quite manage the task of stillness. He admired her carriage, which was as slender and upright as an arrow, and made her appear taller than she actually was.

As he watched her, he found himself unexpectedly assailed by a half recollection. He tried to grasp it – there was something in his past, scratching at his memory. Idly, he wondered whether, if a lot of things had happened to you, they somehow overlaid what had gone before. Why was it, for instance, that he could remember entire pages of medical or archaeological papers word for word, yet forget to put on his socks in the morning? Perhaps you had a certain amount of memories and if there were too many they spilled over, as if from an overflowing bucket. Or perhaps—

Then she turned and, putting back her head, laughed, showing the long, white column of her throat. A flash of movement, the pale arc of an arm, the rustle of silk, and he seemed to breathe in the honeyed scent of hoya. 'Mrs Ravenhart,' he said out loud, but Davey was already crossing the floor to her.

He remembered the night he had met her. It had been in the summer of 1915; the following day he had left Scotland for France. He had spent the next three years with the Royal Army Medical Corps, working at a casualty clearing station near the front line. When the war had ended, he had remained in France, at a hospital in Reims. And then, almost eighteen months later, he had suffered what he had since come to recognize had been some sort of breakdown. He had left the hospital and spent the next few months at his house in Champagne-Ardennes. During the war, the region had been trampled over by a succession of armies, its homes and public buildings commandeered, despoiled or destroyed. The hard work of repairing the house had done him good, exhausting him physically, making him sleep better. A year later, he left France, travelling first to Switzerland, to see the Celtic settlements at La Tène, and then to Italy, and Rome. Eventually, he sailed from the toe of Italy to Cairo. And there, in Egypt, among sand and stone and the artefacts of an ancient, mysterious race, he had seemed to begin to glue himself together again.

He had never forgotten Mrs Ravenhart, partly because she was beautiful, but also because she had represented an end to something – to innocence, perhaps.

Mrs Ravenhart had been wearing black then, too. Martin recalled that she had been pursuing Ralph Fearnley; he remembered the almost military precision of her campaign, the batted eyelids, the alluring smile, the way her small, tapered fingers had stroked poor Fearnley's sleeve. He had disliked her, then. Yet, later that same evening, when he had come across her in the Corstophines' conservatory, guzzling cakes and savouries as though she hadn't eaten for a week, his hostility had lessened. Free from onlookers, free, presumably, from the need to impress, she had had a naturalness and a directness that he had admired. He remembered her licking cake crumbs from her fingers and throwing her head back as she drank from his whisky flask. There had been something attractive and sensual about her unrestrained appetite. Watching her now, he thought she had changed. There was a gloss to her, like a thin layer of lacquer that made her shine brighter, harder.

Davey beckoned to him. 'Mrs Fearnley, this is my friend, Dr Martin Jago.'

Fearnley, he thought. So she had got her man. He said, 'We've met before, Mrs Fearnley. At the Corstophines'.'

She frowned. 'I'm sorry, I don't—'

'It was a very long time ago.'

She turned to Davey. 'You weren't at the ballet last night, Captain Kirkpatrick. Don't you like ballet?'

The Lockhead girls, with their entourage of attentive young men, joined them. Martin noticed how the men brought Mrs Fearnley drinks, lit her cigarettes, and laughed at her pleasantries. And he noticed the blue flash of her eyes and earrings. There was no sign of Ralph Fearnley.

Isabel Lockhead said, 'I read your book, Martin. So clever of you.'

Before he had returned to Scotland, he had published a book about the recent archaeological discoveries in Egypt. To his surprise, it had been a success, capitalizing, he supposed, on the mania for all things Egyptian that had swept the country since the discovery of Tutankhamun's tomb.

Rosemary Lockhead shivered. 'I should be terrified, going

inside a mummy's tomb. Have you ever been inside a mummy's tomb, Martin?'

'Once or twice.'

'The Pharaoh's curse . . .' breathed a young woman, and Rosemary gave a squeal of delight and terror.

Martin shook his head. 'No curses. No ghosts.'

Mrs Fearnley turned to him. 'Don't you believe in ghosts, Dr Jago?'

'No, I don't. Do you?'

She said calmly, 'Of course I do. Our ghosts are always with us. We can never get away from them.'

Rosemary ventured, 'I once stayed at a haunted castle.'

Hester said scornfully, 'And did you see a ghost, Rose dear? Any clanking knights in armour? Any headless spectres?'

'I heard . . . *things*. And there were strange shadows – and it was cold, so cold.'

'Where was this castle?'

'In the Highlands.'

'Which might explain the cold,' said Hester drily. 'I generally wear my coat and socks in bed if I have the misfortune to stay in the north.' There was a ripple of laughter. 'You always did have an overactive imagination, darling.'

'Old houses make strange sounds, don't they?' said Davey. 'The wind rattling the pipes and the floorboards creaking.'

'Or mice,' said Martin. 'I have an army of mice in my rooms.'

'You should find yourself somewhere more salubrious, Jago. No need to stay in that hellhole, surely, now you're a famous author.'

'It's not a hellhole. I like it there.'

Someone put another record on the gramophone. The floor cleared and they split into couples. Martin saw that Davey was watching Mrs Fearnley dance. Then he forgot Davey, and his own eyes followed her round the room. As she danced, the beaded material of her dress swayed, emphasizing the fluidity of her movements. She was sure-footed, keeping perfectly in time with the music. Her skin, which had the colour and smoothness, he thought, of the richest cream, was slightly flushed along her cheekbones, and locks of her dark hair spun out as she turned her head.

A cool voice whispered in his ear, 'Not a hope. Bess Fearnley prefers *expensive* men. You're far too poor for her.'

Martin turned and smiled at Hester Findlay.

'Dance with me, Martin,' she said.

'You wouldn't want me to, Het. I'd tread on your toes.'

'I don't care. My toes are quite tough.' She took his hand.

Beneath the thin fabric of her dress he could feel the bones of her ribcage. 'How's Alex?' he asked. 'I haven't seen him tonight.'

'He's not here. He doesn't like parties. He doesn't like noise. Or crowds. In fact, he doesn't like anything much at all. Which is rather sad, isn't it?'

'Is he seeing anyone?'

'Not at the moment. He's tired of doctors. He's decided to try the sun instead – he's promised me that we'll spend next winter in Menton.' She looked discontentedly round the room. 'I couldn't bear another winter here. The same old people, the same old places.'

They danced for a while in silence, he concentrating,

trying not to confuse the steps, she practised, bored. He asked her, 'Do you know Mrs Fearnley well?'

'Not awfully. Izzy knows her better. She's a little . . .'

'What?'

'Not quite the thing. She works in a nightclub.' Hester shrugged. 'But you know Izzy. She's never cared a bit for what other people think. And Bess is very pretty and utterly charming.'

'Her husband—'

'Which one? I suppose you mean Ralph Fearnley.'

'Did he survive the war?'

'Oh yes. Bess's first husband, the Indian one, died. But Ralph divorced her. Or perhaps he did the honourable thing and let her divorce him. I really can't remember. She has a little girl, you know. And then, of course, there's a string of lovers.' She glanced at him then gave a tinkle of laughter. 'Oh dear, have I spoilt your illusions? You're not in love with her too, are you, Martin?'

'Of course not.' He stood on her toes once more; she sighed, and led him to the edge of the room.

'You really are rather hopeless, darling.'

'I know,' he said humbly. They stood for a few minutes, watching the dancers. Then he said, 'Do many men fall in love with Mrs Fearnley?'

'Dozens. Davey Kirkpatrick is in love with her.'

'Davey falls in love with a different woman each fortnight, you know that.'

'He used to be in love with *me*.' Hester looked suddenly unhappy. 'No one falls in love with me any more. Why do you think that is? Am I too old? Have I grown ugly?'

'Of course not, Het. You're as beautiful as ever.' Though she was too thin, he thought, and there was a bitterness and desperation in her eyes. 'And you are married, of course,' he pointed out.

'Oh, don't be silly, Martin, no one minds about *that!*' She bit her lip, and then she whispered, 'Sometimes I find myself wanting to do something terrible. Do you ever feel that? I want to run down the street screaming. Or set the house on fire. Or chuck a stick of dynamite into some smug little Edinburgh get-together and watch them all burn to a frazzle.'

She was trembling. He took her hand and squeezed it, and then lit two cigarettes and gave one to her. His gaze slid back to Mrs Fearnley, who was now dancing with Johnnie Murray. *Where have you been, my long lost love, these seven long years and more?* How extraordinary that ten years on, he should still recall that phrase, and the sense of yearning it had induced in him.

Davey Kirkpatrick walked her back to her flat; Bess slowed her pace to match his. As they walked, the clouds parted to reveal a full moon, outlining with silver the castle on its rocky promontory. Kate's fairy-tale castle, Bess thought, and smiled to herself. When Kate was younger, she had refused to believe that the distant, turreted, moonlit castle she saw at night, which she thought was peopled by princesses and ogres, could also be the more mundane grey building they sometimes made the destination of their afternoon walks. Edinburgh's old tricks again, its way of deceiving you, of showing different faces, and coming at you in other guises.

When they reached Bess's flat, Davey contented himself with a kiss on the cheek, too much of a gentleman for an undignified tussle at the front door. Bess murmured something pleasant but noncommittal to Davey's suggestion of dinner, and went indoors.

Inside the flat, she went first to Kate's room, where she stroked her sleeping daughter's tangled hair, and then she thanked and paid Annie, the babysitter. Annie was a widow who lived on a small pension in a nearby flat. Kate had known her for years and was very fond of her – Annie had become, Bess often thought, an honorary grandmother to a little girl who had no grandparents.

After Annie left, Bess poured a Scotch, flung herself on the sofa and gave a heartfelt sigh of pleasure. Though she and Kate had lived in the flat for six years now, she suspected that her delight in being in her own home, her own domain, would never lessen. Over the years, she had decorated the rooms to suit her taste. Her Kashmir shawls were arranged on the backs of comfortable chairs, photographs and water-colours hung from the picture rail. She had placed a glass vase filled with pink roses on the centre of the table, and the blossoms perfumed the room.

It was Sunday tomorrow – how glorious to be able to lie in bed late! – though Kate had a way of sneaking into her bed in the early morning, making, at first, heroic attempts at stillness and silence, but then, as boredom set in, fidgeting with the perfume spray or jewellery box until Bess gave up trying to doze and got up to make breakfast.

From Monday to Saturday midday, Bess worked in a dress shop. The shop was owned by Iona O'Hagan, a tall, striking

Irishwoman who, through her instinctive good taste and eye for cut and colour, had made her small shop a magnet for Edinburgh's more stylish and original women. Iona was forthright and warm, and she and Bess had become good friends.

Two or three evenings a week, Bess also worked in a nightclub, the Black Orchid, in Picardy Place. She had met Jamie Black, who owned the nightclub, several years earlier, in the difficult days after she had left Ralph. Returning husbandless to Edinburgh, she had at first endured a period of notoriety. To begin with, she had not cared a jot for the world's opinion. Bruised by a failed marriage, mourning Michael and forced to accept at last that she had lost Frazer, she had welcomed her seclusion. All her thoughts and efforts had been concentrated on survival. Ralph paid for the flat and for Kate's school fees; she herself paid for everything else – food and fuel and Kate's school uniform. She had had enough of dependency; she had learned the hard way that she must have money of her own. If she had had money, she would not have lost Frazer.

In time, she began to miss adult company and tried to pick up the threads of old friendships. The Williamsons had stood by her after she left Ralph, but she quickly discovered that many preferred not to know her. As a divorcee with a child, she existed on the shadowy edge of society. As a divorcee who failed to lead a nun-like existence, who went out to work, who *enjoyed* herself, she soon learned that for Edinburgh's stuffiest, Edinburgh's most self-righteous, she was beyond the pale.

She was snubbed in the street, was the subject of stares

and whispers behind closed hands, and was left off guest lists for parties and suppers. The women regarded her with suspicion, even as a threat, and some of the men looked upon her new status as an opportunity. She learned to deal with those men, became practised at dealing with them. Such men were a tiresome consequence of the ambiguous position in which she found herself since leaving Ralph. The married men were particularly dangerous, and the powerful, conceited married men were the most dangerous of all. They thought they were doing you a favour when they bought you flowers, or when they offered to see you home. Or when they took you to their bed. Give them half a chance and they'd flaunt a desirable woman just as they flaunted their other possessions, their motor cars and their yachts and their shooting lodges in the Highlands. And when they tired of you, they'd not give a damn for your damaged reputation or your broken heart.

Jamie Black had been different. Bess had been working in a tea room when she met him. He sat at one of her tables; when he struck up a conversation with her, he was pleasant and courteous, without a flicker of the suggestive badinage that some men seemed automatically to adopt towards a young and attractive waitress. He visited the tea rooms at the same time every day for a week. When, at the end of the week, he asked her out for a drink, Bess had accepted. She needed company; she needed *male* company.

Jamie was tall and powerfully built, with a face that was craggy and interesting rather than handsome. Now in his early forties, he had a variety of business interests in Edinburgh. He was also married; to his regret, he had no children. Their affair had been discreet and undemanding, and it had lasted as long as it had because of their strong liking and desire for each other, and because they both had busy lives that allowed no place for grand passions or jealousy.

They had been lovers for over a year. Their eventual drifting apart had been prompted by Bess's niggling guilt and anxiety, which had grown, rather than declined, the longer she knew Jamie. There was the fear of being found out, and the fear, however careful they were, that she might fall pregnant. There was also the knowledge of the immense hurt that would be the inevitable consequence of the discovery of their affair. When she eventually found the courage to put an end to it, she hated the loneliness that ensued, and she missed the pleasure they had shared. There were some sorts of love, she thought bitterly, that would always be denied to her. But they had parted on good terms, remaining friends, and when, a couple of years later, Jamie had opened the Black Orchid, he had asked her to work for him.

Edinburgh's young, fashionable and wealthy, spilling out of restaurants and theatres at ten o'clock at night and unwilling to settle for cocoa and bed, headed for the Black Orchid. The Black Orchid operated as a private club, and its licensing hours were extended on condition that food was served. Bess's work consisted of taking customers' drinks orders and offering round trays of sandwiches. *Keep the customer happy*, was Jamie's motto, which meant that she must also smile at the clientele and laugh at their jokes, however unfunny, and make sure they enjoyed themselves so much they would come back again and again.

Bess loved the nightclub. She loved the way the raucous jazz music swept her up, making her foot tap the moment she went through the door. She loved the gaudy glitter of the cabaret, and she loved to see the single spotlight illuminate the performers on the tiny stage, making the plain pretty and the beautiful mesmerizing. She loved the wisps of cigarette smoke that drifted in the changing colour of the lights, and she loved watching the couples on the dance floor, the sway of chiffon and silk and the frenzied rhythm of limbs and swirl of fringe and ribbon.

Hester Findlay had been responsible for the club's decor, and it had been through Hester that Bess had met Isabel and Rosemary. A clique of beautiful and free-spirited people always accompanied the sisters whenever they visited the club. Bess had found herself absorbed into the Lockheads' set, invited to their cocktail parties and dances, fitting easily into their bohemian glamour.

That afternoon, she and Kate had visited Isabel Lockhead at her Moray Place house. After she had given Izzy her birthday present, and after they had put the finishing touches to the party food, they sat out in the garden. Watching Kate play, Bess's heart seemed to swell up with love for her.

At eight years old, Kate was tiny and coltish, all arms and legs and big blue eyes. Her hair, a glorious red-gold, constantly struggled to escape from its plaits, and her clothes seemed always to be in a process of disintegration, buttons flying undone, socks falling down, her blouse untucking itself from her waistband. Because Kate didn't seem to know what to do with her skinny little limbs, Bess had decided to send her to ballet lessons – yet another expense, and another reason why she had accepted Jamie's offer of work at the nightclub.

Ralph had married Pamela Crawford in 1923. Thomas, their first son, had been born less than a year later, Henry a year after that. Kate adored her two half-brothers, and had knitted bootees full of dropped stitches that Pamela, kind Pamela, made sure her babies were wearing whenever Kate went to stay at the Lanarkshire dairy farm that she and Ralph, surprising everyone, had bought shortly after their marriage. Bess was happy for Kate that she had two half-brothers, and ashamed of the rush of resentment and envy she had felt both times she had heard that Pamela had given birth to a son. But it was hard not to think bitterly of the sons she had lost, hard not to brood on how much she would have loved the busyness and clamour of a house full of children – a house full of sons.

After she left Ralph, she had resolved never to marry again. Unfortunately, not wanting to be married hadn't stopped her longing for more children. She had had three babies and had lost two; there was always, at the back of her mind, that fear of the empty cradle. Her dread of loneliness lingered, and with it went a longing for something she had never had – the security of a big, warm family, the comfort of knowing you need never be alone. Which was not, she thought, an unreasonable desire. Most women had families.

But you could not have a family without also having a husband, and, with the passing of the years, her chances of remarriage had shrunk. She was thirty-one now. She knew that a thirty-one-year-old divorcee with a child was to most men a considerably less attractive prospect than a girl of twenty. When, over the past few years, she had received occasional offers of marriage, she had always refused them. She had not loved any of her suitors. She had married without love before and would not make the same mistake again.

Neither would she take any risks with Kate's welfare and happiness. Any future husband must be a good father to Kate. Any future husband must also be a good provider, even-tempered, tolerant and kind, neither extravagant nor mean with money, neither dull nor reckless. Where, at the age of thirty-one and a divorcee with a dubious reputation, would she find such a paragon? Where, among a generation that had been decimated by war and disease, would she discover any such man? Such a person did not exist; she had resigned herself to that some time ago.

She guarded Kate closely, and had vowed that she would have nothing but the best. Kate would not have the short, uncertain, unpredictable childhood that she herself had had. Kate would not learn to flirt at fifteen, and nor would she marry at eighteen. She would not be parcelled off to aunties and friends she hardly knew, and she would always have someone she could turn to, someone to protect her and to give her wise advice.

Long before Kate had gone to school, Bess had taught her her numbers and letters. They had counted the trees in the park and the ducks on the pond. She had read Kate stories, had taught her to write her name, to dress herself and to plait her own hair. Kate must be able to look after herself; Kate must not depend on others for her survival.

In working hard to give Kate all that she could, she was trying to make up for another deficiency. A photograph of Michael stood on the mantelpiece in Kate's room, and his knitted rabbit had its place among the row of teddies at the foot of Kate's bed. What must it be like to lose the person who was your other half, the person with whom you had shared a womb? It would be like losing a part of yourself – it would be, perhaps, like losing a child. Bess shivered, and pushed the thought away.

Kate had another brother, of course. Bess had told Kate about Frazer as soon as she was old enough to begin to understand. She had taken out the atlas to show her daughter where India was, where Simla was. She had shown her Frazer's photograph and the jacket she had made for him, from which the powdery, baby scent had long gone. It had helped her to know that Kate knew about Frazer. It had helped her to feel that, however tenuously, they were all part of the same family.

Frazer was eleven years old now. Often, Bess pictured him, fair-haired, blue-eyed, slight, quick-limbed and spirited, running through the bazaar at the head of a gang of other little boys. He would be fearless and brave, as she herself had been at that age, as Jack must have been. He would be able to swim and to ride a horse. He would scramble up rocks and climb to the tops of the tallest trees. She hoped that Cora had taught him well, and that he knew which streams were safe to drink from and which brackish ponds harboured the larvae that caused malaria. She was sure that Cora would have taught him not to ride through the hills on a misty morning.

Bess wondered whether Cora would send Frazer to boarding school in England, or whether she would keep him close to her in India. *He doesn't know you any more; he doesn't love you at all.* The memory of Cora Ravenhart's words still made her shudder; she strongly suspected that Cora would not let Frazer out of her sight.

It was late, and she was tired. She went into her bedroom and stared in the mirror. She unclipped her diamond earrings and laid them carefully inside their velvet-lined box. Without their reflected light, it seemed to her that there was the suspicion of a shadow beneath her eyes. She gave a hiss and a tut, opened the pot of vanishing cream and began to rub furiously.

There was a small sign, just a stylized painting of a black orchid, which, if you hadn't been looking for it, you would not have noticed. No flickering neon, no brash lettering. Inside, you went through lowish, gloomy passageways and dark anterooms – rather like an Egyptian burial chamber, thought Martin – where your credentials were discreetly checked, and you were relieved of your coat and hat and umbrella.

At the end of the corridor, double doors were flung open and you were assaulted by coloured lights and music, and you found yourself in a room containing a bar and tables and chairs and a small dance floor with a raised dais. A jazz trio played on the dais; the music had a jagged, angular rhythm that sank into your bones. And everywhere there were jostling elbows and voices shrieking over the music, and the glitter of diamanté on the girls' dresses, and the scent of Turkish cigarettes and French perfume, and hostesses carrying trays of drinks which you thought must be dashed to the ground by the crowd and bustle but somehow never were.

Davey caught sight of Isabel Lockhead and called and waved. They wove through the crowd, Davey forging ahead. A tall, majestic woman in dark green velvet, who had a pale, high-cheekboned face, thick copper-coloured hair and a deep, rich voice that cut through everything, waylaid Martin.

'We've just had the most glorious hour trying on gowns in my shop,' she said. 'Don't you adore that blush rose on Rosemary?' She held out her hand to him. 'I don't believe we've met. My name is Iona O'Hagan.'

She had an Irish accent and the look, he thought, of some ancient Irish heroine – Queen Maeve, or Deirdre of the Sorrows.

'Martin Jago,' he said.

'I sometimes feel so sorry for men. Putting on a new dress is so gloriously liberating. A change of colour, the odd pleat or sequin, and you are a different person entirely.'

'Do you want to be a different person, Mrs O'Hagan?'

'We would become very tired of ourselves if we were never able to be anyone else, don't you think?'

A voice at his ear said, 'Martin's like a cat. He has nine lives. Only he likes to keep most of them secret, don't you, darling?'

He turned to see Hester Findlay. 'Not at all. I'm as transparent as glass.'

She kissed his cheek, her lips cool against his skin. 'I'm surprised to see you here, Martin. I thought you'd be doing something noble – curing the sick, making the lame walk.'

'So you're a medical man?'

'Yes, Mrs O'Hagan.'

'That's just one of Martin's lives, Iona. He likes to dig up old bones, too, don't you? And every now and then he disappears to France. You're not hiding a wife and children there, are you, darling?'

'I hate to disappoint you, Het, but no.'

'My dear Dara prefers to stay in Ireland,' said Mrs O'Hagan. 'He collects mosses. There are a great many mosses in Ireland.'

Hester said, 'I wish I had somewhere to escape to.'

'Why?' Martin studied her small, disconsolate face. 'What do you need to escape from?'

She shrugged. 'The weather, this frightful weather. It's supposed to be summer.' Then she brightened. 'What do you think of the decor, darling?'

Black walls, silver and purple lights and purple velvet seats. Silver-framed pictures of orchids, in dark, livid shades, on the walls. 'It's extraordinary,' said Martin.

'Hester did it,' explained Mrs O'Hagan. 'She has an eye for colour, don't you think?'

'Exquisite but decadent, that's what I was aiming for,' said Hester. 'No themes – I am so tired of themes. If I see another papier-mâché Tutankhamun I think I shall scream. And don't you just adore the mirror tiles in the alcoves?' Her eyes scanned the dance floor. 'I'm longing to dance. Won't someone dance with me?'

Martin gave a quick shake of his head. 'You must have learned your lesson the last time, Het.'

'I'll dance with you,' offered Iona.

Hester turned to the men. 'You don't mind, do you, darlings?'

'Not at all.' Davey smiled. 'Run off and dance. We shall enjoy watching you.'

They watched for a while, then Davey went to talk to Alex Findlay. Viewed from his right-hand side, Alex Findlay's profile was handsome and regular, if rather haggard, but from the left the livid scar made by the trench mortar could be seen.

Martin made his way to a quieter corner of the room. He stood in a dark doorway, smoking. Fragments of conversation, and the events of the day, flickered lazily at the back of his mind, like ripples in a pond. *We all like to become a different person every now and then, don't you think . . . Martin's like a cat, he has nine lives.* If you had too many interests – too many lives – did you run the risk of never acquiring true expertise in anything? His mind wandered to the patients he had seen in his surgery earlier that day. The child he had visited that afternoon who had been suffering from rheumatic fever – how extensive was the damage to the heart? The respectable businessman, a mainstay of the community, whom he had been treating for some time and suspected of suffering from syphilis; the tendency of syphilis, at certain stages, to mimic other diseases, making diagnosis difficult. The even more difficult task of breaking the news of his diagnosis to the patient. His promise to look after an Irish wolfhound during a friend's absence in London – what would he do with the creature during the day? Would it pine, enclosed in his rooms? Would it be practical to take it with him while he went on his rounds?

Then he saw her. Bess Fearnley, wearing red this time. A dark, dark blood-red, against which her skin looked bone-white. She was coming away from the bar, a tray of drinks balanced on her fingertips. He saw her pause to speak to someone, flash a smile at someone else, put her free hand on a man's shoulder and stoop to hear what he said to her. He saw the sway of her black hair as she moved, and the way the tasselled ends of the red sash round her hips swung as she slid expertly through the crowd. He put his fingers to his pulse, fascinated by its fast, skittish beat, and took a great breath of hot, smoky air, but it did nothing to quell his giddiness. And then, as she crossed the room, her reflection was caught in the mirror tiles and broken into shards of red and black and white.

A French phrase came into his mind: *coup de foudre*. It meant, literally, thunderstroke. As though the heavens above had opened, forking down fire, changing him, altering his chemistry, the rush of his blood, the beat of his heart. One moment, there you were, happily mulling over this and that, and then the next, after that crash of thunder, you knew that something unalterable had happened, something you could not unpick, something you could not put back and say, *No, this isn't for me, I don't want it*.

Martin Jago had been interested for some time in the diseases that working men and women were prone to – the injuries of the fingers and hands that afflicted bookbinders, the poisons that damaged both the skin and the digestive system of chemical workers, and the chest disorders that so many compositors and typesetters suffered from. There were a great many printing works in Edinburgh, and tuberculosis and its fellow respiratory diseases were responsible for a large number of premature deaths in the city.

Tuberculosis was endemic in the crowded conditions of the Edinburgh tenements, frequently infecting several members of the same family as well as nearby homes. Much of Edinburgh's housing – the same city that boasted the glories of Princes Street and Holyrood Palace – was grossly overcrowded and in poor repair. More than half the population lived in one or two rooms, meagre homes that gave little comfort and no privacy. Birth, copulation and death took place where the family ate, worked and slept. Such hardship showed in the health of the women and children, in particular. The women were prematurely aged by lives of endless physical labour and poor diet, and by long days confined inside their small, cramped, insanitary homes. The children did not grow as well as country children did. At similar ages, city children were several inches shorter and almost a stone lighter than their country cousins from an equally impoverished background. Rickets, too, thrived in the sunless wynds and closes of the city, causing children to suffer the characteristic distended stomachs and bowed legs.

It was frustrating that, all too often, by the time Martin was called out to see a patient, it was already too late. The disease would have run rampant, unsuccessfully treated by a succession of grannies or quacks before a doctor was called in. He saw TB patients treated with brown paper soaked in vinegar, or children suffering from mastoids with bread poultices strapped to their swollen, feverish faces. He knew the reason why, of course. A great many people could not afford the half-crown doctor's fee. Often, he waived his fee, calling back several times to check on a patient without payment.

There were many instances, of course, where the medical profession was helpless. In pneumonia cases, Martin could do little other than administer laudanum in an attempt to see the patient through the crisis. With meningitis or severe chest infections, there was even less that could be done. With luck, with good nursing and a decent standard of care, the patient sometimes recovered by himself – frequently, to Martin's embarrassment, thanking him profusely. Far too often, though, a child from the tenements would die when a child from a more affluent family might have been able to shake off the same disease. It was impossible to nurse a sick child properly in a single-end or two-room home shared, perhaps, with a dozen other people, where water was fetched from a tap in the back yard, and even the air was tainted. However hard parents tried to protect their children – and Martin was sometimes touched almost to tears by their efforts – they were defeated by the environment in which they lived.

His work usually absorbed him, yet after that visit to the Black Orchid, he found himself distracted, dogged by a feeling of dissatisfaction. He felt restless and uneasy, and his concentration was poor. His passions, music and archaeology, failed to give him much solace. He wondered whether he was unwell and took his temperature and pulse and found them to be normal. He wondered whether he should have remained abroad, whether Edinburgh's less attractive

qualities – that streak of Puritanism, that touch of senti-
mentality – had become intolerable to him.

It did not take long, however, for him to admit the cause
of his malaise. Often, and at the oddest times, his thoughts
drifted to Bess Fearnley. Once content with his own company
for long periods of time, he now began to seek her out,
accepting invitations he would not previously have considered in the hope of catching a glimpse of her. He endured
dull conversation and bad music, ate food he did not wish
to eat, suffered company he did not wish to keep, just to
be in the same room as her. Yet when their paths crossed,
he was tongue-tied and awkward. In Bess Fearnley's
company, he spilt wine and trailed his cuffs in his soup.
He wondered why it was that when he talked to someone
he wanted to, if not impress, at least not bore, what wit and
fluency he had deserted him utterly.

He knew that she lived in the New Town and that she
worked in Iona O'Hagan's dress shop in Howe Street, as
well as at the Black Orchid. Walking past the shop one afternoon, he caught a glimpse of her, a shimmer of movement
behind the glass. He knew from Hester Findlay that she
had been first widowed then divorced. Once, in a particularly vicious mood, Hester had also told him the names
of some of Bess Fearnley's lovers. Afterwards, if he happened
to cross the paths of those men, he felt a surge of jealous
dislike.

One evening at the nightclub, he caught Hester studying
him, a measuring look in her eye. 'My, you are smitten,
aren't you?' she said coolly.

He blinked. 'I don't know what you mean.'

'Of course you do, Martin. Bess Fearnley. I've seen you. You can't keep your eyes off her.'

He shook his head. 'I'm not even sure that I like her.'

'You don't have to like a person to love them.' A small smile, then she said, 'There's no need to reproach yourself, you're in terribly good company. Davey Kirkpatrick is absolutely mad about her. Yes, yes.' Impatiently, she silenced him. 'I remember. Davey is in love with half the women in Edinburgh. You told me so.' She took his hand in hers and murmured, 'But you're wrong. This is different. He's serious, this time. He told Izzy so.' Fleetingly, her nails dug into his palm.

After that, he noticed how often Davey was at Bess's side, how often it was Davey who fetched her a drink or walked her home at the end of an evening. He couldn't tell whether or not she favoured Davey. Bess Fearnley smiled her bright smile and laughed her infectious laugh with any number of men.

Walking back to his rooms one evening, he caught sight of Davey through the open door of a Grassmarket pub. Inside, the bar was wood-panelled, the seating round the perimeter divided into booths. Davey was sitting in one of the booths. Catching sight of Martin, he called out to the waiter for another glass of whisky.

As they talked, Davey drank steadily. Conversation drifted to the topic of Davey's sister and her new baby. Davey muttered, 'What I can't understand is how Elspeth can manage it and I can't.'

'Manage what?'

'Family life. There's Elspeth, eight years younger than

me, with a son and a daughter and blissfully happy with dear old Rory, while I'm fast heading for a lifetime of lonely bachelorhood. I can see myself in ten or twenty years' time, wearing the same collar for a week and eating at the same table each night in some dreary club.' He picked up his glass and stared at it, and muttered gloomily, 'If only I knew what she really thought of me.'

'Who? Elspeth?'

'Of course not. Bess.'

Martin's heart gave a little jump.

'If only she'd damn well give me some sort of sign that she doesn't just lump me in a heap with all the rest of them. But then, why should she? I hang around her like the rest of the vultures, don't I? Every now and then she throws them a scrap or two – gives them a smile or lets them fetch her a drink. She keeps them on a string. At least,' he looked suddenly grim, 'I hope she does.'

There were a great many questions Martin wanted to ask. Such as, who does she keep on a string? And, are you and Bess Fearnley lovers? He did not ask them, of course. But something in his expression must have given him away, because Davey stared at him, groaned, and said, 'Oh God. Not you as well.' Then he gave a sour smile and shook his head. 'Always thought you had ice in your veins, Jago. Well, I would say let the best man win. But these things rarely work out that way, do they? Women have the most unpredictable tastes. Just think, right now she could be murmuring sweet nothings to that red-haired idiot who follows her around all day.'

Summer drifted into autumn. Martin began slowly to

accept his situation, as if it were a chronic disease. He would be able to limp on, infected by it, but he would never be cured. He knew that Bess would never reciprocate his feelings for her, and he knew equally well that he would never declare his love for her. He would not behave as the vultures did. He had noticed how they crowded her, pestering her for favours, and how this grated on her.

With acceptance came, at last, a greater serenity. He no longer dropped things at her feet or tripped over his own. He became able to exchange a passably sensible conversation with her. Once or twice they danced, she fluid and graceful, all fizzing, exquisite energy, he concentrating his entire mental capacity on not treading on her feet. As the months went on, it seemed to him that she had begun to look upon him as a friend. He guessed, with a dash of bitterness, that she had discounted him as a lover and, in doing so, had begun to like him better.

Chapter Five

In the Princes Street Gardens in October, leaves hurled themselves from the trees like clothes torn from a washing line. Kate darted through the muddy grass, her plaits flying out behind her.

Someone said, 'What's she doing? Why does she close her eyes whenever she catches a leaf?' and Bess turned her head.

'She's making a wish,' she explained. 'If you catch a falling leaf you can make a wish. Didn't you know that, Dr Jago?'

He had appeared out of the murk, bundled up in a black coat and scarf, beads of mist gathering on the brim of his hat.

'I'm afraid not,' he said. 'And is your wish always granted?'

'Of course. At least, Kate believes so.' Bess raised her voice. 'Kate! Your shoes! And the park keeper will tell you off if you trample his grass!'

'May I walk with you, Bess?'

'Of course.'

They headed along the path after Kate, careful not to entangle their umbrellas. When Bess looked about, it seemed to her that the landscape was nothing more than a blur of grey and brown. 'Wet Sunday afternoons in Edinburgh!' she said disgustedly. 'Can you think of anything more tedious?'

'If you dislike it so, why do you come out?'

'The fresh air's good for Kate. At least I assume it is, though I worry about her catching cold. Still, a brisk walk must be better for her than being stuck indoors with a mother who's slowly going mad with boredom. What do you think, Martin?'

'Oh, a bit of rain never hurt anyone.'

'It's not just the rain. You can't believe that anything exciting – anything new or unexpected, anything *different* – will ever happen again.'

'You can't expect excitement on a Sunday afternoon, Bess – most unsuitable. It wouldn't do at all. There might be a revolution.' She saw a glint of amusement in his eyes. 'And it isn't true that there's nothing interesting to see. For instance, there's a rather fine clump of mistletoe on that apple tree. And see how the earthworms are coming out of the grass because of the rain. And there, look.' He was peering into the dripping shrubs, his hand shadowing his eyes.

'What is it?'

'There's a blackbird with a streak of white on his wing feathers.' He stooped to match her height, his hand resting on her shoulders as he directed her gaze. 'Just there, beneath the laurel.'

'Oh! It looks like a mynah bird. I used to see them in India.' She put up the collar of her raincoat and shivered. 'Days like this, I find it hard to imagine that India still exists. I find myself wondering whether I imagined it. Whether I simply made it up. All that sun, all that colour and heat. I suppose I must have been bored, sometimes, but if I was, I can't remember it.'

'Perhaps boredom by its nature is unmemorable.'

'No. I always remember being bored. I think that's why I try so hard to avoid it, because I remember how miserable it made me feel.'

'If it wasn't Sunday, I'd ask you if it would bore you to let me buy you and your daughter an ice cream.'

She glanced at him. Martin Jago intrigued her; she could not quite make him out. Much of the time he seemed absorbed in a world of his own; he sometimes had an air of distance, almost to the point of unfriendliness. She found it hard to tell whether he liked her or not.

'Ice cream?' she said. 'I'm afraid that even if it wasn't Sunday, I'd have to say no thank you, Martin. It's far too cold for ice cream. Now, a cup of tea – that would be a different matter.'

'That I can manage.' He called out, 'Kate! Would you like to see a Mexican sacrificial dagger?'

'Where are we going?' Bess asked.

'To my lodgings. I'll make you a cup of tea and Kate can learn about the terrible deeds of the heathen Aztecs. You'd like that, wouldn't you, Kate?' His eyes glittered. 'You said you wanted to do something different, Bess. And I can't imagine you've seen *that* many sacrificial daggers.'

It had begun to rain more heavily; water streamed down the gutters, taking with it dead leaves and cigarette ends. Martin Jago's lodgings were lost in a maze of high buildings and narrow wynds. Darkness pooled on the unlit landings. Kate ran up the stairs two at a time.

Inside, the gaslight illuminated a succession of vague, gloomy shapes: flints scattered across the fireplace, a skeleton suspended from a hook on a door, an upright piano, with a sheet of music on its stand, and books, books everywhere, on shelves, stacked against walls, on tables and beside chairs.

Martin shifted a heap of books from the sofa, dusted the cushions, and invited Bess to sit down. Then he opened a velvet-lined box and showed Kate the dagger. 'It's made of black obsidian,' he told her. 'Obsidian is a sort of rock that comes from volcanoes.'

Kate's eyes widened. 'Did they sacrifice *people* with it?'

'Perhaps.'

'Is there blood on it?'

Bess said, '*Kate.*'

'There might be. You could look very hard. But don't touch it because it's very sharp and your mother would never forgive me if you cut yourself.'

He went into an adjacent room; there was the sound of a kettle being filled. Bess wandered round the room, turning the page of a book, brushing the palm of her hand against a bundle of feathers stuffed inside a jam jar. She thought that Martin Jago must be quite poor – the sofa's covering was threadbare and the curtains had seen better days. It must be harder, in some ways, for a man on his own than for a woman. Men did not know how to make do and mend. They did not know how to patch and turn and sides-to-middle and let in and let out, all those tricks that could make anything from a cushion cover to a frock last just that little bit longer.

He came back with the tea, a tin of biscuits, and a glass of milk for Kate. Kate was examining a row of fossils that drifted along a window sill, running her fingertip around the smooth coil of an ammonite.

Bess said, 'You seem to have a great many interests.'

'I suppose I do. They stop me getting bored. Even on a wet Sunday in Edinburgh.'

'Boredom's supposed to be a sign of a light mind, isn't it? A lack of inner resources.'

'I'm afraid so.'

'Perhaps I should take up a hobby. Hen-keeping, like Izzy. Or embroidery.' She made a face.

'What do you enjoy doing?'

'Riding. I love to ride. But I haven't ridden for years.'

'Why not?'

She said frankly, 'Because keeping a horse is ruinously expensive, and even to borrow some poor, hard-mouthed riding-school hack for an hour or two costs far more than I can afford.'

'What else do you enjoy?'

'Oh, plenty of things. I love music, of course. And company. I've always liked to be in company.' She was surprised she had admitted that to him; these days, she rarely let down her guard.

He said, 'I shouldn't have thought someone like you would ever have to be alone.'

'Shouldn't you? Well, you're wrong. I'm very careful in the company I keep.' She spoke sharply. *Assumptions*, she thought, how I detest these predictable male assumptions.

'I meant, you're interesting and intelligent and a good conversationalist. And you seem to have a great many friends.'

'*Friends* aren't available every day of the week.'

'Ah. Sundays, you mean.'

'Sundays are for families, aren't they? Not friends. What do you do on a Sunday, Martin? When you're not walking in the rain, that is.'

'I usually work. People still fall ill on a Sunday. And then there's the archaeological society. If I have the chance, I go and look at something that interests me.'

'What sort of thing?'

'Stone circles, burial chambers . . . Careful, Kate.'

Kate was reaching a jar down from a high shelf; he caught it just as it slipped out of her grasp. 'See,' he said, showing her the jar, 'it's a mouse with two heads, a baby mouse. I found it behind the skirting board.'

'Can I take it out of the jar?'

'*Kate.*'

'I'm afraid not. It's pickled in formaldehyde, which is nasty stuff. But have you ever seen a snake?'

'I saw a grass snake at Daddy's farm.'

'Really? How big was it?'

Kate held her hands two feet apart. Martin said, 'Would you like to see a python's skin? It's *that* big.' He opened his arms wide.

After tea, he insisted on walking them home. The rain had eased but the wind had picked up, making the branches of the trees dance.

Outside her flat, Bess gave him her hand and said, 'Thank you for the tea. Thank you for cheering up a cold, rainy afternoon.'

'Any wet Sunday that you've nothing better to do . . .'

'Of course. I'll think of you, Martin.'

From the front window of her drawing room, she watched him walk down the street. At first, she couldn't work out what he was doing – a curious leaping every now and again, an arm outstretched as if to grasp something. Then she realized that he was catching leaves. He would pause whenever he caught one; she imagined him closing his eyes tightly as he made his wish.

Hester Findlay's visits to Martin's rooms were erratic, at any time of the day or night. If he was working, he would pour her a drink and light her a cigarette, and she would drift round his sitting room like some frail, restless ghost, imparting to him scraps of gossip or finding fault with his housekeeping, while he sat writing at his desk.

'Izzy saw Celia Stewart at the theatre with Lionel Kincardine. He must be about twice her age. I suppose she's getting desperate, poor thing – she must be nearly thirty.' Hester ran her fingertip along a shelf, said, 'Eeurgh! Dust!' and brushed her hands together. 'And Beryl Brown's youngest has had scarlet fever and is now as deaf as a post. I don't believe you can see out of this window, Jago.'

'If you mix up those papers, Het, I shall throttle you.'

'You should get a housekeeper. You don't have to live in a hovel. I bet you've pots of money squirrelled away.'

'Oh, hoards of it.'

'Then buy a lovely house and I'll decorate it for you. I'm awfully good at decorating houses.'

'No, thank you.'

'Why not?'

'Because you'd move all my things and I'd never be able to find them again.'

'I could paint this room a lovely buttercup yellow.'

'Heaven preserve me . . .'

Another time, it was late, almost midnight. She was wearing a short, tubular, bronze-coloured dress. She smelt of wine and Chanel. Standing in his doorway, she did a little twirl.

'What do you think?'

He said honestly, 'You look delectable.'

She came into the room. 'Good enough to eat?'

'Don't tease, Het. Where's Alex?'

'He had a headache. He went home early. Are you busy?'

'Very.'

'What are you doing?'

'Looking through my notes and diaries.' He squinted. 'Trying to read my handwriting.'

'Do you want to know where I was?'

'You obviously wish to tell me.'

'Pour me a drink and then I will.'

He did as she asked. She said, 'I was at the Gilchrists'.'

He must have looked blank because she said impatiently, 'Andrew and Agnes Gilchrist. You must have heard of them.

Andrew's frightfully important, these days. He's quite handsome, I suppose, but he has hard eyes, little black, hard eyes, like chips of granite.' Hester offered her cigarette case to Martin. 'The Gilchrists have an enormous house in Charlotte Square. Agnes hires dozens of servants from Izzy's agency. Agnes is such a wan, pasty little thing, you can hardly imagine her having the strength to plump up the cushions. Her father died a few years ago, so Agnes inherited everything – lucky for Andrew. Well, not lucky. It was why he married her, an only child with a rich, ailing father. She's older than him and so hideously plain. And then, of course, he made a fortune in the war.' She exhaled a thin stream of smoke. 'Funny how things work out, isn't it? Andrew Gilchrist makes pots of money from munitions, and the same war leaves my poor Alex half the man that he was.'

'It's the way of the world, I'm afraid, Het.'

'So it is.' She drew a chair up to the desk and sat down across from him, her chin in her cupped hands. 'I wonder if I'd be happy if I was as rich as the Gilchrists?'

'Aren't you happy, Het?'

'Not really, no.'

'Are you worried about Alex?'

'I'm always worried about Alex. You know that.'

'How is he?'

'Just the same. The Gilchrists' dinner party was the first thing he'd been to for ages. I mean, the first proper thing, not just Izzy's suppers where everyone knows him.' She frowned. 'I've been hoping that Agnes Gilchrist might ask me to do some work for her. I know it's not the thing to talk about it, but we need the money, with Alex not working.' She stubbed her cigarette end into a saucer. 'But he hated every minute of it – he hardly said a word.' When she looked up at Martin, he saw that the artifice had dropped away from her gaze, and had been replaced by fear. She whispered, 'Do you think he'll ever get better?'

He said carefully, 'There's always the possibility of new developments—'

She interrupted, hissing angrily, 'Tell me the truth, Jago!'

He reached across the desk and took her hand. 'It's been, what, eight years now? Eight years since Alex was injured. The human body has a remarkable capacity for recovery. With injuries like Alex's, the medical profession can't really do a great deal more after the first patching up than to stand back and give the body the best chance to heal itself – make sure the patient has a good diet, gets plenty of rest, that sort of thing. Alex may still recover spontaneously. But after such a long time, well, one can't be too hopeful.'

She nodded. 'Thank you for being honest with me. All of the doctors spout such nonsense.' He saw the tears in her eyes as she pressed the back of his hand against her cheek.

With the Lockhead sisters and Iona O'Hagan, Bess danced in nightclubs, played mah-jong, and went out for drives into the Pentland Hills or to the coast, Kate sitting on her knee while the world opened out around them.

Davey Kirkpatrick took her to concerts and red-haired Rob McAulay took her to the cinema. Bess never invited either man to her flat – it was easier that way; they didn't get the wrong idea. These days, she hardly ever invited a man home, though she found herself making an exception for Martin Jago.

It happened at first by accident. They were walking through the park, when Kate, dashing across a gravel path in pursuit of a ginger cat, fell and cut her knee. Blood streamed; Kate howled. Martin carried Kate back to Bess's flat. Kate sucked her thumb vigorously, a baby habit she occasionally reverted to in times of stress.

Martin patched up the wound. 'It's not too deep so it doesn't need stitches, and I've cleaned it out thoroughly. I told her she might have a small scar, which would look rather dashing and piratical, and she seemed quite pleased.' He patted Bess's shoulder. 'Really, she's fine. You mustn't worry. Now, why don't I make us some tea?'

Bess took Kate a glass of milk and some biscuits. Kate was reading a story to her animals; leaving the room, Bess caught sight of her own face in the mirror. She looked pale and tense, a complete fright. She made a quick jab at her hair with her fingers, gave up in disgust, and went back to the kitchen.

'She will rush around without looking! It's so dangerous. I have to watch her like a hawk.'

'She's only eight. You can't expect a great deal of sense at eight.'

'I shall lock her away until she's twenty-one,' Bess said vehemently, hurling knives and forks aside in search of a teaspoon. 'Or we'll go and live on an island, with a big fence all around it so she can't possibly fall into the sea.' She slammed cups on saucers. 'People often tell me that you can't protect children from everything, and I know that, I know it very well.'

She paused, a cup clutched in her hand. The rain was driving down in steel-grey rails, blurring the view through the window. She said abruptly, 'Kate had a twin, a boy, Michael. He died when he was quite little.'

Martin stopped pouring boiling water into the pot. 'I'm sorry. How sad, how very sad. How old was Michael when he died?'

'Almost two.'

'What happened?'

'He caught influenza, at the end of the war.' Though she rarely spoke of it to anyone, she found herself telling him about the night that would haunt her, she knew, for the rest of her life.

'First Ralph caught it, then Kate, then me. Pamela – she and Ralph are married now – looked after us. She told me that he – that Michael – looked perfectly well when she put him to bed that night. But he was gone by the morning – so quickly. And yet he was always such a healthy baby. It was Kate who caught the coughs and colds, Kate I always worried about.' Bess bit her lip. 'It was my fault. If I hadn't been ill, if only I'd been looking after him . . .'

He put a cup of tea into her hands. 'You're cold.'

'I'm always cold. Even in summer.'

'Bess—'

'It doesn't matter.' She turned away. 'It was a long time ago.'

'Bess, listen to me. I was in the RAMC during the war, and afterwards I worked in a hospital in Reims. I saw hundreds of influenza cases. Some lived, some died. A number of the hospital staff died too. And I came to the conclusion that whatever we tried to do for the patient didn't make one iota of difference. I've rarely felt so helpless. The patients with the most severe form of the disease always died, some of them within a few hours of falling ill. Many were healthy young men in their late teens and early twenties. It was a cruel disease. Often, it seemed to take the young and strong and spare the old and weak. Michael was unlucky, that's all – but how dreadful for you, and for Kate. And I quite see that you must want to keep a close eye on her.'

She said, 'I don't know if Kate remembers him. I hope she's forgotten him. If she doesn't remember, it won't hurt.'

Back then, she had learned that there were limits to what she could endure. Kate, and only Kate, had enabled her to survive the loss of Michael and Frazer. That and her secret conviction, which had never faltered, that it would come right in the end, and that, one day, she and Frazer would be together again.

After Martin had gone, she found his scarf, flung over the hatstand. She sent him a note; he called late one evening to collect it, when she was getting ready to go to the Black Orchid. She made him a drink; he talked to her while she stood in front of the mirror, applying her lipstick, a very dark crimson.

That time, he left his gloves behind. She might have thought it intentional, an excuse to call back, had she not noticed that he seemed to leave a trail of scarves, gloves and pens in his wake wherever he went.

They fell into the habit of seeing each other every now and then. It was pleasant to talk to someone before she left for the club. Some nights, when Kate was asleep, the flat was so quiet she seemed to hear the echo of her own footsteps.

On weekends when Kate was staying with Ralph and Pamela, Bess visited Martin's rooms in the Old Town. Martin told her about his work. 'All the great medical discoveries at the end of the last century – Pasteur's work on the transmission of disease, Koch's on tuberculosis, Lister's and Semmelweis's work on the importance of antisepsis – made medicine the field to be in when I was a very young man. It all seemed so glorious, so exciting. When I qualified, I decided to become a surgeon. And then, one day, when I was in France, after the war, I just couldn't do it any more.'

'Couldn't do what?'

'Couldn't operate. I remember going into the theatre, watching my hands shake, and thinking that I was going to be sick. Or pass out. The nurses were all staring at me. God knows what they thought. They probably thought I was drunk. Or insane. I thought I was going insane. I could hardly breathe. I had no idea what was happening to me.'

She remembered how she had felt after Michael had died. She shivered. 'I know just what you mean. Finding that the world doesn't make sense any more.'

'At least the horrors of the war made a dreadful sort of sense, but when you find that you can't even trust yourself—' he broke off and gave a crooked smile. 'Anyway, it's rather tricky to be a surgeon if you can't stand the sight of blood. That's why I went into general practice after I came back here. You have to do a certain amount of surgery – appendices and tonsils, that sort of thing – but I seem to be OK so far.'

She teased, 'Perhaps you'll become one of those very smart doctors with a Bentley and a top hat and a lovely house in Charlotte Square.'

He shook his head. 'I don't think so. I'd be continually losing the top hat, for one thing, and besides, there are certain circles in which I wouldn't be welcome.'

She stared at him. 'Why on earth not, Martin?'

'Because my parents were never married. I'm illegitimate. So there are houses where I wouldn't be received. But I suspect I'd find them insufferably dull, anyway.' He said it matter-of-factly, in the same tone of voice that one might make a remark about the weather.

She said, 'So you're a pariah, like me?'

'Some people make judgements, don't they? But not those worth a candle. In its time, it was a great scandal. But people always tire of scandals.'

'Do you mind?'

'Not at all. I rarely think about it. As for the people who judge me . . . no, I don't care. Not any more. Do you?'

She thought of the women who looked through her in the street and the men who thought that *divorced* meant *easy*.

'Sometimes,' she said softly. 'Sometimes I mind a great deal.'

Martin rationed his visits to Bess – never call too often, never stay too long. At all costs he must not bore her.

Sometimes, he disliked himself. There was something craven and addictive in his need for her, something humiliating in his dependence, which made him ill-tempered and morose. It was a sort of addiction, he thought. In the years after the end of the war, desperate after suffering from insomnia for months on end, he had resorted to taking laudanum. His dose had risen inexorably, and eventually he had made himself give it up. He had felt much the same then as he did now: edgy, irritable, hardly able to know what to do with himself.

What was it that drew him to her so? How could just the sight of someone induce such a mixture of happiness and sorrow and yearning? Could it be the desire for perfection, the search for an ideal? But she was not perfect – her face was a little too broad, perhaps, her mouth a touch too wide. She wasn't tall enough to be ideally beautiful, and her hands – he had noticed that, when she wasn't wearing gloves, she hid her hands. She couldn't afford much help in the house, he supposed – a woman must have servants to have beautiful hands.

When he was with her he sometimes felt a sharp, rare happiness. There was an intimacy about those times, when the winter and the night enclosed the two of them together. He had little experience of intimacy; it was not something he had often sought out. He felt himself changed by her, by her proximity, as though she was peeling the layers from him, revealing parts of himself he hardly knew. He did not know whether she spoke to all men as she spoke to him, whether she exchanged the occasional confidence with them, whether they shared the same jokes. He hoped that she did not.

One night, after walking her home from the Black Orchid, he shared a nightcap with her at her flat. She lay on the sofa, her legs stretched out along the cushions. She had kept her coat on; he knew that she hated the cold. She seemed to peek out at him through layers of material: the shiny red of her dress, the soft brown folds of her coat, and the dark animal gleam of the fur that framed her face.

She yawned. 'Aren't you tired, Martin?'

'Not yet.'

'You're a night owl, aren't you?'

'I'm a chronic insomniac. Very, very occasionally I sleep through the night, just often enough to remind me how glorious it is.' He added, 'It's late. You can throw me out if you want to.'

'It's nice to talk to someone. And you're less tiresome than most.'

He felt a flicker of pleasure. 'Is that a compliment, Mrs Fearnley?'

'Perhaps it is. You don't bother me.' She shivered.

'Shall I rub your feet for you?'

'Please.'

He shuffled up the sofa, and took her feet on his lap. 'You should marry again,' he said. His voice sounded rough, as though he had smoked too much. 'Then you'd have someone to talk to every night.'

She shook her head.

He said, 'Why not?'

'Because I've been married twice and it didn't suit me.'

'Third time lucky?'

'No. Men never want to let women run their own lives. They find that too frightening.'

'You have a poor opinion of our sex.'

'No, I don't. I like men. I enjoy their company. They can be more straightforward than women.'

'Simpler, you mean?'

She smiled. 'You're not simple, Martin, not at all. I'm never sure what you're thinking.'

He was thinking that he would like to kiss her toes, one by one, to run the tip of his tongue along the arch of each foot. But he said, 'Perhaps not all men view marriage in such a way. Perhaps not every husband is possessive.'

'Perhaps. But most are.' She shuffled up the sofa and began to pull the pins from her hair. Then she said carelessly, 'And besides, if I did marry again, then I'd marry a rich man.'

Something inside him seemed to die a little. He looked at her for a moment, dishevelled in furs and scarlet satin, her black hair tumbled round her shoulders, then he rose and went to the window, glancing out over the darkened street.

'Do you care about money so much?'

'I've been penniless, and I wouldn't choose to be so again. I wouldn't choose poverty over comfort.'

He thought she sounded hard. He erased the disappointment from his eyes, and was able to turn to her and say lightly, 'So you'll wait till you find your rich man?'

'Rich men can pick and choose. They don't marry women like me. They make women like me their mistresses, not

136

their wives.' She shrugged. 'It's how things are. I learned that a long time ago.'

After work one evening, Iona held out to Bess a gown covered in tiny silver beads.

'Try it. We've had it in stock for ages and no one will buy it. It's rather outré, isn't it? It needs a certain type of look to carry it off. If you like it, you can wear it to the club tonight.'

Bess let the dress slide over her head. The beading made it heavy, and the silk lining felt cool against her skin.

'There,' said Iona, with a smile. 'I knew it would work on you. Have a look at yourself.'

Bess glanced in the mirror. There was a Greek motif picked out in darker silver beads around the hem, which fell to just below the knee. The dress was sleeveless and low-necked, revealing her arms and throat. She saw how it shimmered as she moved, catching the light.

That night, the club was busy, every seat taken. Girls dressed as butterflies, their chiffon wings glistening with sequins, danced on the tiny stage. A man sang a risqué song and plucked silk handkerchiefs from the pockets of the audience. There was a whoop of delight and a ripple of applause as he pulled, apparently from the air, a trio of doves, feathers dyed pink. Nights like this, Bess loved the club. It made her feel alive; it had a magic that transformed the wettest, greyest Edinburgh night.

After the cabaret, Jamie Black drew her aside at the bar.

'Table number five,' he murmured to her.

She peered through the crowd. 'Four men. Are they new members?'

'Yes. And very well heeled. Between them, they prob-ably own half Edinburgh – and a chunk of Glasgow too, I shouldn't wonder. So we'd better make sure they enjoy themselves tonight.'

'Do you want me to keep an eye on them?'

'If you would. You know the routine, Bess. Make sure they always have a drink to hand. I don't doubt they'll leave you a nice fat tip. The dark-haired, heavyset one's called Gilchrist, by the way.'

She smiled at him. 'Keep them happy.'

'That's right. Good girl.' He touched her cheek. 'You look particularly stunning tonight, my darling. You wouldn't reconsider . . . ?'

'No, Jamie.'

'Ah well.'

She did as Jamie had asked, glancing frequently towards table number five and taking orders for drinks whenever their glasses were empty. She felt the men's eyes following her as she walked back to the bar.

It was past midnight when Andrew Gilchrist beckoned to her. As she reached the table, he said, 'Dance with me.'

'I'm sorry, Mr Gilchrist, I can't. I'm rather busy.'

'Later, then. When you're not so busy.'

She explained pleasantly, 'I'm afraid I never dance with customers.'

'Then I shall have to hope that we run into each other some other time.' He raised his glass to her. 'I'm sure we will.'

'I look forward to it, Mr Gilchrist.'

'Andrew,' he said. 'You must call me Andrew.'

After that evening, he began to pursue her. Whenever Gilchrist came to the club, his eyes followed her; when there was a cabaret, he insisted she sit next to him. She was used to that, it was what men did. They made declarations of undying love, and then, sooner or later, discovering that she would not give them everything they wanted, they grew bored, and found another pretty girl to pay compliments to.

Andrew Gilchrist seemed to bring a different group of friends with him each time he visited the club. Jamie told her who they were. They were Edinburgh businessmen – publishers, brewers, the owners of factories and mines and transport and construction companies. They were short, stocky Glaswegians, who surveyed the club with swift, curious glares before knocking back their shots of whisky in one mouthful, betraying little pleasure. They were local dignitaries and lawyers – 'Now, that wee man's what's known as a hanging judge,' Jamie murmured to Bess one evening. Jamie's gaze focused on the fat, red-faced, white-haired man who was dancing a jig on top of a table, surrounded and cheered on by Gilchrist and his cronies. Jamie smiled to himself. 'He's sent more poor souls to meet their Maker than any other judge in Scotland. Still, if he keeps on that way at his age, and with that weight on him, he'll soon be going to the same place himself, won't he?'

Sometimes Gilchrist's party included girls, slender, beautiful girls with platinum-blonde marcel waves and flesh-coloured silk stockings. Girls whose short skirts barely skimmed their knees, girls whose peals of laughter trilled through the evening like a descant over the clamour of the club, but whose eyes never betrayed a glint of amusement.

Gilchrist's wife never came to the club. Bess asked Jamie about her. 'Agnes?' he said. 'This place is far too sinful for her. I've heard she's worn her knees out with praying, that woman.' Jamie's eyes rested on the blonde, the redhead and the brunette who were sitting at Gilchrist's table, sharing his champagne. He murmured, 'I wonder what Agnes Gilchrist would make of those three lassies with her husband. No doubt they're all good, church-going girls, don't you think, Bess?'

Once, she met Andrew Gilchrist at the Kincardines' house. He asked her to dance; she had a sudden instinct to keep her distance from him. But that was foolish – Gilchrist was wealthy and powerful, and it didn't do to offend men like that. It was far better to keep them happy. After all, she was practised in keeping men happy, and practised also in keeping them in their place. You let them go so far, you let them hope they might get close to you, and then you drew a firm line. They didn't, in her experience, mind too much, but accepted it with reasonable grace, knowing that it was all part of the game.

When she danced with Andrew Gilchrist she was aware of his height and strength, of the firm grip of his hand as he steered her round the room. She felt a tension; he spoke little, and her own conversational forays were met by short replies and a touch of amusement, as though he indulged her chatter for politeness' sake.

Then she saw Martin Jago. He was standing on the perimeter of the room. Each time she circled the floor, she caught his eye. When she rolled her eyes, or winked at him, or yawned, he made a face back at her and she had to stifle a burst of laughter.

Later, Martin walked her home. He asked, 'The man you were dancing with, who was he?'

'He's called Gilchrist, Andrew Gilchrist,' she said uninterestedly. 'Sometimes he comes to the club.'

One man was always with Andrew Gilchrist on his visits to the Black Orchid. Simon Voyle was a small, thin, rat-faced Englishman. He never danced, drank little, and had a nervous habit of biting his nails. Every now and then he would scurry off to reclaim coats or make a telephone call, or dash out of the building to take a message. On the morning of her birthday, Bess answered the doorbell and discovered Mr Voyle standing outside, almost buried beneath a huge bunch of carnations and lilies. 'Mr Gilchrist wishes you many happy returns of the day, Mrs Fearnley.' After she had taken the bouquet from him, she saw the orange powdery marks on Simon Voyle's coat, where the lily stamens had brushed against the fabric.

Andrew Gilchrist did that once in a while, unnerved her by revealing that he knew something about her that she had never told him. *Knowledge is power*, he once said to her. She supposed it disturbed her because she had learned to run her life by dividing it into compartments, disclosing a different part of herself to different people, because different people were for different things. Kate was for love. Iona, Isabel and Annie were for friendship. Martin Jago was for long, late-night conversations, conversations that meandered enjoyably, arriving at unexpected places.

She tolerated Andrew Gilchrist's company partly because it was her job to do so, and partly because wealth and influence gave him a touch of glamour, and there was a certain satisfaction in receiving the admiration of such a man. She was not attracted to him – he took himself too seriously, and was too lacking in both humour and kindness for her to wish to be closer to him. And besides, she had crushed that part of herself ruthlessly, all too aware of the dangers of a relationship outside marriage – and of the impossibility of marriage itself.

Chapter Six

Someone on the council was digging in his heels over planning permission for one of Andrew Gilchrist's sites. The delay aggravated him. He had bought the land a year ago, swiftly clearing it of the small workshops and paper mill that had formerly stood there. Since then, he'd been forced to wait, cooling his breath, while some planning committee or other dithered endlessly. Many of the committee members were in his pocket – a backhander here, an offer of a share in the profits there. But every so often you'd find some sanctimonious bastard who liked to keep to the rules, some smug socialist or self-righteous Christian who couldn't be bought.

Gilchrist put his head round the door of his office and called for Simon Voyle. Voyle came scuttling along the corridor. A slight, pale man with a permanently hunted air, he had worked as Gilchrist's assistant and general factotum for the past ten years.

It was six o'clock on a Friday night. Voyle was wearing

his outdoor coat. Gilchrist drawled, 'Am I keeping you, Simon?' and Voyle flushed.

'Not at all. I have an appointment but I'm at your service.'

'I'm pleased to hear it.' Gilchrist glanced at a sheet of paper. 'Josiah Patterson – do you know him? What sort of man is he?' Gilchrist reached for his own coat and Voyle hurried to help him into it. 'I want to know everything about him,' Gilchrist said as he folded a silk scarf about his throat. 'I want to know his little secrets. The woman he keeps in Fountainbridge. His loans from Jews or sharks. His hobbies. Perhaps he enjoys a game of cards. Or perhaps he has a liking for boys.'

'Yes, sir.'

'And quickly. He's losing me money.' Gilchrist patted Voyle's cheek. 'Now, run along. Mustn't keep the little lady waiting, must you?'

Walking home, Gilchrist felt, as always, a swell of pride as he turned into Charlotte Square. He had felt the same pride when he bought the house three years ago. He had stood in the hallway and let his gaze run from the black and white marble floor to the high plaster cornices and the crimson-carpeted stairs, and he had felt a warm glow of self-satisfaction.

As well as the house, he owned half a dozen tenement buildings, a construction company and an iron foundry in Portobello. His wife, Agnes, had brought him the foundry and one of the tenements on their marriage; the others he'd acquired himself. He had started with the little square of land that contained the printing works his father had been so proud of. The day after his father's funeral, he had closed down the printing works and sold the land off to the highest bidder. It was a good piece of land, in the middle of an up-and-coming residential area, and with the profit he had earned he had bought more land. That was how you made money; he'd learned that while he was still a boy. You didn't bother making things – books or furniture or pearl buttons, or whatever nonsense – oh, no. You bought up unprofitable land, light industrial or agricultural, and you sold it off as building land. That was where the money was, in building land. Edinburgh was bursting at the seams, hungry for land to house the workers who were needed to run its factories and to serve in its shops and houses. The city encroached into the surrounding countryside like a dark ink blot spilling over clean paper.

He had an eye for land, a knack of knowing which area to buy into next. After a while, you could *make* an area go up. Get a name for yourself, get a reputation for having a nose for it, and the dogs would come snapping at your heels, hungry for crumbs, jostling to buy where you were buying.

Sometimes he sold on the land straight away, sometimes he put up a tenement, for the rents, for the steady cash. Over the years, he had learned the tricks of the trade, and he had made sure to get to know the right people. He had also learned that everyone had a weakness, that only saints were pure in heart, and that you didn't meet many of them in his business. He could spot hypocrisy, greed, corruption and snobbery a mile off, and he knew how to take advantage of each vice. He reserved his deepest contempt for the idle, arrogant aristocrats, the landed gentlemen who'd never done a day's work in their lives. Overbred, lily-livered weaklings the lot of them; it gave him satisfaction to note the steady erosion of their power.

Marrying Agnes had been a coup, lifting him several rungs up the ladder. The woman had a face like a bowl of cold porridge and an unpleasant, whining voice to go with it, but Andrew Gilchrist doubted if there were many now in Edinburgh who remembered him as the son of the owner of a small print works in Canongate. And at least Agnes, for all her failings, had done her duty and given him three sons.

The bell rang for dinner. As he glanced round the table, a little of his satisfaction ebbed away. Niall and Sandy, his elder sons, were already in place, but the fifth seat was empty. 'Maxwell?' he asked. 'Where's Maxwell?'

As the maid served the soup, Agnes sent a servant in search of her youngest son. The family ate in silence. Agnes dipped her spoon tentatively into her bowl every now and then, eating little but dabbing her lips frequently with her napkin in a way that grated on Andrew's nerves. Niall, who was dark and thickset, like his father, spooned up his soup quickly, as if afraid that his dinner would be snatched away from him. Fair, sharp-featured Sandy hunched over his bowl, his eyes flicking every now and then to the door.

They had almost finished the first course when Maxwell came into the dining room. Maxwell Gilchrist had had the good fortune to inherit his father's dark hair and even features and his mother's slightness and blue-green eyes. Now, at the age of fourteen, he was a boy of exceptional good looks.

'So, Maxwell,' said Andrew. 'You've decided to grace us with your presence.'

Maxwell smiled blithely. 'Yes, Father. Sorry, Father. I was . . .' he cast a glance round the room, as though searching for inspiration. 'I was busy.'

'Busy?' repeated Andrew, heavy with sarcasm. 'Studying, I don't doubt.'

Maxwell's wide gaze met his father's. 'Yes, Father.'

Sandy spoke for the first time. 'You were with Dougie Ferrers. I saw you.'

Dougie Ferrers had once worked as a boot boy in the Gilchrist household. He had been dismissed for stealing cigarettes.

Andrew said, 'Is that true, Maxwell?'

'Yes, Father.'

'Then you're to go to bed without any dinner.'

'Yes, Father.' Maxwell reached across and lifted the lid of the serving dish the maid had brought in. 'I don't mind,' he said. 'It's mutton. I hate mutton.'

It was the insolence in those lucent green eyes that infuriated Andrew as much as his son's words. He gave a roar of anger and made to clip Maxwell across the ear, but Maxwell was quick on his feet and darted out of the room.

Andrew Gilchrist's ill humour lasted throughout the remainder of the meal. Maxwell had a knack of riling him. It irked him that the only person who failed to show him the respect due to him should be his youngest son. Niall and Sandy were different, dull and dutiful the pair of them. Niall had recently begun to work for the business; Andrew had started him off in the foundry – best to throw him in

147

at the deep end, among the dirt and noise and heat, to knock the softness out of him. All three of his sons were soft, he thought irritably. It was Agnes's fault, she had spoiled them.

His gaze slid round the table to rest on Agnes, who was stirring her rhubarb and custard into a mess. 'For God's sake, woman, can't you even eat properly?' he barked, and saw her and the boys flinch.

After dinner, he had a servant bring him a Scotch in his study. He drank and smoked a cigar and ran a quick eye over the latest figures from his accountant, but he felt restless and, unusually, he found his mind wandering. He knew what the trouble was – it had been a while since he had had a woman. Sharing a bed with Agnes had never been an attractive prospect, and these days it was like making love to a bag of dried-out old peas. He'd do it if he needed to, but it was hardly a pleasure.

He thought of Bess Fearnley. Now, there was a woman. He felt a rush of desire, and his fingers clenched round the glass. The intensity of his longing for her took him by surprise. He was not a sentimental man; he had always despised those who let their desires get the better of them. It lost you the upper hand; it lost you control.

He had wanted Bess since the first time he saw her. Yet she had so far proved maddeningly unobtainable, refusing to dance with him at the nightclub, and leaving before he could offer to walk her home at night. He knew that he would have her, though. It was only a matter of time. It was the waiting that grated, this playing of a game that they both knew must end with only one outcome.

But if that was the sort of woman she was, the sort of woman who liked a man to run after her, to flatter and coax her, then he'd play along with her, for a while at least. And besides, there was a little milliner in Gorgie who would always accommodate him. He swallowed the last of his drink, put on his coat and hat, and left the house. But, later, as he watched Kitty Green unlace and unbutton her layers of satin and frills, and then as he made love to her, he found himself thinking of Bess, only Bess.

Summer came early that year and, with it, newspaper headlines that spoke of a general strike, and of revolution. Martin called at Bess's flat one evening.

'Sarah Williamson has filled an entire cupboard with tins of soup,' she told him. 'Do you think I should buy dozens of tins of soup, Martin?'

'I think that if you did, then you'd get very tired of soup.'

He watched her circle the room, tidying up books and teacups. She was wearing a pale blue floaty dress; her silver bangles slid up and down her wrists as she moved. He thought how often he had sat like this, talking of soup or some such nonsense, watching her, unable to drag his eyes away from her, longing for her.

'How's Kate?'

'In heaven. Ralph and Pamela have just had another baby, a little boy. Ralph drove Kate down to the farm this morning so that she could see him.'

'Kate must enjoy having three little brothers.'

'Yes.'

That was all. *Yes.* He remembered the baby she had lost, Kate's twin. Now she was standing at the mirror, checking her hair. He said, 'Do you miss her?'

A quick glance around the room, as though she was searching for something. 'It's very quiet when Kate's not here. But I can catch up on things. Seriously, though, Martin, do you think I should be stockpiling food?'

'Because of the general strike?'

'Do you think it'll happen?'

'I suspect so, yes. The government seems determined to stand its ground. And the miners are desperate. They've been pushed into a corner and they haven't really anywhere else to go. But, no, I don't think you need worry about buying in extra food.'

'I have to think of Kate.'

'Neither the government nor the TUC will want to stop essential supplies getting through. That would turn public opinion against them. Both sides count on gaining the public's sympathy.'

'Do you sympathize with the strikers, Martin?'

Outside, couples in evening dress strolled along the pavement. Cabs rolled up and down the street; behind the glass, you could glimpse their top-hatted, silk-scarved passengers. Revolution seemed a long way away.

He said, 'The mine owners are asking the miners to work longer hours for less money. Baldwin claims to detest industrial strife, yet he can't seem to appreciate its underlying economic causes. We live in a wealthy country and yet a great many men earn barely enough to feed their families. The miners are asking for a share in the country's wealth,

which seems reasonable enough to me. I see the consequences of poverty every day in my work. When I set up
my own practice—'

'Is that what you mean to do?'

'Yes. I've been thinking about it for some time. It was
why I came back to Edinburgh. I mean to set up my own
clinic. Somewhere that everyone can come to. If you can
pay, you pay, and if you can't, it doesn't matter.' He grinned.
'I suppose I may have to badger the great and the good to
help finance it. Dear God. Can you see me, dressed in my
best, trailing round Edinburgh's finest, trying to charm Lady
So-and-So out of a few shillings to help the poor?'

Bess had gone back to the mirror. 'I didn't think you
possessed anything that was *best*, Martin. Help me with my
necklace, would you?'

He clasped the necklace for her; her skin was cool against
his fingers. He wanted to close his eyes, to press his lips
against the smooth curve of her neck.

Instead, he stepped back and said, 'You look as lovely as
always, Bess.'

'They're paste,' she said dismissively. 'Almost all my jewels
are paste. But they look all right from a distance.'

The general strike began on 3 May. Throughout Great Britain,
almost two million workers downed tools. Transport,
printing, building, industrial and utility workers were called
out first. In the very early morning, the streets were eerily
quiet. No trams clattered along the rails, and no trains let
off steam or billowed clouds of smoke into the air at
Waverley station. The rollers and presses of Edinburgh's

many printing works fell silent. Then, as businessmen, clerks and shop assistants struggled to work by whatever means they could, the better off driving private cars, others cycling or walking the miles from the suburbs, the city streets became filled with great columns of motor cars, crushed nose to tail, moving at a snail's pace, and the silence was gone, and in its place was the clamour of horns, the rumble of engines.

The government news-sheet, the *British Gazette*, screamed of revolution but Martin thought that, to begin with, Edinburgh took on something of a holiday air. The brilliant early summer weather seemed to emphasize that these were exceptional times. There was a promise of excitement, of change. Some old barriers tumbled: bank managers in Bentleys gave their clerks lifts into work from the suburbs, and buses driven by student volunteers wove eccentric routes, dropping their passengers off outside their homes.

As the days went on, though, there was a gradual souring of mood. Martin had to put a dozen stitches into the head of a plasterer who had been struck by a brick during a scuffle over blackleg labour. Rising early one morning to attend to a woman in childbirth, he came across a street obstructed by vans and trucks, their drivers forced out before the vehicles were set alight. Violence jangled in the bright May air; you could feel it. Not, he thought, the violence of revolution, but a violence born of desperation.

His work went on much as before. No doctors or nurses were to be called out. He spent a futile morning telephoning every sanatorium in Scotland, trying to find a bed for a young woman with a tubercular spine; in the afternoon, he was summoned, far too late, to the bedside of a child with a badly swollen jaw, the consequence of a mouthful of decayed teeth. There were four other children in the family, and the parents had treated their son by binding a woollen sock filled with hot salt to the side of his face. The infection had spread into the jawbone; the boy had a high fever and tremors. Martin did what he could and had the child admitted to hospital but doubted whether he would survive the night.

His frustration was not shaken off by the long, brisk walk back to his rooms. He threw his jacket onto a chair and poured himself a whisky. Then he noticed the folded sheet of paper that had been pushed under the door. The note was from Hester Findlay. *Dearest Martin, I must see you, Het.* That was all.

He glanced at his watch; it was almost ten o'clock. He put his jacket back on anyway and walked to Eglinton Crescent, where Hester and Alex lived.

The maid showed him in. Hester was in the drawing room. Her dark hair was scraped back into an unflattering knot, and she was wearing navy-blue trousers and a navy and white striped jersey. The maid went to put on the lights – the room was half dark, with only a single reading lamp lit – but, with a shake of her hand, Hester said, 'No. Leave it. I prefer it like this.'

'Can I get you anything, Mrs Findlay?'

'We'll look after ourselves. You go to bed, Miller. It's late.' The maid left the room.

Hester said, 'So sweet of you to come, Martin. You'll have a drink, won't you?' She opened a cabinet; he noticed how her hand trembled as she poured. Noticed, too, her reddened eyelids, her pale, taut skin, the shadows under her eyes.

'What's happened, Het?'

She made a sound somewhere between a laugh and a gasp. 'Alex has gone.'

'Gone? Where to?'

'I don't know.' There was a blank emptiness in her gaze. 'We had the most frightful quarrel.'

'Do you mean that he's left you?'

'I don't know, I tell you! I don't know where he is!'

He said comfortingly, 'He's probably staying with friends or relatives.'

'No. I've phoned everyone, simply everyone. His mother's as frantic as I am.' Her face crumpled. 'I'm afraid he'll do something stupid. Perhaps he's done it already. And all because of me.'

'Hester—'

'I've been such a rotten wife.'

'Nonsense.'

'It's true. In sickness and in health, that's how it's supposed to be, isn't it?'

'You've been a wonderful wife. No one could say you've had an easy time of it.'

She pressed the heels of her hands against her face. She whispered, 'What if he never comes back?'

'Of course he'll come back. Just give him a few days to cool off.'

After a silence, looking down at her glass, she murmured, 'Alex is trying to make me leave him.'

'Surely not.'

'He knows I want children, you see.'

'And he doesn't?'

'He *can't*.'

'But surely there's no physical reason—'

'I mean, he can't – we don't . . . you know.' Suddenly, she looked angry. 'And don't you dare tell me it'll just take time! I am so sick of people telling me everything will just take time!'

'I'm wouldn't dream of telling you that, Het.'

She said miserably, 'Sometimes I'm afraid he just doesn't want *me*.'

'I'm sure that's not true.'

'I almost wish it were.'

He looked at her sharply.

She shrugged and said, 'I think he believes that if he's really horrible to me then I'll leave him and get a divorce and I won't feel guilty about it. I think he thinks I only stay with him out of pity.' She gave a short laugh. 'It would be easier, wouldn't it, if we hated each other. I won't do it, of course, I won't leave him. But he can be so beastly sometimes. The thing is, the silly thing is that I still love him, no matter what he does. Yet I do want children.' Her expression altered. She said softly, 'I always thought I'd have half a dozen. But it doesn't look as though I'll even manage one.' She bit her lip. 'I'm afraid I'm running out of time. Alex and I have been married for twelve years. I'm thirty-three.' She looked up at Martin. 'How old are women before they stop having babies?'

'Forty-five or so. So there's no rush.' He squeezed her shoulder. 'Alex will come back, Het. Of course he will. And meanwhile, I'll keep an eye out for him, if you like. I'll ask around. So you mustn't worry.'

Martin checked for Alex Findlay at the hospitals and was relieved to find no trace of him. In the evening, he tramped round pubs and clubs and came up, once more, with nothing.

As the general strike went into its second week, riots, vicious and prolonged, broke out in the city. Martin was on his way home from visiting a patient when he heard the roar of angry voices and the crash of breaking windows. A mob slewed across the narrow street. There were two vans struggling to gain entrance to a building site. The gates of the works were open, and a man, a security guard, perhaps, lay beside the gate, blood flowing from his head. The mob had surrounded the vans, and the shout of 'Scab!' filled the air. Missiles – bricks and setts, prised from the road – clanged against the sides of the van. Martin saw that a little further down the street a bus was pushing its way through the fracas. At the driver's wheel, he thought he recognized Alex Findlay. He had to squint and look again to check that he was right.

He waved to Alex and shouted his name as he began to push through the melee in the direction of the fallen man. He found himself sucked up into the motion of the crowd, borne along by the impetus of it. The hundred or so individuals had formed into a single, monstrous mass, with a mind and force of its own. Martin had always hated crowds and the way they made people do things they wouldn't otherwise have done, but he made himself press on. The bus was forcing its way through the crowd and was now much nearer to him, near enough to see, in Alex Findlay's one good eye, an expression of deep, dark delight.

Some of the rioters fell back, pushed aside by the weight and bulk of the bus. Martin saw a clear path to the gates, and took it. The guard was unconscious, but alive. Martin dragged him away from the gates, making for the bus. The mob, the direction of their anger altered, turned on the bus, giving the vans, with their cargo of blackleg labour, time to get through the gates to the site. To his horror, Martin saw Alex climb out of the cab. Someone raised a stick to strike him; he heard Alex say, 'It's me, Rentoul. You remember me, don't you?' and the stick was lowered.

They hauled the guard into the bus. Alex pulled away from the gates; the crowd parted. 'Is he dead?' he called over his shoulder to Martin.

'Not yet. What happened, back there?'

'Oh, Rentoul was in my regiment. We were at Arras together. I know some of the others, too. Decent fellows.'

'Are you all right, Alex?'

A sharp glance. 'Have you seen Hester?' Martin nodded. 'How is she?'

'She's fine. But worried about you.'

Alex smiled. 'You wouldn't think driving a bus could be so much fun. They almost didn't let me do it, because of the eye, but I insisted. I can't see anything on my left side and I'm forever veering into pavements and scraping the thing on walls, but people are pretty good at scarpering out of my way. I've had the best time I've had in years.'

He glanced over his shoulder again. 'We'd better get that poor chap to the infirmary. Hold on tight.'

The bus veered along a steep street, tyres bouncing against the kerb, cyclists and pedestrians scattering. They reached Lauriston Place and carried the security guard into the hospital. After he had seen his patient into the admissions ward and had spoken to the doctor on duty, Martin left the hospital. He found Alex sitting on the steps outside, smoking. The rush of excitement that had sustained him through the riot must have ebbed, because he looked deathly white. His hand shaded his eyes, as though he couldn't bear the sunlight, and when he offered Martin a cigarette, he was shaking too much to flick the lighter.

'Hell,' he said.

'Is your head bad?'

Alex nodded, then flinched.

Martin said, 'You should go home.'

'Not yet.'

'Hester misses you.'

'Does she? I doubt it. Sometimes I think we just bring out the worst in each other. Most of the time I think she'd be better off without me.'

'Perhaps you should leave it to Hester to make up her mind about that.'

Alex closed his eyes. Then he said, 'I will go back, but not yet. When I've thought what to do.'

'If I see her, do you want me to give her a message?'

Alex thought for a moment. 'Tell her I'm fine. And give her my love, if she'll take it, Martin.' He sounded suddenly wretched. 'And tell her I'm sorry for – well, everything.'

'Is there anything else I can do?'

Alex managed the ghost of a grin. 'Well, you can drive the bloody bus back to the depot for me. When I'm like this, I can hardly see a thing.'

Hester was waiting at Martin's rooms when he came back. He said, 'I've seen Alex. He's fine. He's driving a bus.'

'A *bus*? Alex is driving a *bus*?'

'Only while all this goes on. Lots of people are helping out. I think he's rather enjoying it.'

He saw from the flare of anger in her eyes that he had said the wrong thing. He added quickly, 'I think it makes him feel useful. And he probably hasn't felt useful for quite a long time.'

She was prowling round the room, fidgeting with the pens on the desk, the fragments of pottery and stone on the window sill. 'What else did he say?'

'That he sends his love.'

'And? Did he say when he was coming back?'

'Not exactly.'

'*Martin.*'

He sighed and said, 'He said he needed time to think things over.'

'Time to think about *me*,' she said bitterly. 'Time to think whether he wants to come back to *me*.'

'Het,' he said gently, but she gave a short, humourless laugh.

'I wonder whether we'd have been all right if the war

hadn't happened. You can never tell, can you? I thought we were all right, but perhaps we weren't, perhaps I just couldn't see. Perhaps he'd have got sick of me anyway.'

'Let me get you a drink, Het.'

He poured out two glasses and gave one to her. She sat on the arm of the sofa, tapping her foot. 'What a mess of a marriage!' she said softly. 'We were married in nineteen fourteen, you know. Six weeks afterwards, they sent him to France. And he didn't have a scratch for more than three years. Terrible things were happening to everyone else, but not to Alex. I started to hope that he was going to be all right. I used to pray for him every night – I thought that God was protecting him. And then he was wounded and I went to see him in the hospital in France. They didn't know whether he was going to live or die. I still prayed for him. I thought if I prayed enough he'd get better. But he didn't get better. He'll never get better.'

She sounded hopeless, beaten, all her usual bravado and brightness knocked out of her. His heart ached for her; he put his arms round her and hugged her. She leaned against him, her face buried in his shirt. After a few moments, she said, 'Kiss me, won't you, Martin?'

He kissed the top of her head. She looked up at him. 'Not like that. Kiss me properly.' Her lips brushed against his, and he found himself responding to her – such a long time since he had kissed a woman, and she was, in her unique way, quite beautiful.

Yet when he kissed her, he thought of Bess. And reason reasserted itself, and he drew back and said, 'Hester, what do you want?'

'I want you to love me, Martin. I'm tired of being on my own.'

A moment of temptation, and then he saw consequences rolling out before him, all of them unwanted, all of them involving betrayal and deception.

'It's very sweet of you to ask, Het, and I'm immensely flattered, but I don't think it would be a good idea.'

She was running her hand through his hair. She paused, clenching a lock of it in her fingers. 'Why not?'

'Because of Alex, for one thing. He's your husband.'

She gave a short laugh. 'He'd probably be relieved if I had an affair. Then he could divorce me without feeling guilty.' Her brows lowered. 'What is it, Martin? Don't you like me?'

'You know that I like you.'

Her eyes narrowed, became hard. 'But you don't love me.'

'As a friend. I love you as a friend.'

'Liking, loving, friends, lovers – what's the difference? I love Alex, and a great deal of the time it makes me miserable. What's the point of loving someone if it makes you miserable?'

'I don't know. Maybe there's no point to it. We don't choose who we love, do we?'

'Why have you never married, Jago?'

He said lightly, 'Because I'd have to find someone to put up with me.'

She stood up; he heard the snap of her cigarette lighter. 'Someone like Bess Fearnley? It's because of *her*, isn't it? You don't love me because of *her*.' She smiled unpleasantly. 'Shall

I tell you a secret about her? Well, not so much of a secret. Everyone's talking about it.'

He thought of Bess, lying on the sofa nestled in furs and velvet. And he remembered Davey saying, *She keeps them on a string. At least, I hope she does* – and he seemed to taste something sour.

'I don't want to know,' he said. 'And I think perhaps you should go home, Het. I'll call you a taxi.'

'Why is everyone in love with Bess Fearnley? She's a slut, a common slut.' Hester was biting her thumbnail, staring at him. 'I think I'll tell you my secret anyway. You do know that Bess Fearnley is Andrew Gilchrist's mistress, don't you?'

He froze. She said, as she walked out of his door, 'You should come to the Black Orchid more often, Jago. Bess Fearnley and Andrew Gilchrist are always together. They're as thick as thieves. Everyone says so.'

Sometimes she felt as though she was running, hardly able to pause or look back or consider her direction. There was Kate and her work, and she had her worries, just now, about both of them.

She started at the Black Orchid at ten o'clock; most nights she stayed there until after one. She could never sleep straight after coming home; her head seemed too full of the jangling music and the bright lights. When she did eventually drop off, she was woken a few hours later by the alarm clock going off at seven. Then she must cook Kate's breakfast and see her off to school and quickly get herself ready before dashing out to Iona's shop. By the afternoon it was a battle not to yawn, to remain bright and enthusiastic with the customers. Often, during the weekends that Kate spent with Ralph, Bess slept through the morning, thankful for the chance to catch up on some sleep.

If she hadn't needed the money, she would have told Jamie that she could no longer work at the club. But she did need the money; she needed it for Kate. The general strike had come to an end after ten days. The newspapers wrote of a humiliating defeat for the unions, with only the miners still out, betrayed and isolated, faced with penury and perhaps even starvation. Though Bess sympathized, it seemed to her that trade unions and politicians made little difference to women's work. Through revolution or war, women still had to care for their children, clean the house, cook meals and do the washing – endless, unpaid work. The tighter the budget, the harder the work, because if you hadn't much money you couldn't eat out and you couldn't afford a maid.

And if you were hard up and proud and you wanted to give your only daughter the best of everything, then it was sometimes very difficult indeed. Over the last few months balancing the budget had become near impossible. Kate, who had always been small for her age, seemed to be growing at last. The girls' school she attended demanded that its pupils have both indoor and outdoor shoes, and then there were ballet shoes and wellingtons and gym shoes – five pairs of shoes to be replaced. She must also buy Kate a school blazer and panama hat. Having recently been put up a class, Kate was to learn tennis this term, and though Bess had managed to find a second-hand racket, the cost put a further strain on her purse. In the new class, the pupils had to wear stockings instead of socks – yet more money, as well as a great deal of misery for poor Kate, who loathed the clammy constriction of liberty bodices and suspenders and whose stockings sat in grey wrinkled folds round her skinny little ankles, making Bess think of elephant skin.

Bess herself possessed three evening dresses. Over the past few years, the hems of the dresses had been taken up several times as skirts became shorter, and the collars and trimmings had been altered according to fashion. All three dresses were showing their age, the seams wearing thin, the fabric losing its shape. You couldn't look glamorous in an old, worn frock and, working at the Black Orchid, she must look glamorous. She often wondered how she would have managed if she had not worked at Iona O'Hagan's shop. Iona liked to lend her dresses – 'You're a grand advertisement for the place, Bess,' she said. 'Women will see you wearing my frocks and want to buy one just the same.'

She could, of course, have asked Ralph for help with the cost of Kate's school uniform. But something in her shrank from doing so. She had her pride, and besides, there was always the fear at the back of her mind, the fear that Ralph might disapprove of the way she lived, that he might sue for custody of his daughter and that she might lose Kate as she had lost Frazer. She knew that her fear was irrational, and that Ralph, dull, kind Ralph, would be far more likely to offer her money to help her out – but that, too, would in its way have been unendurable.

So she had to keep working at the club. She had no

alternative. Yet she found herself enjoying it less than she had, partly because she was tired, she supposed, and partly because of Andrew Gilchrist. Gilchrist was too free with his hands – a pat on the bottom to speed her on her way as she went to get drinks for him, and a tendency, when she was sitting beside him, for his knee to brush against hers beneath the table. She found herself disliking him. Plenty of the men who visited the club treated her as Andrew Gilchrist did, their manner patronizing and possessive, verging on the overfamiliar. She was used to that, and used to tactfully keeping them at a distance. Yet even more than most of his sex, she sensed that Andrew Gilchrist valued women for their looks and nothing else. A woman could have a head as empty as an electric light bulb and Gilchrist would still have wanted her for her full breasts, her rosebud lips. That was what had begun to repel her, that to Gilchrist she was no more than a voluptuous body, a pretty face. She had no soul, no spirit, no character, no intellect. He dehumanized her, making of her a thing, an object, a cartoon figure. Making of her something that could be bought and sold.

You do know that Bess Fearnley is Andrew Gilchrist's mistress, don't you? Hester's words battered at the back of Martin's mind, like a moth caught in a jar.

At first, he didn't believe her. Hester's sharp tongue had run away with her; she had lied to him. Or, if not *lied*, then exaggerated. Wounded by the breakdown of her marriage, piqued by his rejection of her, Hester had set out to hurt.

Yet he couldn't forget what she had said. The moth buzzed

and whirred, its dark, hairy body hammering against the glass, clamouring to be let out. At the nightclub one evening, he saw how Bess smiled at Gilchrist and how often she paused at his table to talk to him, and how, while the cabaret performed, she sat at his side. And how, every so often, Gilchrist touched her – his fingertip running down the inside of her arm, his hand covering hers as it lay on the table. When she stood up, Gilchrist's palm traced the curve of her hip just before she walked away.

In the cloakroom, Martin sluiced cold water over his face. His reflection in the mirror reminded him why Bess Fearnley would always choose someone else over him. Hester had lied to him, he told himself once more. But the words sounded hollow and, just then, it seemed all too possible that Bess Fearnley might take Andrew Gilchrist to her bed. She liked rich men; she had told him so. There was a ruthless, avaricious side to Bess's character – he had witnessed it the first time they had met, many years ago, at the Corstophines' house. That night, she had said to him, *Innocent young debutantes calculate their marriages just as carefully as experienced adventuresses do.* Which was she? He already knew the answer. It was just hard, he thought bleakly, to accept that she had made a career of it.

Kate was unwell, with vague stomach aches and headaches, which always came on in the mornings before she went to school. Bess took her to the doctor, who found nothing wrong with her and prescribed a few days' rest and a simple diet. Because Annie wasn't always available, and because she didn't like to leave Kate at home all day on her own, Bess took her with her to Iona's shop. Kate was no trouble; she just sat on the floor and drew or read while Bess attended to the customers, but it was distracting, and Bess knew that she was neither looking after Kate properly nor doing her job well. If Martin had called she would have asked him to take a look at Kate, but she hadn't seen Martin for more than a fortnight.

After work one day, Annie drew Bess aside when she came home from the shop. 'Kate's a wee bit upset,' she said.

'What about?'

'I don't know, she won't tell me.' Annie was putting on her coat. 'Came home from school with her eyes all red, the poor wee thing.'

'Arithmetic,' suggested Bess. 'She does so hate arithmetic. Perhaps there was a test.'

Annie pulled on her hat, an uncompromising black felt. 'I don't think so. I've never seen a wee girl that upset about her sums.'

Kate was in her room, hunched on the bed. Though she turned aside as Bess came in, Bess had time to see that her face was red and swollen with tears.

'Kate honey, what is it?'

'Nothing.'

Bess sat down beside her. 'Tell me, darling. Is it because you were put up a class? Is the work too difficult?' Kate shook her head. 'Is it your form teacher? Don't you like your new form teacher?'

A muttered, 'She's all right.'

Bess racked her brains. 'Have you quarrelled with Caroline?' Caroline had been Kate's best friend since she had first gone to Bryan House.

'Caroline's still in 2B,' said Kate, rather impatiently. 'People from 2A aren't friends with people in 2B.'

'Oh.' Bess looked closely at Kate, who was wiping her nose on the sleeve of her cardigan. 'Hanky, darling . . . Is that why you're upset? Because you and Caroline aren't friends any more?'

'I haven't got *any* friends!' A sudden wail of misery.

'I'm sure that's not true.'

'It is! Everyone hates me! Marcia Kennedy hates me! She's invited everyone to her party except me!'

'Surely not, Katie.'

Kate was crying openly now. Between sobs, Bess made out the words, 'She gave out the invitations today – at break – everyone else had one – all the others – not me – so beastly!'

'Perhaps Marcia forgot. Or perhaps it's because she hasn't known you long. You've only just moved up—'

'I told you, she hates me!' cried Kate angrily. 'She said her mummy said—' suddenly she broke off, looking down, picking at a scab on her knee.

'She said what, Kate?'

'Doesn't matter.' Bess only just caught the mumbled words.

'I think it does. Tell me.' There was a cold feeling in Bess's stomach. '*Katie.*'

Kate said reluctantly, 'Marcia said her mummy said that she can't think why Miss Gibson lets that woman's daughter go to Bryan House.'

Bess felt shock, quickly followed by anger. She wanted to slap snobbish Mrs Kennedy and her obnoxious daughter.

She wanted to storm up to the school and tell Mrs Gibson that she had decided to take Kate away from Bryan House.

Yet a moment's bleak reflection told her that she should do neither, and her anger mutated painfully to guilt. If Kate was ostracized then it was because of her, because of the way she lived. Because of the choices she had made, the respectability and stability she wanted so much for Kate might always be out of reach.

When she drew Kate to her, kissing and cuddling her, it was to comfort herself as much as Kate. Eventually, Kate agreed to come into the kitchen and help make a cake. But, watching her, Bess knew that the wound had gone deep.

That night, Andrew Gilchrist was waiting for her outside the club after she finished work. She had no alternative but to let him walk her home. They had reached the block of flats where she lived when he pulled her to him, pressing his mouth against hers. His tongue forced her lips apart and his fingertips dug into her spine.

She squirmed from his grasp. 'Andrew, please, not in the street.'

He stood back, gasping. 'Then let me come in.'

'No.'

'I want you, Bess. Let me in.'

'No, Andrew.' Her voice was cold. 'I mean it. I never invite men up to my flat.'

'Really? Well, I'll take your word for it. But you could make an exception for me.'

'I can't. You must understand—'

'Oh, I do. I understand perfectly. You want to keep me waiting. Very well, if that's how you choose to play it, Bess.

But know this. I won't be kept waiting for ever.' He turned and walked away.

She let herself into the building. Running upstairs, she wiped the back of her hand against her mouth, to take away the taste of him. The key fumbled as she fitted it to the front door of her flat and she found herself glancing back down into the darkness, her heart pounding.

A measles epidemic, rippling through the city like a dark, salty wave, was snuffing out the lives of infants and children. Martin almost welcomed the night calls; he couldn't sleep anyway.

He met Davey in the Grassmarket pub. Davey said, 'You should know that I'm out of the race. I asked Bess to marry me.'

'And?'

'And she said no.' Davey gave a hollow laugh. 'Knew she wouldn't have me. Been obvious for months that she wasn't interested. Still, one always likes to think hope can triumph over experience. Only somehow it never damn well does.'

'I'm sorry, Davey.'

'Are you? I should have thought you might be pleased. Leaves the field open.' Davey raised his glass. 'She asked after you. Said she hadn't seen you for a while. She wondered whether you'd gone away.'

Martin shook his head. 'Still here.'

There was a scuffle at the bar, and as the landlord, a short, burly man whose head was as bald as an egg, threw two of the combatants out into the street, Davey said, 'I don't suppose either of us ever had the slightest chance. I sometimes wonder whether she's sick of the lot of us.'

'Perhaps Bess has made her choice. Someone told me she was seeing Andrew Gilchrist.'

'Gilchrist? Rubbish,' said Davey, very definitely. 'Who told you that?'

'It's not important.'

'Well, they're wrong. Anyway, he's married.'

'Bess doesn't want marriage. She told me so.'

Davey stared at him. He shook his head slowly. 'No. She wouldn't. Not Gilchrist.'

'Do you know him?'

'A little. Our paths have crossed, shall we say.'

'Professionally or socially?'

'Both. Gilchrist's a self-made man. Humble beginnings but now he's as rich as Croesus. Makes his money from property. He buys up land cheap, then he gets rid of the tenants by bribery or, more often, by threats. I'll torch your factory if you haven't moved out in a fortnight, that sort of thing.'

'Pleasant chap, then.'

'Oh, quite charming.' Davey's lip curled. 'Anyway, when he's got the land, he makes sure that the council grants permission for a change of usage. Then he slings up tenements, shoddily built tenements, and crams as many people into them as possible. Afterwards he sells on the land at a profit, or hangs on to it, waits till property prices go up.' Davey lowered his voice and leaned closer to Martin. 'I'll tell you something interesting about Gilchrist. There was a fellow named Patterson on the planning committee.

Patterson knew what was going on, tried to stand up to Gilchrist. Then, a few weeks ago, Patterson resigns from the committee and Gilchrist gets his way, everything tickety-boo, planning permission granted.'

'Why did Patterson resign?'

'That's the question, isn't it? Everyone thinks they know the answer but no one dares say it.'

'Gilchrist bribed him, or threatened him?'

'You said it, not me. Personally, I wouldn't dream of making slanderous accusations about Andrew Gilchrist. He uses lawyers like other people use guard dogs. You wouldn't want their teeth in you.' Davey shook his head. 'You're mistaken, Martin. Bess wouldn't look at a man like Gilchrist.'

Once again, Martin found himself remembering the first time he had seen Bess. She had glittered – with sequins and diamonds and a barely contained energy. He hadn't been able to look at anyone else in the room. He said, 'If Gilchrist is rich—'

'She's not a whore. She wouldn't sell herself.' Davey looked angry. Then he said less heatedly, 'Bess has a sort of innocence, I've always thought. You want to look after her. You want to protect her.'

Beer tankards were flying through the air. Martin smiled. 'The places you choose, Davey. This is what I came back to Edinburgh for. The culture. The refined pleasures.'

Later, walking back to his rooms, he knew that there wasn't just desire, that there was concern, understanding, liking, all those awkward emotions that got in the way of just letting things go. If Bess was involved with Andrew

172

Gilchrist – if Davey's estimation of the man was correct – then he found that he was afraid for Bess. *Bess has a sort of innocence* – Martin knew exactly what Davey meant. Sometimes she had a bruised look, as though life hadn't always treated her too kindly. He had seen that bruised look about her eyes when she had told him about the baby who had died, Kate's twin. If Hester had been telling him the truth about Bess and Andrew Gilchrist, then it was possible that Bess didn't understand Gilchrist's nature, possible that she wasn't much of a judge of men. When she had spoken to him about her marriages, she had as much as acknowledged it.

Bess had an impulsive side to her character; it was one of the things he loved her for. He himself lacked spontaneity and calculated carefully before taking action. He was not accustomed to being at the mercy of his emotions – these last few months he had felt as if he was drowning. Yet he had learned a long time ago that action was the best answer to melancholy. Now he must act – to save Bess from herself, if necessary.

The doorbell rang at nine o'clock, when Bess was getting ready to go to the club. She ran downstairs to answer it. Martin Jago was standing on the doorstep. 'I must speak to you, Bess,' he said.

'Goodness, Martin. So dramatic.'

Seeing him cheered her up. They would talk and they would have a drink or two and then they would talk some more, and by the time he left, though she would have forgotten much of what they had spoken of, they would have laughed and argued and she would not have been bored for so much as a minute.

She chatted to him as she led him upstairs to her flat. 'I haven't seen you for ages. I've missed you – I thought you must have gone away, that you must be digging up your old pots. Can I get you a drink?'

'No thanks.'

'You look tired.' He looked dreadful, she thought, thinner than ever, his clothes in need of a good pressing.

He said, 'Bess, I came here to warn you.'

'Warn me?'

'About Andrew Gilchrist.'

She stiffened, her good mood abruptly extinguished, the sound of Gilchrist's name recalling to her that unpleasant incident in the street the other night.

'I know,' he said quickly. 'What you do in your private life is none of my business.'

She was putting on her earrings. 'I couldn't have put it better myself.'

'He's a friend of yours, though, isn't he?'

Friend was not the word she would have chosen. But she said, 'I met him at the club, yes.'

She could see Martin reflected in the mirror behind her. He ran his fingers through hair that was dishevelled already, making tufts of it stick up on end. He said, 'Do you know what sort of man Gilchrist is?'

'He's some sort of businessman, I believe.'

'Davey told me about him. And then I did a bit of digging myself. Gilchrist is the landlord of half a dozen of the most overcrowded tenements in Edinburgh. Much of the work

I do is a wasted effort while tenements like Gilchrist's exist. Poverty and tuberculosis go hand in hand.'

She clipped the second earring in place. It sent out sharp rays of light. 'Martin—'

'Of course, the middle classes bear a responsibility too – the small *rentiers* and bondsmen who have a vested interest in keeping Edinburgh's housing exactly as it is. But it's land speculators like Gilchrist who pay for their mansions and their motor cars with children's rotting lungs.'

She turned to face him. 'Why are you telling me this?'

'Because I want you to know where his money comes from.'

An unpleasant flutter of suspicion stirred, something she had not expected to feel towards Martin Jago. 'Why should that interest me?' she said coolly. 'Why should I care where Andrew Gilchrist gets his money?'

'Because I'm concerned for you.'

'I don't want your concern. I can look after myself. I always have done.' She turned back to the mirror, but her hand shook as she unscrewed her lipstick case. She remembered the gossip that had reached even Kate, at school, and she said harshly, 'I ask you again, Martin, why are you telling me this?'

He said slowly, 'Someone said that you and Gilchrist – well, that you were close.'

She had to force herself to keep her voice low, afraid of waking Kate, in the next room. '*Close*,' she repeated. 'You aren't usually so mealy-mouthed, Martin. Why don't you say it? Why don't you say that you think I'm his mistress?'

His eyes, watching her in the mirror, were like chips of

slate after the rain has washed over them. He said, 'Are you?'

'How dare you?' she hissed. She spun round to him. 'My God! And I thought you were my friend! But you're just like all the rest! Thinking the worst of me, with no reason, no evidence whatsoever.'

He said flatly, 'I saw you with him.'

'Where? At the club?' She gave a short laugh. 'Don't you know that's what they pay me for? Don't you know that's how I earn my living – by being nice to men like Andrew Gilchrist?'

'But I don't know,' he said heavily, 'just how nice you are to him.'

In the silence, his words seemed to reverberate, almost as if she could see them hanging in the air. 'I think you should go, Martin,' she said coldly. 'I'd like you to go.' When she glanced in the mirror, she saw that her face was white, with two angry red spots on her cheekbones.

She heard him say, 'After all, there was Ralph Fearnley.'

'Ralph? What has Ralph to do with any of this?' Crossing the room, she flung open the door. She said softly, 'How dare you judge me, Martin? I am so tired of being judged by men. They want me and at the same time they disparage me. It's as if they're ashamed of wanting me. As if they think that wanting me makes them weak. You thought that I'd sell myself to Andrew Gilchrist, to a man I detest. And I thought you were different. But you're just the same as all the other gossipmongers. So we were both mistaken, weren't we?'

After he had left the flat, she stared out of the window

through the crack between the curtains to the darkened street below. She watched Martin Jago leave the building and head down the street. And then, with a sharp flick, she drew the curtains shut, and he was gone.

Andrew Gilchrist was at the Black Orchid that evening. Bess saw him as soon as she entered the room, sitting at his usual table, holding court, surrounded by his flunkeys. There was a girl beside him, a girl with frizzled curls and too much kohl round her eyes and the reek of cheap perfume whenever you passed the table. When the girl laughed, she put her hand over her mouth to hide her bad teeth, and, with the other hand, she squeezed Gilchrist's sleeve. Martin Jago thought that she, Bess, was the same as the kohl-rimmed girl, fawning, pathetic, *cheap*. Just now, she couldn't decide which man she hated most, Martin Jago or Andrew Gilchrist. At least Gilchrist made no pretence of hiding his vileness. At least Gilchrist was perfectly blatant about what he wanted.

There was a cabaret that night. Girls in high heels and short scarlet frocks danced on the stage. A tiny, dark-haired woman, covered entirely in sequins, writhed on a trapeze. The audience roared and howled, loving it. Other nights, she might have loved it too. Tonight, she saw the beads of sweat on the dancers' foreheads, the bulges of flesh through their fishnet stockings, the marks that age and exhaustion had made, the tired, bruised skin and the purple veins, the mouths that, like hers, feigned a smile. Understanding piled on understanding. Martin had talked to Davey Kirkpatrick about her. Martin had spied on her at the club. Martin had listened to gossip and had believed every word of it, without questioning it.

As for Gilchrist, she found that she could hardly bear to be near him. She saw him now for what he was: greedy, grasping and careless of everyone's desires but his own. She saw with what contempt he treated Simon Voyle, and she saw his equal contempt for the girl sitting beside him, the girl he'd probably take to his bed that night. Though she would have preferred never to speak to Andrew Gilchrist again, that was impossible. *Keep him happy*, Jamie had said, and if she went bleating to him that Gilchrist had tried to kiss her, he would think her a fool. That was what men did, they tried to kiss women, and any woman worth her salt, any woman who was more than a silly girl, learned very quickly how to deal with it.

Gilchrist stopped her as she carried a tray of glasses back to the bar. 'Sit with me, Bess.'

'I'm afraid I'm rather busy.'

'Then you can stop being busy. I'm sure no one'll mind.' His small, dark eyes rested on her. 'You're not avoiding me, are you?'

'Of course not, Andrew.'

'Then sit down.' He gave the girl beside him a little shove; she pouted and moved to another chair.

Bess sat down at Gilchrist's table. There was a large black woman on the stage singing 'The St Louis Blues', and the timbre of her rich, husky voice sent shivers along Bess's spine. The kohl-eyed girl's cloying perfume filled the air, and Andrew Gilchrist's hand rested heavily on her shoulder. She wanted to swipe it off, as though it was unclean.

Bess felt a wave of misery. Tears stung her eyes; she blinked hard. I thought you were my friend, Martin, she muttered under her breath. She felt sick. It must be the perfume.

When the song finished, she heard Gilchrist drawl, 'Women like that should stay at home with the curtains drawn,' and the men sitting at the table sniggered.

Simon Voyle said, 'You'd turn the lights off, wouldn't you, Andrew?' Through louder laughter, Andrew Gilchrist said angrily, 'Good God, you don't think I'd take that ugly black bitch into my bed, do you? You're a fool, Simon. You should keep your mouth shut.'

And Bess felt the nausea rise, scorching the back of her throat, and she found herself standing up, shaking off Gilchrist's hand and walking away.

There was a dark maze of corridors where the offices and storerooms were. She blew her nose and walked about a bit and stole a quick slug of gin from one of the bottles to calm her nerves. It surprised her that she minded so much. It surprised her that she minded so much that Martin Jago should think badly of her.

She heard footsteps; looking up, she saw Andrew Gilchrist.

'You walked away from me, Bess.'

'I had work to do.' She grabbed a bottle or two from the rack.

He said, 'Women don't walk away from me.'

Her temper, raw since she and Martin had quarrelled, rose. 'Don't they?' she hissed. 'Well, there's a first time for everything, isn't there, Andrew?'

He gripped her upper arms. 'You're driving me mad,

Bess, don't you know that? Is that what you wanted to hear – that I'm mad for you?' His fingers dug into her flesh. 'Don't you play games with me. And don't you dare go cold on me. I won't have that. Not after you've been leading me on for months.'

She said icily, 'I haven't been leading you on, Andrew. I'm afraid you're mistaken. If I've been pleasant to you then it's only because it's my job to be pleasant. And actually, the job's beginning to bore me. Men like you are beginning to bore me.'

His hands fell away. He took a step back, his mouth slack, his eyes disbelieving. 'I bore you?'

'Yes. Sorry.'

Pushing past Gilchrist, she went to find Jamie. After she had given him her notice, she put on her coat and hat and walked home, taking in lungfuls of cool night air. Stars were scattered across the navy-blue sky. She found herself thinking of the sky at Simla, how the moonlight had outlined the peaks of the Himalayas. No night sky since had ever seemed so shimmering, so vivid. She remembered the last time she had seen Simla, looking out from the window of the railway carriage as the roads and buildings disappeared behind the curve of the hills. She remembered how the pain of leaving her child had torn at her heart. Nothing since, neither the passing of the years nor the crushing of hope, had lessened that pain.

At the flat, she scrubbed off her make-up and took off her dress and jewellery. She wished she could scrub away the memory of Martin Jago saying *after all, there was Ralph Fearnley*. The blue diamond earrings lay in the palm of her hand. She stared at them. She had worn them the night Ralph had proposed to her, the night she had first met Martin Jago. She seemed to see a quick, vivid picture of herself, silk and diamonds sparkling, brushing a lock of hair out of Ralph's eyes. Martin had assumed that she was pursuing Andrew Gilchrist just as, once, a long time ago, she had pursued Ralph. She had felt angry with Martin; now the anger transmuted into shame. She must speak to Martin; she must try to make him understand.

She still felt sick. But it wasn't the perfume that nauseated her; it wasn't even Andrew Gilchrist. She sickened herself.

Chapter Seven

Bess was waiting for him when he came back to his rooms. Martin saw her before she saw him; she was sitting on the top of the flight of stairs that led to his rooms. Her arms were looped round her knees and there were shadows like bruises beneath her eyes.

She looked up. 'I need to explain about Ralph,' she said.

'You don't have to.' He sat down beside her. 'I was a pompous idiot, lecturing you like that.'

'It doesn't matter.' She pushed back her hair, which lay loose over her shoulders. 'Of course, you were right. Not about Gilchrist,' she added quickly. 'But Ralph.'

'As you pointed out, it's none of my business.'

There was a silence. Then she said abruptly, 'I want to tell you about my son.'

A quick look. 'I remember. Michael.'

'Not Michael. He's called Frazer. He lives in India.'

He blinked. 'Bess, I don't understand.'

'Frazer is Jack's son.'

'Jack . . .'

'I was nineteen when Frazer was born.'

'I didn't know—'

'Not many people do. Just Ralph and Pamela. And Kate, though I don't think she really understands.'

'You have a son but he doesn't live with you?'

She said slowly, 'After Jack died, I was penniless. My mother-in-law offered to look after Frazer while I went to England to find my father. But when I found him, he was very ill. He died six months after I came here.'

She remembered her journey to Scotland, to Ravenhart House, with its turrets and gables and countless windows and the mountains soaring up all around it. And she remembered how the darkness had flooded over the house, shutting out the sun.

She heard Martin say, 'I think I'm going to have to eat something. And have a drink. It's been a long day.'

He gave her his hand to help her up. In his kitchen, he opened cupboards, peered into tins and discovered a piece of pie and a lump of cheese, hairy with mould.

'You don't look after yourself properly, Martin.'

He said vaguely, 'There's a lady who shops for me but her daughter's unwell . . . Two sons. Michael and Frazer.'

'Yes. I married Ralph because of Frazer.'

'Cheese?' He was scraping off the mould.

'No thanks. But a drink might help.'

He poured two glasses of port. As he swept the sofa free of books and papers, he said, 'When we first met you told me you wanted to go back to India.'

'What an extraordinary memory you have. I had to go

back to India because of Frazer. I had to fetch him, you see.'

'But you didn't?'

'I *couldn't*. Because of the war.' Looking Martin Jago in the eyes, she said proudly, 'I don't regret marrying Ralph. I'd do it all over again if I had to. I married him for his money, it's true. But I didn't marry him so that I could have a wardrobe full of clothes and a big house. People thought so, but they were wrong. I married him for Frazer. I needed money so that I could go and get Frazer.'

'So what happened?'

She looked suddenly stricken. 'My mother-in-law was supposed to bring Frazer to Scotland that summer so that I could collect him. But she never came. I realized that I would have to go back to India to fetch him myself. That was when I married Ralph.' Her hands were clenched, the knuckles white. 'All those years of waiting – I'll never forget them. All that longing, all that loneliness. Ralph wouldn't let me go to India – he was afraid my ship might be sunk. I'd have taken my chance, taken the housekeeping money to pay my fare, but I couldn't risk anything happening to Frazer. And then the twins came along, and you can't travel halfway round the world with two little babies. And by the time the war had ended and I saw Frazer again, it was too late. He had forgotten me. He loved his grandmother. She'd made sure of that. It would have broken his heart to take him away from her. And I couldn't do that, I just couldn't.' She looked up at him, her eyes defiant. 'I did what I did for love. I wanted you to know that. Only for love.'

He pushed aside the plate; he wasn't hungry any more.

He said slowly, 'What do we know of each other? Hardly anything at all. My father was ruined by his association with my mother. She died a few years after I was born. Some people said that she died of shame. I choose to think that she died for love. Most of the time, we only see what's on the surface. We rarely understand one another's deeper motives.'

She fumbled in her bag and took out an envelope. 'Look,' she said.

She handed him a photograph. He looked down at it, and saw a plump, fair-haired baby dressed in velvet and lace, and said, as he knew he must, 'He's beautiful.'

'Isn't he?' She smiled. 'Frazer and I will be together again one day, I know we will. I feel it in my heart. I feel it *here*.' She put her fist to her chest.

Towards the beginning of July, Andrew Gilchrist had a letter from Maxwell's headmaster asking – insisting – that he take Maxwell away from the school. Andrew drove out to the godforsaken, windswept valley in Lanarkshire where the establishment stood, confident that he could persuade Dr Nicholls to change his mind.

He endured an aggravating hour in the headmaster's study as Dr Nicholls listed Maxwell's crimes – answering the French master back, visiting the pub in the nearby village, and some sort of dalliance with one of the younger maidservants. Though Andrew offered him money – a donation towards the library or swimming pool or whatever – Dr Nicholls was adamant. With the sort of supercilious glare that made Andrew long to punch him, Dr Nicholls said, 'I'm afraid you must understand that nothing will persuade me to keep Maxwell at this establishment, Mr Gilchrist. I have to consider the school's reputation.' Andrew heard himself blustering – he would knock some sense into the boy – but Nicholls looked away, murmuring, 'I have tried, God knows I have tried. But the boy is undisciplined, he is wild.' Then he made it clear that the conversation was closed, leaving Andrew inwardly seething with rage.

Shortly afterwards, Maxwell and his overnight bag were flung into the car. The rest of his belongings would be sent on later. On the drive back to Edinburgh, Maxwell's expression and demeanour showed not a hint of remorse. Andrew felt his fury boiling up inside him.

At home, he dealt with Maxwell, administering his own form of discipline. Then he went into dinner. He and Agnes dined alone. Niall was in London on business and Sandy was still at boarding school. As for Maxwell, he would go to bed without his supper for as long as it took to make him mend his ways. For some time they ate in silence, the awfulness of the day hanging over them, and then, irritated by the way Agnes picked at her food, Andrew said, 'Well? Don't you want to know what that fool of a headmaster said to me? Don't you want to know what he said about your son?'

Then he told her. That Maxwell was deceitful and manipulative, and she said, startling him, 'If he is, then it's because he has learned it from you.' Then, shockingly, she began to laugh, and he reached across the table and slapped her face, and the laughter stopped as suddenly as it had begun.

There was a sound. He looked up and saw Maxwell, standing in the doorway. Maxwell's clear green gaze jumped from his mother to his father. Andrew made to hit him, too, but Maxwell was quicker than Agnes, and ran away. But not before Andrew had the satisfaction of seeing tears in his son's eyes, tears he had refused to let fall while his father had thrashed him.

His sour mood lingered. After the general strike, Andrew Gilchrist had sacked all his labourers – he'd warned them, any man who downed tools wouldn't receive another penny from him – and he'd kept his word. There were plenty of others to take the place of those he'd laid off. Work was hard to come by; the country had limped along, dipping in and out of recession for several years now. But it took time to train up workers, and some of the new lot still weren't pulling their weight.

It wasn't only his work and his family that were making him foul-tempered, though. No, it was that bitch, Bess Fearnley, leading him on and then throwing him aside as though he was nothing. He knew what she wanted, of course, but he wasn't going to give her the pleasure of yielding to her easily. If you waited, you got a better bargain, and besides, he wouldn't have a woman call the tune.

Sometimes, half unwillingly, he found himself admiring her spirit. Not many women had the courage to stand up to him. Though Bess Fearnley might drive him wild, though she had angered him, it made a change from Agnes's mewling humility or Kitty Green's transparently grasping flattery. He knew that Bess was only playing a game, and she was playing it well – again, he found himself reluctantly acknowledging her expertise. It wasn't often that he met his match.

He could feel his resolve crumbling, ready to give her what she wanted. And it wasn't, after all, as though he couldn't afford it.

Bess had tidied things up, sorted things out. She and Martin were friends again, and she had spoken to Kate's form teacher, Miss Dunbar, and had explained to her that Kate was finding it difficult to fit into her new class, and Miss Dunbar had somehow smoothed things over and Kate seemed happier.

Then it was the end of term and Kate was to stay with Ralph and Pamela at the farm. Pamela insisted Bess stay overnight, wouldn't hear of anything else, so she slept in a whitewashed, low-ceilinged room and woke in the early morning to the sound of cows lowing and the newest baby, Archie, crying in the next room. Though she went in to him and rocked his cradle, he only cried louder, so she picked him up. He snuggled into the hollow of her shoulder and the crying stopped. He had a fuzz of red hair and when she stroked his head with the palm of her hand it felt like velvet.

After breakfast, she politely turned down Pamela's suggestion that she stay longer and caught the next train back to Edinburgh. She had expected to feel relieved to be back in the city, away from babies and small children and all the difficult, conflicting emotions they stirred up inside her. But without Kate the flat seemed too empty and still, and though she filled the day writing letters and catching up on housework, she was relieved when Monday came and she went back to work.

There was a garden party in Morningside the evening before Kate came home. Dark green leaves hung motionless in the warm midsummer air and the heavy heads of the roses drooped. A string quartet played on the terrace, waiters with trays of champagne moved among the guests. Bess's escort melted away into the crowd not long after they arrived. She had thought that Iona and the Lockhead sisters would be at the party, but she could not find them. These days, when she went out, she seemed to feel eyes following her and she thought she caught words, phrases, whispered behind raised hands. *That woman . . . leading me on . . . someone said . . .* After a while she wandered away, heading through the garden to the terrace, and found herself face to face with Andrew Gilchrist.

'Bess,' he said.

She was halfway up the stone steps. Below, tall spikes of hollyhock and delphinium rose into the air; above them, the quartet was playing '*Eine Kleine Nachtmusik*'.

They must be civilized, she thought, two acquaintances passing the time of day at a party. 'Andrew,' she said. 'How are you?'

'Missing you.'

She gave her best social smile. 'It's been an age, hasn't it? And now I'm afraid you must excuse me – I have to dash.'

'Why don't you come to the club any more?'

'I gave in my notice.'

'Why?'

'I never meant to stay there long.'

His voice lowered. 'I must see you, Bess. You shan't fool around with me. I won't have it.' Couples passed them, hand in hand, and three girls ran up the steps, their arms linked, giggling. He said, 'How much do you want?'

There was the hum of a bee out hunting for pollen, and his eyes burning into her as he murmured, 'A bigger flat? I can do that. I've got a nice little place I could move you into tomorrow. New frocks – you'd like some new frocks, wouldn't you? You wouldn't have to work in a shop any more – no more flattering fat old biddies who can't hold a candle to you.'

Now the scent of lilies choked her and the music seemed repetitive, irritating and overfamiliar. She said slowly, 'You're offering me money to go to bed with you?' and she saw him smile, showing perfect, even teeth.

'I wouldn't have put it quite so bluntly. But you're a good businesswoman, Bess.'

And then she slapped his face hard – a crack that made everyone around them stare – and in the seconds that followed, she saw on the faces of the guests shock and amusement and curiosity, and the silence seemed to reverberate until it was broken by a burst of laughter, quickly stifled. She saw the rage in Andrew Gilchrist's eyes as he put his hand up to where she had hit him, and whispered, 'You bitch. You little bitch.'

At first, he felt only fury and humiliation. Plenty more fish in the sea, he told himself, gritting his teeth as he flung a glare at anyone who dared catch his eye. Plenty more who'd be only too happy to do whatever he wanted for the price of a new frock. Inside the house, in the cloakroom, he found that he had spilled wine over his sleeve, so he wiped it off with his handkerchief, and then crushed it into a ball as he caught a glimpse of himself in the mirror and saw the scarlet stripes her fingers had made across his cheekbone.

Once or twice over the next few weeks he found himself walking past the O'Hagan woman's shop. Or standing on the far side of the road, watching, while Bess and her daughter left their flat. *Kate*. Simon Voyles had told him about Kate Fearnley. And a few other things about Bess Fearnley's colourful past. Knowledge was power.

These summer evenings, the light lingered late, and Bess did not draw her curtains, and every now and then, looking up, he caught a glimpse of her behind the glass. Something seemed to ache inside him, and he wondered whether he, who was never ill, was ailing.

One evening, he saw a man stop outside the block of flats and ring the doorbell. He watched, sinking back into the shadows as Bess opened the door. There was a brief exchange of words and then the visitor went into the flat. Gilchrist felt a surge of uncontrollable rage. He caught a fleeting sight of the two of them together, upstairs, just before she drew the curtains. *I never invite men up to my flat*, she had told him. What a liar she was! Such a liar. How dare she make a fool of him? How dare she laugh at him and think she could get away with it?

Now his fury was mixed with hatred. He knew that he must find a way to pay her back, to make her sorry for what she had done. No one got away with making a fool of him in public. At night, the longing persisted, and he dreamed about her, dreamed about her slender white limbs and her fall of black hair, dreamed about taking her to his bed and doing what he needed to her. His imagination conjured up pictures of her obliging, obedient and compliant, submissive at last, no longer able to blow hot and cold as it suited her.

He knew that he had never wanted a woman as much as he wanted Bess Fearnley. He hated that she had done this to him. And she a slut who teased men for money.

Edinburgh seemed empty; those who couldn't afford to go away rattled around the city like coins in a child's money box. The summer disappointed, low cloud and fine rain casting a chill over the closes and alleyways. Days like these, Bess remembered a sun so hot you had to take shelter at midday, and skies so blue they almost hurt your eyes. She remembered lotus blossoms the size of dinner plates, floating on limpid olive-green water, and the gold and emerald shimmer of a bird's wing as it darted through the highest branches of the trees.

She didn't go out much – invitations always tended to fizzle out in August, and besides, there was the memory of the fury in Andrew Gilchrist's eyes when she had slapped his face. The venom in his voice: You bitch. She didn't want to risk running into him again. Gilchrist wasn't a man who would take kindly to public humiliation. Sometimes she found herself glancing over her shoulder as she walked from the shop to the flat. But she never saw him.

She didn't miss the parties and the nightclubs; she seemed to have grown tired of all that. She and Kate walked to the castle or played ball in the park and, sometimes, late at night, Martin Jago called and they played a hand of cards. Just now these things were enough for her. She could see her life going on like this for years, she and Kate and a few good friends, and her work, and the occasional visit to Ralph and Pamela and the boys when she needed hills and open spaces. It pleased her that her life had settled into a pattern at last, that she had put behind her the uncertainties and upheavals of her earlier years. And if, sometimes, she felt a flicker of melancholy for all that might have been – a snapshot of a baby in velvet and lace, the swirl of an Indian shawl, rich with the colours of Kashmir – she brushed it aside.

So she forgot about Andrew Gilchrist, and made a small, mental letting out of breath in acknowledgement that a disturbing episode was over. After work one Friday, she gave Kate her tea, then they played happy families and Ludo and listened to the wireless, and then Kate had her bath and went to bed. Low, dark clouds had gathered over the city, spitting rain, and every now and then there was a rumble of thunder. Bess put Kate's discarded clothes away and cleared up the tea things – Martin had said he might call later, though why she tidied up for Martin, who was even untidier than Kate, she did not know; habit, she supposed. She had the wireless down low, so as not to disturb Kate, and she had opened the windows to try to make the flat airier; there was the low drone of cars and lorries and the shriek of a pair of tomcats as they fought.

She was in the hallway, hanging up sou'westers and putting umbrellas back into the stand, when there was a knock on the door. Her hands full of things, she pulled the door open and said, 'You're early. I thought—'

It was Andrew Gilchrist. She tried to shut the door, but he pushed past her, into the sitting room. She dropped the umbrella and raincoats – what a stupid, stupid mistake, she thought later, to have dropped the umbrella – and ran after him.

'What are you doing?' She wasn't frightened yet, just shocked and angry. 'How dare you barge your way in here? Who let you in?'

A shrug of the shoulders. He said, 'I waited till someone came out of the building and then I slipped inside while the front door was open. These things are easy if you put your mind to it.'

'I told you not to come here. I haven't changed my mind. You must go.'

'I don't think so. You see, Bess,' and he smiled, 'I'm not used to taking no for an answer.'

He was strolling round the room, his gaze raking over her possessions. He seemed out of proportion, too large for the small sitting room. Beside him, the chairs and table and bookshelves looked fragile and spindly. He took a step towards her; involuntarily, she shrank back. Then he turned the key in the door.

Now she was frightened. Why had he come here? What did he mean to do? 'Andrew,' she whispered. 'You have to go. Please go.'

He shook his head. 'Not till I've had what I came for.

You've made a fool of me once too often, Bess. No one makes a fool of me and gets away with it.'

She remembered the garden party, the crack of her hand against his face. 'I'm sorry – what happened – I shouldn't have done that.' Fear made it hard to get the words out; it seemed to paralyse her throat. 'It was wrong of me.'

'Make it up to me then. I'm giving you the chance to make it up to me.'

'I said I was sorry.' She heard the rise of her voice, the fluttering edge to it.

'Not enough, Bess. Nowhere near enough.'

When he ran his fingertip down the side of her face, along the curve of her jaw, she shuddered. She smelt the drink on his breath. 'No,' she whispered. 'Please, no.'

'Ah, nice and polite now. Such a change. Virtuous little Bess. Pity you're such a liar.'

'I've never lied to you—'

The palm of his hand struck her across the mouth and she heard herself cry out with shock and pain. 'Liar,' he hissed. 'I saw you. *I never let men into my flat.*' His voice had taken on a falsetto whine. '*I know.*'

Then he hit her again. It was as though, once he had started, he got a taste for it. There was blood in her mouth and she knew that something unspeakable was about to happen, something that would change everything. She fell against the table; Ludo counters scattered and dice rolled.

Then she was lying on the floor and he was pinning her down with one hand and tearing at her clothes with the other. Cards were scattered around her: Mrs Bun the Baker's wife, Mr Bone the Butcher. She opened her mouth to scream and felt his hot breath at her ear as he whispered, 'You don't want to wake your daughter, do you, Bess? You wouldn't want her to see what I'm going to do to her mother, would you?'

The scream died; she did not struggle any more.

Then he raped her.

When he was gone, she crawled to the front door and pushed it shut. She tried to slide the bolt home, but her hands were juddering too much to grip it. When, eventually, it was done, she sat, her back against the door, her knees hunched up to her chin, shaking. Then she thought, *Kate*, and tried to pull herself to her feet using the door handle.

She had to prop herself against the wall as she walked. She couldn't seem to stand upright properly. A momentary relief that Kate was still asleep – and then she went into the bathroom. There was blood on her face, blood between her legs. Crouching beside the lavatory, she vomited.

After she had stopped being sick, she washed herself. Every inch of her body, over and over again, till her skin was red and raw. Rubbing him out of her. It hurt to touch her face: her left eye was already puffing up, starting to close, as if it wanted to shut out the evidence of what had taken place. When she was done, she dressed. Pyjamas, jersey, dressing gown, because the cold seemed to have got inside her. It took a long time to dress because of the shaking. It was hard to tie tapes, to do up buttons.

In the sitting room, she gathered up her clothes. The room, which had once been her sanctuary, was despoiled and diminished; she knew that she would never feel safe in it again. She didn't think she would ever feel safe anywhere again.

She dropped her clothes into the kitchen bin, filled up the kettle, and put it on the hob. When the water was boiled, she tried to fill up the hot-water bottle, but the boiling water splashed, scalding her. She began to cry, and could not stop.

The cloud that had hung over the city cleared, giving way to blue skies and soft, warm air. Clerks and shop assistants flung off their jackets as they walked home from work. In the parks and gardens they sat on the grass, eating ice creams, putting up their faces to the sun. Edinburgh looked its best; the castle, on its volcanic outcrop, glittered, as though it was made of glass.

Late on Monday afternoon, Martin called at Iona's shop. There was a stout lady in lilac tulle emerging from a dressing room; he kept a respectful distance.

The stout lady left the shop. Iona said, 'One moment, Martin darling,' and disappeared back into the dressing room, emerging shortly afterwards, her arms full of gowns in bright, slithery fabrics.

'She will insist on scarlet satin. And really, who can blame her? I fully intend to wear scarlet satin when I'm seventy.' She kissed his cheek. 'How lovely to see you, darling. But if you've come for Bess, she isn't here.'

'She's left early?'

'She didn't come into work today. Or Saturday.'

'Is she ill?'

'I don't know.' Iona frowned. 'It's not like Bess. I thought the child must be unwell perhaps, so I sent a note, but I haven't heard a thing. She's usually so reliable. Have you seen her, darling?'

Martin shook his head. 'I called at her flat the other night – Saturday? Or perhaps it was Friday? But no one was in. I'll try again.'

He was within a short distance of Bess's flat when he caught sight of Kate. She was skipping along the pavement; he noticed that she was avoiding the cracks between the stones. She was carrying a wicker shopping basket; when he caught up with her, he saw inside it a bottle of milk and a loaf of bread.

He said, 'What happens if you step on a crack?'

'Bears eat you.'

'Bears? In Edinburgh?'

She said, with a kindly and pitying air, 'It's only a story, Martin.'

'Still. I'll be more careful.' He walked beside her; they reached the block of flats where she lived. 'Is your mother in?'

Kate pushed open the front door, which had been left ajar. 'Mummy fell over. She's got a black eye. I had to buy steak from the butcher. Why does steak make a black eye better?'

He followed her up the stairs. 'I suppose,' he said absently, 'there must be chemicals in the steak that make the swelling go down.' Then the door of the flat opened, and he saw Bess. 'Mother of God,' he whispered.

* * *

Bess shot a swift, fierce glance at Kate.

He recovered himself and said, 'Kate was explaining to me about bears in the pavement. May I come in?'

She didn't want to let him in – she didn't want to let anyone in – but Martin Jago could help her, perhaps; he could tell her how to stop the thing that frightened her most of all.

He followed her into the flat. He said, 'Kate told me you had a fall.'

'I fell downstairs. So silly.'

She knew that he didn't believe her. She saw him fish in his pockets and draw out a magnifying glass, an old fob watch and a handful of toffees, and give them to Kate. Then he followed her into the kitchen and shut the door behind them.

'What happened, Bess?' When she did not answer, he said gently, 'Those are not the injuries you'd get from falling downstairs. What happened?'

She did not reply.

He asked, 'Have you seen a doctor?'

She shook her head. He went to her, but she jerked away, hissing, 'Don't touch me!'

She saw him step back, saw his gaze run round the room and take in the washing-up in the sink, the bottle of aspirins on the table, the bottle of gin on the draining board. He said, 'Someone hurt you, didn't they?' and eventually she nodded.

'Who was it?'

'It doesn't matter.'

'It matters. Of course it matters.'

She met his eyes. 'Whatever I do,' she said levelly, 'whatever I say, it will still have happened.'

'Even so. Tell me.'

'Why, Martin? What will you do? Will you kill him?'

'Perhaps. If you like.'

After a while, she shook her head and muttered, 'No. I don't want you to do that. But I need you to help me.'

'Anything.'

'Anything? Then tell me how not to have a baby.'

She saw the dawning horror in his eyes, and she went on, her voice low and only a little unsteady, 'I won't have his baby. I couldn't bear it. I'd rather die. Only there's Kate. I can't leave Kate. You must know, Martin, you're a doctor. You must be able to tell me how I can make sure there's no baby. You'll help me, won't you?' She drooped against the table, wrapping her arms round herself. She was exhausted; she had hardly slept since it had happened. She murmured, 'And I have to go away. I hate it here. I don't feel safe any more. I'm afraid he'll come back. Every time I hear footsteps on the stairs, I think it's him. I have to go away, Martin. I have to.'

You could think several things at the same time: you could put aside the sickening sense of shock, file it away for later, just as you could put aside your rage, which was the last thing Bess needed now, and make yourself deal with practical, resolvable problems.

He helped Bess pack a bag for herself and Kate, and then he hailed a taxi to take them to his rooms in the Old Town. There, he borrowed a camp bed and put it up for Kate in his bedroom. He would sleep on the sitting-room sofa. He dressed the cut over Bess's eye and gave her a sleeping draught. He explained to her that it was too early to tell whether she was pregnant or not, that she must wait a few weeks, and meanwhile try not to worry.

Over the next few days, he spoke to Charlie Campbell and made telephone calls. By Wednesday evening he had found a locum. Back in his rooms that night, he took Bess's hands in his and told her that they were going to France. 'I have a house there,' he said. 'You can stay as long as you like. It's a beautiful place – you and Kate will love it, I promise you. There are woods and fields and it'll be warm and sunny. We'll leave tomorrow morning.'

All the time, names ran through his head. One of them kept coming up again and again. As he made his arrangements, as he lay awake at night on the slippery, lumpy sofa, he thought about who might have done this to her. And what he would do to him when he knew.

Chapter Eight

Martin Jago's house in France was called Les Trois Cheminées. It was three-storeyed, with a tiled mansard roof and small-paned windows with green shutters. The house stood between Metz and Reims, in rolling countryside of woodland and fields. Vineyards pleated the sides of the hills that faced the sun, and in the orchard behind the house the gnarled branches of the trees were heavy with apples. There was a farm half a mile away; on the first morning Martin took Kate to fetch milk and bread. Madame Lemercier, who lived at the farm, and who looked after the house in Martin's absence, embraced both of them and exclaimed at Kate's skinniness, and then fed Martin coffee and Kate milk and rolls, her small, dark, inquisitive eyes flicking all the while between the two of them, and eventually concluding, Martin supposed – perhaps with some disappointment – that flame-haired, restless Kate could not possibly be his natural daughter.

Madame Lemercier found a kind-hearted young woman

called Marie-Yvonne to cook and clean for them. Kate quickly made friends with Emilie, a granddaughter of Madame Lemercier. Emilie was a prim and proper girl, who wore clean white ankle socks and neatly darned gloves, and whose hair was dressed in a complicated arrangement of plaited loops and whorls that Kate tried to copy. Kate's open adoration of Emilie was based, Martin suspected, on her admiration of Emilie's impressive array of material possessions – a writing desk with a pot of ink and a supply of dip pens, and the hoard of prayer books, medals, crucifixes and lace veil, accumulated at her recent confirmation.

Emilie occupied Kate for most of the day, which left Martin free to be with Bess. He showed her round the house and gardens, and saw her effort to pretend interest, to jerk her mind away from the horror he knew she must think about all the time. He put a comfortable chair in the orchard and a heap of old books and magazines beside it, and she curled up in the chair while he went about various small repairs to the house. The weather was fine, and he saw how she pushed up the sleeves of her blouse and closed her eyes and let the sun lull her to sleep.

When she wasn't sleeping, he talked to her. He knew how you could brood when something appalling had happened to you, something that shook your view of the world, your view of yourself, to the core. Better to think of other things, better to paper over the cracks, however wide they gaped beneath. He talked to her about anything and everything. He took her on walks and showed her the swallows that nested in the eaves and the purplish-blue chicory flowers that grew at the side of the road. He told her about the bats that roosted in the attic, like rows of little crumpled black silk purses, and about the slow-worms which, when he was a child, had used to startle him, cutting across the narrow footpaths through the woods behind the house. He explained to her that he had been brought up in this house, that it had belonged to his French grandmother, who had left it to him, and he told her about Sunday visits to aunts and cousins, who had made a fuss of him, plying him with cake and pastries until he had thought he would burst. He told her how, after his grandmother had died, he had been sent to school in England, and how, though he had by that time a good working knowledge of Latin, he had known hardly a word of English.

They had been at the house for a week when she told him that she was not pregnant. They had just had breakfast; Kate and Emilie were playing in the garden. He felt a wash of relief. Marie-Yvonne came in to clear up the breakfast things; when she was gone, he said, 'It was Andrew Gilchrist, wasn't it?' and he heard Bess's small, sharp intake of breath, saw the flash of fear in her eyes.

A few days later, he explained to her that he had to go back to Edinburgh. The locum had been engaged only for two weeks, and besides, he had business to attend to. Marie-Yvonne would look after her; Pierre, the handyman, would make sure there was enough fuel for the stove and oil for the lamps. There was a heap of francs in the drawer in his study – she must help herself to whatever she needed. He would return as soon as possible.

In Edinburgh, he went back to work, and he watched and waited. He let weeks pass, waiting until he knew the bars where Gilchrist liked to drink and the tenement rooms in Gorgie where his mistress lived. He would wait until Gilchrist had too much to drink and was clumsy and careless. Gilchrist drank a lot, like a man with a bad conscience.

One night in September, Martin followed Andrew Gilchrist through the narrow alleys of the Old Town. Enclosed within the wet, dark walls of a courtyard, he said Gilchrist's name. When Gilchrist turned and stumbled, his eyes blearily raking the darkness, Martin struck him in the solar plexus. Gilchrist was heavier and stronger, but Martin knew where to hurt so that you couldn't draw breath enough to hit back. He stood over Gilchrist as he lay on the ground, choking. 'This is for Bess,' he said, and hit him again. When Gilchrist was able to listen, he stooped down beside him and hissed, 'Touch her again and I'll kill you, Gilchrist. Never doubt that I will.'

Footsteps in the distance. Martin walked home.

She kept thinking that she should go back – Kate and school, Iona and the shop – but she did nothing about it. A lassitude seemed to have settled over her and, for the first time she could remember, she did nothing. The cuts and bruises faded until there was only the narrow white line of a scar above her left eye. Still she stayed in France, eating the daubes and ragouts that Marie-Yvonne made, going to bed early and rising late. She kept to the house and its immediate environs, rarely walking further than the farm, watchful of strangers, checking obsessively each night that the doors were locked and the windows were shut.

Summer drifted into autumn. Kate went to the village

school with Emilie; now, her speech was peppered with fragments of French. In the fields, they had taken in the grapes; at the time of the vendange even the air seemed rich and heavy with wine. The sun lingered. For the first time since she had left India, Bess felt satiated with warmth, satiated with sun.

In October, Martin returned to the house. One morning, he went out early and came back later riding a horse, a spectacularly bony, ugly horse that nipped him as he dismounted. Bess found herself laughing, the sound creaking in her throat as though she was out of practice.

'What do you think?' he said.

'He's hideous.' She rubbed the horse's neck. 'And very impolite.'

'Horses always dislike me. I seem to bring out the worst in them. As for camels . . .'

'What's he called?'

'Pegasus. He's called Pegasus. I can't think why you're laughing, Bess.'

They borrowed a saddle and bridle from the farm. She had no riding habit, so she searched through the chests of drawers in the house until she found a pair of corduroy trousers that she cut down and took in. With them she wore an old jersey and tied back her hair with a length of ribbon. 'I must look a sight,' she said to Martin, but one day, returning to the house after riding along the narrow, chalky tracks that threaded between the fields and woods, she saw the way he looked at her, and felt a flicker of surprise.

He went back to Scotland. The leaves, first turning gold,

then copper, drifted from the trees. In the mornings, Bess rode through land that still bore the scars of war – trenches dug alongside a copse, a vast heap of tin helmets in the corner of a field.

The sun retreated, and, in the evenings, she lit the wood-burning stove in the sitting room. She asked Marie-Yvonne to teach her French – she had no French at all – but her mouth seemed to mangle the words, and they both became helpless with laughter. So Marie-Yvonne taught her how to cook instead, French provincial cooking, glorious fluffy batters and light, golden pastries, and rich, aromatic stews.

When Martin next returned, he had parcels for them both. Kate unwrapped hers first, squealing with delight as she uncovered a fountain pen and a leather-bound note-book. Bess's parcel was large and soft, tied up with tissue paper and string. Inside was a coat of crimson cloth with a fur collar.

'Iona chose it,' said Martin. 'Do you like it?'

She put it on and looked at herself in the glass over the mantelpiece. The glossy dark fur was the same colour as her hair, and the cloth was soft and warm and light – cash-mere, surely.

She ran the back of her hand along a sleeve. 'It's beautiful, absolutely beautiful. But you don't have to bring us gifts, Martin.'

'I don't do it because I have to. I thought you'd need a winter coat. You brought only summer things. As for Kate,' she had run off to fetch a bottle of ink, 'I would have bought her a writing desk, she lusts after Emilie's so, but it wasn't practical.'

'She wants a lace veil to wear to church. It'll be crucifixes and holy medals next.'

When he went away, she missed him. He wrote several times a week, amusing letters in an angular hand that was hard to decipher – doctor's writing, she thought. Whenever he came back to France, there seemed to be a holiday air about Les Trois Cheminées. Once, she was pulling off her boots in the porch after a long ride, when she heard him playing the piano. She stood in the doorway, listening, watching him as he bent over the keyboard. Somewhere in the distance a door slammed, and she ran away, quiet in her stockinged soles, before he saw her.

He told her about his early years in France, about playing at the Lemerciers' farm, and going with his grandmother to the village church each Sunday. He had liked the candles and the incense, he said, adding, 'I suppose I lost what religion I had in the war. A lot of men did.'

It was evening; they were in the sitting room. The stove cast an orange light over the room, and long, black tongues of shadows were painted over the floor. Bess was curled up on the sofa, her feet tucked beneath her. 'You never talk much about the war, Martin.'

'Words never seem to match up to the most extreme experiences, do they?' He put another log on the fire and refilled their wine glasses before he sat down. 'I tell people that I was in the RAMC, and I can see them assuming that I worked behind the lines, so although it was messy and bloody, it was, at least, fairly safe. But sometimes you had to treat your casualty before you could move him. And then it wasn't safe at all. And the injuries . . . we had to learn quickly. We were seeing things we'd never seen before.' He paused, his long, thin hands wrapped round the wine glass. 'One day, I came across a man with severe abdominal wounds. I knew he hadn't a chance, and that he was in great pain. He begged me to finish him off. And so I did. I shot him in the head. There I was, sworn to preserve life, and I shot him.' Martin's face was set. 'I've never told anyone else that. I dream about it a lot, though. I see him.'

'You had no choice.'

'True. But afterwards I felt . . . adrift. Nothing seemed predictable or safe any more. I knew that anything could happen – that I could betray my most fundamental prin- ciples. I suppose that's why I broke down, because I had nothing to hold on to. It was a long time before I was able to go back, pick up the pieces again.'

She said slowly, 'And now . . . do you still feel like that now?'

He met her gaze. 'No. Now there are things I wish to hold on to.'

'What things?'

'Love,' he said simply. 'It's always love, isn't it, that keeps you going.'

There were other questions she might have asked him. Such as who do you love, and how much do you love them? But she hadn't the courage. She turned aside, changing the subject.

After he went away, the first frosts greyed the fields and hills. When she walked through the orchard, blades of grass crunched beneath her feet. She wore the red coat, the fur collar turned up round her face. She saw Marie-Yvonne

209

gaze with longing at the coat, so she let her try it on. On Marie-Yvonne's squat, full-bosomed shape the coat swept the ground and failed to do up round the middle, but Marie-Yvonne smiled conceitedly into the mirror and fluffed up her hair and walked a few steps with a sway to her stride. Then she said something in French. Seeing that Bess did not understand, she translated, 'Monsieur Jago –' she always pronounced the J as a Y, giving the name a rather sinister, Spanish cast – 'Monsieur Jago, 'e . . .' and Marie-Yvonne clasped her hands over her heart and made a swooning face.

'Nonsense, Marie-Yvonne,' said Bess sharply. 'Martin and I are just friends.'

But Marie-Yvonne shook her head, gave a knowing smirk, and returned the coat to Bess before tossing flour and butter into a bowl to make pastry.

The frost got a grip; when she and Pegasus rode out now, Bess was careful of the pearly opaque ice that gathered in the ruts between the tracks. Kate was reading French storybooks; she confided to Bess that she was keeping a diary in the notebook that Martin had brought her; she would write it in French so that it was secret.

The next time he visited, there seemed to be an electricity between them. Their eyes would meet, and then they would look away. His gifts appeared carefully chosen – a tortoiseshell comb, leather riding gloves, half a dozen pairs of stockings. The sort of gifts a lover might bring.

Over dinner the first evening, she told Martin about her parents, about her mother, who had died of cholera when she was ten, and about her father, whom she had loved, but who had so often disappointed her – his sudden whims, his changeable affection for her, all too often overtaken by his next grand passion, for a woman or a place or a new business venture. 'We were never settled,' she explained to Martin. 'Even when my mother was alive we were always moving from place to place, and after she died I doubt if we lived anywhere for more than a year.'

She told him about the heat of the central plains of India and the crisp, cold promise of an early morning in Simla. She described Fenton and Cora's bungalow in Simla, and Sheldon Ravenhart's house in the Highlands. 'It was like something out of a fairy tale,' she said. 'Beautiful and haunting and magical, like a fairy tale, but it had a malevolence, too. How extraordinary it would be to know that you belong to such a place. I envied the Ravenharts that. Since I left India I've always felt as though I was in exile.'

'Don't you think, though, that sort of belonging brings with it a loss of freedom?'

'I hadn't really thought of it like that.'

'Being attached to a place ties you to it. You can't move away, you can't move on. However much of a burden it might become, you could never leave it.'

'Don't you love this house?'

His glance trailed round the room. 'I'm very fond of it. I don't know that I *love* it. I don't love easily. There have been times when I haven't visited this place for years.'

The lethargy that had come over her since she had arrived in France had been replaced by restlessness. She continued to ride in the mornings, and in the afternoons they went on long walks, he stopping every now and then to examine a twig, a beetle, a bird's nest, she jumping from one foot to the other to keep warm.

Overnight, it snowed, a white covering that iced the branches of the trees and the red roofs of the houses. Before dusk, they put on their coats and boots and went out. Kate ran ahead, making tracks in the snow, tracks that ran parallel to the small arrowhead footprints of hare and fox. At the top of the rise, they saw how, in the distance, the hills folded upon each other, those furthest away matching the heavy grey of the sky. It began to snow again, a light sprinkling of flakes that floated in the cold air. Martin delved in his pocket for his magnifying glass – each snowflake, he explained to Kate, had its own unique design. Kate caught snowflakes, peering at them through the glass.

When the snow thickened, they headed to the farm, where Kate was to stay overnight with Emilie. The sun was dipping below the horizon and the sky was a heavy iron grey as Martin and Bess walked back. At the house, Bess peeled off her gloves, scarf and coat. Martin took her hands in his, rubbing them warm. She saw the deep blue-grey of his eyes, the long, dark lashes, and the fine chiselling of nose and cheekbone. How had she ever thought him ugly or strange-looking? 'You should go and sit in front of the stove, warm up,' he said. His voice sounded thick. The cold, perhaps.

In the sitting room, she pulled off her stockings and held her bare feet up to the wood-burning stove. Her hair was coming down, falling round her face in wet hanks; she tugged out the tortoiseshell comb, laying it on the arm of the chair. When he came back into the room he had a towel and a bottle of cognac. She sat at his feet while he towelled dry her hair.

She put up her hands to her head. 'I must look like a witch.'

'Keep still. I'll comb it for you.'

He drew the comb through her hair, freeing the tangles. She closed her eyes, leaning back against his knees. She felt him lightly run his fingers the length of her hair.

They ate bread and cheese and soup and drank cognac, sitting on the rug in front of the hearth. The cognac was strong and fiery and burned the back of her throat. When the clock chimed midnight, he said, 'You should go to bed. It's late.'

'What about you?'

'I'm going to work for a while.'

She gathered up her stockings and comb and looped her shawl round her shoulders. Then she kissed him on the cheek.

'Such a lovely evening, Martin.'

In her bedroom, she took off her clothes. Since Andrew Gilchrist had violated it, she had hated to look at her body. These past months, getting ready for bed, she had undressed beneath her nightgown, like a girl at a convent school. Now, though, she looked down at herself. There were the marks that childbirth had made – the tiny white stretch marks at the sides of her belly, the breasts that were heavier, slacker, than when she had been a young girl. But there was still that narrowness of waist, that voluptuous curve of hip, and the fine, pale softness of her skin. Did he want her? She thought that he did. And she knew that she had begun to want him. She ran her hands down her body, from breast to thigh. Could she bear to let a man touch her? Could she bear to let any man touch her ever again?

She pressed her knuckles against her mouth, trying to decide. Then she put on the red coat with the fur collar and went downstairs. The door to his study was slightly ajar; she stood there for a moment, watching him. He was sitting at the desk; the oil lamp cast a soft gold light over the room. She said his name, and he started, turning to her.

'Come to bed, Martin,' she said.

'Bess . . .' He was still for a moment, frozen, and then he rose from his seat.

She put the palm of her hand against his face. 'Come to bed, my dear.'

A feather bed, which smelled of summer: Marie-Yvonne put dried lavender in the airing cupboard. The fire in the grate, the embers dying, turning pink. Kneeling on his bed as he opened her coat and saw that she was naked beneath. His eyes, dark with desire, and his voice, saying her name, a sound between a sigh and a groan.

His mouth, kissing her mouth, her neck, her breasts, her belly, and then returning, hungry for more, to her lips. His hands running over her skin, then flinging off his own clothes in a tearing of buttons and ripping of cloth. His body, long and thin and tapering – why did men's bodies always look as though their Maker hadn't quite troubled to finish them off? His eyes, questioning her as he lay down beside her again, and her small nod of the head as she wrapped her arms round him, holding him close to her so that he could not see the fear in her eyes.

The warmth of his body against hers and the neat fit of him inside her. And the utter relief of knowing that it was all right, that every time would not be like that last unspeakable time, that she could still find pleasure in love, that Andrew Gilchrist had not taken that, too, away from her.

He woke her in the early morning. It was hard to drag herself out of her deep, dreamless sleep; it took a moment or two to remember the events of the previous night. A woman from one of the neighbouring farms had gone into premature labour, he explained; her husband had asked him to attend because the local doctor had slipped on the ice the previous day and had broken his ankle. He kissed her, a long, lingering kiss. He would be back as soon as he could, he promised. She heard the front door close and then the sound of horse's hooves as he was driven away in a pony and trap.

She had the house to herself – it was Marie-Yvonne's market day and Kate was still at the farm. After breakfast, Bess wandered around, peering into rooms she had scarcely entered since she had first arrived at Les Trois Cheminées. She went into the library, with its rows of leather-bound volumes. She opened the door to a bedroom, full of spindly old furniture and a press of embroidered linen and a prie-dieu on the wall. The room must once have belonged to Martin's grandmother, she guessed. Then she peered into the attics, with their jumble of boxes and chests and broken umbrellas, and a crinoline, like the ghost of a woman, abandoned on a stand in a corner.

Pausing at the door of Martin's study, she remembered how, last night, he had turned in his chair and how he had looked at her. Her gaze ran over the animal skulls arranged on a window still, the bone of the smallest creatures as thin as paper. She saw the scattering of potsherds on the hearth and the artefacts that he must have brought back from his travels – a scarab, a blue and white and gold ceramic tile, a vase with stylized figures drawn in black upon the terracotta clay. Idly, she turned the page of a book that lay open on the desk. The paper smelt old and musty, and the print was small and close, the language impenetrable to her.

She sat down on the window sill. Outside, the snow had begun to thaw, dripping from the bare black branches of the trees. There were questions she must face, however little she wanted to, however much she would have liked to put them off for a day, a week, a month. The events of the previous night meant that she could defer them no longer.

When Martin came back to the house he would ask her to marry him. He was an honourable man, and he would not spend the night with her and then let things drift, returning every now and then to visit his mistress in France. No, he would ask her to marry him. What would she say when he did?

If she married Martin Jago, she would have the status that only marriage could bring. She would no longer suffer the powerlessness that had too often been her lot since she had left Ralph. Her compromised social position had made it doubly impossible for her to claim custody of Frazer. Any competent lawyer would make her out to be a scarlet woman – worse, a scarlet woman who had abandoned her child.

And then there was Andrew Gilchrist. She had not told the police that Andrew Gilchrist had raped her because she had known that she would not be believed. Her reputation, her work as a nightclub hostess, would have undermined everything she said. She would only have given Gilchrist further opportunity to humiliate her. *She asked me to*, he would have said. As for the cuts and bruises: *she likes it rough.*

If she married Martin Jago she would have some protection against men like Gilchrist. And if she married Martin Jago, she would be financially secure. Martin wasn't a poor man, as she had once assumed. She would no longer have to worry about the price of a loaf, the cost of a new dress. She would no longer feel that curling anxiety in her stomach when Kate needed a new pair of shoes or an unexpected bill arrived. And, most importantly, Martin, who was kind and tolerant, would make a good stepfather to Kate.

Could she marry him? She pressed her knuckles against her teeth, thinking. This house, this study, told her what sort of man he was. In Edinburgh, he had revealed only a part of himself to her. He had hidden his complexity beneath a gauche, untidy, unsociable exterior, perhaps because it suited him to do so. Here, he was different. Here, he was unruffled and confident, seeing to the affairs of the house with easy competence, switching from one language to another as unthinkingly as she might have threaded her needle with another colour of cotton.

Here, she saw him more clearly, just as she saw more clearly than ever her own limitations. Martin Jago was an intelligent, educated man, a man with a curious mind and a multitude of interests, a man who liked to travel, to see the world. He was a man who hated to be tied down. What had he said to her? Attachment brings with it a loss of freedom. However much of a burden the place you loved might become, you could never leave it.

Houses . . . people . . . both could be burdensome. If he married her, might she become an encumbrance to him, something taken up out of duty, out of conscience, forever regretted, to be silently endured? He had never sought marriage and family – he had made it clear to her the first time they met that he believed himself unsuited to marriage. He might desire her – but did he love her? Last night proved nothing – what man, seeing her standing in front of him half naked, would have turned her down?

What had she to offer a man like Martin Jago? Passion might not be enough. Marriage was supposed to be a meeting of minds, yet she neither shared his interests nor spoke the language of his upbringing. What would they talk about, over the countless breakfasts and suppers that decades of marriage entailed? How long would it be before desire faded to irritation, boredom, indifference? When would he begin to resent the restrictions that her presence placed upon his life, and how would she feel when she saw his desire for her mutate to disappointment and disillusion or, worse, dislike?

She felt a surge of anger at herself. Why did she still rush into things without thinking them through? Had she learned nothing from the mistakes of the past? Would she, out of a need for human closeness, a need to prove to herself that she was still capable of love, commit herself to yet another imperfect alliance? Would she make yet another wrong choice, in a life that sometimes, looking back, seemed nothing more than a succession of wrong choices?

No, she would not. She rose from the seat and stared out of the window at the snow-covered countryside. Her clenched fists pressed against the glass as she recalled the cool wind in her face when she rode through the autumn woodland, and the delight of drinking in the first sharp frosty air of the day. She had arrived here bruised, beaten and defeated, all her courage, even her sense of self, knocked out of her. Yet this place – this man – had allowed her to remake herself. Though she knew that some of the deepest wounds would always remain, the months she had spent here had been neither barren nor wasted. Her gaze focused once more on the gentle curve of the hills, with their pattern of path and wood and vineyard, and she felt a wash of regret and grief, knowing that she must leave France. The sparse, wintry landscape matched the hollowness in her heart.

Yet still the memory of a fair-haired little boy, weeping in a room scented with lilies, was always with her. She must go back to Edinburgh because of Frazer – because, having made that most disastrous of wrong choices in leaving her son with Cora Ravenhart, she must not fail him again. If – when – Frazer searched for her, he would surely come to Edinburgh. It had been in Edinburgh that they had last met. Though Frazer himself might not remember that last meeting, though Cora would try to make him forget, a maidservant or his ayah might recall it. When he came of age perhaps. Or when a lawyer, picking over a will in the event of Fenton or Sheldon Ravenhart's death, reminded Frazer that he still had a mother.

She must go back to Edinburgh, though she dreaded to. She went up to Kate's room and began to fold blouses, to pair socks. She knew that to spare Martin the slow, chronic ache of disillusion, she must now be cruel. And as for herself, whatever desire or fondness she had for him must be put aside, crushed as though it had never been.

By the time he returned to the house, Kate had come back from the farm and their bags were packed and waiting in the hall.

Martin said, 'A boy, and he should, God willing, survive. I'm sorry I was so long, I—' he broke off, seeing the bags. 'Bess?'

'I've decided to go home, Martin. I've trespassed on your kindness long enough.'

'You're going back to Edinburgh?'

'Yes.'

She was glad of Kate, stuffing notebooks and pencils into a case in a corner of the room. She said, 'I'm deeply grateful for everything you've done for us, but it's time we went home.'

'*Grateful* . . .' he repeated. She could hear the shock in his voice. 'I don't understand, Bess.'

'I can't stay here any longer. I really can't.'

He crossed the room to her, and said softly, 'Last night—'

She made herself meet his eyes. 'Last night was a mistake, Martin.'

His expression made her shrink back. He said coldly, 'I'm sorry that you think so.' His gaze flicked from her to Kate to the bags, and he said, 'If this is what you truly want, we'll leave tomorrow morning.' Then he walked away from her.

The journey was dreadful, strained and silent, their sparse conversation unnaturally polite. Every train was late, and the Channel crossing was an ordeal of choppy grey waves and the nauseating rise and lurch of the boat on a stormy sea.

In Edinburgh, her flat was cold and neglected. It seemed smaller than she remembered, the rooms cramped, dust dulling the furniture, the view from the window all greys and browns. The evidence of her hasty departure four months earlier – an open chest of drawers and the cups and saucers still stacked on the drainer – made her shiver. Outside, a sharp wind seemed to chase her along the roads and across the squares. She longed for woodlands of gnarled oaks, and for chalky tracks between fields of vines.

Kate was miserable, difficult, given to sulks and outbursts of tears. She missed Emilie; she didn't want to go back to Bryan House – she hated Bryan House. Kate had had too many changes in her short life, thought Bess, guiltily. Adding an extra spoonful of guilt at the thought of the damage to Kate's education, she gave in to the tears, agreeing that Kate need not go back to school until after Christmas.

Though she tried to pick up the pieces, her old life didn't seem to fit any more. She went to see Iona at the shop and Isabel Lockhead in Moray Place, but their lives had moved on during her absence. Iona was thinking of selling up the shop and moving back to Ireland – 'Dear Dara doesn't remember to eat when I'm not there, he's wasting away, the poor fellow, and I do so love the old place.' Izzy and Davey Kirkpatrick, surprising everyone including themselves, had fallen in love with each other, and now wafted around in a happy haze, oblivious of everyone and everything else around them.

Weeks passed. Bess felt unwell, off her food, tired all the time. She had not seen Martin since they had returned to Edinburgh – not a visit, not a note. If she had been able to forget how deliberately and deeply she had hurt him, she might at least have the comfort of being able to tell herself she had done the right thing. As it was, misery mixed with the nausea and fatigue, a potent mixture that made her feel as though she carried a black cloud around with her throughout the day.

One Saturday morning, Ralph came to collect Kate to stay at the farm. Bess saw her off with a mixture of relief and loss. Kate's absences always reminded her of the endless absence that must eventually occur when Kate married and left home, and when she, Bess, would always be on her own.

She wandered round the flat while her stomach turned and coiled. She must have eaten something, she thought. Or she was so upset at the thought of not seeing Kate for a week that it was making her physically sick. Or . . .

She had to sit down, her hands pressed against her mouth, suddenly hot and faint. She did not keep a diary, and there didn't seem to be a calendar in the house, and besides, she had never been good at keeping track of the mundane workings of her body. Was it possible? Could she be expecting Martin Jago's baby? And why hadn't she considered the possibility before, the same possibility that had filled her with such dread after Andrew Gilchrist had raped her?

Because this baby, if there were to be a baby, would be Martin's, and therefore she would be able to love it wholeheartedly. A dangerous thought – she pushed it away, and tried to calculate, counting up on her fingers, but the numbers muddled up in her head and she was relieved when she glanced at the clock and saw that it was past ten. She had offered to help Iona at the shop that day – the Saturday before Christmas was always a busy time. She would think about it later, she told herself. She would work out what to do later.

Yet the day seemed interminable and, every now and then, doing up hooks and eyes or coaxing an undecided customer to try on a frock, she felt such a mixture of conflicting emotions – fear, delight, confusion – that it was hard to concentrate on her work.

She was in the changing room, helping a pretty, freckled girl into a frock of apricot silk, when she heard his voice. She fumbled the pins, dropping them, stabbing herself as she gathered them up.

Iona put her head round the changing-room door. 'You've a visitor, Bess – Martin's here. It's almost five – you run along now. I'll finish in here.'

She took a deep breath and went out to the shop. 'Martin,' she said.

'I have to talk to you, Bess.' He glanced around. 'Not here – there's a cafe over the road.'

The small tables were covered with brown oilcloth, and the steamy smell of hot food and wet coats and cigarette smoke clouded the room. A waitress in a white apron and her cap too low over her forehead licked her finger to turn the pages of her notepad.

Martin ordered tea and cakes. The waitress went away. He said, 'When we left France . . .' She had noticed that the shoulders of his mackintosh were soaked, as though he had been walking for a long time. 'That night . . .' Again, the sentence died, incomplete. He scowled, digging his fingers into his damp hair. 'Do you mind if I smoke?'

'Of course not.'

He offered her a cigarette; she shook her head. He went on, his voice low. 'I've been trying to work it out. At first, when I came back here, I was angry with you. I thought of going away, going abroad for a while, perhaps. But then I began to wonder. To wonder whether you meant to make me think that what happened meant nothing to you.'

'Martin—'

'The thing is, I don't believe that's true. Because I don't believe you're like that. You might pretend to be, but I don't think you are.'

She looked down at her hands. 'Perhaps you don't know me as well as you think you do.'

'Perhaps.' His frown deepened. 'Or perhaps you thought I might feel obliged to marry you.'

She felt herself flush – she was too hot, the place was airless and the smell of food intolerable. She heard him say, 'Was that it, Bess? Am I right?'

'What if you are?'

'I do want to marry you. But not out of a sense of obligation.'

She said coldly, 'I can't possibly marry you, Martin.'

'Why not?'

'It simply wouldn't be a good idea.'

'How can you say that? Have you even properly considered it?'

'I don't have to consider it. I know that it would be ridiculous. I know we wouldn't suit each other. I know that it wouldn't work at all.'

'Why wouldn't it?'

'I should have thought that was obvious.'

'Not to me.'

'Do I have to spell it out to you? We're too different. We like completely different things. I'm not as clever as you – I haven't read all those books, I can't speak all those languages—'

'Can you really think that I'd want to marry some female equivalent of myself? Can you really think that?' He spoke too loudly and angrily; the people on the adjacent tables turned to stare at them. Bess looked away.

She said quietly, 'I would bore you.'

'Never.'

'How can you possibly—'

'You could never bore me. I would never feel that I knew you completely.'

Tears pricked, not so far behind her eyes. She dug her nails into her palms. 'I know you mean to be kind, but I can't let you do this.'

'I'm not asking you to marry me out of kindness.'

'You are making this so difficult.'

'No. It's you who are making it difficult. It's you who are so wretchedly obstinate.'

She bit her lip, evading his gaze again. The diners at the next table were eating pie and chips, and her eye was caught by the gleam of gravy, the pale line of fat frilling a piece of meat. She swallowed, and felt a trickle of perspiration run down the back of her neck as she pulled at the collar of her jacket.

'Bess? What is it?'

'Nothing. I'm fine.' She tried to think clearly, to find the right words, the words that would stop him making a terrible mistake. She said, 'Martin, this is very sweet of you, but you wouldn't be happy, I know you wouldn't. And I can't get it wrong again,' but she couldn't quite keep the tremor out of her voice. And everything in the cafe – the smells, the loud chatter, the line of sweat just visible beneath the waitress's cap – grated on her nerves, and, as her stomach lurched, she shut her eyes, concentrating hard. She must not be sick, she must not faint, that would be too awful, in front of all these people, in front of him.

'Bess,' he said.

She opened her eyes. He flung down a handful of coins on the table and helped her out of her seat. In the street, she leaned against a wall, taking in lungfuls of cool, fresh air.

He asked, 'Are you ill?'

She shook her head. 'No, Martin, I'm not ill. Actually, I think I'm pregnant.'

They walked in the Princes Street Gardens. It was dark and a soft rain fell; he held his umbrella over both of them. Women pushing prams and shop girls hurrying home passed them as he listed all the reasons why she should marry him.

'It wouldn't be like either of your other marriages. I've never wanted to control anyone in my life. What money I have would be yours, too. I wouldn't expect you to account to me for what you spent. I think you know me well enough by now to realize that I haven't the slightest interest in that. And if you don't want to live in Edinburgh then we could live somewhere else. We could live in London, Paris, wherever you like. We needn't be constantly in each other's pockets – I understand that you've led an independent life for a long time. And you know how fond I am of Kate, and I believe that she likes me. I would love her as my own child.'

He peered at her. 'Would you like to sit down? Or shall I take you home?' She murmured a refusal. 'As for the child – our child – I know what it means to be born out of wedlock. I wouldn't choose that for any child, least of all my own. Come, Bess, you surely cannot want a lifetime of – of opprobrium at worst and grudging acceptance at best for our child.'

Our child. A sudden thrill of optimism: if she married Martin, she need not settle for a half-lived life. She need not dread the loneliness that would follow Kate's leaving home. She was still young enough to have half a dozen more children. She could have what she had always wanted.

Her own family. Her own sons.

But she said, 'Why should you feel responsible for us? Why should you choose to fit a woman and a child into your life? You've lived alone for years – I don't think you've paused to consider how marriage would change your life. And a baby, too – do you know how babies disrupt a household? I don't suppose you do for a moment!'

'I could learn.'

'Why should you have to learn? It seems a hard price to pay for one night's pleasure. A night that was my fault.'

'Oh, *Bess*.' He smiled. 'Do you think I didn't want you? Do you think that being so close to you all those weeks didn't torment me? My God, how many sleepless nights did I endure, thinking of you just across the landing? How many dry-as-dust academic papers did I read to try to take my mind off you?'

She said curtly, 'That's just desire.'

'Do you discount desire, then?'

'No, of course not. But . . . thrown together like that, naturally you wanted me. And desire isn't enough. It doesn't last.'

'This time it will last. This time will be different. You told me yourself that you had your own reasons for marrying Ralph. And you were very young when you married Jack – too young to know your own mind, perhaps. We're neither of us children, Bess, and we're neither of us innocents. Perhaps experience has its uses. Perhaps we don't have to repeat our mistakes. Perhaps if we marry then marriage can be what we choose it to be, and not what the priests and moralizers tell us it should be.'

They had reached a roofed iron bandstand. They went inside. She sat down; he stood in the doorway. She watched the rain gather and slide from the roof as he spoke.

He said, 'If we married, I would never try to hold you back. I would never limit your freedom. Why should I? It's your spirit, your courage, that has made me love you.'

She heard her own sudden indrawn breath, but before she could speak he went on, 'I understand that I'm probably not the sort of husband you had in mind. I daresay you'd prefer a man who could manage a few of the social niceties. But I would do my best, I promise you, I would take you to parties if you wanted me to, and I would—'

'Oh, Martin, I don't care about *parties!*'

He looked at her, blinking. 'Then what is it you want? Tell me.'

'I'm afraid.'

'Afraid of what?'

I am afraid to love, she thought. If she let herself love Martin Jago then she needed to know that weeks, months, years in the future she would not find herself without love once more. She had lost love too often to lightly take it on again. Here, in the rain-swept park, she realized that what she felt for him was neither fondness nor merely desire, it was love, as deeply ingrained in her as dye in a fabric. But love brought with it its own risks, risks of rejection and loss. Once, she would have seized it, gathering it up with both hands without thinking twice. Now, she faltered, knowing the price you paid for love.

She looked up at him. 'I won't marry without love, Martin. I did that before, and it was a terrible mistake. I'm sorry, but I can't do it.'

'It wouldn't be without love. Not on my part, anyway.'

Her heart leapt; she took a step in the dark. She whispered, 'Nor on mine.'

'Bess?' The umbrella slipped from his fingers and rain dripped from the brim of his hat as he clasped her hands in his. Then, 'Marry me, Bess,' he said. 'Please marry me.'

Chapter Nine

They were married six weeks later. Bess wore a dress and coat bought from Iona's shop, in pale blue cloth edged with black velvet ribbon, her favourite colours. They honeymooned for a week in Largs, walking on an icy, windswept beach where the grey sea licked their toes and the waves scraped and sucked on the shore. After the baby was born, they would have a proper honeymoon, Martin said. They would go to India, perhaps.

When they returned to Edinburgh, it was to a four-storeyed stone house in the Old Town. The house had five bedrooms, two rather grand reception rooms, and a scrap of walled garden in the back. Martin's consulting room and the waiting room were on the ground floor and there was a dispensary in the basement. Bess engaged a cook-general and a daily woman to do the rough work.

The baby was due at the end of August. Bess was certain that it was a boy. She had forgotten how tired pregnancy made her feel – but then, ten years had passed since she had been pregnant with the twins. She spent the latter half of her pregnancy lying on the sofa, reading. She had never been much of a reader – she had always needed movement, company – but something seemed to have settled inside her, as though she had been searching for a very long time and had found what she was looking for at last. Besides, there was still a wisp of a suspicion at the back of her mind that Martin would one day grow tired of her, tired of her lack of education, her ill-informed mind. Now she had the chance to make up some of the deficiencies of her past, she seized it with both hands. Books that were dry or pompous disgusted her and she flung them aside after a few pages. But others absorbed her, carrying her into a different world. She began to read *Jane Eyre* the day she went into the nursing home to await the arrival of her baby. She was weeping over Jane's wedding day when she went into labour.

Eleanor Louise was born on the first day of September. The exhaustion of a long labour, and the shock of discovering that she had had another daughter rather than a son, were forgotten as soon as she held her baby in her arms. After all, there was plenty of time for more babies, more sons. Eleanor was a long, thin, wriggling infant, almost bald at birth, with a large head and blue eyes. Those blue eyes were generally open and wakeful, squinting at this and that as Eleanor gave a drunken half-smile that the nurse said was wind and Bess knew was not.

Eleanor's presence changed the house for ever. Nights were punctuated by her loud, lusty cry; by day, a trail of bottles, blankets, toys and little cardigans snaked through the house like a paper chase. A restless child, Eleanor continued to wake during the night long after the monthly nurse had gone. Those blue eyes, which darkened to Martin's slate-grey as the months passed, often contained a sharp, curious expression, and those little hands reached out, stuffing anything she found into her mouth. Eleanor was cheerful, robust and as bright as a button. But it was just as well, Bess sometimes reflected, that both Martin and Kate also adored Eleanor, because Eleanor exhausted her in a way that even the twins had not. When Martin sat his daughter on his knee and showed her the pictures in her rag book, or played 'This Little Piggy' with an unlimited patience that Bess found infinitely touching, or when Kate came home from school and pushed Eleanor round the garden on her little wooden horse, Bess would sink into a chair, a cup of tea to hand, too tired to read, almost too tired to think.

Because Eleanor had an adventurous spirit, she became prone to accidents as soon as she could crawl. There were three flights of stairs in the house, and, during the first year and a half of Eleanor's life, Bess reckoned she tumbled down each of them. Bess would be watching her, and then the doorbell would ring or Mrs Tate, the cook-general, would ask her to run her eye over the menus, and Eleanor would be off like a streak of quicksilver, pulling saucepans off the kitchen table, or hurtling towards an electrical socket, her fingers outstretched. The patients in the waiting room used to cluck with sympathy at the sight of Bess, with a wailing Eleanor in her arms, rushing into the consulting room to seek Martin's opinion after yet another bump or graze. That she never injured herself seriously was, Bess often thought, merely a matter of luck.

Afterwards, she always wondered whether it was because of Eleanor's accident that she lost the next baby. It was March 1929, too early for the pregnancy to show, and she felt unusually well, not sick at all. She hadn't felt sick with Frazer, so she felt hopeful that, this time, it was going to be a boy. Then, one afternoon, Eleanor, who, at eighteen months old, walked with a hurtling, single-minded speed that left her no opportunity to notice obstacles in her path, tripped in the garden, hitting her head on a stone bench. There was a very long indrawn breath, and then a howl of pain and fury. Eleanor's face was pasted with blood and tears; as Bess carried her into the house, Eleanor handed her something that looked like a fragment of apple peel, but was a piece of her gum. Martin was out on his rounds, so Bess telephoned Charlie Campbell, who came to the house straight away and patched Eleanor up. When Martin came home, Bess and Eleanor were curled up together on the sofa, asleep, a large plaster over Eleanor's cheekbone.

By the time Bess woke, the cramps had begun. Martin sent her to bed, telling her not to worry, but she had lost the baby by the morning. Afterwards, Martin took her in his arms and they both cried – all that promise, all that excitement and hope taken away in a rush of blood, a tearing pain. They would try again, he promised, but she must wait six months, until she was well again. Eleanor recovered, with only a small scar on her cheekbone and a front tooth that was grey rather than pearl-white, because the root had been damaged by her fall. But Bess always thought that a little piece of her had been ripped away, much like the fragment of gum that Eleanor had handed her.

At around that time, Martin began to work for the Medical Officers of Health, at the same time as running the practice and the free clinic. Bess knew that Martin, who had avoided emotional entanglement for such a long time, felt the loss of the baby deeply. She wondered also whether for him work was a distraction, the place where he could escape from the turmoil of family life. The Medical Officers of Health were responsible for public health concerns in the city. Martin had never sought position or power but he knew that the city's poor would continue to suffer ill health so long as they lived in overcrowded slum conditions. The role brought with it some influence, he explained to Bess, a chance, perhaps, to curb the worst excesses of the property developers.

Though neither of them said his name, Bess knew that they were both thinking of Andrew Gilchrist. Through the dying years of the twenties and the early 1930s, Gilchrist's rise to power seemed inexorable. Along with other city landlords, Andrew Gilchrist sat on the Lord Provost's Committee, the Treasurer's Committee, and the Plans and Works Committee. Every now and then, Bess noticed the Gilchrists' names listed in the newspaper as guests at charity balls and recitals. Occasionally there were photographs of them, Andrew a massive, bull-shouldered presence, Agnes gaunt and shadowy beside him.

And it was inevitable in a city the size of Edinburgh that their paths should sometimes cross. When once, in Jenners department store, she found herself standing only a few feet away from him, she seemed to shrink inside herself, trying to make herself small and tight and impervious to him. She could taste her fear and her hatred, and they drained her.

The collapse of the Wall Street stockmarket in October 1929 was followed by a sharp rise in unemployment. Over breakfast, reading newspaper leaders that deplored the idleness of the working classes and described their comfortable lives on the dole, Martin was unable to contain his anger. When, in the late summer of 1931, the newly formed National Government cut unemployment benefit by introducing the Means Test, his anger deepened. We treat the poor as if they were less than human, he said. We pretend that they have different motives, different aspirations from us. It suits us not to acknowledge that they feel the same as us, that they too can suffer cold, hunger, fear and loss.

They were trying for another baby, but in the two years since her miscarriage Bess had failed to become pregnant again. She wondered whether she was too old to have another child – she had turned thirty-seven that year. Now, when they made love, she was aware of a sense of desperation. The start of every monthly period brought with it a feeling of failure and despondency. When Martin told her not to worry, she wanted to scream at him that she would be forty in three years, that she was running out of time.

Each year since their marriage, they had spent the month of August at Martin's house in France. When they arrived at Les Trois Cheminées that summer and were greeted by Madame Lemercier and Marie-Yvonne, a weight seemed to slip from Bess's shoulders. Her small worries about the girls, even her failure to become pregnant, drifted away in the languorous warmth. After escorting his family to the house, Martin went back to Edinburgh, returning to France for the final fortnight of the holiday. During those first two weeks there was a delicious freedom in having no husband to please, in being able to think only of the children and herself. They wore old clothes and got up and went to bed whenever they felt like it. When Eleanor had a restless night – she was still a poor sleeper – Bess took her into her own bed. By day, they paddled in the stream, walked in the woods and went on picnics as the corn grew tall and puffy white clouds drifted across a sapphire blue sky.

Except at mealtimes, Bess hardly saw Kate, who dashed off to the farm and Emilie the morning after they arrived. At fourteen years old, Kate was still slender and loose-limbed, and now almost as tall as Bess. She had recently persuaded Bess to agree to her having her fine, red-gold hair bobbed. Though Bess had been reluctant at first – Kate's hair was her chief beauty and, besides, why would a young girl want to look like a boy? – she had to admit that the style suited Kate's heart-shaped, elfin face. By day, Kate and Emilie wandered around the farm, exchanging secrets, bursting every now and then into uncontainable giggles. In the evenings, they retreated to the attic, where they had hauled up a couple of old seats and a table. Bess offered to teach Kate to ride, but Kate refused. Ballet dancers mustn't ride, she explained to Bess, with an air of patiently instructing one who understood breathtakingly little; it spoiled their turnout. Though Kate had no interest in sport

– her school reports wrote of a lack of team spirit and a tendency to daydream on the hockey pitch – she still loved her ballet lessons.

They went back to Edinburgh. By the end of September Bess knew that she was pregnant. She was euphoric with happiness, and confident that, this time, the baby would be a boy. As the pregnancy went on, she became prone to fainting fits as well as the occasional small loss of blood, which frightened her so much she obeyed Martin's injunction to rest each afternoon. In January, when she was four and a half, Eleanor started at nursery school. Though Bess worried that she might find it hard to settle, she sailed through her first morning, hardly looking back as Bess left her at the school gates. As Bess walked home, there was a flicker of the old fear: that she would be left alone. Superstitiously, her hand went to her belly, which had, at almost five months, only the gentlest curve. She must keep this child, she must.

The baby was born at eight months. When her pains began, knowing that it was too soon and remembering her long labour with Eleanor, she left it too late to reach the nursing home, so Rebecca Elizabeth was born at the Royal Infirmary. Bess herself was too ill to see her newborn child for nearly a week. Only when, at last, she was able to hold her baby in her arms did she completely believe in the infant's survival.

It was easy to love Rebecca, who was an infant of exceptional beauty. Her blue eyes were framed by a starburst of long black lashes and her dark hair was straight and fine, like silk. Strangers in the street commented on her loveliness. A neat and tidy child, her smocks and pinafores remained crisp and white, unlike Eleanor's, which were always torn and grubby by nightfall.

But, perfect though Rebecca was, she was not a boy, was not the son Bess longed for. When Rebecca was six months old, Bess spoke to Martin about the possibility of trying for another baby.

The strength of his response took her by surprise. 'No,' he said. 'No more children.'

They were in the bedroom; she was unbuttoning her blouse.

She stared at him. 'What, never?'

'You are almost forty, Bess,' he said bluntly. 'And the last child nearly killed you.'

'But, darling, just one more . . .'

The expression in his eyes made her falter. 'They thought you would die, did you know that? Can you imagine what that was like, knowing that I might lose you? It was only by the grace of God that you survived. Do you think I would choose to go through that again? No, I will not be instrumental in you killing yourself, Bess. We have three beautiful daughters, aren't they enough for you?'

She kept it to herself that they were not. She would wait; he would change his mind. She had always been good at making men change their minds. Yet Martin remained implacable, and, as the months went on, she was aware of a growing frustration. She must have a son; she had waited so long, had endured so much. The disagreement put a small wedge between them, the first cracks showing in a marriage that had, up until then, been happier than she could have imagined. She began to feel a flicker of resentment – why must he be so unreasonable? Why must he withhold the one thing she longed for?

With the coming of spring 1933, her spirits lifted. She had always loved the sun, even this pale northern sun. But Martin's mood darkened. At the end of January, Hitler was appointed Chancellor of Germany. In May, the newsreels at the cinema showed pictures of SA men and students making bonfires of books in Munich and Berlin. Martin spoke of the possibility of another war. Bess did not believe him – the Great War had been the war to end all wars, hadn't it? And the politicians could not possibly be so foolish as to court all that grief, all that destruction again, could they? They were just going through a bad patch. Now that the Nazis had gained power in Germany, they would surely moderate their demands and find accommodation with the other European countries.

And besides, all that seemed so distant, so far away. Most days, she struggled to find time to read a newspaper, or to keep up with her letter-writing to friends and family. Davey and Isabel had married, and had two children. Ralph and Pamela had sold up the Lanarkshire farm and had bought a larger dairy farm in the south of England. At the end of the summer term, Tom, Henry and Archie came to stay with the Jagos overnight while Ralph and Pamela attended a friend's wedding in Glasgow. Though the small, mean part of Bess that envied Pamela's easy ability to produce sons might have liked to label Ralph's boys stolid or boorish, she couldn't help but acknowledge that all three were well-mannered, attractive and bright. Sharing the tea table with

Ralph's sons and her own daughters, their ages ranging from one-year-old Rebecca, sitting in her high chair, to sixteen-year-old Kate, with Tom, Henry, Archie and Eleanor fitting neatly in between, Bess felt a deep contentment.

By the time they went to France in the summer of 1934, Rebecca was a gloriously pretty two-year-old, more self-contained than her sisters, yet with a deep seam of stubbornness that sometimes seemed at odds with her beauty. Rebecca liked to have her own way, and because hearts melted at the sight of her, she tended to get what she wanted. On the rare occasions she was crossed, she was capable of throwing spectacular tantrums. Eleanor would stare open-mouthed as her little sister lay on the floor and screamed and beat her heels. All two-year-olds were wilful, Bess told herself. Rebecca would soon grow out of it.

Eleanor would be seven the following month. She was tall for her age, with a mane of unruly brown hair. She had a physical confidence and fearlessness that both her sisters lacked. Eleanor turned nut-brown that summer as she climbed trees and swam in the silky green river and learned to ride on a squat, fat pony that Bess borrowed from one of the neighbouring farms. Her long, thin legs were always covered with grazes and bruises, and Bess had learned to have a plentiful supply of plasters and iodine with her to patch up her wounds.

And then there was Kate. Kate was now seventeen and a half, not yet a beauty – she was still too tentative and unsure of herself for beauty – but striking, certainly, with her gorgeous rose-gold colouring. Bess had met Jack Ravenhart when she was seventeen, and had married him at eighteen. Had any boys come to call on Kate, Bess would have made it very clear to them that they were not welcome. Fortunately, there were no boys; Kate seemed uninterested in boys. Though eventually – in five or six years' time, perhaps – Kate would settle down with a pleasant, sensible man, she must now think of a career, nursing, perhaps, or a secretarial course. Or she could use her fluent French and train to be a teacher. Bess sent off for college brochures for Kate, who glanced at them uninterestedly and then forgot about them. Kate's indecisiveness on the subject of a career worried Bess. Kate mustn't just drift. Kate must have direction and ambition, and she must have training, skills, and a useful job. Bess knew too well what happened to girls who lacked those things, knew how limited their choices were.

Kate still had time to make up her mind. In September she would return to school for her final year. *September* . . . This September, Frazer would come of age. He would be an adult, no longer at Cora Ravenhart's beck and call. In the quiet of Martin's study at Les Trois Cheminées, among the bones and books and pots, Bess wrote a letter to her son. She had wondered whether she would be able to find the right words, but they flowed, covering the pages as she offered Frazer congratulations on having reached his majority, and tried to explain to him the events that had followed Jack's death. She knew that she must not blame Cora Ravenhart – Frazer, after all, loved his grandmother. She knew that, most importantly, she must tell him how much she loved him, and how much she missed him.

As always, Martin returned to France for the last two

weeks of August. The house retained a special magic for them – it was the place where they had fallen in love, and where both their daughters had been conceived. She wanted her son, too, to be conceived at Les Trois Cheminées. Martin could not really have meant that he wanted no more children – she had broached the subject too soon, when the trauma of Rebecca's birth had been too fresh in his mind. She was aware of a sense of urgency, that she would leave it too late, that she was growing too old. With the passing of each month, chances slipped away from her – last chances, perhaps. She had turned forty earlier that year. It became harder, people said, to conceive a child once a woman had passed forty.

The night Martin arrived at the house, she sent the girls to stay at the farm. After dinner, they sat in the room with the wood-burning stove, drinking wine. Bess wore her nicest dress and her diamond earrings and just a spray of L'Heure Bleue. She knew by the way his eyes followed her that he wanted her. When, later that night, they were in bed, and he asked her whether it was safe, she said, 'It's fine, darling. It'll be fine.' A little lie, but she knew he would forgive her when he held his son in his arms.

Les Trois Cheminées worked its old magic and, six weeks later, she knew that she was pregnant. When she told Martin, he said, 'I see,' and then, after a short, heavy silence in which she felt the first murmurings of unease, he added, 'When is it due?'

'May.'

She saw the quick flicker of his eyes as he calculated. 'So it was conceived in France?'

She nodded. He went to the window. His back to her, he said, 'You knew, Bess, didn't you? You knew that it wasn't safe.'

When he turned, she saw the anger in his eyes, and it shocked her. He left the room without saying another word. After his study door closed behind him, she felt hollow inside. He'd come round, she comforted herself; he just needed time to get used to the idea of another baby.

Yet, though Martin was solicitous of her health, recommending a good obstetrician, there remained a distance between them, a distance that unnerved her, making her doubt herself. Suffering badly from nausea and faintness, and confined yet again to the sofa for much of the day, she began to wonder whether she had made a mistake in embarking on a sixth pregnancy. Perhaps she was too old to have another baby. Perhaps Martin hadn't loved her in the first place, but had only married her because she had been expecting his child. Perhaps he resented the domestic responsibilities marriage had burdened him with.

And still there was no word from Frazer. She felt a rush of excitement whenever she saw the postman, an excitement that was replaced by a black gloom as soon as she had riffled through the letters and found nothing. Each slow day passing reminded her of the months she had spent in London, looking after her dying father, and waiting, waiting, waiting for a letter from Cora Ravenhart. Perhaps Frazer hated her. Perhaps he would never forgive her. Perhaps the Ravenharts had moved away from Simla and she would never find him.

Or perhaps he was dead. Perhaps Frazer had died years

ago from malaria or yellow fever or enteric fever, or he had been thrown from his horse like Jack, and Cora Ravenhart hadn't troubled to tell her. Whenever *that* thought crossed her mind, she pushed it quickly away.

And if he were to come to her, would she know him? Would any sympathy exist between them, after such a long separation? She had always believed that it would. Frazer was her child, her first-born son, and she would never stop loving him. But had she any right to lay claim to him when another woman had brought him up, had cared for him when he was sick, had taught him to tie up his shoelaces and to write his name and to ride a bicycle? Who was Frazer's mother now – herself or Cora Ravenhart?

That part of her life – the India part – was long gone. She was a different person now, and she belonged to a different place. Bess Cadogan, Bess Ravenhart, Bess Fearnley were each done with, finished, never to exist again. She was Bess Jago now, the mother of three daughters, with another child on the way, the wife of a man she loved deeply, even though she sometimes found him hard to understand. And she had learned that though you might satisfy some desires, others withered on the bud, failing to flower, however much you longed for them. She might never have another son – although she was sure, so sure that this baby would be a boy – and she might never return to India. The second honeymoon they had planned upon their marriage had been postponed again and again. Something always intruded – the children, Martin's work, the unending hurly-burly of family life.

Christmas and New Year came and went; in January, Kate

and Eleanor went back to school. The weather was a foul mixture of sleet and rain, driven by a spiteful north wind. The castle, perched on its rock, was curtained in swirling shades of grey. All three girls caught head colds. One afternoon Bess left Kate looking after Rebecca at home while she went to meet Eleanor from school. The sleet had hardened to snow, which darted beneath her collar and cuffs. As they walked back to the house, Eleanor's hand in hers, Bess worried about Martin, driving on slippery roads as he went on his rounds.

They were in the lobby, peeling off wellingtons and gloves and coats, when there was a knock at the door. Bess opened it. A young man was standing on the doorstep. She thought, if he's selling encyclopedias . . .

Then, looking at him properly, her heart seemed to still. Jack, she thought, for a fleeting, unreal moment.

'Frazer,' she said.

Part Three

Frazer Ravenhart

1935–1937

Chapter Ten

When her mother told her who he was, all Kate could think at first was, *oh no, not another brother*. After all, five brothers and sisters – six, soon – were surely enough for anyone.

Her next thought was that at least this brother was older than her, not younger. It was rather wearing, always being the eldest. And a phrase from *Paradise Lost*, which they were studying that term with Miss Rattray, who taught English, came into her head: *the lost archangel*. Because Frazer Ravenhart was such a handsome, golden, almost *mythical* being.

She heard Frazer say, 'Perhaps I should have written. Only I wasn't sure . . .'

His voice trailed away and her mother said quickly, 'No, no, not at all! It's so wonderful to see you! So marvellous!' Then her voice cracked and frayed a little, and she gave a little cough and seemed to recover herself, and said, 'Frazer, you must meet my children. You must meet your sisters. Kate—'

Kate shook Frazer's hand, then sneezed. 'Sorry. I've a beastly cold.'

'Bad luck,' he said. 'I had a frightful cold, sailing from India. I thought I'd see the most marvellous things but all I did was sit in my cabin and cough.'

He had a lovely smile. Kate saw that he, too, was finding this all rather an ordeal, so she said comfortingly, 'I shouldn't bother meeting Eleanor and Rebecca. Eleanor only ever wants to talk about horses and Rebecca just talks nonsense.'

Her mother said, 'Kate.'

Kate sighed. 'Yes, Mum.' She stuck her head round the door and called for Eleanor. Then she went down to the kitchen, scooped Rebecca off the floor where she was banging pot lids together, and asked Mrs Tate to bring tea and cakes up to the sitting room. She was pleased with herself for thinking of tea; her mother seemed to have forgotten it. As she piggybacked Rebecca upstairs, she wished that Martin was here, because Martin was always so calm, and you couldn't possibly have called any of the rest of them calm, and just now they needed someone who was calm.

But Martin was out on his rounds, and actually (a weasel word, Miss Rattray called it, but Kate found it useful, *actually*) it was quite handy having Eleanor and Rebecca around. They were both perfectly disgusting, as always – Eleanor sniffing throatily because she had lost her handkerchief, and Rebecca rolling the icing from her cake into a ball and then threatening to throw a tantrum because there were crumbs stuck to it – but at least scolding them filled in the silences. Kate would have thought that if you hadn't seen your son for *decades*, you would have had a lot to say to him. But the conversation was halting and, after a while, finding herself wanting to curl up with embarrassment, she leapt into the breach.

'Is this your first visit to Scotland, Mr Ravenhart?'

'Yes,' he said. 'Well, the first that I remember. But please call me Frazer. We are brother and sister.'

He sounded as if he didn't quite believe it himself. She asked curiously, 'Did you *know* you had three sisters?'

'Not till I found the letter.'

'Letter?' Bess repeated.

Frazer smiled. 'The letter that you wrote to me on my twenty-first birthday. That's how I knew where to find you. It must have been delivered when my grandmother was ill. I found it in her desk, after she died.'

'Cora's dead?'

'She died in November.'

Bess turned white. But she remained sitting ramrod straight, as she always did in company, and she said stiffly, 'I'm sorry for your loss, Frazer.'

'Thank you.'

'And your grandfather?'

'He died five years ago.'

'It must have been a very difficult time for you.' She pressed her handkerchief against her mouth.

Kate said, to fill in another silence, 'I have three brothers as well – Tom, Henry and Archie. I don't know whether they're your brothers, too. It's rather complicated. Are they, Mum?'

Her mother didn't answer. She was staring at Frazer, her

eyes filled with a mixture of shock and joy – as though he was a ghost, a revenant come back from the dead, thought Kate ghoulishly.

Frazer said, 'I was already intending to travel to Scotland when I found the letter, because of Ravenhart. So after I spoke to Mr Daintree, I thought—'

'Mr Daintree?'

'He's Uncle Sheldon's solicitor.'

Her mother looked as confused, Kate thought, as she herself felt, and she was quite relieved that Eleanor chose that moment to stab herself with a cake fork and had to be taken off to be patched up.

'She's always doing things like that,' Kate confided to Frazer when her mother and Eleanor had gone. 'Martin says it's because she's left-handed. You'll be thoroughly sick of sisters soon, I should think, and wishing you were an only child again.'

'Oh no,' he said seriously. 'You're so lucky, having a proper family.'

Kate made a snorting sound, that, had her mother been there, she would certainly have been told was vulgar. 'Honestly, Frazer, they are an utter trial. You can't imagine.'

His gaze, which was both earnest and tentative, came to rest on her, and she thought how handsome he was. He had the sort of face you would have been happy to look at for a long time, had staring not been rude.

He said, 'I haven't any family at all. At least, I thought I hadn't. After Grandmother died, I realized I was the last one, the last Ravenhart. Uncle Sheldon's son died in the war, you see. That's how I've inherited Ravenhart House.'

Now she stared at him, she couldn't help herself. 'You have an *inheritance?*'

'Yes. Uncle Sheldon left me everything. That's why I came to Scotland.'

'To claim your inheritance? Oh, Frazer, how romantic!'

'It's a castle,' he said, in an offhand way, as though one inherited castles any day of the week. 'It's miles and miles away from here. I'm not really sure where it is, to be honest. Mr Daintree told me, but I've forgotten.'

Kate drew for Frazer the family tree of the Ravenharts and the Fearnleys and the Jagos, showing how they connected, and who was who. She liked drawing family trees, had enjoyed plotting out the intricacies of succession when they had studied the Wars of the Roses at school.

'Your grandmother . . .' she prompted him.

'Cora Ravenhart.'

She pencilled it in. 'And your father was called Jack, wasn't he?'

'Yes.'

'Mum told me about Jack. And your grandfather?'

'Fenton. And Sheldon was his elder brother.'

'And the son who was killed in the war?'

'Lewis. Lewis Ravenhart. His mother's name – Sheldon's wife's name – was Anna, Anna Faversham. Anna died years ago, and Lewis was an only child.'

A spider's web of lines branched over the paper. Kate added more names. Her mother's parents – her mother had been born in India, like Frazer. Her own brothers, and Pamela's brothers – Uncle Douglas and Uncle Fergus, and their wives

253

and children, and Archibald, the eldest, who, like poor Lewis Ravenhart, had died in the war. Looking down at all the names, Kate thought that when she and her brothers and sisters married, there wouldn't be room enough to fit their children on.

She and Frazer studied their reflections in the mirror, trying to see connections, similarities. His mouth was wider than hers, and his nose was Roman, while hers was retroussé. They had the same fair skin, though she had freckles, which he didn't. Her mother said she should bleach her freckles with lemon juice, but she never seemed to get round to it, there were so much more interesting things to do. His features seemed to fit together, to be carved from the same stone, in a way that hers did not. She envied him his hair, which was pure gold, whereas hers was the colour of marmalade. 'Carrot-top, ginger-nut,' she muttered disgustedly, looking at herself. 'If only I had your hair, Frazer.'

She found kinship only in their eyes. His were a deeper blue than hers, but they were the same shape, and their brows were the same straight, uncompromising sweep of gold. She wondered what it would have been like to have grown up knowing him, knowing his face almost as well as her own. He had come out of the shadows; before, he had been a ghost, one of a pair of old photographs, Frazer and Michael, all lace and white muslin and fat little faces that she had never been able to see her own in at all. Sometimes, when she was little, she had muddled them up in her head, the brother who was lost, the brother who was dead.

She showed Frazer her city – the secret gardens and the narrow, odd little streets and wynds she wasn't supposed to go down on her own but sometimes couldn't resist, even though they scared her, and the peaks of the castle and Calton Hill, from where, on a sunny day, you could see the sea sparkling like diamonds.

Even though Frazer was three years older than her, and even though she felt very unsophisticated compared to him (India, and inheriting a castle), he never tried to rub it in, as some of the girls at school did, girls who were already allowed to go to cocktail parties and who went on skiing holidays. He was an easy person to talk to; he seemed to fill some gap she had hardly known was there. She knew that when, in time, Frazer left Edinburgh to go and live in his castle, she would miss him. But then, she never expected things to stay the same. Parents remarried and brothers and sisters were born and you left one house and went to live in another, and no one tended to ask your opinion of it all.

She told Frazer how school no longer seemed to fit her, how it pinched and squeezed and irked like an old dress she had grown out of. And how far away the end of the summer term seemed, when she would leave school.

'What will you do then?' he asked her.

They were walking along the Grassmarket, eating chips. The cobbles were slippery with rain, but the sun had come out, making light flash from the raindrops caught on railings and branches.

'My mother wants me to be a teacher,' she said. 'Or a secretary.'

'Is that what you want to do?'

She shook her head. 'Not in the least.'

'What, then?'

'When I was younger, I wanted to be a nun.' Kate threw a small pinch of salt from her chips over her shoulder. It kept the devil away. Not that she really believed in the devil – she had given up all that when she had stopped wanting to be a Roman Catholic – but you never knew. 'And after I changed my mind about being a nun, I wanted to be a ballet dancer. But then I grew too tall.'

'I was going to be a soldier,' said Frazer. 'My grandfather wanted me to join the Lancers, like my father.'

She studied him. 'I don't think being a soldier would have suited you.'

'I don't think being a nun would have suited you, Kate.' He gave her his glorious smile. No one else smiled like Frazer, so bright and eager to please, like the sun coming out. He took a silver case out of his pocket. 'Cigarette?'

She had taught Frazer to eat chips out of newspaper, and he had taught her to smoke. A fair exchange. She held the cigarette carefully between her first two fingers, and every now and then flicked the ash into the gutter. When she blew the smoke in a thin column between her pursed lips, she could feel herself changing, becoming someone different.

Having an elder brother was useful. Quite soon after Frazer's arrival, it occurred to Kate that she could say she was meeting him when, in fact, she was walking round the city on her own, looking at this and that. Sensing that her mother wasn't herself these days, that she was unwell with the coming baby and exhausted by Eleanor and Rebecca and distracted with joy at Frazer's presence, Kate felt ashamed of the little lies she had begun to tell, and every now and then tried to stop herself. But those odd scraps of the day, those portions of time that were hers alone, pleased her too much to give them up.

Martin was paying her ten shillings a week to type up the book he was writing about crannogs, which were a sort of island that people had built in lochs thousands of years ago. Martin was a dreadful typist, his pages scattered with corrections like crumbs on a white tablecloth after Eleanor and Rebecca had had their tea. Kate liked the look of the printed words on the page – they seemed to make the people, and their strange, watery dwelling places, real. Roaming round the city, she explored the second-hand bookshops, and with her earnings bought books, lovely old books which smelt musty and whose dog-eared pages were bound with leather, and whose frayed spines were embossed with the remains of gold leaf.

She and Frazer were now the grown-up part of the family; she could feel herself pulling away from her little sisters. At school, she noticed how the girls in her class preened themselves and smiled at Frazer whenever he met her outside at the end of the afternoon. Girls who had never sought her friendship now did so, angling for invitations to tea or to accompany her and Frazer to the cinema. She felt proud of herself, as though she was responsible for bringing this glorious, golden creature into everyone's lives.

He had brought a magic with him, this long-lost brother, he had worked a transformation. It changed her to have kinship with someone so marvellous, so princely. That was how she thought of him sometimes: Frazer Ravenhart, serene and regal in his castle, surveying his domain. The sorts of things that worried Kate, that reduced her to childish clumsiness or an inarticulacy that made her despair of herself, never seemed to bother Frazer at all. Frazer was always beautifully dressed – his buttons did not fly from his shirts as Kate's did from her blouses, and no ink stains or biscuit crumbs marred his crisp white cuffs. When he took her out dancing, she saw girls' heads turn, their eyes filled with envy. When he walked into a shop, the assistants came smartly to his side. In restaurants, he always knew which wine to order, and he had no qualms about sending back food he did not consider perfectly cooked. Kate supposed it was something in the way he carried himself, something in the way that he spoke, that made him attract service and deference.

Frazer lived in a suite in the North British Hotel. His rooms were crowded with plump chairs and sofas and side tables of a red-brown wood so deeply polished Kate could see her reflection in it. Chinese vases were filled with vast, stiff arrangements of flowers, and stacked in the writing desk were sheaves of smooth cream-coloured notepaper with the hotel's address printed at the top. Kate would have liked to pull off her stockings and sink her bare toes into the thick wool rug. If Frazer wanted anything – a glass of brandy or a lemonade for Kate – then he picked up the telephone receiver and the bellboy arrived in minutes. Once, when Kate broke a glass, Frazer stopped her picking up the shards herself and called housekeeping, who sent a maid who knelt on the carpet, carefully gathering up every fragment of glass, while Frazer continued to describe to Kate the fancy-dress ball he had once attended in Simla.

Everyone liked Frazer. Bess never refused him anything. Sometimes Kate felt a stab of envy – her mother's voice often followed her, reminding her of homework undone or of the need to come home from school promptly. But then she disliked herself, because Frazer was simply too nice to envy.

It was only after she had known him for a couple of months that Kate realized that Frazer wasn't quite how he seemed to be on the surface. When Frazer spoke to her about his grandmother's long illness, and when he described the paperwork that he must go through with Mr Daintree, his solicitor, she saw the look of dismay – panic, almost – in his eyes, and she felt sorry for him. It must be hard for a boy, because boys were supposed to be brave. Much later, she realized that was what made her love her brother, discovering that chink of doubt in his golden armour.

Bess's last daughter was born at the beginning of May. When they placed the infant in her arms, she felt none of the immediate love and tenderness she had experienced with her previous children. There was the disappointment of Aimée not being a boy, and, added to that, she was such an odd little thing. Aimée was ugly, there was no other word for it. She was small and scrawny, barely five and a half pounds at birth, with a fluff of white down on her head and swollen eyes screwed up in a pink, bruised face.

'They had to deliver her quickly,' Martin explained. 'The

bruises will go down. Then she'll be as beautiful as the others.'

Privately, looking at her daughter with dismay, Bess found that hard to believe. She let Martin take Aimée from her and put her in the cot.

She watched him stroke his daughter's face with his fingertip. She said, 'Have you forgiven me yet?'

A sharp glance. 'Forgiven you?'

'For having her.'

'Bess.' She saw him frown. 'There's nothing to forgive.'

'But you were angry with me. Because of the baby.'

He came to sit beside her. Just for a moment, she glimpsed the sadness in his eyes. 'I'm not angry about the baby, how could I be? She's perfect. I was angry that you lied to me about the possibility that you might conceive another child. It hurt that you should choose to lie to me. I thought we were better than that.'

She held out her hand to him and he took it in his. 'I'll never lie to you again, Martin,' she whispered. 'Never, I promise you.' She felt the pressure of his fingers and the sting of tears in her eyes.

Mr Daintree, Frazer's solicitor, often invited him to supper in the evenings. At the Daintrees' house, Frazer met Mr Daintree's wife and his daughters, Janet and Maisie, who were large, rosy-cheeked girls in their early twenties. Janet and Maisie and their friends had a passion for amateur dramatics. When Frazer mentioned that he had taken part in a play or two at the Gaiety Theatre in Simla, he found himself roped into charades and sketches, as a desert sheik, draped in bedspreads and curtains, or as a vicar, his collar turned back to front.

It was only when Maisie flung herself into his arms in the cluttered privacy of the box room where they kept the costumes that Frazer discovered that he had misunderstood the situation. Maisie's soft, lipsticked mouth slithered over his face and her large breasts pressed against him as, between gasps, she told him that she loved him. He didn't know whether to kiss her back, though the warm clamminess of her skin repelled him, or to remind her that her parents were in the next room. In the end, he did the latter, and Maisie said, 'Oh, don't be silly, Frazer – they like you awfully, you know,' and began to kiss him again. Suddenly finding the whole thing intolerable, he blustered an excuse and made a run for it, tripping over the trailing fringe of a curtain as he headed for the safety of the drawing room. He left the house as soon as decently possible, the recollection of the scorn in Maisie's eye all too vivid.

Back at his hotel, Frazer had room service bring him a drink. But the walls seemed to press in on him, and the silence persisted. He was alone, and he had always hated to be alone. He found himself thinking of Nana, and how dreadful the last months of her life had been, and he had to press his knuckles against his forehead to stem the tears.

Since his grandmother's illness and death he had felt stranded, adrift. Her passing had left a hole in his heart. She had acted as a barricade between him and the rest of the world, and her death had left him with an endless series of tasks that he felt unprepared for and unsuited to. Sometimes, waking in the morning, it was all he could do not to pull the blankets over his head and stay curled up in bed. At night, when he had bad dreams, he longed for Nana's touch, for her to stroke his forehead as she had used to do and whisper the nightmares away. His grandfather's estimation of him, overheard once during a hissed exchange between his grandparents, still rang in his ears: *The boy's a lily-livered weakling – he must be sent to school, Cora, to knock some of the nonsense out of him.* Much to his relief, his grandmother hadn't sent him to school but had employed a tutor instead. But the words remained, needling him, making him question whether he was really up to things.

Frazer put his coat back on and went out, crossing the North Bridge into the Old Town. He thought of going to see Kate, but it was late – too late, he suspected, for Kate to be allowed to leave the house. And he could not just then face the prospect of sitting in the Jagos' comfortable drawing room with this family who did not yet really seem to be his family. When, before meeting her, he had thought of his mother, he had pictured a younger version of his grandmother, dignified and serene, someone who would make him the centre of her life. Yet his mother wasn't like Nana at all. For one thing, she was far younger than he had imagined. She dressed differently to Nana, spoke differently, even *smelled* different. Since the new baby had arrived, his mother had rushed around more than ever, and often, when he called, she had the baby in her arms as well as the little girls hovering at her skirts. Their conversations seemed to be carried out over a babble of interruptions and crying.

Walking through the city, Frazer was aware of a loneliness

that made him feel not only far from home but also marked out from his fellow human beings, different in some not quite acceptable way. He needed another drink, so he dropped into one of the pubs that lined the High Street. There was a roar of noise from the adjacent public bar, and, once he had swallowed the whisky and had had a smoke, his unhappiness seemed if not to ebb, at least to blur.

He moved on to several more pubs. In each of them, he looked around the bar, studying the clientele. In one establishment, a tart with a painted face and bleached hair approached him. He left quickly. In the next bar, his gaze once again ran round the small, dim room, drifting from face to shadowy face. The men's heavy stomachs strained at their braces, and their red, swollen noses spoke of too many hours in the pub. The women beside them were cold-eyed and narrow-lipped, their fat, soft, abundant bodies a series of folds and bulges. Their clothing spoke of their low class and lack of refinement. He thought how ugly they all were – like Nana, he loathed ugliness. He didn't see a single person he would have wanted to pass the time of day with.

Then, when the loneliness had begun to eat into him once more, his eye was caught by a young man sitting at the bar. There was a row of glass tumblers lined up in front of him and he was working his way from one end of the line to the other, dropping his head back, swallowing the drink, and then sitting very still and blinking for a moment before picking up the next glass.

Frazer watched for some time, fascinated by the swift, purposeful movement of the arm, the small shake of the dark, curling hair as the last drop of whisky was swallowed.

When he reached the end of the line, the young man waved an empty glass at the barman and fumbled in his pockets – for change, presumably. As he was doing so, he looked round the room. Frazer's heart speeded, willing this stranger's eyes to meet his own. When, eventually, they did, Frazer smiled. Then he stood up and crossed the room to the bar.

'Let me buy you a drink,' he offered.

'Good of you,' said the young man, and frowned. 'Have we met before?'

'I don't think so. My name's Frazer Ravenhart.'

'Maxwell Gilchrist.'

A hand was extended, Frazer shook it. Maxwell Gilchrist's eyes were a changeable mixture of green and blue and grey, which made Frazer think of the sea. He glanced at the row of glasses and said, 'Are you celebrating?'

Maxwell shook his head. 'I've just been to my mother's funeral.'

'I'm sorry. How frightful. Perhaps I should go.'

'No, please don't.' Maxwell swept back a lock of dark hair that had fallen over his forehead. 'What did you say your name was?'

'Frazer Ravenhart.'

'Ravenhart . . . where are you from?'

'India,' said Frazer. 'Simla.'

'Good Lord. Why are you here?'

'My grandmother died. And afterwards the bungalow seemed so empty. And India's not like it used to be . . . too many troublemakers, trying to stir things up.' Frazer looked at Maxwell, who was, he guessed, about his own age, maybe a year or two older, and said, 'You must miss your mother dreadfully.'

'I don't know. Do I miss her?' Maxwell frowned, as though trying to work out a knotty problem. 'You're supposed to love your mother, aren't you? But sometimes I hated her. She never even tried to keep Father off my back.' He shrugged and added conversationally, 'My father's a pig, you see. It's a pity it wasn't him we buried today, but people like him go on for decades, they always do. My mother used to pray for him to change. But he never will. *Families*. Like being slowly suffocated. I shall never marry, never.'

He looked suddenly depressed, darkness clouding his eyes, and Frazer, searching for something to comfort this stranger, said, 'I was always terrified of my grandfather. But he died – he choked on a fishbone.'

Maxwell laughed. 'God, if only my father would. Perhaps I should take him out to dinner, treat the old bastard to a nice sole meunière.' He took out a crumpled packet of cigarettes and offered them to Frazer. 'How I'd love him to die in some hideously unheroic way – on the lavatory, perhaps, or fucking his mistress . . .' His long lashes batted over his eyes. 'I'm sorry, I've had rather a lot to drink.'

'It doesn't matter.'

'Or,' carried on Maxwell, warming to his theme, 'throttled in one of his lousy buildings by a disgruntled tenant. My father made his money through property. He's trying to become respectable now. I'm sure he sees himself as the next Lord Provost. He'd love that – badges of office and people kowtowing to him. I think he means to found a dynasty. Niall and Sandy and I will carry on the glorious name of Gilchrist.' Maxwell's eyes glittered. 'All of his sons are a disappointment to my father. And I intend to be the greatest disappointment of all.'

Frazer said, 'I met my mother for the first time a couple of months ago.'

The blurred green gaze attempted to focus on him. 'Really?'

'Mmm. The first time since I was a baby.'

'Why? Where had she gone? Do you mean that she didn't bring you up?'

'She abandoned me after my father died.'

Frazer saw that Maxwell was impressed. During the time he had spent in Scotland he had noticed that other people seemed to think that there was something extraordinary, romantic even, in his story. He felt a particular enjoyment in having Maxwell Gilchrist's attention; his mood lifted.

'She just walked out,' he said. 'She never wrote or came to see me. There I was, in India, all on my own. I could have died.' He slipped easily into embroidering a little – his mother's version of events was rather different. She had told him that she had had to leave him with his grandmother because of financial constraints. Which was abandonment in all but name, Frazer thought.

'I wish my parents had abandoned me,' said Maxwell wistfully. 'So much better to have been consigned to an orphanage.' His gaze sharpened. 'You didn't know your mother *at all*?'

Frazer shook his head. 'No. Actually, I assumed she was dead. My grandmother never talked about her. But she's married, and she has four daughters.' He frowned. 'I wasn't sure whether to go and see her or not. After all, after so long . . .'

Maxwell asked the question no one else had dared to voice. 'Do you like her? What if you hated her? What if you were reunited with your mother after years and years and then you couldn't stand her?' He crushed the stub of his cigarette into the ashtray. 'I suppose you could always go back to India and just send the odd postcard.' He looked at Frazer closely. 'Do you hate her?'

'No, not at all. Only I don't . . . I don't . . .'

'You don't love her.'

Frazer was silent, turning his cigarette lighter, which was lying on the bar, over and over. He had only ever loved one person in his entire life. Nana had been everything to him: his comforter, his teacher, his companion, a bulwark against a sometimes confusing world. Though, as he had told Maxwell, Nana had hardly ever spoken of his mother, she had talked a lot about Jack, his father. Jack had seemed quite alarmingly perfect – brave and fearless, all the things Frazer often suspected he was not.

Maxwell said, 'So I've just lost my mother and you've found yours. What a coincidence.' He raised his glass. 'To coincidence.'

Their glasses clinked. Maxwell said, 'Won't you go back to India? It must be so much more fun there.'

'I don't know. I haven't decided yet. I suppose it depends what the castle is like.'

Maxwell gave his head a little shake, as if to clear it. 'Castle?'

'I own a castle – well, it's really a house, Ravenhart

House, in Perthshire. I'm the last Ravenhart, you see.' Frazer took Nana's old photograph of Ravenhart House out of his wallet and handed it to Maxwell. 'This is it.'

This time, Maxwell's awe was almost palpable. 'Good God, it's huge. And it's yours?'

'Oh yes. And there's a gatehouse and a hunting lodge and acres and acres of land. And some farms, I think. The house looks rather marvellous, doesn't it?'

'How many rooms are there?'

'I don't know.'

'You haven't counted them? I would have counted them. I would have wanted to know exactly how many there were.'

'I haven't been there yet.'

Maxwell looked puzzled. 'You've been in Scotland for months and you haven't gone there yet?'

'I've only been here since January.'

'*January. It's May.*'

Frazer said, rather huffily, 'I've had a lot to do. Financial affairs—'

'But even so.'

'My solicitor keeps reading me out long documents,' said Frazer evasively, 'all about trusts and bonds and things, and I haven't a clue what he's talking about. And it's all so dull.'

But Maxwell, accurately pinpointing the problem, said, 'Don't you want to go and see it?'

Frazer sighed. 'I suppose I do, in a way. But it's a bit . . .'

'What?'

'Well, it's rather a long way away, for one thing. And I don't know anyone there.'

'But think of the fun you could have.'

Frazer's lashes lowered. 'Not on my own,' he murmured. 'Now, if I had a friend in Scotland, if I had company . . .'

Maxwell's eyes lit up with enthusiasm. 'Imagine the parties you could have. Imagine what you could do, with your own castle. God, how I'd love it, to have my own place and no one to bother me.'

'I hadn't thought of it like that.'

'I wonder if there are any ghosts.'

Frazer snorted. 'My Uncle Sheldon died there. Maybe he haunts the place.'

'What was he like?'

'I never met him. Grandmother disliked him. He sounded as though he was a bit potty. Collected stamps and butterflies and didn't change his clothes often enough.'

Maxwell smiled. 'A smelly ghost with a butterfly net – I should have thought we could do better than that.'

We, thought Frazer, with a rush of delight. He said offhandedly, 'I was thinking of driving up soon. You wouldn't care to come along, would you?'

Explaining to Frazer Ravenhart that he didn't actually live anywhere in particular at present, and that the easiest way of letting him know which day they were to drive to Perthshire was to leave a message at the Two Magpies cafe in Guthrie Street, proved more complicated than Maxwell Gilchrist had anticipated. Frazer's blue eyes were wide and bewildered as he said, 'But you *must* have a home – you must live *somewhere*,' and Maxwell, torn between irritation and laughter at Frazer's incredulity, had to smooth things over by explaining that he was temporarily between lodgings.

He had been between lodgings for some time now; his efforts to sort himself out never seemed to come to anything. The unexpected would happen – in Maxwell's experience life was endlessly unpredictable. A girlfriend would find fault with him and throw him out of her rooms, or he'd meet a girl in a cafe or a pub and end up sleeping in her bed. The difficulty was that his belongings rarely seemed to keep up with him; he pictured books and clothes dotted in little heaps all over the city, mementoes of his brief stay in one lodging house or another. He wondered whether that was why he never seemed to succeed in anything; sometimes he imagined an attic room, for instance, with a bed and a cupboard and a table all of his own. He possessed a fierce desire for success and fame – he was not yet sure quite at what he would be famous, something glorious or something shocking, he didn't care which – and it often seemed to him that in that quiet attic room he might be able to gather his thoughts and make a start at last.

At present, he survived by writing pieces for journals and news-sheets – mostly left-wing publications, and under various pseudonyms, which meant attending political meetings in smoky rooms above pubs, where the comrades made passionate speeches denouncing capitalism. Maxwell was all for denouncing capitalism, and for putting the bosses and profiteers up against the wall, his father first, preferably, but there was something funny about all that anger, all that passion, contained in so small a room, and sometimes he found it hard to keep a straight face.

When the writing didn't pay enough (it hardly ever did), he worked in pubs or washed up in cafes for extra cash. And every now and then his father sent him money, which he knew he shouldn't accept because it came with an entire cat's cradle of strings, but somehow he always ended up doing so.

Meeting Frazer Ravenhart in the pub had been fortuitous. Maxwell had been down to his last shilling. He had spent the interval between his mother's death and the funeral in a haze of alcohol. It had been the only way he could get through it. Though he prided himself on his ability not to show his drink (essential because of Father), he remembered telling Frazer that he had hated his mother, so he must have been even drunker than he had thought he was. He hadn't meant to make such a confession, such a loathsome, slithery confession, to a stranger – or to anyone else, for that matter.

And had he truly, honestly hated his mother? Some of the time he had loved her. He still recalled with perfect clarity the rare occasions when she had showed him affection or sympathy. His mother had been ill for as long as he could remember, had seemed too ill to notice himself or his brothers. Her death had been a final erasure of a line that had always been faintly sketched. Maxwell remembered the heavy, clotted air in his mother's bedroom, and the rows of medicine bottles, with their sweet, sticky syrup, on the mantelpiece. He had tried the laudanum once, and it had given him the most extraordinary dreams.

Much of the time, he had felt sorry for her. What hell, to be married to his father. He had treated her like a dog

– worse than a dog, he seemed to quite like dogs. He hadn't hit her often, just the odd slap now and then, but when he had hit her it had made Maxwell feel far worse than being hit by his father himself, because she had seemed so defenceless, he supposed, so lacking in any knack of avoiding his father's ire. And perhaps also because it had brought home to him how useless he was at protecting her. At protecting anyone, for that matter, himself included.

His encounter with Frazer Ravenhart saved him from having to prowl the city in search of friends who would buy him a drink. Maxwell had plenty of friends; he made a point of cultivating those his father would disapprove of – the artists, the idle patricians and the nancy boys (his father's term for anyone who lacked his own bullish, overly masculine sort of brutality). Frazer Ravenhart fell into, thought Maxwell happily, two of those categories – the well born and the soft. There had been men like Frazer at school – odd that his father, with his prejudices, should have sent him to the sorts of establishments where he was bound to meet the very people he despised. Thirteen years old, and newly arrived in a cold, bleak building filled with hundreds of boys bigger and older than himself, some of the senior pupils had bewildered Maxwell at first. They had plied him with sweets and invited him for tea in their studies. He had been frightened because he had not been able to understand their interest in him, and because he had not known what they wanted. He had learned quickly enough though, and, knowing himself to be powerless, it had not occurred to him to refuse them. It had been some time before he had understood the value of his looks, and what they could do for him.

Frazer Ravenhart, too, was quite startlingly good-looking – and rich. With his expensive clothes and plump wallet, it had been immediately obvious that he wasn't short of cash. And then Frazer had shown him the picture of the house. Ravenhart House had seemed to go on forever, all turrets and crenellations and wings and gables. You could have fitted the Gilchrists' Charlotte Square house into it several times over. Looking at the photograph, Maxwell had felt, intermixed with envy, a sort of longing.

Frazer Ravenhart owned a Lagonda sports car, too. Sitting in the passenger seat as they drove out of Edinburgh, Maxwell felt a deep stab of envy. He had only a *bicycle*, and a rusty, third-hand one at that, handed down to him from Sandy and Niall.

In spite of the glorious Lagonda coupe, and even though they had set off at some godforsaken hour in the morning, the journey north seemed to take for ever. They didn't talk much because of the noise of the wind and the rattle of the wheels on roads that became narrower and more tortuous and more potholed the further they travelled. Maxwell had never before driven so far north. He had never been anywhere much, only to London, with friends, which he had enjoyed immensely. Quite soon, he meant to go everywhere, to Paris and Provence and Morocco and dozens of other places.

They stopped in Perth for lunch. In the restaurant, Frazer said, 'Apparently there is a factor, Ronald Bain. He lives at the gatehouse. My lawyer, Daintree, has been keeping an eye on the estate since Uncle Sheldon died. The rents from

273

the tenant farms pay for Bain and the housekeeper and the other servants.'

Maxwell said, 'How extraordinary, to be going to a home you've never seen before.'

Frazer looked alarmed. 'Is it my home? I hadn't thought of it like that.'

'Well, unless you're going to keep on living in a hotel for ever. And only rich, seedy old men who don't know how to look after themselves do *that*.'

The road out of Perth climbed through the hills, swooping and curving in blind summits and circuitous bends. Maxwell was impressed by the scenery, and by the immensity of the hills – or mountains, perhaps. When did a hill become a mountain? Must a hill be a rocky peak topped with snow to qualify as a mountain? Snow lay like fragments of white cloth on the summits, and paled the sunless corries.

The car sped around outcrops of rock and across bridges spanning narrow gorges, where rivers funnelled beneath in cascades and waterfalls. Small hamlets and isolated farmhouses peeled past them, livestock and children scattering out of the path of the Lagonda. Most of the houses were squat and stone-built, with slate or tin roofs. Every now and then they saw oblong lines of stones, marking where a house had once stood but had since fallen into decay. Once, Maxwell glimpsed the stark upright of a menhir, silhouetted by the folds of the hills.

Maxwell almost missed the turn-off to Ravenhart House, he was so absorbed in everything he saw. There was a small, stone church, and a pub and a bridge, and then he caught sight of the gatehouse, and called out to Frazer to turn.

They stopped outside the gatehouse. Maxwell stayed in the car while Frazer knocked on the door. The gatehouse was a substantial cottage, with stepped gables and two chimneys and a round turret stuck on one side, a touch of whimsy that appealed to Maxwell.

Frazer reappeared with Mr Bain, the factor. Maxwell climbed into the narrow back seat while Mr Bain, a stern, weather-beaten man, took his place in the front. He sat stiffly, as if unused to motor cars; Frazer's attempts to engage him in conversation, as they drove along the track that led to the house, met with little response. Maxwell suspected that Mr Bain, in his tweeds and gaiters, would have been happier striding around the moorland, shotgun in hand.

The drive must have been more than a mile long, running beside a shallow-banked river that was fringed with birches and rowans. Imagine, thought Maxwell, awed, having a front path that was a mile long.

And then he saw the house. There was a bend in the road and the fir trees parted, and there was Ravenhart House, with its roofs and towers and many, many windows. Maxwell whistled. You lucky devil, Frazer, he thought, you lucky, lucky devil.

The housekeeper welcomed them, and a maid brought them tea and sandwiches and cakes in the drawing room. Afterwards, Frazer had to spend some time closeted with Mr Bain, so Maxwell took the opportunity to explore.

Ravenhart House was a feast of late Victoriana, Scottish baronial at its most confident and flamboyant, all dark wood panelling and swagged crimson curtains and enormous faux medieval fireplaces. Antlered stags with sad glass eyes gazed down from the walls. Ancestors (whose ancestors? wondered Maxwell; the house couldn't be more than fifty or sixty years old) in lace collars and ruffs preened themselves on the portraits lining the main staircase, and glaring, fierce-beaked birds – ravens, he supposed – perched on the finials. At the top of the stairs, Maxwell ran his hand over a raven's head and felt the carved wooden feathers smooth beneath his palm.

He walked down passageways and peered into rooms. Staircases branched dizzily off from corridors, leading him higher and higher. He came across a desk in an alcove; opening a drawer, he discovered pencils and sketchbooks. Window seats strewn with cushions of faded velvet were accompanied by yet more fraudulent ancestors: Regency misses with pink and white complexions, and Gainsborough homages of ladies in wide silk skirts. The place was cold, bloody cold. There were no radiators, only huge fireplaces, few of them lit. Though the early evening sunlight poured through the windows, in dark corners the air seemed chilly, as if nothing much had moved there for a very long time.

In a gloomy, panelled room, Maxwell pulled out one narrow shelf after another, and saw the butterflies displayed beneath the glass covers. There were hundreds of them, the colours of their outstretched wings dulled, their sheen gone.

A spiral staircase led up through a turret. Maxwell rested his elbows on the window sill and looked out at the glen and the mountains. All sorts of muted colours seemed to merge into each other: russet and mauve and lovat green and grey. The turret smelt damp, and black mould bloomed beneath the window. Maxwell wondered how long it was since anyone else had been there. Fancy, he thought, owning a house so large you never went into some of the rooms.

He meandered back through the main body of the house. A door led him to a wooden staircase that took him up into the attics. Two black trunks with the name RAVENHART stencilled in white across the top lay at the sides of the attic like sarcophagi. A tight little ball of lacy bones told him that an owl had feasted on the mice that made their home here. Dead flies littered the eaves and, when he brushed against a heap of yellowed, dusty linen, a cloud of moths flew out, tiny autumn leaves blown up by a breath of wind.

In a corner of the room, he found an old photograph album, shrouded in cobweb. He leafed through it. Glum females encased in whalebone and crinolines glared at him disapprovingly. Tweedy men stood triumphantly over a small hillock that he realized, peering at it, must be composed of dead grouse. A family party feasted in front of a stone lodge beside a river: a table had been placed on the rocky ground and, even in the wilderness, the white tablecloth was uncreased, the cutlery placed with precision.

He glimpsed a small door, only a couple of feet high, in the wooden wall dividing one attic from the next. He opened the door and squinted into the black interior. A narrow ladder led upwards. He wormed through the door and shinned up the ladder. There was an unpleasant moment when he couldn't open the trapdoor at the top of the ladder, and he thought how old and rotten the treads must be and felt himself caught in the spidery, dusty darkness. Fall and break a leg here and they might not find you for months. They might not find you until time had spat you out in bones, like the owl's prey.

Then he gave the trapdoor a hard shove, and it opened, and he saw blue sky broken up by puffy, marshmallow clouds. He was on the roof, on a flat platform edged with a low stone balustrade. Maxwell sat against a chimney stack, getting his breath back. He was aware of a sudden, rare feeling of peace. He closed his eyes, breathing in the cold, sweet air. He thought of all the things he must do, such as amass enough money to leave Edinburgh, and find somewhere decent to live. Then, for once, he put aside his scheming and calculating, and seemed to relax, and he opened his eyes and looked out at the view, and saw the mountains and the valley and yes, surely, the hunting lodge from the photograph, embraced by a bend in the river.

Kate left school at the end of the summer term in July. There was something disappointing and anticlimactic about it. So many of the other girls in her class were going to do so much more interesting things than she was. Some were holidaying in Capri or Nice before attending finishing schools in Paris or Switzerland; others were going to stay for the summer in country houses. Two girls were already engaged to be married. In comparison, the secretarial college at which she was to start in September seemed unbearably dreary.

But before secretarial college there was France. Kate had always loved their annual summer holiday, but this year, Les Trois Cheminées, too, disappointed. Emilie had acquired

278

a boyfriend, and seemed unable to think about anything else. Emilie had kissed Félix, which she described to Kate in great detail, who had to pretend interest even though she couldn't imagine why anyone would want to kiss Félix Morin, who had boils on the back of his thick, red neck, and who liked to show off, riding his motorbike very fast along the muddy road between the farm and Martin's house.

It was Martin who noticed how she felt. She and Martin had a tradition of going for long walks, just the two of them, when they were in France. Martin was focusing his binoculars on a little brown speck of a bird wheeling high in the sky, when he said to Kate, 'You must be rather at a loose end, with Emilie being so taken up with Pierre's grandson.'

Kate shrugged. 'I don't mind.'

'Are you looking forward to secretarial college?'

She said honestly, 'Not really.'

'I can't see it being quite right for you. You don't have to go there, you know. It's not too late to change your mind.'

'I can't think what else I could do.'

'You could go to university.'

She stared at him. 'University?'

'Yes, why not?' He looked suddenly cross. 'That school of yours, they didn't even seem to consider university as an option. You have a good brain, Kate, so why not use it? You could sit the entrance exams in the autumn and go up next year.'

The thought of more exams filled her with horror. She shook her head. 'It's all right, Martin. Secretarial college will be fine.'

He looked as though he was going to say something more, but then he seemed to change his mind. They walked in silence, taking the twisting path through the woods. Then he said, 'Well, while you're here, why not ask Marie-Yvonne to teach you to cook? It would stop you being bored, and then, if you found that secretarial work didn't suit you, at least you'd have an alternative. And it's a useful skill.'

Kate did as Martin had suggested and, rather to her surprise, found that she enjoyed cooking. By the time they went back to Scotland, she could make quiches and daubes, éclairs and madeleines, and a rather lovely pudding called floating islands. Then she began her secretarial course, and she knew by the end of the first fortnight, though she would never have admitted it to anyone, that Martin had been right. Not wanting to take more exams hadn't been a good enough reason for embarking on something that bored her. The despondency that had seized her in France seemed to swamp her again, and, this time, her mother noticed and suggested a tonic. But Martin said firmly, 'All Kate needs is a change of scenery. A week away, perhaps.'

Bess had wanted to visit Frazer at Ravenhart House for ages, so she wrote a letter to him, asking him if she and Kate and the little girls could come and stay for a week at half-term. But then Rebecca fell ill at the last minute, and, after telegrams had flown to and from Ravenhart House, and after endless warnings about not talking to strangers and never being alone anywhere with a man, Kate was allowed to visit Frazer on her own.

She felt a rush of excitement as the train headed out of

Edinburgh. Sitting in a compartment shared with two elderly women, she gazed out of the window, watching the city speed away.

Perth looked lovely, the sun glinting on the stone buildings, but she had only time to buy a sandwich and a cup of tea in the station waiting room before catching the train to Pitlochry, where Frazer met her at the station.

'My favourite sister,' he said, and kissed her. He asked after the others.

'Mum was sad not to be able to come. And Rebecca's all right, just a bit poorly. Mum's afraid it might be whooping cough but Martin doesn't think it is.'

Frazer showed her round the house and garden. A cedar tree cast its long, dark shadow over the easternmost part of the building; ivy ran green tentacles along the tumbled granite blocks that were the last remnants of the old house that had stood on the site before Sheldon Ravenhart's father had bought up the estate and pulled it down. On the outside of the house hung a large old bell – used, Frazer explained to her, by his Ravenhart forebears to call the hunters in from the moors in time for meals. When he rang the bell, the booming echoed round the valley, startling a flurry of jackdaws in the trees, so that they rose into the air like fragments of ragged black cloth.

Ravenhart House was marvellous, breathtaking, even better than Kate had imagined. Frazer showed her the signet ring he had discovered among Sheldon Ravenhart's belongings; with its raven and heart engraved in gold, it was too large for any of Kate's fingers. He told her his plans for the house – he was going to have the principal rooms redecorated. He would whitewash the gloomy oak panelling and replace the heavy swagged velvet curtains. Flinging open a tall cupboard in the warren of rooms at the back of the house, he showed Kate stacks of china plates and bowls and serving dishes, all bearing the insignia of the raven and the heart, just like his ring.

In one of the reception rooms on the ground floor, empty wine bottles stood by the fireplace and the ashtrays overflowed. A silk scarf lay abandoned behind a sofa, and records, out of their sleeves, were scattered beside the gramophone. Frazer frowned at the mess, scratching his head. 'Some of my friends came up from Edinburgh. They left this morning. I asked Mrs McGill to find someone to clear up, but she can't have got round to it yet,' he added, rather peevishly. Kate opened the windows to let out the stale air and helped Frazer carry the wine bottles to the pantry.

Frazer let her choose her bedroom, so Kate plumped for a hexagonal room in one of the towers. The room was huge, far bigger than her bedroom at home, and she had her own bathroom, a cavernous, clanking affair; it took half an hour to fill the bath with tepid, peaty water. At night, the wind snapped round the roof, making the panelling and the floorboards creak, so that she woke every now and then and wondered about ghosts. She wouldn't have changed the room for anything, though; she loved her high, pinna-cled chamber tagged on to the side of the house, like a boat precariously moored in a stormy harbour.

They walked up the glen, where the stream rushed through a narrow, fern-fringed gorge, and the fallen leaves of the birches littered the ground like golden pennies. Lower down in the valley, the burn wound sluggishly through damp, marshy land. A slow burn, Ronald Bain, the factor, called it. Reddish-brown spikes of grass warned them of the marshland, where there were holes deep enough to swallow a man up. To reach the derelict farms and ruined houses of the abandoned hamlet they had to wade through the stream and then pick their way across the treacherous, changeable ground. They paused, balancing on seemingly solid clumps of grass, throwing pebbles that were swallowed up soundlessly.

This part of the valley always seemed to be in shadow, as though the grief of the families who had been forced to abandon their homes had stained the air black. Long shadows fled away across the grass, and ivy twisted round ruined walls and fallen roofs. Weeds – bramble, nettle and dock – grew in tumbledown byres and in the gaps between blackened hearthstones.

'The villagers left because of the red deer,' Frazer explained. 'The deer ate their crops.'

Kate found herself listening for other voices. 'Perhaps there are ghosts,' she whispered, and Frazer laughed.

'I shouldn't think so.'

Frazer showed her on a map the boundaries of the Ravenhart estate, and pointed out to her the tenant farms that clung to the slopes of the mountains. In the fields, shepherds tipped their caps as they drove past, and the village women nodded their heads.

One morning, they walked to the hunting lodge, which was caught in a loop of the river. The house could be reached only across stepping stones; the broken remains of a bridge, swept away by some long-ago storm, stood upstream. 'We'll have picnics here in the summer,' Frazer said. 'We'll catch fish. Maxwell and I are going to do the place up.'

She asked, 'Who's Maxwell?'

'Maxwell Gilchrist. He's a friend of mine.'

Kate typed letters for Frazer, sitting in his study. She wondered whether Frazer was lonely, living here with only the servants for company. She wondered why he didn't come and stay with them at home – Mum was always asking him to – and guessed that she knew the answer: that Frazer would have felt as she did sometimes, almost boiling over with the need to escape from her mother's loving, protective eye, a need that made her feel both guilty and resentful at the same time.

The morning Kate left Ravenhart House, a sharp frost greyed the valley. Frost flowers bloomed on the inside of the windows in her bedroom, and the cold air, as she walked out of the house carrying her small suitcase, seemed to bite into her. Bundled up in her old school coat and a scarf, her teeth chattered as Frazer drove her to the station at Pitlochry.

There, he bought her a bar of chocolate, which she slid into her coat pocket. She danced from one foot to another, trying to keep warm, as a train pulled into the opposite platform.

When it drew away, they both saw through the cloud of smoke the figure on the far side of the rails, heading for the footbridge. Frazer whooped, and lifted an arm in salute.

'Who is it?' asked Kate.

'It's Maxwell. He didn't tell me he was coming.'

Kate could see her own train, the plume of white smoke in the distance swelling as it drew nearer. Her gaze was drawn to Maxwell Gilchrist, who was crossing the bridge. She watched him pause and lean precipitously over the parapet, his dark curls blown about by the breeze.

'Max,' called Frazer. 'Over here, Max!' He had never sounded happier.

Maxwell waved and then ran down the steps towards them.

Frazer said, 'This is my sister, Kate. Kate, this is Maxwell Gilchrist.'

'Ah, the famous Kate. Frazer has told me so much about you,' said Maxwell.

She looked up at him. Kate fell in love three times that year. The first time was with Frazer, whom she loved because, for as long as she could remember, her mother had spoken to her of her lost brother, who came to her possessing the allure of one who has stepped out of the void, trailing the mystery of a far-off, exotic land. As she came to know him, she loved him also because he was strong and handsome and kind, and because she recognized in him a deep desire, a longing to be loved.

The second time she fell in love was with Ravenhart itself. Ravenhart swept her up into its haunting magic, showing her something other than the mundane, the everyday. With its fairy-tale towers and empty valleys and mountaintops tipped with snow, Ravenhart filled a need she had hardly known was there.

But she had not bargained for falling in love with Maxwell Gilchrist. On a windswept platform at Pitlochry station, she learned what it was to look at someone and love them, in an instant, in the dumb, dizzying meeting of a gaze, as her blue eyes met sea-green, and she was lost.

Chapter Eleven

When Bess eventually visited Frazer at Ravenhart House, it was like reliving an old nightmare. So many years had passed, she hadn't thought she'd mind so much.

'What do you think of it?' Frazer said, as they stood in the room with the panelling and the stags' heads.

'Of course, I've been here before,' she told him. 'I visited your uncle once, Frazer, during the war' – and she remembered Sheldon Ravenhart's uninterested dismissal of her, and the shock of discovering that Cora and Frazer were still in India, and how small she had felt compared to the vast, stony bulk of the building. And how the house had shut her out, its doors and gates closing and the curtain of trees folding around it, excluding her.

For Frazer's sake, she hid her dislike of the place. Each time she saw him she felt a confusion of joy and pain. Though he acknowledged her as his mother, Bess knew that she had not yet earned the rights of a mother. She must not push too far, must not assume an authority she was not due nor demand an intimacy Frazer was not yet able to give. Though he seemed fond of Kate, Frazer was ill at ease with his younger sisters. He had little experience of infants, Bess supposed, brought up by his grandparents in the rigid formality of their bungalow in Simla. Though she had invited him to stay with them whenever he visited Edinburgh, Frazer had not so far chosen to, preferring to take a room in a hotel. Bess could not blame him – she still remembered the smoothly running silence of the Ravenharts' bungalow, where sometimes, in the deep lazy quiet of the afternoon siesta, you could have heard a pin drop. For a man who must be accustomed to peace and quiet, staying with the Jagos would be like moving into a zoo.

Ravenhart House still had the air of dusty neglect that Bess recalled from her first visit. She ran her finger along the mantelpieces to check for dust and annoyed the house-keeper by peering into the kitchen cupboards. Apart from Mr Bain, the factor, the Ravenhart servants were a ragtag lot. Bess suspected that they took advantage of Frazer's lack of experience and good-natured innocence, so she tried to lick them into shape herself. She had Mrs McGill and Phemie, the slow-witted kitchen maid, scrub out the larders, which were scattered with crumbs and smeared with grease stains. She organized the housemaids to take outside the dirtiest rugs and curtains and beat the dust out of them.

She knew that, in part, she kept herself busy because she could not bear to be idle. She could not sit and read, could not even enjoy these rare few days away from her small, demanding daughters, looked after this weekend by Kate and Martin. Though she appreciated the immense pleasure of a night's uninterrupted sleep, much of the time she felt a vague melancholy. It was the house, she decided – all those ponderous, echoing rooms, all those dead faces staring out at her from photograph and portrait, and all those memories that lingered for her.

In her heart, she knew that it was not only the house that oppressed her. Though she had always imagined that her reunion with Frazer would be a time of undiluted happiness, there remained a distance between them, which gnawed at her. That first night he had come back to her, she had knelt on the floor of her bedroom and thanked God for such a gift. Her joy in the arrival of her tall, handsome son – a son that any mother would be proud of, a son that any other mother must envy – had almost overwhelmed her. A terrible wrong had been put right; at last she could break the shackles of the past.

Yet as time passed, her happiness had not been unmixed. You could not expunge a twenty-year absence in a few months. The long parting had scarred both of them. She experienced an awkwardness and diffidence with Frazer that she had never felt with her daughters. She sensed that he did not absolutely trust her, and feared that he in some way blamed her for leaving him. Though he was never hostile to her, the warmth that Frazer offered her was only the same pleasant-mannered geniality that he bestowed on anyone he considered his equal, the smiles that he gave her only the same brilliant smile that he offered everyone else.

Bess knew that Aimée's birth, so soon after Frazer's arrival in Scotland, had complicated matters. The return of her longed-for son and the arrival of her newborn baby had cast her into an emotional turmoil that had sapped her reserves. She had felt as though she had been swallowed, chewed up, and spat out in little pieces. Though she had always assumed that her capacity to love was infinite, she had seemed to lack the energy to bond with her newborn baby and had felt herself clumsy with Frazer, unable to find the words that would make him see that, in spite of absence and parting, she had always loved him – unable to find the words that would make him love her. Frazer's perceptible discomfort with physical contact made her hold back from throwing her arms around him and hugging him as often as she wanted to. It frustrated her that love must so often be wrapped up with guilt. It made her angry that the vigour and drive she had always taken for granted should have deserted her when she needed them most.

Love for her last daughter had grown in time, though she still thought Aimée odd and strange-looking, a changeling child, different from the others. Frazer's love was less easily acquired. Sometimes it saddened her that he seemed to accept Kate more readily than he accepted his mother. Sometimes Bess was afraid that the distance between them would never be narrowed. In her darkest moments she feared that in his heart Frazer cared little for her, and that he might drift away from her once more, and that, one day, she might lose him all over again.

Maxwell Gilchrist attended the reception held at the Charlotte Square house to celebrate his father's fiftieth birthday because Barbara had asked him to. Barbara was Niall's wife, and was the only one of the four – his two brothers, and Sandy's wife, Avril – that he liked. Barbara was round and plump-cheeked and full-bosomed. Maxwell had often wondered what it would be like to go to bed with a sensible, motherly woman like Barbara. Once, at a grim family Christmas, in a spirit of boredom and mischief and curiosity as much as desire, he had made a pass at her – just his hand on her arm and a certain look in his eye and a few murmured words – and she had said, 'It's very sweet of you to offer, Maxwell, but I don't think Niall would like it.' Then she had looked at him more closely. 'Or would you prefer me to be shocked? I will if you want,' and he had found himself laughing, and she had laughed with him. Then she had ruffled his hair and kissed him on the cheek, which had made him want her all over again.

Since then, they had been friends. So when Barbara said, 'Max, your father would like all three of his sons to come to his birthday party, and if you aren't there, he'll be angry and that may spoil the evening for the rest of us,' he had, to please her, agreed.

It crossed his mind to do something outrageous – get raging drunk or turn up with a Princes Street whore on his arm – but, to keep the peace, he regretfully discarded the idea, and escorted Virginia Pagett instead. Ginny was an artist's model; she was tall, dark and opulent, and her lazy, heavy-lidded gaze seemed to hint of passion, if only she could be bothered.

Barbara had been roped in to act as hostess for the evening. The reception room of the Charlotte Square house glittered with cut glass and chandeliers, and black-uniformed maids trotted round with trays of champagne. Plutocrats and politicians rubbed shoulders with some of the businessmen and fixers Andrew Gilchrist had made use of in his rise to the top. A butler had been hired for the night, to announce the names of the guests as they entered the room. You could trust Father not to get a thing like this quite right, thought Maxwell with a smirk, as the guests made their entrance. It was all just ever so slightly overcooked.

Maxwell introduced Virginia to Niall and Sandy, noting with pleasure the envy on his brothers' faces. Niall's brown hair had begun to recede already – he was only in his early thirties – and his eyes, which always made Maxwell think of those of a ferret, were dark and darting and voracious. Sandy, the middle brother, was slight and stoop-shouldered. When Sandy's wife, Avril, spoke to Maxwell, her tone was a mixture of condescension and wariness, such as one might use to a slightly mad relative. He must have done something dreadful at some point, Maxwell supposed, though for the life of him he could not remember what. Avril was terrified of her father-in-law and flinched if he so much as looked at her. Most of the time, Andrew Gilchrist ignored Avril, who was, Maxwell suspected, too easy a target. His father only troubled to inflict his amorality and his strength on those who thwarted him. Niall, Sandy, Barbara and Avril would never cross him because his money paid for their homes, their motor cars and their children's schooling.

Barbara beamed. 'Such a good turnout! Your father will be so pleased.' Neither of his daughters-in-law ever called him Andrew, or, God forbid, Father – their evasion was a way, Maxwell had concluded, of distancing themselves, of keeping the monster at arm's length.

Sandy eyed his canapé suspiciously. 'What on earth is this?'

Avril peered. 'Oysters and bacon.' She went green.

'My dyspepsia . . .'

Barbara took the canapé from Sandy and hid it in a pot plant. 'Are you quite well, Avril?'

Avril had gone to stand at the open window, and was taking deep breaths. Barbara patted her arm solicitously. Sandy's sallow, freckly skin had turned pink. He said coyly, 'We're expecting a happy event.'

'Oh, how lovely!' cried Barbara. 'Such good news!'

A voice said, 'Good news? What good news?'

It was impressive, Maxwell thought, how Father could cast such a chill on things by his mere presence. There they were, having what passed for a conversation in the Gilchrist family, and then Father came along and it was as though they had been put under a spell, tongue-tied, awkward, their knuckles whitening as they gripped their glasses.

Andrew Gilchrist had always been tall and heavily built, but over the last few years he had put on weight. His face had filled out round the jaw and eyes, reducing his gaze to two dark, sharp fragments of basalt as he studied his sons.

'Well?'

Sandy said, 'Avril's expecting a baby, Father.'

'About time. You've been married – how many years is it?'

'Three, Father.'

'Took a while, didn't you?' Andrew Gilchrist surveyed Avril, who was standing at the window, dabbing her mouth with a handkerchief. He muttered, 'Should have married a woman with a bit more meat on her bones.'

'Yes, Father.' Sandy's flush had deepened. 'If it's a boy, we'd like to call him Andrew, after you, Father.'

A grunt. A *flattered* grunt, though, thought Maxwell. Good old Sandy, always the sycophant.

'At least you've managed to find a wife. Can't be said for all my sons, can it?'

Maxwell said demurely, 'I think I'm still too young to settle down, Father.'

'Too young? You couldn't find a respectable woman who'd have you.'

'Well, there's Ginny.'

Father's gaze travelled to where Virginia Pagett was standing in a corner, surrounded by men. 'Her? She's a slut.'

'Yes, Father. But a very *obliging* slut.'

Andrew Gilchrist's eyes narrowed, anger sparking in them. He put his hand on Maxwell's shoulder, steering him to a quieter corner of the room.

He said, 'Look at the state of you. You look like a scarecrow.'

Maxwell had lost his dinner suit somewhere on his travels; for his father's party, he had borrowed clothes from a friend at the cafe. The trousers were too long for him and fell in buckled folds, and the cuffs of the jacket had frayed.

His father's gaze ran over him. 'I suppose you're short of money.'

'Yes, Father.' Maxwell added hopefully, 'If you could lend me a few pounds . . .'

His father's gifts were randomly munificent, their quantity and quality never predictable, always bestowed at times of Andrew Gilchrist's own choosing. He expected gratitude, but poured scorn on what he saw as grovelling. He loved to be capricious; he considered obliging people, including his sons, weak. He gained his family's obedience by dangling in front of them the possibility of wealth and comfort, and then despised them for their greed and their servility. If he knew they wanted something, he'd hold it to their heads like a gun. Andrew Gilchrist's anger was equally indiscriminate. Maxwell had concluded long ago that his father ruled by uncertainty, which was why Niall drank too much and Sandy's nails were bitten to the quick and why he himself suffered from headaches.

His father said slowly, 'Now that's an interesting word, lend. You're proposing to pay me back, are you?'

'Yes, Father.'

'When?'

'As soon as I can.'

'Got work, have you?'

'Some.' He added honestly, 'Not much.'

'I've a proposition for you, Maxwell. Come and work for me, like your brothers. Earn your living instead of cadging it.'

They had had the same conversation countless times over the years. It wouldn't be worth it, he wanted to say. He'd rather die of starvation and be gnawed by rats in a cellar than end up like Niall and Sandy.

'No, Father.'

Andrew Gilchrist's lip curled scornfully. 'I've worked my fingers to the bone to give you and your brothers a home. There's thousands out there who would give their eye teeth to live in a place like this. But you turn up your nose at it.'

Maxwell could feel his composure slipping away from him. Charlotte Square had never been a *home*. A home, surely, should be more than a collection of rooms and regular meals.

But he said, making a play of scanning the room that his father was so proud of, 'It's not really to my taste, Father. A bit overfurnished. Too much gilt.'

'Don't be so bloody cheeky,' hissed his father. There was a silence. Maxwell could hear his father breathing heavily, struggling to control himself.

Then Andrew Gilchrist said, 'There's a position free in the office at the moment. Might suit you – it's book work, so you wouldn't have to get your hands dirty. It's yours if you want it.'

Maxwell shook his head. 'No thanks. I can manage.'

Andrew Gilchrist's eyes hardened. 'Then I'm afraid I can't help you, Maxwell. Come and see me again when you've begun to see sense. I've no doubt you'll soon be back, begging me to bail you out.' He turned away, merging into the crowd.

The champagne had given Maxwell a headache, and he felt a sudden self-loathing. His gaze slid round the room. He wondered how many of the hundred or so guests wanted something from his father, and how many his father wanted something from. He used money to cement his ownership, of things and people.

Maxwell headed out of the reception room in search of something stronger than champagne to drink. He was passing his father's study when he heard a sound from inside. His curiosity sparked, he opened the door a crack. In the sliver of light he saw Simon Voyle, sitting in his father's chair, his feet on his father's desk and a glass in one hand.

When he coughed, Voyle shot to his feet. Maxwell shut the door behind him. 'It's all right. I won't tell.'

There was a beading of perspiration on Simon Voyle's forehead. 'I was just—'

'Reading Father's private papers and drinking his whisky,' supplied Maxwell, surveying the desk. The open bottle was a 25-year-old Scotch.

Voyle was bundling papers back into a drawer. Maxwell found a glass and poured himself a drink. 'Find anything interesting?'

'Your father's business dealings are always interesting,' said Voyle, with a cackle. Then he wiped his brow with his handkerchief.

'Don't worry, Voyle, I won't go running to Daddy.'

'Your brothers—'

'And neither will I say a word to dear old Sandy and Niall. We all know who jerks their strings.'

'And mine,' said Voyle viciously. He laughed again. 'And yours.'

'Not me. I've got away from him.' The disbelief on Voyle's face made Maxwell angry. 'You'll be at his beck and call till you draw your old age pension.'

Voyle shook his head. His expression became secretive, preening. 'I can leave here whenever I want.'

'Who'd pay your mortgage, Simon? Who'd feed your family?'

Voyle tapped his breast pocket. 'You don't think I haven't taken out insurance, do you?' Then his mouth clammed up and he sidled out of the study.

Good God, thought Maxwell, what has the little toad been up to? He sat still for a moment, thinking hard. Then he poured himself another drink. Voyle's assumption of his own subserviency rankled. He knew that he was different from Sandy and Niall. He hated to be classified with them, even by Simon Voyle.

He could feel his mood plummeting, the headache pushing at his eye sockets as a black depression crept up on him. He found himself thinking of Ravenhart House. When he was there, he didn't feel quite so – so *grubby*. Something about the Charlotte Square house and its occupants seemed to have left its mark on him. In this house, he was always vigilant and on edge. He had learned since childhood to watch himself, as if from the outside, to estimate his father's reaction to what he did, what he said. Yet however much he might hate the house, it was still part of him; it seemed to trail behind him, like dirty footprints. Only when he was at Ravenhart was he able to believe that he had escaped.

Maxwell swallowed down the rest of the whisky, and was about to put the bottle and glasses back in the cupboard when he decided against it. Let Father know that someone had violated his sanctum, he thought. Then he went to find Virginia.

*   *   *

In the six months since he had come to live in Perthshire, Frazer had begun to try to bring Ravenhart House up to date. Though the house appeared imposing, inside it was uncomfortable, gloomy and old-fashioned. His first Scottish winter showed up the inadequacies of the heating and electrical systems. The house's hot water came from a coal boiler, its lighting from an oil-fired generator. When the first snows fell, covering the hills and the glen with a thin blanket of white, Frazer woke in the morning to a trickle of cold water in the bathroom and ice glazing the insides of the windows. 'Och, the place always freezes up when winter comes,' said Mrs McGill, as though it was normal for one to have to endure cold baths and rooms of sub-zero temperatures in midwinter, adding as an afterthought that more coal must be fetched because they were almost out.

As Ravenhart House had no telephone, the coal merchants must be visited in person to place an urgent order. In India, Frazer couldn't help thinking, they would have sent a boy. Here, though, he ended up driving to Pitlochry himself – one could hardly send Mrs McGill, with her bad leg and rheumatism, on a ten-mile walk through the snow, and Phemie would have forgotten her message by the time she was a few yards out of the house. And none of the other servants – the disparate collection of housemaids and kitchen maids that Frazer sometimes encountered scrubbing steps or pegging washing on the line in the back garden – had appeared that morning, preferring to remain, he guessed resentfully, in their comfortable, warm cottages. As for Ronald Bain, he would have thought the job beneath him. Frazer was a little afraid of his factor – sometimes, in Mr Bain's eyes, he thought he glimpsed something close to contempt.

So he hauled the Lagonda out of the garage, and set off for Pitlochry that afternoon. By the time he returned to the house, after a twenty-mile round trip in which he had had to concentrate hard all the time so as not to skid off the narrow, icy road and be swallowed up by a bog or river, it was dark, and he was exhausted. Peeling off his scarf and gloves, he went indoors. Ravenhart House was always gloomy, but that evening it looked positively funereal. None of the electric lights were on. Candles lit the entrance hall. Frazer cursed as he tripped on the curled-up corner of a rug. The great hall was illuminated by candles also. Frazer roared for Mrs McGill.

That thing – Mrs McGill's term for the generator – had stopped working, she told him. She looked almost pleased – Mrs McGill feared and disapproved of the generator. 'Don't we possess any oil lamps?' Frazer demanded, exasperated, and she scuttled off and eventually Phemie appeared, clutching two dusty lamps.

Frazer ate his supper of soup, bread and cheese sitting as close as he could to the fire. At some point in the evening, Mrs McGill muttered something about visiting a sick relative and disappeared along the drive. Not long afterwards, Frazer, heading upstairs in search of a thicker sweater, heard a sniffling sound and discovered Phemie, hidden behind a curtain. Phemie's plain little face was blotched with tears. After much coaxing, she told Frazer that she was afraid to go upstairs to her attic room because of the ghosts. Frazer patted her shoulder and made soothing noises; then, with an inward sigh, he gave her his torch and, as an after-thought, a handful of toffees – Phemie had a sweet tooth.

Later, Frazer sat in the great hall while the house creaked and murmured and ink-black shadows gathered in corners. Outside, the wind whistled, hurling a fresh fall of snow at the windowpanes. It was all too easy to imagine some rest-less spirit prowling along the unlit corridors, opening doors into empty rooms. He seemed far away from any other human being, and many, many miles from anyone he might call a friend. He felt lonely and miserable, and found himself, not for the first time, wondering whether he should sell up – always assuming anyone would want to buy the place – and move somewhere civilized: London, perhaps, or Paris.

But he knew that he would not. The thought of starting all over again, in a place where he didn't know a soul, and where no one knew who he was, appalled him. And besides, Ravenhart was his. He was the last of the Ravenharts.

Ravenhart House had also brought him Maxwell Gilchrist. Frazer had never forgotten Max's expression of shock and admiration and envy the day he had seen the house for the first time. There was a part of Maxwell – quite a large part, Frazer thought fondly – which would have liked to have been landed and rich.

To please Max, Frazer had put a room aside for him, a big, comfortable room at the front of the house. Max's life seemed so chaotic, such a muddle of moving from place to place; Frazer had not previously encountered anyone who lived such a transient, unrooted existence. Max needed somewhere, thought Frazer, that he could call his own. After he had given him the room, Max spent more time at Ravenhart. When Max was there, all Frazer's doubts dissolved, and he felt happier than he had been since he was a small boy in India, cared for by his grandmother and sheltered from every difficulty. Maxwell had a way of transforming everything; in his company, Frazer's lingering uncertainty disappeared, and he felt confident of his own worth, almost as if he could see himself through Maxwell Gilchrist's laughing, sea-green eyes.

Would Maxwell have been his friend if he had not owned Ravenhart House? Frazer was never sure. He had come to learn, over the six months of their acquaintance, that Max was changeable, subject to sudden depressions and changes of mood, which rattled him. Every now and then, Max would suddenly and without warning disappear from Ravenhart, and Frazer wouldn't see him again for weeks on end. He never told Frazer where he was going, or who he was with. Frazer supposed he was with a woman.

When Maxwell was away, Frazer was obsessed by the possibility that, this time, he would not return. A month ago, Frazer had driven to the railway station at Pitlochry to meet Maxwell's train. The arrangement had been long-standing; there was to be a party at the house that night, a party conceived and organized by Maxwell himself. At the station, first one train and then another had arrived. Maxwell had been on none of them. Frazer had found himself resenting the passengers that the trains disgorged – the hikers, with their rucksacks and mackintoshes, and the shoppers, back from a day out in Perth or Edinburgh. Why should they have got here and not Max? Between trains, he had passed the time wandering around Pitlochry, a dispiriting little place, full of boarding houses and tea shops, which he had begun to detest by the time he turned back to Ravenhart in case Max had sent a telegram.

There had been no telegram, and the workmen who were decorating the great hall had taken advantage of Frazer's absence and downed tools early, leaving a litter of paint cans and brushes and ladders and dust sheets slung anyhow over the room. Frazer had taken a rapid drink or two and then his temper had boiled over and he had given vent to his anger and misery by kicking a paint can. White paint had bled over the floor. He had yelled for Phemie, who had scurried around, mop and bucket in hand. Frazer had poured himself a drink as Phemie sloshed water and spread the white paint in a larger circle. It was infuriating of Max to be so unreliable. If you thought about it, Max owed him – there wasn't only the bedroom, there were also the restaurant meals Frazer treated him to, not to mention the odd handout of cash. Frazer took a few mouthfuls of Scotch and managed to control his temper sufficiently to thank Phemie for clearing up the mess. She bobbed a curtsey and ran away.

Frazer hadn't enjoyed the party that evening – the gaiety had seemed forced, and most of the guests had been Maxwell's friends anyway. When, a few days later, Maxwell had eventually appeared, Frazer had felt annoyed all over again, until Max, thoroughly contrite, charmed him out of it.

The night of the snow, he went to bed early, sleeping beneath a heap of blankets to keep out the cold. Overnight, the storm thickened, and the next morning, peering shivering out of a window, Frazer saw a landscape of icing-sugar whorls and crests. The Lagonda would no longer be able to make the journey to Mr Bain's gatehouse, let alone Pitlochry. Icicles grew like glistening daggers from the guttering, and the summits of the mountains were lost in greenish clouds that were swollen with the next snowfall.

Huddled beside the fire that evening, Frazer decided that he would take a train to Edinburgh as soon as the roads were clear enough for him to reach Pitlochry, and that he would stay there until the house was bearable again. Then a hammering on the door made him jump and spill whisky onto the hearth. Through the windowpane, he could make out only the swirl of the snow and the endless expanse of night-dark sky. His fingers trembled as he slid the bolt on the front door, imagining – what? The ghosts that Phemie feared, or a pack of red-eyed wolves, which had once roamed these desolate hills?

He opened the door. 'Max,' he said, and gave a gasp of relief.

Then Maxwell was in the hall, shaking snow onto the stone flags. Snow frosted his shoulders and clung to the tips of his dark curls.

Frazer gazed at him open-mouthed. 'How did you get here?'

'I hitched rides from Perth. The snow's not so deep further south. I had a ride on a horse and cart the last few miles. It was fantastic. Like suddenly finding yourself in another century.'

He was shivering, so Frazer helped him out of his wet coat and scarf. In the great hall, Maxwell stood in front of the fire, warming himself, while Frazer poured him a drink.

Maxwell looked around the room. 'It's a bit *crepuscular*, isn't it?' His eyes glittered. 'I couldn't resist coming here when I knew there was snow. Isn't it marvellous?'

'Marvellous,' echoed Frazer. And, placing the glass in Maxwell's cold hands, seeing his glorious Ravenhart through Max's eyes, realized to his delight that he meant it.

Kate hadn't thought that falling in love would be like this. The books she had read had not implied that it would be so. She had assumed there must be something more, some extraordinary event, some bolt of lightning. Now, if he had pulled her from a swirling torrent or scooped her off a runaway horse . . . But to fall in love on Pitlochry station, with a handshake and a few words – *Ah, the famous Kate. Frazer has told me so much about you* – threw her into confusion.

She wasn't sure what to do with it, this new thing which had come upon her like a bout of measles. He crept into her thoughts in every little crack and crevice of the day, so that she thought of him last thing at night and the moment she woke up in the morning. It made her angry, resentful, that she, who had long ago lost half of herself, should redis-cover this feeling of incompleteness, of loss and joy and longing, all over again. She seemed to burn, a fire had been lit. When she remembered how she had blushed and how she had not been able to think of a word to say to him, and when she thought how dreadful she must have looked, bundled up in her old school coat and a scarf that Pamela had knitted for her, something seemed to curl up inside her.

For the first time, she began to pay attention to her appearance. She babysat for neighbours and, with the money she earned, bought herself clothes – a pair of silk stockings, a blue velvet beret, a canary-yellow artificial silk blouse from a street market. She grew out her fringe and let her hair fall to her shoulders. Sometimes, when she looked in the mirror, she thought she might be pretty.

It was February, and she was walking down the High Street late one afternoon, when she saw Maxwell Gilchrist, wearing a grey overcoat and with his dark head uncovered, coming towards her. Though it was very cold, and fragments of snow were dancing in the air, her face went hot and her heart raced. As he passed within a few feet of her, she did not dare acknowledge him – she knew he would not remember her.

And then, out of the corner of her eye, she saw him pause, swivel on the balls of his feet and walk back to her. 'Kate,' he said. 'Kate Ravenhart.'

'Kate Fearnley, actually.'

'Really?' He looked at her, frowning. 'Still, Frazer's Kate. What are you doing in Edinburgh?'

'I live here.'

'Fancy that. I sometimes live here too.'

'Sometimes?'

'I've been at Ravenhart, helping Frazer with stuff,' he explained vaguely. He shivered. 'Damnably cold, isn't it? You don't fancy a coffee, do you?'

She almost said automatically, *I have to go home because my mother is expecting me*, but managed to swallow the words.

'That would be lovely,' came out in a croak.

They went to a little cafe called the Two Magpies. There were portraits on the walls in pastels and oils of sullen-looking women curled up on sofas and languid young men gazing through windows. Some of the figures in the paintings had splodgy orange and purple faces. A gramophone was playing 'Mack The Knife', and a black cat was coiled on the counter, beside a plate of buns.

The cafe's customers – men wearing collarless shirts beneath threadbare overcoats and girls in black jerseys or blouses of brilliant colours – all seemed to know Maxwell Gilchrist, and waved and called out greetings to him. Maxwell scrabbled in his pockets for change and, finding a threepence, said, 'I'm sorry, I seem to have come out without any money,' so Kate paid for the coffee.

After he had sat down, he wrapped his hands round his cup to warm them up, and said, 'Kate *Fearnley.*'

'Yes.'

'But you're Frazer's sister. You can't possibly be married, can you? You're much too young.'

She giggled. 'Goodness, no. Frazer's father was called Jack Ravenhart and mine's called Ralph Fearnley, that's all. I suppose we're half-brother and -sister really.'

'How complicated,' he said.

She noticed that there always seemed to be laughter in his eyes, as though he was on the verge of finding everything a great joke. Afraid that the pause in the conversation might go on too long, and that the laughter might be replaced by boredom, she added, 'I have four half-brothers and three half-sisters. Both my parents married again, you see.'

'Heavens.'

'My mother's Mrs Jago now and Dad's married to Pamela. So Pamela's Mrs Fearnley, instead of Mum.'

The little crinkles beneath his eyes deepened. 'You've lost me.' He opened a packet of French cigarettes. 'I don't suppose you smoke, do you?'

'Yes, please.'

He struck a match. When he lit her cigarette his fingers brushed against hers. He said, 'Augustus John's supposed to have fathered dozens of children, so – eight of you, wasn't it? – isn't too extraordinary.'

'Augustus John?'

'The artist.'

'Oh yes. Of course.'

'Aren't you interested in art?'

'Oh I am, terribly.' She admitted honestly, 'But I don't know a lot about it.'

'What do you know a lot about?'

'Not much, really. Ballet. I like ballet. And I like to read.'

'What are you reading now?'

'Byron,' she said. There was a book of Byron's poems in her coat pocket.

'Byron.' He quoted, '"So we'll go no more a-roving, so late into the night."' Then his eyes narrowed, the laughter in them now barely contained. 'He slept with his half-sister, you know.'

She felt herself blush again, and was thankful when a girl stopped at their table and said, 'Maxwell. Where have you *been*?'

He said, 'Oh, here and there, Jen.'

The girl was short and buxom. She was wearing paint-stained trousers and a rather holey knitted top the colour of blackberries. Her untidy black hair was pushed behind her ears and her fringe was too long. She said, 'Well, it's too bad,' and flung a sulky glance at Kate.

'Jen, this is Kate Fearnley. Kate, this is Jenny Watts. Don't be cross with me, darling Jenny. You know I hate it when you're cross with me.' He took her hand and pressed his lips against her palm.

Jenny seemed to soften; she wound her arms round Maxwell's neck. 'You're such a wretch, Max. But you can come to supper tonight if you promise to be good.' She gave a lock of his hair a little tug just before she walked away.

Afterwards, Kate lurched between elation and despair. Elation because Maxwell Gilchrist had remembered her, and because he had wanted to buy her a cup of coffee – even if, strictly speaking, she had ended up buying the coffee herself. Despair because she had seen quite plainly that he put her into a different category to Jenny and her ilk. Too young to be married, too young to smoke, too young, perhaps, to be his friend. Remembering how he had kissed Jenny's hand, Kate closed her eyes and pressed her own mouth against the palm of her hand, over and over again. She felt giddy with longing, shocked and half drowned by it.

He was there the next time she spent a weekend at Ravenhart House.

The morning after she arrived, all three of them went

for a walk, following the path of the burn as it snaked through the valley. Every now and then, covertly, carefully, she looked at him. She might, after all, be mistaken. He might not be as she had remembered him to be. She might have imagined the plane of cheekbone and chin, the way he could never be still, or the dark, amused timbre of his voice. Yet, watching him, she knew that she was not mistaken, that she knew him by heart already, had known him from the moment he had taken her hand, the wind raking them among the confused busyness of the station platform.

The hunting lodge was a mile and a half from Ravenhart House, between the confluence of two rivers. One of the rivers leapt down the mountain in a series of waterfalls and pools. They followed the ravine cut into the rock, threading uphill between the scattering of firs and birches that grew on the banks. The fast-running burn had sculpted cascades and runnels out of the soft, red-brown sandstone, and the force of the water had hollowed out the bases of the boulders that caged the torrent, making dark overhangs which ate back an unknown distance into the hillside. Branches, blown from the trees by the winter's storms, jammed and caught between rocks, jostled by the passage of the river.

Beyond a high outcrop of boulders, a circular pool had been scooped out of the mountainside by the waterfall that plunged from the rocks high above. Sunlight dropped in shafts through the trees and was broken into shards by the movement of the water, where it lay glittering on the surface. Hidden by the cleft of the rock and the fringe of

trees, both waterfall and pool were invisible from the valley below. A deep silence lingered, broken only by the splash of the water and the creak and murmur of pines. It took Kate a few moments to realize that she was holding her breath.

Maxwell was circling the pond, moving from rock to rock.

When he threw a pebble into the water, it was swallowed up with hardly a splash. It seemed to Kate that the stone took an age to drift to the bottom of the pool. A cloud covered the face of the sun, erasing the diamond glitter of the water, darkening the gorge. Kate shivered.

They climbed away from the river, breaking through the band of trees. Down in the valley, the hunting lodge could be seen, bordered by rivers on two sides. The men led the way. Seeing them together, Kate thought how glorious they were, and how well they went together, like the sun and its shadow: golden Frazer, taller and broader-shouldered than the dark, mercurial Maxwell. The breeze blew fragments of their conversation back to her.

'They used to have banquets down there – I found photographs . . .'

'We could have a banquet . . .'

'Why not? In the summer.'

'What does one eat at a banquet?'

'Haven't a clue. Roast suckling pig, d'you think? Pike? Peacocks?'

Another weekend. Food and champagne from the best Edinburgh stores, candles in sconces and fires lit in a dozen

rooms. From the hillside across the valley, the windows must blaze scarlet light.

All the other guests were older than Kate. The women moved with a languid elegance in their long, slinky, figure-revealing, bias-cut dresses. Kate did not possess a long, slinky, bias-cut dress. For Frazer's party, she wore her best dress, which was navy-blue velvet with a white Peter Pan collar and puff sleeves, and made her look, she thought glumly, about twelve.

After the guests had arrived, they went into the great hall, where Kate perched on a window sill as Frazer opened bottle after bottle of champagne. Then they danced. She loved to dance with Frazer, who was tall and graceful and who danced as well as any man in the room. Yet she longed to dance with Maxwell. Why didn't he ask her to dance? Because he preferred those glossy, sophisticated women, she supposed, with a stirring of jealousy that stabbed her heart. Why should Maxwell Gilchrist dance with Frazer's little sister, in her puff sleeves and navy-blue velvet?

Someone threw quoits at the stag's head above the fire-place; the crowd cheered whenever one hooped round an antler. Kate felt sorry for the stag, whose expression was such a mixture of dignity and mournfulness. Maxwell was always in the thick of things, dancing, drinking, mimicking Ronald Bain, his voice broad Scots and his features taking on Mr Bain's stony glower. 'Do Mrs McGill, Maxwell,' a girl coaxed, and his voice rose a couple of octaves and became shrewish, hectoring. He seemed to move round the old house like a bright naphtha flare, always an object of atten-tion and always surrounded by people, making the party

come alive. Her own eyes were constantly drawn to him – how dreadful, she thought suddenly, if someone should notice the direction of her gaze, and how much more dreadful if, noticing, they should laugh at her.

The night lengthened. Guests wandered away from the reception rooms; the corridors of the house echoed with running footsteps and half-stifled laughter. The fires died down and the candles burned to a stub and no one thought to replace them. It was growing cold; Kate went upstairs to find a cardigan. On an upstairs landing, a couple were locked in an embrace, their hungry eyes and mouths devouring each other, and their breath making the air shiver with passion. If I was older, she thought. If I had platinum-blonde hair. If I had a gorgeous satin dress.

In the darkness, someone complained, 'Max, where *are* you? Don't be a bore,' and Kate turned a corner, and there he was, sort of semi-upright, leaning against the wall, his tie undone and his collar unstudded, his shoulders resting against the panelling.

'Kate,' he murmured, opening one eye. He smiled. 'Little Kate.'

'Hello, Maxwell.' She looked at him. 'Are you all right?'

He rubbed his eyes. 'A bit tired. What time is it?'

'Almost three o'clock.'

There was the sound of footsteps, and he whispered, 'Come with me,' and took her hand. They ran up a staircase and along a succession of corridors. Another, narrower, staircase took them into the attics. Dark shapes loomed in the dim light. It was cool and quiet in the attic, and she could sense him, very close to her.

Maxwell opened a tiny door in the wainscotting. 'Come on.'

'In there?' Beyond the door it was pitch-black, and there was a damp, musty smell.

'You'll like it. Promise.'

She had to go on her hands and knees to squeeze through the little door. When he closed it behind them the darkness fell around them like a blanket. She heard him say, 'I'll open the trapdoor so that we can see what we're doing,' and she felt Maxwell brush past her. When her eyes became accustomed to the dark, she could just make out the ladder on the far wall. Maxwell climbed up it and pushed open the trapdoor, and Kate saw above her a square of black sky, embroidered with stars.

There was a moment when, near the top of the ladder, she looked down into the void, and her stomach lurched. But then he reached out his hand and pulled her through the trapdoor, and the sharp, cold air struck her.

'Oh,' she gasped.

She was standing on the roof. A full moon outlined the distant mountains. She saw the lacework of the stone balustrade, just a few yards away, and, far, far below, the dense, dark shrubs that grew round the gravel forecourt. The ground seemed to loom up at her; she shrank away from the edge.

Maxwell had sat down, his back against the chimney stack. Kate sat beside him. For a while, they did not speak. Every now and then, their shoulders and elbows touched, and she was aware of the warmth of him, and the faint, salty scent of his sweat.

'Isn't it glorious?' he said. 'And so nice and quiet.'

'I didn't think you liked quiet.'

'You shouldn't judge by appearances, Miss Fearnley. Deep down, I'm a contemplative soul.' He pressed the heels of his hands against his eyes and then ran his fingers through his tangled hair. 'Are you cold?'

She was shivering. 'A bit.'

'Bloody Scotland, still perishing in what passes for spring. Here.' He wrapped his jacket round her shoulders. His hand brushed against her hair; he caught a few strands between his fingertips. He said, 'Such gorgeous hair.'

'I detest it.'

'Course you don't.'

'I do. Everyone detests having ginger hair.'

'Men might. Not women. Sign of a passionate nature, you know. The heroine of my novel has red hair.'

'You're writing a book?'

'It's a detective story.' He lit two cigarettes and passed one to her. 'It's not as easy as you'd think. There's the murder, for a start. You can't just clock someone on the head with the nearest blunt object, though I daresay most murders are as banal as that. How would you do it, Kate? How would you kill your most hated enemy?'

'I've never really thought about it. I don't think I've ever actually *hated* anyone.'

'Haven't you? I have. I hate lots of people and I've thought of lots of interesting ways to finish them off. I'm using poison, administered with a blowpipe – rather good, don't you think?' He smoked for a while in silence. 'Anyway, your hair's not *ginger*. It's the colour of—'

'Marmalade, my father says.'

'Apricots. It's the colour of apricots.'

Far below them, a peal of laughter split the night. A couple were crossing the lawn, their movement uncertain, zigzagging. 'Three sheets to the wind, I fear,' said Maxwell lazily. 'Perhaps they'll fall into the burn and drown themselves. Now, that would be handy. I'd be able to find out what policemen do. Sudden deaths and all that – it'd be useful to see at first hand. I don't know any policemen, I'm afraid. I know hundreds of people but not one single policeman.'

She said, 'I suppose we should go down.'

'Why?'

'Because of Frazer. He'll miss us.'

'There's plenty of others.'

She turned to look at Maxwell, at the clean lines of his profile and the sleepy, half-veiled sea-green of his eyes. She wondered whether he knew what it was like to look at someone and to ache for them. She wasn't sure, now that she thought about it, whether Frazer liked any of the others. Not like he liked Maxwell, anyway.

She started to rise, but he put a hand on her arm, stopping her. 'I'll go.'

She watched him disappear through the trapdoor. It occurred to her that it was in some ways even more lovely when he wasn't there, when there was just the recollection of their conversation and the memory of his fingers stroking her hair. When he was beside her she was aware of a sense of danger, as if he – or she – might venture too near the balustrade, and slip and fall.

She heard footsteps on the ladder, and then first Maxwell, closely followed by Frazer, came through the trapdoor. Maxwell had a bottle of champagne in his pocket. They sat to either side of her and passed the bottle from one to the other. The fires must have died down by now, Kate thought, and all you would be able to see from the hills would be a scattering of pinkish squares, like pieces of rose quartz on black velvet.

Bess said how pleased she was that Kate and Frazer got on so well, and Kate suppressed a squirm of guilt. She hadn't told her mother about Maxwell Gilchrist. At first, there had been no need, Max was Frazer's friend, and she had been only a tolerated third. The guilt had lain in how she felt about Maxwell Gilchrist, which no one, no one at all, must ever know about.

Over the next few months, however, almost imperceptibly at first, something changed. Frazer – and Maxwell, too – began to *expect* her to visit. Both men met her at Pitlochry station, both kissed her cheek. All three of them dined together at the big old mahogany table laid with the Ravenhart china. When the better weather came, they cleared out the hunting lodge together, ridding it of old perambulators and chipped pieces of crockery, and jumping back in alarm when a swarm of bees boiled up into the air after Maxwell poked at a piece of decaying plaster. At the end of the day, they flopped, exhausted and dirty, on the flat stones by the river, passing a bottle of wine from one to the other and eating the sandwiches that Phemie had made.

Kate knew that though her mother was pleased that she

visited Frazer, she would be far less pleased to know that her daughter spent her weekends with Frazer's friend, an unmarried man of twenty-four. She also knew that she herself edited for her mother her accounts of how she passed her time at Ravenhart House. Her mother didn't know, for instance, about the parties. Frazer's parties weren't like the parties that Kate was allowed to go to in Edinburgh. Images crept into Kate's mind when she thought about Frazer's parties: Maxwell, his hair tousled and his collar undone, leaning unsteadily against a wall; Frazer looping a quoit round the stag's antler, the room a mess of empty champagne bottles and discarded glasses.

As for Maxwell himself, Kate had a strong suspicion that her mother wouldn't approve of him, that he wasn't the sort of man mothers approved of. She couldn't even be sure that, if, for instance, she invited Maxwell home to tea, he would behave himself. He was unpredictable, capricious. And would Martin like Maxwell? Martin's opinion had for some time been her litmus paper, her test of what was true and good.

The trouble was that telling her mother the truth now about what really went on at Ravenhart House would mean admitting to a great many evasions in the past. Her mother would, Kate suspected, be furious. She might even forbid her to visit Ravenhart House. And then she would not see Frazer and Maxwell any more. And that would be unbearable.

One Saturday in July, Frazer and Maxwell carried chairs and rugs from Ravenhart House to the hunting lodge, while

Kate ran alongside, her arms full of treasures – a vase, a looking-glass, a sinuous candelabra, hung with glass drops. Every now and then they would stop, red-faced and sweating, and collapse in the chairs until they got their breath back. There was something freakish and funny about them sitting on chairs in the wilderness while a peregrine falcon circled overhead.

They built a bonfire of old furniture and packing cases on the flat stones beside the burn and shoved the rubbish that couldn't be burned into the outhouse at the back of the lodge. Kate swept out the dust and dead leaves and spider's webs, Frazer hauled outside the huge stones that had fallen from the chimney stack, while Maxwell crawled precariously over the roof, pushing loose slates into place. It was a warm day, and he took off his shirt while he worked.

When he came down the ladder, Frazer traced with his thumb the criss-cross of white scars over Maxwell's shoulders. 'What are these?'

'My father, I should think.' Maxwell shrugged on his shirt.

The next day, Kate and Maxwell walked back to the hunting lodge while Frazer discussed estate matters with Ronald Bain. In the valley, the air was hot and still and sweetened by the honey smell of heather, but on the hilltops anvil-shaped clouds had begun to bubble up.

'Thunderstorm soon,' said Maxwell. He looked cheerful. 'I love a good thunderstorm.'

Kate put the picnic basket in the lodge. When she went back outside, the heat seemed to strike her and cling to her.

They walked up the burn to the pool with the waterfall. Kate watched Maxwell prowl round the boulders that circled the pool, his body casting indigo shadows on the stone.

'It's so hot.'

'Come for a swim then.'

She was not a strong swimmer, and had not yet swum in the pool. Swimming in the river at Les Trois Cheminées, she had always avoided the deep cut where your feet couldn't touch the bottom and pond weed wound round your legs like an octopus's tentacles. And there was something about the pool that she distrusted, its unpredictability, the way it could appear silvery and inviting one moment and dark and unfathomable the next.

'I can't. I haven't brought a swimming costume.'

'Kate,' he said mockingly. Then, without warning, he stepped off the rock into the pool. She heard herself gasp, and then, several long seconds later, his head broke the surface of the water.

He held out a hand to her. 'Come on.'

She shook her head. Her heart was pounding: the heat, and the way the pool had swallowed him up.

When he pulled himself out onto the bank, his footsteps were wet on the stones. Water ran off him in rivulets. He unbuttoned his shirt and it flopped damply to the ground. She saw how the droplets of water gathered in the tiny ridges and hollows of the scars that Frazer had noticed.

'Max?'

'Yes?'

'Those scars. When you said that your father—'

320

His eyes veiled, their green almost hidden beneath black lashes. Kate said quickly, 'I'm sorry. I expect you don't want to talk about it.'

'I don't mind.'

'Then – what did you mean when you said that your father did that? Did you mean that he hurt you? *Deliberately?*'

A small smile. 'Well, I doubt if one beats one's children accidentally.'

A breeze had got up, ruffling the ferns that grew between the rocks. Kate wanted to sit beside him, to rest her head against his shoulder, to press her lips against the scars.

Instead, she remained sitting on a rock a few feet away, her feet dangling in the water. 'Why did he beat you?'

'Oh, I don't know,' he said vaguely. He gave his head a shake; drops of water spun into the warm air. 'I can't remember. Sometimes he got a bit carried away. He has a temper, my father. I've forgotten the particular occasion.'

She felt dizzy – with the heat, and the heaviness of the clouded sky, and with rage. She thought of Eleanor and Rebecca and Aimée, and how deeply she loved them, even though they were often infuriating. Just the thought of anyone ever hurting them made her blood boil. *I don't think I've ever actually hated anyone*, she had said to Maxwell, weeks ago, on the roof of Ravenhart House. Yet she hated now, hated someone she had never even met.

'I don't know how someone could do that to their own child,' she said. 'I mean, a smack, perhaps, when they're very naughty. But not *that*.'

'I expect I'd done something dreadful.'

321

She stared at him. 'Max, you don't really believe that, do you?'

He shrugged. 'Sometimes I try to please people, to say what I think they want me to say. And sometimes I try to annoy them – him, most of all. Living with my father is like waiting for a thunderstorm to break. You start wanting to make it happen. You know that it's going to happen anyway so you might as well get it over and done with.' He pushed a lock of damp hair out of his eyes. 'I can't remember not hating my father,' he said meditatively. 'I sometimes think it wears me out, hating him so much. Sometimes I can't think of anything else.'

Kate thought of her own father, his gentleness, his utter dependability. She missed him all the time they were apart; she had never doubted his love and protection.

'What about your mother?'

'Oh, she was under his thumb.' Maxwell smiled. 'Under his jackboot, perhaps I should say.' He dropped a pebble into the pool. 'Tell me about your family, Kate. Tell me what a nice, normal family *does*.'

'I don't know that you'd call us normal,' she said dubiously. 'Martin has a room full of skulls and bits of pottery. And my mother's been married three times. And my sister Eleanor keeps frogs as pets and Rebecca has the worst temper you've ever seen. And Frazer—'

'Frazer's not remotely normal, I grant you that.' There was a crackle of thunder and the first raindrops fell, making fat dark spots on the stone. 'As mad as a hatter, playing at being the laird in his castle while the world falls to pieces around him.'

322

She looked at him sharply. 'You do like him, don't you, Max?'

'Of course I do.'

But not as much, she thought with sudden uncomfortable intuition, as he likes you.

It began to rain harder, the force of the drops whisking up bubbles in the pool. The branches of the firs swayed in the cold wind and the boulders were hot and wet under their feet as they dashed down the path to the hunting lodge. There was only the rush of the water and the drumming of the rain and the crack of lightning and the fast beating of her heart. And his hand, holding hers, as they ran for shelter.

At the lodge, Maxwell leaned against the doorjamb, watching the rain, while he caught his breath. Outside, in the burn, the stepping stones were almost lost beneath the churning water.

She whispered, 'Perhaps we'll be stranded.'

'Perhaps.' He turned to face her. He was frowning.

Her fingers were still entwined with his. He moved closer to her. She saw his eyes dip and scan the length of her body, and she became conscious of the rivulets of water running from her hair, and the way the wet folds of her dress clung to her.

'Kate,' he said softly. 'Dear little Kate.'

Then a voice cut through the rain. 'Max! Kate!'

Maxwell said, 'The poor bugger's survived his interview with Mr Bain.' His frown deepened, he blinked, and ran the tip of his index finger slowly down her face, from brow to chin. 'It's probably just as well,' he said softly. 'You are almost nice enough to eat, darling Kate. And I'm feeling very hungry.'

They crossed the burn to meet Frazer. Water swirled round their ankles. She thought she might fall, thrown off balance by the force of the water.

Frazer smiled his familiar glorious smile, and said, 'You should come here in August, Kate. There'd be just the three of us. I won't ask anyone else. It'd be fun.'

Maxwell Gilchrist's gaze slid to her again. 'Why not?' he said.

Chapter Twelve

Frazer's idea seeded and grew. At breakfast one morning, Kate spoke to her mother.

Her mother's reply was predictable. 'Of course you must come to France with us, Kate. There's no question of you not coming.'

'I don't want to go. It was boring last year.' The wrong approach: her mother's brows snapped together. Kate added quickly, 'And if I don't go to Ravenhart House for August, Frazer will be all on his own.' A lie: the first lie.

'His friends—'

'They've all gone away. That's why he asked me to come and stay.'

Her mother said sharply, 'Don't do that with your egg, Rebecca. If you've finished, Eleanor, you may get down from the table and wash your hands.' She shovelled another spoonful of mush into Aimée's mouth. Her frown deepened. 'I invited Frazer to come to France with us this summer, but he said he couldn't. I wonder whether I should write to him again.'

Oh no, please no. The summer would be unbearable if she did not spend it at Ravenhart House — if she could not spend it with Frazer and Maxwell.

'Frazer's very busy, Mum,' she said quickly. 'All the things he's doing with the house. I said I'd help him.'

'What's this?' Martin had wandered into the dining room.

'Kate wants to go to Ravenhart House instead of coming with us to France.' Her mother sounded upset and Kate felt a stab of guilt.

'Why not?' Martin was picking up heaps of books and peering behind the breakfast china. 'We would miss you, of course, Kate.'

'But you love France, you know you do.'

'It's always the same — so boring.'

'You never used to think it was boring. Martin, what are you looking for?'

'My stethoscope. Frazer is Kate's brother, Bess. Presumably he can be trusted to care for her.'

'That's not the *point*.' Bess mopped Aimée's face with a napkin. 'I put your stethoscope in your consulting room. No, Kate, it's out of the question.'

'Mum.'

'Who else will be staying at the house?' Martin asked.

Kate made herself meet Martin's eyes. 'No one.' Beneath the table, she crossed her fingers. 'It'll be just us.'

Martin nodded. 'Then I don't really see the harm.'

'Rebecca, I told you not to play with your egg!' Bess tapped Rebecca's hand, and Rebecca threw her head back, set her body into a rigid line, and screamed.

Martin picked her out of her chair and tucked her under

one arm. Rebecca yelled and beat her feet against him as he said calmly, 'It's not impossible that Kate would like a break from family life. That the prospect of a month spent with one civilized elder brother is more appealing than a month spent with three remarkably badly behaved little sisters.'

'I'm not bad, Daddy,' said Eleanor smugly.

'Of course you are. You are quite shockingly bad.' Martin hauled a howling Rebecca out of the room. Eleanor's lip quivered.

Kate not coming to France made Bess feel as though there was a knot in the place between her heart and her stomach. Kate had often gone away before, of course, for weeks and fortnights, to stay with Ralph and Pamela, and with Frazer. But never for a month. And never instead of their holiday in France, which had always seemed to Bess the best part of the year, and about which, until now, she had always assumed that Kate felt the same way.

Kate left for Pitlochry the day before the rest of them travelled to France. Which meant that seeing Kate off at Waverley station had to be fitted into all the preparations necessary for a family of six – no, dear God, only five this year – to go away. Their cheerfulness at breakfast seemed artificial, and was punctuated by Bess saying things like, 'And you have packed enough handkerchieves?' and, 'You must remember to send a telegram as soon as you get to Pitlochry.' Then, suddenly, it was only half an hour until Kate's train. Eleanor and Rebecca both insisted on coming to the station to see Kate off, so there seemed no point in not taking Aimée as well. Aimée had to be bundled into the pram and Rebecca and Eleanor into their sandals and cardigans. And in no time at all, and without her having had the chance to finish saying all the things she needed to say, the train was pulling out of the station, and Kate, her beautiful daughter Kate, was a little gold dot waving from a window, growing smaller and smaller in the distance. And there was a hole the size of an ocean in her heart. Something irreplaceable was ending, she thought.

They never seemed to run out of things to say to each other, and the mountains walled them off from the outside world, so that sometimes it seemed as though only they existed. They rarely left the valley, only venturing out occasionally to fetch supplies from Pitlochry or Braemar. Sometimes Frazer drove the Lagonda, sometimes he let Maxwell. In the evenings, after dinner, they lounged on the flat part of the roof until the sun went down. By day, they bathed in the pool or picnicked at the hunting lodge.

Sometimes, in the early mornings, Kate walked up Ben Liath, the highest mountain in the glen. She took an apple and a chunk of bread from the kitchen, and left the house while Phemie was lighting the stove and muttering to herself. Kate thought that this was one of the best parts of the day, when everything was glistening and new and a silence hung over the valley. Sometimes she walked to the hunting lodge and sometimes she scrambled up the glen, to where the cleft in the rocks narrowed the burn to a fierce, rushing succession of torrent and pool and waterfall. Sun filtered through the branches of silver birch and rowan, making shadows move over the grass and rocks. Where the woods thickened, they were made green-black by conifers. Shafts of light pierced the open spaces between the trees.

Once, entering a clearing, Kate came across a red deer, standing almost motionless, quivering, antlers proud, only a few yards away from her through the ferns and bracken. They seemed to look at each other, her eye and its great, startled dark eye meeting for an instant, and then it was gone, and only the sway of the leaves and the echo of hooves proved to her that it had ever been there at all.

Maxwell strolled back along the drive after calling at the village to buy cigarettes and a newspaper. He crossed the little stone bridge and walked round the bend in the road. Frazer's ancestor had had a flair for the dramatic. You couldn't see Ravenhart House at all, and then, without warning, the fir trees parted, and there it was, all fairy-tale turrets and the roof gleaming silver in the sun. Maxwell glimpsed Kate in the front garden. When he had first met her, Kate Fearnley had generally been bundled up in coats and cardigans like a badly wrapped parcel. Now, she was wearing khaki shorts, a white blouse knotted round her waist, sunglasses, and a wide straw hat. Her long, slim legs seemed to go on forever. Maxwell watched her appreciatively.

The straw hat tilted back and Maxwell saw the red-gold hair beneath it. He smiled to himself. He remembered how he had almost kissed Kate in the hunting lodge. He remembered the way her damp dress had clung to her, outlining the slender contours of her figure, and how strands of her hair, darkened to chestnut by the rain, had clung to her face. Her mouth had been only a few inches from his and he had known that she had wanted him to kiss her. If he had taken her in his arms, her body would have been soft and pliant. He had been almost unable to resist her, she was so glorious, all pink and gold and inviting, like a bowl of strawberries and cream.

But then Frazer had turned up, which had probably been just as well. Maxwell knew that Kate was too young, too inexperienced, too nice for him. Maxwell also suspected that Frazer wouldn't be keen on him kissing Kate; after all, Frazer was Kate's brother, and, in his experience, brothers could be possessive, proprietorial. And it wasn't as though he had any intentions where Kate was concerned, so no point stirring things up. Kate would just be nice to kiss, and he liked her a lot, because she was kind and gentle to him in a way that few other people ever had been. He never expected kindness; he expected desire or irritation or anger – he habitually provoked those emotions, if he was honest with himself.

It was a hot day, so he stooped beside the burn and cupped water in his palms. The water was ice-cold; it still tasted, he thought, of winter. The breeze flicked at the newspaper. He scanned the headlines on the front page: there had been a military coup in Greece, and France had closed its borders after the outbreak of civil war in Spain the previous month.

Maxwell lay on his back on the grass, looking up at the clear, cloudless blue sky and the peaceful green swell of the mountains, and thought of war and rumours of war, and how, sooner or later, they would all be swept up in it. Often, lately, he had had a feeling of urgency, as though he shouldn't count on having too much time left. So much talk of war, he supposed – at twenty-four years old he knew himself to be cannon fodder.

It was almost the end of August. At the hunting lodge, Frazer and Maxwell made a fire of twigs and peat on the flat stones beside the burn; bottles of wine cooled in the shallow water. Kate cooked sausages in a pan; the skins blackened and split. After they had eaten, she paddled in the stream, her heels sinking into the bed of gravel and the stones smooth beneath her toes. The water was so cold it made her feet ache. She climbed out of the river, her footprints revealing her path along the stones. Some of the stones glittered, fragments of quartz encased in them.

She put on her sandals and headed along the path that led away onto the hillside. She felt drowsy with the heat, the wine, and the honey smell of heather. The air seemed to shimmer, to contain a lustre. Far beneath her, Maxwell lay on a flat rock beside the water, his eyes closed, his limbs flung out and his shirt unbuttoned. Kate's sunglasses hid her gaze, which focused on the brown of his skin, the musculature of his torso, and his damp, dark curls.

She turned away and continued up the hill. Rocks burst through the grass like splinters through skin. The air became cooler the higher she climbed, a breeze picking up as she left the shelter of the valley. The angle of the incline sharpened; her legs ached and she could hear her breathing. When next she looked down, Frazer and Maxwell were matchstick figures beside the silver curve of the burn and the grey oblong of the hunting lodge. Frazer had abandoned the fishing rod and was sitting on the rock beside Maxwell. Their heads almost touched, the black and the gold. Kate called out and waved her arms and they both looked up. Then she plodded on up the hill, past the shielings, the shepherds' summer pastures on the high slopes. Sheep dotted the more distant slopes like puffs of smoke from a shotgun.

She kept thinking she'd reached the summit, only to find, as she climbed over the next swell, another crest beyond. She saw that Frazer and Maxwell were coming after her, their longer legs allowing them to gain on her. She speeded up; it was suddenly important to her that she reach the summit first. The ground became rougher and she had to scramble up a cluster of tumbled boulders. The wind pushed at her, making her teeter as she perched on an outcrop of rock, the valley spread out beneath her.

At the summit, her breath caught in her throat as she looked down to the next valley, and from there out to where the hills rose one behind the other like huge blue-grey waves. It seemed to her that she was standing on the edge of the world. She swayed. Through the whine of the wind, she heard Frazer and Maxwell scramble up the final slope. One of them came to stand behind her. 'I won't let you fall,' said Maxwell. His hands rested lightly on her hip bones, his fingertips stroked her waist and she felt herself tremble.

I can't bear it, she thought. I can't make do with these little pieces any more. These touches of the hand, these brushings of skin against skin, they are no longer enough. Sometimes she was frightened of herself. Of what he might do; of what she might let him do.

They didn't go back to the house that night. They simply didn't seem to get round to it. There was too much to talk about and too much to see, and enough food left in the picnic hamper, and Maxwell standing thigh-deep in the pool, fishing, swearing that he was going to catch something. When he failed to land even a tiddler, he threw the fishing rod aside and dived down to the bottom of the pool. Frazer dived in after him, and Kate, sitting on top of a boulder, saw their forms shift and mingle, deep beneath the surface of the water.

They dried in the sun, and then they walked down the hillside to the lodge. Frazer lit a bonfire and they sat beside it, eating the remains of the food and drinking the wine they had left cooling in the stream. They smoked to keep the midges away while they played poker and pontoon, and when Maxwell lost, he muttered, 'Every time we play you fleece me, Frazer, every time,' and Frazer's face broke into a broad grin and he ruffled Max's hair. And then it was late and dark, and there didn't seem, they agreed, much point in stumbling back along the path to the house when they had the lodge. So they spread out a blanket on the floor, and Kate lay between Frazer and Maxwell – to keep her from the wild animals, said Frazer.

Not that she slept much. Not with the noises of the night – the rush of the burn and the call of an owl and the scurry of small feet as a mouse or a vole scuttled across the floor.

Not with two of the people she loved most in the world sleeping to either side of her, so close that she could feel the warmth of their bodies and hear the soft rise and fall of their breathing.

Sometime in the night, Maxwell moved closer to her. She felt his mouth touch the back of her neck, his hand run along her bare arm. When she turned to him, his lips brushed against her cheek, then her mouth. She closed her eyes, dizzy with longing. When he put his hand at the back of her neck and drew her to him, kissing her harder, she heard herself moan. His fingers dug into her hair and she felt his body, hard against hers. She wanted to go on kissing him forever, but she wanted something more as well.

Then Frazer muttered something and moved restlessly and Maxwell lay still, his arms round her, her head fitted into the hollow of his shoulder. Eventually, Kate knew that he had fallen asleep again, but she remained motionless, not wanting to disturb him, her eyes open, sensing the utter impossibility of sleep and watching through the open door of the lodge the rising sun coat the distant hills with silver.

She must have dozed off for an hour or two, because when she next opened her eyes, she was alone, and someone had tucked the blanket over her. She could see Frazer, stooped by the burn, sluicing his face. Maxwell was a few yards away, smoking a cigarette.

Kate sat up, bits of straw from the floor clinging to her clothes. She thought that what had happened that night must show on her face; her mouth felt bruised with kisses. Yet Frazer just smiled at her, and said, 'You look a bit the worse for wear, Katie. Still, I suppose we could all do with a bath.'

Maxwell yawned and stretched his arms wide. 'God, I'm starving.'

Frazer combed his wet hands through his hair. 'We'd better go back. Some of my tenant farmers are calling this morning. To talk to me about sheep or something.'

They headed back along the path to the house. They hardly spoke, and Kate's head ached – she had drunk too much wine, she supposed. She seemed to see everything with increased clarity: the fat grey clouds rushing through the sky and the purple heather, ruffled by the breeze. There was a sharpness, a vividness, that she had never noticed before, and which exhilarated and exhausted her.

As soon as they reached the house they saw the open-topped motor car parked in the forecourt. A man was lounging against the bonnet. Kate recognized him from one of Frazer's parties. A woman wearing a straw hat was wandering round the courtyard, her high-heeled shoes crunching the gravel as she glanced in a desultory fashion at the plants in the tubs.

'Good Lord,' said Frazer. 'It's the Lamptons.'

Kate's gaze was drawn to the second woman, sitting in the back of the car. Her hair was covered by a cream silk scarf, her eyes by dark glasses, and she wore a dress of cream linen. A small grey and white long-haired dog was curled in her lap. Looking at her, Kate was suddenly conscious of her own bare legs and wet sandals. She ran her fingers through her sleep-tangled hair and made a doomed attempt to straighten her crumpled clothes.

Frazer said, 'Charlie, Fiona. I didn't know you were coming.'

'Fee and I thought we'd look you chaps up. We've been motoring round your neck of the woods for a day or two.' Charlie spoke with a patrician English drawl. 'Couldn't raise anyone in the house.' His sharp pale eyes moved slowly over Frazer, Maxwell and Kate, questions contained in them. 'Been out for a ramble?'

'We camped out for the night.' Frazer shook Charlie's hand and kissed the woman in the straw hat.

Charlie said, 'This is a friend of ours, Naomi Jennings.' He held open the back door of the car. As Naomi stepped out, the dog jumped from her lap and ran across the courtyard.

'This is my sister, Kate,' said Frazer. Naomi's gloved hand briefly touched Kate's.

Then she removed her sunglasses, revealing dark, lustrous eyes. 'Susie!' she called to the dog. 'Susie, come here!'

Maxwell scooped up the dog and crossed the courtyard to her. 'Yours, I think,' he said, and smiled.

'So sweet of you,' murmured Naomi. Her dark eyes studied Maxwell as he dropped the dog into her waiting arms.

He said, 'What on earth is it?'

'Susie's a shih-tzu. Aren't you, darling? A chrysanthemum dog.' Her gaze dropped at last; she planted a kiss on the dog's head.

Frazer found himself inviting them all to stay. They seemed to expect it. He chased up the lad who helped in the garden to carry in their bags, and told Mrs McGill to make up two of the bedrooms. Then he and Maxwell showed the Lamptons and Naomi Jennings round the house. Charlie and Fiona, who had, after all, seen the place before at one party or another, drifted off quite soon to sit outside under the cedar tree, so there was just Frazer and Maxwell and Naomi left. Frazer wasn't sure where Kate had gone – to have a nap or a bath, perhaps.

Naomi admired the house. Every now and then she would say, in her low, throaty voice, 'Too stunning – such a view,' or, 'These old places – so divinely romantic.' After a while, Frazer, who had the dazed, jumpy feeling that comes from not enough sleep, fell silent, and he let Max point out the interesting bits. Pieces of Max and Naomi's conversation pierced the silence of the corridors as they walked from room to room.

Then the tenant farmers arrived, and Frazer had to endure their moans about the recent rent rise as well as all their niggling concerns about grazing rights and access paths and hikers letting dogs off the leash, all served up in the locality's thick, clotted accent, so that he had to concentrate hard to make out what they were saying. And then, when at last they left, Frazer was able to share with his guests a dreadful lunch of stew and gritty rice pudding – Mrs McGill's revenge for the arrival of three unexpected visitors, he supposed. There was some talk of a walk, which never came to anything because the weather had begun to turn, clouds gathering and blotting out the sun, and besides, a languor had fallen over the company, so they sat instead in a room at the back of the house, leafing through magazines and drinking coffee, their chatter, of friends and weddings and holidays, becoming more and more disjointed inside Frazer's head until eventually he dozed off.

He must have slept soundly, because waking was like forcing himself up out of the deepest part of the pool. He blinked, trying to get his bearings. The clock on the mantelpiece said it was almost four o'clock. All the other chairs were empty. When he looked out of the window, he saw that Charlie Lampton's car had gone.

He wandered up through the house, searching for everyone. Eventually, out of a back window, he caught sight of Max and Naomi, small, dark figures against the purple heather on the hills. They had been to the hunting lodge, he guessed, which for some reason rather took him aback – perhaps because it was hard to imagine Naomi with her high heels and her pale, well-cut clothes, tackling the stepping stones across the burn. Frazer watched them walk along the path. The dog skittered beside them, and Frazer noticed, not for the first time, the way Max's hands always moved as he talked.

Something jarred; he couldn't quite pinpoint it. At dinner that night he found that the contentment of the summer had evaporated; he felt irritable and sluggish with having slept deeply in the wrong part of the day. He thought that some of the others shared his mood – Kate hardly said a word, and Charlie and Fiona had come back from their drive fractious and sharp-tongued, and carried on their quarrel in a muted way throughout the meal.

Only Max and Naomi seemed untouched by ill feeling. Naomi laughed and purred, and Max was on form, telling funny stories and doing the tenant farmers to a T. It was almost, Frazer found himself thinking as he watched them, as though none of the rest of them were there at all.

Much later, looking back, Kate saw how inevitable it was that Maxwell and Naomi Jennings should fall in love with each other. Though perhaps love was the wrong word, because love surely implied tenderness, consideration, gentleness. What Max and Naomi, those kindred spirits, felt for each other had no softer components. Their passion was something darker, like the void in the heart of a whirlwind, born of hunger and desire and a recognition that, beautiful and damaged, they were made for each other. At the time, she didn't know that, of course. Kate knew only that something was out of joint; she blamed numbers, timing.

The Lamptons headed off early the following morning, leaving Naomi at Ravenhart. A small hand squeezed Frazer's arm and great dark eyes stared at him imploringly. 'Such a gorgeous house. I can't possibly leave so soon. I'll take a train or something home. You don't mind, do you, darling Frazer?' And Frazer, polite, generous, obliging Frazer, said, 'Of course not, old thing. The more the merrier.'

Where once there had been three, now, on this precious last day of Kate's holiday, there were four. Naomi Jennings' husky voice echoed in Ravenhart's rooms; her scent, sharp and floral, lingered in the corridors. There was the obligation to entertain her, their guest, to offer walks and drives, to dine at the big mahogany table instead of cooking sausages on a bonfire by the burn. The obligation to try to find a neat frock and an unladdered pair of stockings from her jumble of clothes, clothes which had unaccountably, during her month at Ravenhart House, shed buttons and acquired grass stains. And all the time, Kate seemed to move around in a daze, as though she had been woken too suddenly out of a particularly pleasant dream and couldn't quite readjust herself to the ordinary day. At lunch, she knocked over the sugar bowl and spilt coffee into her saucer. Her efforts to make conversation were stumbling and clumsy. After a while, she left it to the others.

She had believed that the night that she and Maxwell and Frazer had spent at the hunting lodge had been a beginning. It took her a long time to accept that it had been, in fact, an end. She had slept in Maxwell Gilchrist's arms and he had kissed her, yet only a day later she found herself doubting her memory of what had happened. Maxwell neither spoke of their kiss nor touched her again. He had had no opportunity to, she told herself, because of the Lamptons and Naomi Jennings.

The weather had broken, rain sweeping across a grey sky. In the afternoon, while Kate packed, Frazer lent Maxwell his car so that he could take Naomi out for a drive. They were gone for most of the afternoon; eventually, Frazer went to stand at the window, watching for them.

After a while, Kate heard his sharp indrawn breath. Looking out, she saw that the Lagonda had burst through the curtain of fir trees and was veering down the driveway, weaving from side to side. 'Something's wrong,' said Frazer sharply, and hurried outside. Kate followed him.

The car slewed across the drive and over the lawn, towards the cedar. Kate saw that Naomi, not Maxwell, was driving.

Maxwell reached over and grabbed the steering wheel from Naomi, and the car came to a halt a yard away from the tree. Naomi flopped over the steering wheel, shaking. Kate thought at first that she was crying. It was only when she and Frazer had almost reached the car that they heard Naomi's peal of laughter.

The following day, the day she had to leave Ravenhart, she discovered at breakfast that Naomi and Maxwell had gone out already. She was sure he would be back in time to see her off, couldn't believe that he had forgotten that she was going home that day. She kept looking out of the window, certain that she would see him, coming back along the hill path. Even when Frazer told her that they must go or she would miss the train, she was sure Max would be waiting for her beside Mr Bain's lodge, or even – a wild, stupid thought – that he would somehow have travelled the ten miles to Pitlochry, and would be waiting for her on the station platform.

But he wasn't, of course, and the train arrived, though even when she'd found a seat in a crowded carriage, there was still a small part of her that thought she'd see him. She stared out of the window, as though the intensity of her thoughts could conjure him up. The train pulled out of the platform and her gaze lifted up to the bridge, to the parapet. But he was not there, and as the train gathered speed, the shops and houses of the town were replaced by trees and fields. Stupid, stupid, Kate, she thought, and closed her eyes tightly, biting her lip hard. Something must have held him up; it didn't *mean* anything that he had not seen her off.

When she was sure she would not cry, she opened her eyes again. Images from her month at Ravenhart still reeled across her mind, like a film set too fast. Maxwell and Frazer, blurred by the deep water of the pool; Maxwell bending over her in the darkness of the hunting lodge; Naomi Jennings' small hands caressing her dog. And the fury in Frazer's eyes as he watched his car skid across Ravenhart's lawn.

In September, Kate started a secretarial job. It was good for Kate, Bess thought, to be doing something sensible and settled. For work, Kate wore a smart skirt, blouse and cardigan. In the evenings and at weekends, Kate had taken to wearing rather odd clothes – brightly coloured blouses with bead necklaces picked up from rummage sales, or hopsack skirts and black jumpers which she made herself. Sometimes Kate borrowed one of Bess's Indian shawls, looping it round her narrow shoulders; sometimes she wore trousers. Bess had only ever worn trousers for riding or, during the war, when she had gardened at Hollins Lodge. It seemed contrary of Kate, who was growing into such an attractive young woman, to choose to look like a barrow boy.

When Eleanor went back to school in September, Rebecca joined her for the mornings in the nursery class. At four and a half, Rebecca was heartbreakingly pretty, with large deep blue eyes and long dark hair that Bess combed into beribboned plaits. Rebecca was all girl – she adored pretty clothes, often insisting, with tears or tantrums, on wearing her party dress to go to the shops. Bess hoped that nursery would settle Rebecca down, and would modify that touch of autocracy in her nature. Kate, Eleanor and Rebecca were all, in their different ways, determined and driven. If they wanted something, they wouldn't rest until they had got it. Bess supposed that her three eldest daughters had inherited their will and their stubbornness from her.

Aimée was different; Aimée was Martin's child and lived much of the time in an inner world. Like Martin, Aimée possessed a distance, a self-suffiency, that Bess sometimes found frustrating. In the course of a year and a quarter, Aimée had grown a head of hair so fine and pale it was almost colourless, and her eyes had become the colour of agate. She was a fair, slight, little thing, as insubstantial as thistledown. A freakish-looking child, Bess still thought privately, with those strange eyes too large for her head and that fringe of silvery hair. Amiable by nature, she had fitted easily into the family, content to be picked up and played with by sisters and friends and made a fuss of by the steady stream of visitors who had recently come to stay.

Their visitors were old friends or colleagues of Martin's from Germany. They would arrive at the Jagos' house at any hour of the day or night. They were academics or doctors, Jews or Communists or trade unionists, or just misfits, driven out of the country of their birth by the new laws that the Nazi government had put in place. Sometimes they were alone, sometimes they had their families in tow, their quiet wives and their confused, frightened children. They stayed in the slope-ceilinged attic rooms at the top of the house, rooms that offered them a little privacy. Some of them spoke English, and Martin had good German, and every now and then they would seem to relax a little, and they would talk about archaeological expeditions or about happier days in Berlin or Frankfurt. But often, at night, Bess heard them moving about, their footsteps padding quietly on the ceiling above her, sleepless in a strange house, a strange city. And after a few days or weeks they always moved on, sometimes to other parts of Britain, sometimes to America.

Now, the attic rooms were a temporary home to Gregor and Resi Schmidt. The Schmidts were in their late twenties. Resi was small and slender, her blonde curls tumbling to one side of her face. Her eyebrows were plucked to thin, high Marlene Dietrich arches, and she never left her room without face powder and lipstick, expertly applied. Resi's clothes were always smart and well pressed; Bess noticed that Resi kept Rebecca and Aimée at arm's length, as if afraid of creases or grubby fingermarks on her pale green linen skirt.

Gregor Schmidt was short, dark and broad-shouldered. In Berlin, he had worked as a stage manager in a theatre, which was where he had met Resi, who was a dancer. His nose, which must once have been Roman, veered off to the side of his face, a legacy of the year he had spent in Dachau concentration camp in punishment for his Communist sympathies. If you spoke to Gregor, you must stand to the left of him, as his right eardrum had been permanently shattered in Dachau.

The Schmidts had been staying with the Jagos for almost a fortnight when Gregor left the house early one morning to visit his shipping agent to arrange their passages to the

United States. Bess took Eleanor to school and, after picking up some shopping, returned to the house. There was no sign of Resi, who had not come down to breakfast. At ten o'clock, Mrs Tate always made coffee – Martin could not get through the morning without hourly cups of strong, black coffee – so Bess went up to the attics to ask Resi whether she would like a cup. When there was no answer to her knock, she pushed open the door. It took a shocked, nauseating moment to accept that what she saw, lying on the bed, was Resi. There seemed to be blood everywhere – Resi's jaunty curls were stained with blood, and her neat clothes were clotted with it. The metallic smell of blood pervaded the room. Bess ran downstairs to get Martin.

Through the jarring chaos of the next few hours, as the ambulance arrived to take Resi to hospital, and as she helped Mrs Tate clean the Schmidts' room and wash the bedding, Bess kept seeing it over and over again, Resi Schmidt, lying on the bed, bathed in blood from her slit wrists. Smart, pretty little Resi, who hadn't liked the babies near her because she worried about damp patches and jammy fingers.

Martin returned to the house shortly after seven o'clock. The younger children were in bed and Mrs Tate had gone home. Bess and Kate were in the kitchen, clearing up a supper that neither of them had much wanted to eat.

Martin took off his coat. 'They think she'll pull through. She's very weak, of course, but she's come round. Gregor's sitting with her.'

Bess felt shaky with relief. 'Thank God.'

Kate opened the oven. 'Supper, Martin?'

'What is it?'

'Shepherd's pie.'

'Some bread and cheese later, maybe.'

'I don't blame you,' said Kate, hanging up the tea towel. 'There's butter beans in it.' She made a face.

'Perhaps a brandy.'

'I'll get it.' Kate left the room.

Martin sat down beside Bess. 'I'm sorry.'

'What for?'

'For bringing such tragedy into our home.'

She whispered, 'I thought she was dead.'

'If you hadn't found her when you did . . .' The sentence died, incomplete.

Kate came back into the room with the brandy bottle and glasses. She unstoppered the bottle and poured out two measures. Then she said to Martin, 'Why did Resi do it?'

'I don't know.' He took off his spectacles and rubbed his eyes. 'One never really knows. I blame myself. I should have seen it coming. I should have guessed.'

His voice was flat, and he looked drawn. These days, there was more than a feathering of grey round his temples, and hard work and time had carved deep lines into his face. There was grey in Bess's hair, too, which took her by surprise every time she saw it, brushing out her hair at night. How could she, Bess Jago, be growing old?

Kate said, 'We were trying to help her. Why did she try and kill herself when we were trying to help her? When they'd got away from Germany – when they were *safe*.'

'I suppose she was desperate.' Martin gave a fleeting smile. 'We say that about such little things, don't we? About missing a train, or about wanting something very much.

But true despair, the feeling that it might be preferable to be dead, we don't experience that often, thank God.'

'Do you think that Resi felt desperate because they'd hurt Gregor?'

'It could have been that, yes, Kate. It's hard to see someone you love suffer. Particularly when, as with Gregor and Resi, there's nothing whatever they can do. No possibility of vengeance.'

'Or justice,' said Kate.

'Or justice,' acknowledged Martin. 'Germany's a dictatorship. One man makes the laws. Gregor and Resi fell foul of those laws.'

Kate was turning the stopper of the brandy bottle over and over in her hand. 'They hurt him deliberately,' she said slowly. 'How could they do that?'

Bess took the shepherd's pie dish out of the oven. The topping had charred and the gravy was congealed. She scraped it into the bin and put the dish in the sink. She said, 'Really, darling, you must try not to worry about it.'

'I want to know, Mum. Why do people want to hurt other people?'

Martin was polishing his spectacles with a rather grubby handkerchief. 'Sometimes it's to reinforce authority. If you make people afraid, they'll do as they're told.'

'Do you think some people like hurting other people?'

Bess filled the dish with water. 'Kate, you mustn't think about things like that.'

'But do they?'

'Perhaps.' Martin sighed. 'Yes, I'm afraid a few people do.'

'But why?'

'It could be because they themselves feel powerless. They take out their rage on those weaker than themselves. And there are people who enjoy violence for its own sake. I hope there aren't many of them, but I know that there are some. A system of government such as Nazi Germany's allows them a voice – and power.'

'But I still don't see why.'

'I don't really know, Kate – childhood trauma, perhaps. If you're treated cruelly as a child, it sets up a pattern. Perhaps you think of violence as normal, acceptable, even. I can recommend you some psychology textbooks to read, if you wish. Freud said . . .'

Bess went outside. In the basement courtyard she felt as if she could breathe again. She had filled the small, paved area with terracotta pots of jasmine and lilies, and their scent perfumed the air. She closed the door behind her to shut out the voices. Sitting down, she drank her brandy in an attempt to quell the panicking, unsteady feeling that had settled in her stomach since she had pushed open the door of Resi Schmidt's room.

She found herself thinking of the two times in her life she had despaired, as Resi Schmidt must this morning have despaired. The first time had been after her visit to Sheldon Ravenhart, when she had known that Cora Ravenhart had taken Frazer from her. The second time had been after Andrew Gilchrist had raped her. Both times she had felt powerless. Both times, something irreplaceable had been taken away from her, some spark, some piece of herself. She never, ever wanted Kate to feel as she had then. She never, ever wanted any of her children to feel as she had then, and she would do everything in her power to ensure that they never did.

Yet some things were beyond her control. Any hope that she had once had that the Nazis would moderate their views when they were in power had long since been dispelled. The hope of the left-wing, that Hitler would prove himself incompetent and would be voted out at the next election, had also foundered. Elections, along with every other trace of democracy, had been banished from the German political system.

The newspapers daily reported wars, coups, and outrages against civilian populations. Civil war had broken out in Spain in July. Backed by the army, General Franco had risen against the democratically elected Popular Front. Towards the end of August, Franco's Nationalists had bombed Madrid, using German warplanes. Hundreds of civilians had been killed and thousands wounded. In a shuffling of position that had deepened Martin's pessimism and alarmed Bess, Germany and Italy had aligned with General Franco. The Soviet Union backed the Republic, while Britain and France had chosen to remain neutral. British politicians warned of the impossibility of stopping the bombing, and spoke of the many civilian casualties that would inevitably result if Britain became involved in another European war. The goverment's announcement that every Briton must be trained in the use of gas masks sent a chill down Bess's spine.

No one, this time, viewed the prospect of war with enthusiasm or with confident expectation of easy victory, as they had in 1914. Bess would have liked to join the pacifists, the Peace Pledge Union, perhaps, which already claimed hundreds of thousands of members. But something held her back. What could pacifism, however fine its motives, achieve against those who caused despair? Neither reason nor self-abasement had saved her from Andrew Gilchrist. Men who hated, men who wanted to hurt, were not swayed by negotiation or appeasement.

And yet the thought of another war appalled her. Her memories of the last war, and of the absences and losses it had inflicted, were far too strong for her to view the possibility of further conflict with anything other than deep repugnance. Thank God I have daughters, Martin had said to her one evening, after he had switched off the wireless. *Frazer*, she had said, *and Ralph and Pamela's boys*. He had put his arms round her and held her to him.

All those years she had fought to protect her children. All those years she had waited for Frazer to come home. The thought of losing him now to some quarrel made of other men's greed and hatred was unbearable. She thought of all the men who had been broken by the Great War. She thought of Alex Findlay's years of suffering, and of what war had done to both Martin and Ralph. She knew that Frazer was not made to be a soldier, any more than they had been.

Naomi Jennings' family lived in Virginia Water, in Surrey. Her father, who worked in a merchant bank, was busy and distant; her brothers, Simon and Julian, were some years older than her. She was her mother's longed-for daughter, but Naomi had always sensed that she disappointed. Her mother would have liked a pink-and-white, biddable sort of girl, who played with her dolls and could be shown off to friends. Instead, she found herself with a tomboy who climbed the trees in the Jennings' large garden, and who preferred to play with her brothers' friends rather than with the polite little daughters of her mother's set. And there was something unsuitable, slightly common even, about Naomi's excitable, emotional nature.

The mismatch worsened throughout Naomi's adolescence. Entering her teens, Naomi often felt as though she was enveloped in a haze of boredom. As she grew older, some experiences pierced the cloud. She discovered that she loved to be driven fast and to sail in a fast yacht. She adored drinking champagne and smoking cigarettes and the company of people who possessed a reckless courage similar to her own.

When she was sixteen, she discovered sex. Her first lover was the son of a colleague of her father's. Naomi lost her virginity in the stables of a house in Buckinghamshire; for months afterwards, the smell of hay brought back the mingling of pain and pleasure that characterized that encounter. She saw her lover a few times afterwards, stolen meetings that involved her slipping out of her boarding school on Sunday afternoons, and which eventually led to her expulsion. Her parents found her another school; she did not hear from the boy again.

Other boys followed, in Surrey, and then in Paris and in Switzerland, where she was sent to finishing school. After a year abroad, groomed from head to toe and knowing how to cook a mushroom soufflé and how to step out of a motor car without showing too much leg, she returned to England. She spent the next two years going to parties and to weekends in the country. In a futile attempt to keep boredom at bay, she helped in a friend's hat shop and briefly worked as a mannequin, a job that consisted of parading in expensive frocks in front of a handful of wealthy ladies and their debutante daughters in the private room of a London department store.

She also took lovers. Boys her own age at first, and then, when they began to tire her, older, sometimes married men. There was still that underlying restlessness, that discontent that, after a few weeks or months, poisoned the first rapture, pointing out to her the dullness of her lover's conversation, or making her focus on the imperfections of his appearance, the flush of pimples on the back of his neck, the bushiness of his eyebrows. She always broke it off before they had a chance to finish with her – she had learned that from her first love affair.

Then, a year ago, she had been unlucky, and she had got caught, and had found herself vomiting up her breakfast in the morning. Her mother had correctly diagnosed her daughter's complaint before Naomi herself had understood that she was expecting a baby. In the green and cream perfection of the Jennings' bathroom, her mother, her face twisted with anger, screamed at her, 'Who's the father? Who?' and then, after Naomi blurted out that she wasn't absolutely sure, her mother recovered her customary composure, and said, coldly, 'You silly little slut. You're not to tell anyone, ever, do you hear? Daddy will have to know because of the money, but no one else, not your brothers, not Tessa or Hazel, no one at all.'

The next day, Naomi was whisked off to a clinic in Harley Street; the day after that, they rid her of her baby. She spent five cold, silent days in a small hotel in Bournemouth, recuperating, and then she and her mother went home. It took Naomi a while to realize that nothing would ever be the same again. Her father, who hardly spoke to her now, slashed her allowance; her mother, her eyes set like stones, watched her like a hawk. Her parents' hopes of a grand marriage for their beautiful daughter were forgotten; anyone would do so long as he had money, so long as he came from a respectable family. Mrs Jennings surveyed their circle of stockbroker and banker friends with a calculating gaze, judging which of their sons might be secured for Naomi.

The baby was never mentioned. It might, Naomi often thought, never have existed. Only she seemed to mourn it, tears oozing silently from her eyes when she woke too early in the mornings. She had never been interested in babies before, but now she felt as though something important had been taken away from her, something that might have quelled the boredom.

It took her months to shake off her wretchedness. Trapped in the dull, comfortable prison of her home, her parents' disapproval of her – dislike of her, perhaps – seemed an almost tangible thing. Lack of money put paid to her usual diversions of buying new frocks and going to nightclubs, but she sometimes thought that even if she had had a purse full of banknotes, she still wouldn't have cared much for new clothes or for going out.

One afternoon, she burst into tears at one of her mother's bridge parties. Once she had started crying, she couldn't stop. Her mother slapped her face and sent her to bed; the doctor prescribed rest and a change of scenery. A few days later, her mother told her that she was to holiday in Switzerland with her brother and his wife. Among the mountains and lakes she had always loved, she began, at last, to feel better. There would be other babies, she told herself, babies she could keep. She would marry, and have a family and a home of her own. It was the obvious answer.

On her return to England, her mother relaxed her vigilance – wary, Naomi suspected, of another embarrassing outburst of emotion. The Jennings didn't *do* emotion. They distrusted it. Figures, balance sheets, were so much more reliable.

In August, she toured Scotland with the Lamptons, who were old friends of the family. Naomi discovered that she adored Scotland as much as she had loved Switzerland. She loved the wild scenery and the extreme weather, the rainstorms and the hailstorms, and the soft shallow sunlight of the north.

She became tired of Charlie and Fiona quite soon. They bickered constantly, and once, when Fiona had gone up early to bed and she and Charlie were left alone in the drawing room of the hotel, he made a pass at her. Though she gave him the brush-off, something in his knowing expression left her wondering whether some rumour of her disgrace had reached his ears.

The next day, they drove to Ravenhart. The castle, with its arrow-slit windows and fairy-tale pinnacles, took Naomi's breath away. The setting, in a valley surrounded by mountains, seemed to her incomparably romantic.

And then she saw Maxwell Gilchrist. He had the sort of looks she liked, dark and gypsyish, and, that morning, his blue-green eyes were heavy with sleep, his clothes crushed and rumpled, as though he had slept in them. Frazer Ravenhart owned the house; Frazer's sister, Kate, was staying there for the summer. As Charlie introduced her, Naomi found her gaze darting between the three of them, Maxwell and Frazer and Kate, wondering what was going on. Because there was *something* going on — she always had a sense for these things — though she couldn't quite work out what.

She would have wanted Maxwell Gilchrist even if she had not first seen him backed by Ravenhart and its mountains and glens. He was what she had been searching for all these years. She hardly glanced at Frazer, though he was, in his utterly different way, just as handsome as Maxwell. Yet it was Maxwell who suited the house, not Frazer. There was something brooding about it, she discovered, a dangerous edge. Stairs spat you out in unexpected places, lose your footing and you might tumble to your death. High on the roof, only a shallow balustrade divided you from the precipice.

Meeting Maxwell Gilchrist made Naomi feel as though a light had been switched on, a light that had been extinguished for a long time. There was a sensation in the pit of her stomach that she had almost forgotten, the twist of excitement she felt when someone she desired looked at her. And he did look at her, she could feel the heat of his gaze.

She knew, though, that you didn't get a man like Maxwell Gilchrist by throwing yourself at him. And she had learned to be wary, not to give away too much, too soon. Not till she was sure. She had just enough insight to know how brittle she was, like a flawed piece of glass that would shatter at the smallest touch.

Chapter Thirteen

Kate couldn't at first work out why Frazer tolerated Naomi Jennings' presence at Ravenhart House, and then, of course, thinking about it, she knew that it was because of Maxwell. Frazer was afraid that if he refused to invite Naomi to Ravenhart, he would see less of Maxwell. Though Kate had known for a long time that Frazer was fond of Maxwell, it shocked her to realize that Frazer was so fond of him he would, for Max's sake, have someone he actively disliked to stay in his house.

Because Frazer *did* dislike Naomi. Though he made some attempt to hide it, Kate saw the way he looked at Naomi, the coldness in his eye and the way his knuckles whitened or he shifted in his chair the moment she came into a room. Kate wondered at first whether Frazer, too, was attracted to Naomi – love made you behave oddly, she had learned that, and perhaps Frazer disliked Naomi because she had chosen Maxwell and not him – but then she noticed how he shrank away from Naomi's touch. Every so often,

Naomi would make some coquettish gesture to Frazer – a seductive smile and a squeeze of his hand – and Frazer's lip would curl in distaste. Naomi's little hands ruffled Frazer's hair as her throaty voice cooed, 'I'm so bored. You'll lend us your lovely car, won't you, darling?' and Kate saw the flicker of anger in his eyes.

Kate wondered whether Naomi's caresses were intended to repel, whether it amused her to see Frazer squirm. Or whether the person Naomi was really taunting was Maxwell, to make him jealous. If so, it didn't work, because Maxwell just went on smoking or drinking or eating his dinner, or, at the most, drawled, 'Put the poor chap down, Naomi. I'll fetch your dog if you need something to torment.'

Which made Kate, to begin with, feel relieved. Maxwell could not be in love with Naomi if he spoke to her like that. His lack of reaction sometimes provoked in Naomi sulks or outbursts of temper, which Maxwell on the whole ignored. Surely, if Maxwell loved Naomi, he would not laugh when she refused to speak to him or when she flounced out of the room, the dog tucked under her arm.

Her relief was momentary, though. Frazer might shrink away from Naomi, but Naomi and Maxwell were unable to stop touching each other. They seemed to stick together, like the tiny claws on a zip. Passing Maxwell in a room, Naomi's fingertips would drift across his shoulders, lingering on a sleeve, as though she could not bear to relinquish that small, final touch. Beneath the dinner table, Maxwell would run the tip of his toe along the arch of Naomi's foot. Walking along the hill path together, their fingers entwined and clung, only separating when forced to do so by the terrain. They murmured endearments, gave each other pet names. Once, they swam in the pool, and Kate saw how, in the depths, their bodies twisted round each other like two serpents spiralling together. Afterwards, when they were sitting on the bank and Naomi was shaking because of the cold, Maxwell dried her, wrapping the towel round her, helping her on with her sweater. When, back at the hunting lodge, they lit the fire and he combed out Naomi's thick, dark hair, Kate had to look away, to dig her fingernails into her palms, to force herself not to cry out.

Kate had been working since the beginning of September for a firm of solicitors. She had known from her first day that the job wasn't right for her. Though her colleagues were perfectly pleasant and her boss wasn't overly demanding, there was something missing. Her mind was only half occupied, her passions hardly engaged at all. Part of her knew that she had made a dreadful mistake and that she should have done as Martin had suggested a year ago and tried for university. A lack of courage had made her accept second-best, and she disliked herself for that.

It was lack of courage, too, she later acknowledged, that made her continue to visit Ravenhart House long after she had ceased to feel happy there. At the back of her mind she suspected that nothing would ever be the same any more, and at Ravenhart, where everyone drank too much and smoked too much and hardly seemed to sleep at all, there seemed often to be a scent of disaster in the air, yet she still took the train up to Pitlochry on a Friday evening after work once or twice a month.

But it was hard to accept that she was not important, that she had been pushed to the periphery, an insignificant onlooker in a drama in which the three main participants were absorbed only in themselves. Seeing Maxwell and Naomi together, witnessing their mutual obsession, was like running fingernails across already grazed flesh. She went back, she supposed, because she had to know, and because she could not yet rid herself of the ragged remnants of hope.

One evening, she went up to the flat roof. She was halfway through the trapdoor, hidden by shadows, when she realized that she was not alone. Silhouetted against a churning purplish-grey sky, Naomi was standing on the balustrade, the sheer cliff edge of the wall of the house a single step behind her. Maxwell said sharply, 'For Christ's sake, Mimi, get down from there,' and Naomi, laughing, held out her arms to him.

'Come and get me, Max.' Then she swayed.

The breath caught in Kate's throat; she saw Maxwell dart across and catch Naomi round the waist.

'You stupid cow. You stupid, stupid cow.'

Then he kissed her, a long, deep kiss, their bodies moulding against each other, fitting into each other's hollows and swells. When they separated, Maxwell put his hand to his mouth. As he drew it away, Kate saw the scarlet staining his fingertips.

'You bit me. Jesus, Mimi, you bit me.'

But he did not sound angry.

Another time, late at night, she heard raised voices along a corridor. Kate stood motionless, letting the darkness settle round her, stilling the rustling folds of her silk dress with her flattened hands.

Maxwell first, as a door was flung open. 'You don't own me.'

'Don't I?' Frazer was speaking, his voice rough and angry. 'What about the loan, Max? Of course, loan is hardly the appropriate word, is it?'

'As soon as I've got some cash – when I've finished the book—'

'You'll never finish it. You know that yourself. You never stick anything out.'

A curse – 'Be damned to you, then' – footsteps heading down the corridor, a slammed door.

In her room, Kate took off her dress. It was violet-blue silk – she had chosen and bought the material herself, and her mother had helped her make it. She had wanted a new dress so that Maxwell would notice her again, so that he would take a strand of her hair between his fingers and say, *such gorgeous hair, like apricots.*

The next day, at breakfast, Maxwell and Frazer were sour, unspeaking, brittle. Only Naomi, humming as she fed Susie scraps of toast under the table, seemed untroubled. The men started drinking before midday; over lunch, the conversation drifted to the civil war that was raging in Spain. Kate heard herself filling the silences, making soothing, conciliatory remarks, trying to stave something off.

Maxwell said suddenly to Naomi, 'What's wrong? Nothing to say?'

Naomi pouted. 'You know I'm not interested in politics, Max darling.'

There was a dark glitter in Maxwell's eyes. 'What about you, Frazer? Have you been keeping up with international events? Damned confusing, I'll grant you that. All those different factions – can you tell your anarchists from your anarcho-syndicalists, Frazer?'

'I haven't a clue. Does it matter?'

Maxwell shrugged. 'All Reds, aren't they? And an awfully long way away. The only thing is, there's Germany and Austria and Italy fallen to the Fascists already, and if Spain were to go too, it would seem to tip the balance in a rather horrible way. And maybe make another war unavoidable.' His voice softened; he leaned across the table to Frazer. 'But then, it probably is, anyway. And perhaps you wouldn't mind. Perhaps you've a penchant for the strong leader and a bit of whip-cracking and shiny leather boots? For myself, I couldn't stand the uniforms.'

Frazer flushed. 'Of course I don't think that.'

Maxwell leaned back in his chair. 'Perfectly understandable if your sympathies are with the Nationalists. Got to look after your own, haven't you? Anarchists have been picking off landowners in Spain with the bullet and the bomb for quite a while now. How would you feel if they did that here?'

'I should hate it, of course. It would be unthinkable.'

'I suppose it would.' Maxwell emptied his glass. 'Just think, fifty years ago some rich Ravenhart who's made a packet through his cotton mills or coal mines decides he fancies living in a castle, buys up a bit of cheap land in Perthshire, throws up his Victorian monstrosity and brings in a herd of red deer so that his friends can have fun taking pot shots at them when they come to stay for the weekend. But then the red deer eat the crops that belong to the poor bastards who've been farming the land for decades and suddenly they can't feed their families any more. I wonder if, when they were packing their bags to leave their homes, any of them thought of putting a knife in *your* ancestor's belly, Frazer?'

Frazer's eyes met Maxwell's. 'It was *his* land.'

'True enough. But it was *their* homes.'

There was a silence. Then Maxwell rose unsteadily to his feet, muttered, 'Got to get some air,' and left the room. Naomi ran after him.

Frazer's gaze followed them. There was the sound of the front door opening and closing. Frazer threw back his head and swallowed the remainder of his wine and then roared for Phemie to fetch another bottle. When he had a drink in his hand again he muttered, 'Winds him round her little finger. He can't keep away from her. I've never seen him like this before. I mean, he likes women, I've always known that, but I've always assumed he beds them and then forgets about them.'

A jolt: that Frazer, her polite, courteous elder brother, should talk to her like that. For the first time Kate realized how drunk he was.

He began to speak again, the words slightly slurred. 'He's let that creature get under his skin.' A croak of laughter, and then his eyes narrowed. 'Perhaps he hasn't bedded her. Perhaps that's her secret. She might look stupid, but maybe she's cleverer than I thought. Perhaps old Max has met his match at last.' He shook his head slowly. 'No, he's had her

363

– you can tell, can't you? He can't get enough of her. And doesn't she know she's got him under her thumb.'

'You shouldn't talk about Max like that, Frazer. He's your friend.'

'And yours too, Kate?'

She looked away, seeing the knowledge in his eyes. She heard him say mockingly, 'Oh dear, you haven't gone and fallen for him too, have you?'

'Frazer—'

'More fool you if you have. Bad mistake. And you such a sensible girl.'

'Stop it, Frazer.'

'Now, any chap with any sense would prefer you to Naomi, but I don't know that Max *has* a lot of sense.'

'I said, stop it.' She put her hands over her ears; she was almost in tears.

He moved unsteadily to the sofa and sat, one arm flung along the back. Then he said, almost to himself, 'D'you know what really browns me off? When I think of everything I've done for him and then half the time he can't even manage to turn up when he says he's going to.'

'You don't do things for people – for friends – and expect some sort of *payback*.'

'How very idealistic you are, Kate.' Frazer's gaze, resting on her, had become cold. 'You'll see. Max'll come running when he wants something from me. It's always the same. Just a question of waiting it out. Waiting out his little enthusiasms.'

Kate wanted to run from the room, to escape the bitterness in Frazer's voice and the disillusion in his eyes.

But she said, 'Friendship isn't about *money*, it isn't about *possessions*.'

'Of course it is.' His tone was contemptuous. 'It's about what you can get. Money, a decent dinner, something to take your mind off all the things you'd rather not think about.'

'But what about affection? What about companionship?'

'How many of the people who visit me here would bother if I hadn't the house and the money? They're here because of what I can give them, that's all. How many of them would come all this way to see me if I lived in a slum?'

She said angrily, 'Then perhaps you should find other friends.'

'You make it sound so easy.' His tone was vicious. 'Like picking out new shirts in a shop.'

'No.' She shook her head. 'No, it's you who thinks that friendship can be bought.'

He looked down at his glass. When he spoke, his voice was so low she had to strain to hear him. 'But you have to pay more and more, don't you? The price always seems to go up.'

She felt nauseated. But beneath his scorn, she recognized his intense loneliness. She went to sit beside him, and said gently, 'You have a family, too, Frazer. You've got us.'

'Have I?' His cornflower-blue eyes returned to her, cool and questioning. 'You managed without me for long enough, didn't you? If I went away, how long do you think it would be before you forgot me again?'

* * *

365

Afterwards, Martin Jago looked upon the year of 1936 as a dividing line, a watershed. Before, though there had been a darkening of the skies, he could still believe that the worst might be avoided, that the world might yet see sense before it was too late. By the time the year ended, a year in which horror had followed closely upon horror, it was hard to maintain hope. He was aware, much of the time, of a deep sense of dread, and an expectation of worse to come.

In his work, the old frustrations persisted. Huge strides had been made in medicine during the last decade. Following the discovery of insulin, the diagnosis of diabetes was no longer a death sentence. The use of sulphonamides had greatly reduced deaths from puerperal fever following childbirth, and had even lessened the huge toll exacted by pneumonia. But what use were such advances to families who could not afford to call out a doctor? No medicine could counteract ignorance or poverty. Because of the continuing economic depression, the living standards of the poorest had worsened, rather than improved, as the decade had gone on. Though there were always queues of patients at his free clinic, and though he worked long hours, Martin knew that he only scraped the surface. He held the free clinic three times a week; the remainder of the time he must attend to his paying patients. There was, after all, food to buy and school fees to pay. And Edinburgh's ills were reproduced over and over in towns and cities the length and breadth of the country. It would take a revolution – or a war – to shake up the old system and change it for ever.

He found his escape, as before, in archaeology. Once

every few months, when he had a free weekend, he drove out into the countryside in his Austin 7 to research his book on the prehistory of Scotland. He suspected that he might never finish the book; it had already grown far beyond his original intention, dividing and multiplying with amoeba-like rapidity. Yet his visits to the mountains and lochs restored him, blowing away some of the dust of the city.

His trips away served another purpose, too. He had never reneged on his promise to Bess to recognise her need for independence, her need for freedom. He acknowledged the danger of living in each other's pockets, that she would grow tired of him, that the spirit and fire that had originally attracted him would dim, constrained by domesticity. He had always made sure to give her the time she needed to spend by herself or with the children or friends. Mostly, he thought it worked well.

They had been married for almost ten years. The first eight of those years had been happier than he could ever have imagined. He had never expected happiness; he had learnt a long time ago that it came in little sparks and alterations of mood, that it took you by surprise, unexpectedly lifting a day out of the ordinary. The change had come with the arrival of Frazer and the birth of Aimée. He had seen it often enough in his work, the one child too many who tipped a tolerable domestic life into one which scarcely allowed time to breathe. Though nobody could have called Aimée a demanding child, Martin had seen that her birth had exhausted Bess far more than those of her sisters.

And then there was Frazer – Frazer, whose existence and

arrival had forced Bess to revisit a difficult past. Martin knew that Frazer was charming, personable, generous and eager to please. But, over the past year, he had seen that Frazer was spoilt, and had come to suspect that he could be weak. He had not spoken of his concerns to Bess. He hoped that Kate, who was level-headed and sensible, would provide a settling influence on Frazer.

He knew that Bess would hear no criticism of her son. Frazer's failings must be added to the list of things they never talked about: Andrew Gilchrist, and the fear that came to Martin when he was particularly tired or despondent, that Bess had only married him so that she could have more children, to quell her fear of the empty cradle. He knew that his doubts were born of his own insecurity, his conviction that he could never be enough for her. But he had come to suspect that her strongest feelings were reserved for her children. He remembered the lengths to which she had gone to get Frazer back – marriage to a man she had not cared for, years immured in an existence that must have stifled her.

As for Gilchrist, Martin had always respected Bess's decision never to mention his name. *Whatever I do, whatever I say, it will still have happened*, she had said to him, all those years ago, and he had seen perfectly what she had meant. If never referring to Andrew Gilchrist's violation of her made it easier for her to endure the memory of it, then what right had he to question that? Yet he had seen how Gilchrist had changed her, that she was no longer as outgoing, as blithely sociable as she had been when he had first met her. He had loved her from the first for her emotional generosity, yet Gilchrist had forced her to rein in that part of herself.

Gilchrist had taken something from Bess, and every now and then Martin found himself wondering whether he should have killed him when he had had the chance. Snapped his spine, broken his windpipe. The reflection always jarred him, forcing him to acknowledge the seam of violence in him. Yet it might have provided a finish, might have rubbed away a shadow.

On a wet, blowy day, Martin explored a souterrain in Perthshire. Souterrains were sunken, stone-lined passages, many of which had been discovered towards the end of the previous century. Their purpose was unknown, their exploration often only achieved through low-ceilinged passageways. Towards the end of the afternoon, emerging from the dank, dark structure, torch in hand, Martin saw that it had begun to rain. He shook off the worst of the earth, stretched out his cramped limbs, and set off south.

The tyre punctured as he rounded a sharp bend in the road through a narrow valley walled with hills. The Austin spun out of control, its back wheels veering round. When it came to a sudden halt, Martin thudded against the steering wheel.

He sat still for a moment, getting his breath back. His ribs were bruised, he thought, rather than broken. He climbed out to inspect the damage. It was raining heavily by now. The car's front wheels were dug into the shallow, boggy stream that ran alongside the road.

The front nearside tyre was flat, its outer rubber casing split. He took out the spare and had the good fortune to be able to hail a passing carter, who helped him push the vehicle out of the ditch and change the tyre. The front bumper had struck a rock and hung at a drunken angle, and one of the headlamps was shattered. The carter recommended a blacksmith in the next village who would be able to repair the bumper.

It was late evening by the time the car was roadworthy again. Heading south once more, he was aware of a deep weariness. Once, he began to nod off, but the shriek of a barn owl jerked him awake. Shining his torch on his map, he realized that he was within ten miles of Ravenhart House. He was aware of a feeling of relief; he longed for sanctuary, for rest.

A party at Ravenhart House: after searching for some time, Frazer found Max in a room at the back of the building. A whisky bottle stood on the sill; Max was drinking its contents with conscientious application.

Max's head jerked up when Frazer came into the room. 'Something I have to tell you.'

Frazer thought he sounded nervous. 'Fire away, then.'

'It's Naomi. We're going to get married.'

Somehow, Frazer managed to keep his expression unaltered. He sensed that he teetered on a knife edge.

'Married,' he murmured. 'This is rather unexpected.'

'Mmm.' Max ran his fingers through his hair. 'For me, too.'

'When?'

'Soonish.'

Frazer battled down his anger, and, his voice low and level, said, 'She won't make you happy.'

'I haven't the smallest expectation that she will,' said Max lightly. 'But there you are. I'm going to marry her.'

Frazer looked at Maxwell closely. 'Do you want to?'

'Not at all. I've never wanted to marry anyone.' He smiled fleetingly. 'When she spoke to me, all I could think was that I should run away to Spain and join the Republican Army. Marriage – I shall hate it, I know I shall. I shall feel like I'm suffocating.' A rushed succession of phrases, and his hand, as he picked up the glass, trembled.

Then he laughed. 'I've never thought of myself as husband material. I mean, *really*, can you imagine? I've always preferred to enjoy the pleasures of marriage, shall we say, without actually having to go through the process itself.'

'Is she forcing you into this?'

Maxwell shrugged. 'In a way, I suppose.'

'You don't have to do it.' Now, Frazer could no longer keep the anger out of his voice. 'You don't have to go on like this, doing whatever she wants.'

Maxwell said flatly, 'She says she'll kill herself if I don't marry her, you see.'

The manipulative bitch, thought Frazer. 'You shouldn't listen to her. She's lying. She wouldn't do it.'

'Oh, she would.' Maxwell's voice was bleak.

'That's blackmail. You don't have to give in to blackmail.'

'Frazer, she's pregnant.'

Frazer stared at him, shocked. 'Are you sure?'

'Yes.' His tone was final, brooking no argument.

And is it yours? But Frazer thought that if he voiced that question Maxwell would walk out and he would never see him again. Instead, he said slowly, 'And she wants to keep the baby?'

'Yes. She had an abortion before, you see, a year ago. She found it very – very upsetting. She refuses point-blank to go through it again.' He swallowed more whisky.

'She's bluffing. You shouldn't take any notice. You should tell her to sort it out herself.'

Maxwell frowned. 'That is *exactly* what my father would do.' A long silence, then he said, 'If I refuse to marry her I honestly think she might do something dreadful. It's not an empty threat, Frazer. I believe her capable of taking her own life. And however shabbily I've behaved in the past, I can't quite go along with that.'

Frazer went to the window and looked out. It was still raining; water was gouting from a blocked gutter and churning up yellow puddles in the gravel. He said, 'Do you love her?'

'Love?' Maxwell repeated the word as though he wasn't certain what it meant. 'I don't know.' Then his head dropped. He said softly, 'The thing is, she seems to *draw* me. I can't explain . . . she fascinates me. And sometimes, just sometimes, I think – well, perhaps I'm being given a chance.'

'A chance?' said Frazer blankly.

'To change.'

Maxwell's gaze met Frazer's; Frazer dug his nails into his palms. He heard Maxwell's outward exhalation of breath. 'Anyway, I've thought and I've thought and I can't see what else to do. So I've come to ask for your help.'

Frazer managed to stifle his sudden impulse to laugh. 'My help? What sort of help?'

'Oh, the usual, I'm afraid. Money. You can tell me to jump in a lake, if you like, but I can't see who else I can turn to. The idea of asking my father is so frankly appalling – it would mean working for him and I think, I honestly think, that I'd rather die. And apparently Mimi isn't exactly in her parents' good books at the moment. And they're going to have to know that we've, well, jumped the gun rather, and can't hang about while they plan a big wedding. Which won't go down too well, I daresay, so not much hope of financial help there, Mimi thinks. And neither of us has much in the way of money in the bank – Mimi hasn't a clue what she has, actually, but I suspect that she doesn't have two pennies to rub together. So I wondered whether you could help us out, Frazer. Just for a while, until I've sorted myself out. A frightful nerve, I know, after everything that's happened, but . . .' His voice trailed away.

Frazer said, 'How much do you need?'

'I have to find us somewhere decent to live. Mimi lives with her parents, you see, and the room I've got in Edinburgh isn't suitable – it isn't suitable at all for her. Or for a child.' White-faced, he shook his head. Then he muttered, 'Jesus, what a mess, what a bloody awful mess.'

Frazer stared out at the sodden garden. The rain was like an opaque veil, walling the house off from the rest of the world. When it was like this he couldn't think why he had ever come to live here. It was Max who had made Ravenhart bearable, Max who had made it fun. An only child brought up by his grandparents, Frazer hadn't a great deal of experience of having fun. He'd had a better time in the last year and a half than he'd ever had before.

I need to find somewhere decent to live. Suddenly, he saw what he must do. He wondered whether he could bear it, having that fat, dark-haired creature around all the time. Yet if he could, it would mean that Max would remain at Ravenhart, and that he wouldn't be on his own, that everything would be just the same.

Well, not quite the same, of course. Max would have a wife and child. And Max would be beholden to him.

Martin headed up the narrow, winding road that took him towards Glenshee. He would stay overnight with Frazer and set off for Edinburgh the following morning. Kate was staying with Frazer for the weekend – they would be able to travel home together.

A feeling of relief came over him when, through the rain, he made out Mr Bain's gatehouse. He turned off from the main road and headed along the track beside the burn. When he reached the house, he saw the motor cars parked in the forecourt. Lights blazed in the windows of the house – Frazer must be entertaining friends. Martin felt a flicker of irritation – he longed only for a hot bath and bed; instead, he must endure polite conversation and introductions to people whose names he would instantly forget.

He had to ring the doorbell several times before it was answered. Light and music flooded into the courtyard; a yellow-haired girl in a peach satin dress stood in front of him.

'Dickie, darling, you're been hours—' she broke off, staring at him, her lower lip sticking out disconsolately, then said, 'You're not Dickie.'

'I'm Martin Jago, Frazer's stepfather.'

Her eyes widened. She giggled. 'Frazer's stepfather? I didn't know he had one.'

'Is he in?'

'Somewhere, sweetie,' she said vaguely, and he followed her inside.

Swing music was playing very loudly on a gramophone; the syncopated beat echoed against the panelled walls. Empty glasses and bottles littered the passageways; at the top of the stairs a girl sat weeping, mascara running down her cheeks. Ravenhart's rooms were stale with cigarette smoke, their contents rumpled and disordered.

Martin searched for Frazer and Kate. Opening a door, he saw a couple entwined on a sofa; the woman's halterneck dress had become unfastened, displaying her breasts. He closed the door quietly, he did not think they had heard him. Loud whoops and roars of laughter drew him to a long passageway to one side of the house. Men, their jackets discarded and shirtsleeves rolled up, were bowling a cricket ball at the empty champagne bottles that had been set up at the far end of the corridor. The ball skated along the polished wood floor, then struck the bottles. The litter of broken glass showed where some of the bottles had smashed on impact. Frazer and a dark-haired young man were standing nearby. When a ball knocked over half a dozen bottles at once, Frazer cheered and flung an arm round the dark-haired man's shoulders.

Frazer looked up, caught sight of him, and struggled to focus. 'Martin. Good God.'

Martin picked his way through shards of glass. 'Frazer.'

'I wasn't expecting—'

'You must excuse me for turning up unannounced. I had a motor accident, and I came to ask whether you could let me have a room for the night.' His eyes flicked over the scatter of broken glass; he knew that his repugnance must show on his face. 'But I seem to have turned up at a bad time.'

Frazer's friend said quickly, 'Oh, most of this lot will be gone soon. There's another party at the Hardacres' place. I'm sure there'll be plenty of room for you, Dr Jago.' He gave Martin a conciliatory smile. 'You are Dr Jago, aren't you? Kate has told me so much about you.'

Has she now, thought Martin. He said, out loud, 'I don't believe we've met.'

'I'm Maxwell,' said the dark-haired young man. He crunched through broken glass to offer Martin his hand. 'Maxwell Gilchrist.'

Gilchrist. The name jarred. Martin said, 'Where's Kate?'

Half an hour ago, Frazer had announced Maxwell and Naomi's engagement and had toasted the couple with champagne. Yet it wasn't the fact of Maxwell's engagement, or even the not-so-softly murmured scandal, whispered in rooms and corridors, that Maxwell and Naomi had to get married because Naomi was expecting Maxwell's child that had shocked Kate most.

The worst thing was that Frazer was going to give Maxwell and Naomi the gatekeeper's lodge on their marriage. After the champagne had been drunk, after everyone had dispersed through the house, Kate had gone to find Frazer.

'Are you all right?' she asked him, and he nodded.

'Of course I am.' Yet she saw from the lack of focus in his eyes and the slight clumsiness of his movements that he was very drunk.

Then she said, 'You don't really mean to give Max and Naomi Mr Bain's house, do you?'

'Yes, I do.'

'Frazer, you can't.'

'Oh, I can.' He lit a cigarette, his hands fumbling with the lighter. 'It's my house. I can do what I like with it.'

'But Mr Bain's lived there for years – for *decades*. It's his *home!*'

After she understood that he would not change his mind, she walked away from him. Unable to bear to be in the house a moment longer, she stood outside on the fore-court, listening to the drum of the rain on the stones, closing her eyes and holding her face up to the sky.

Then she went back to her room in the turret. After a while, there was a knock on the door. She didn't want to answer it at first, and then a voice called out, 'Kate? Are you in there?' and she thought, *Martin*, and was aware of an extraordinary mixture of relief and alarm.

She opened the door. He said, 'Hello, Kate.' She saw him taking in her wet hair and clothes. 'How are you?'

'Fine.' Though she was not fine, not fine at all. And then suddenly she couldn't quite pretend any more, and she said rather tremulously, 'Actually, I've rather a headache.'

'You're shivering.'

'I went for a walk in the garden. I got a bit wet.'

'You'll catch a cold. You must get changed into dry things.

I'll see if I can make us a hot drink. Come down to the kitchen when you're ready.'

When Martin had gone, Kate changed into trousers and a jersey and towel-dried her hair. It was good to have someone tell her what to do. Since Maxwell had announced his engagement to Naomi Jennings, she had seemed to lose some sort of internal compass. Every now and then she remembered the hunting lodge and Maxwell's kisses in the darkness. *So we'll go no more a-roving, so late into the night.*

She found Martin in the kitchen, heating a pan of milk on the stove. While she drank the hot milk and swallowed the aspirins he offered her, he explained about his motor accident.

'We'll head off in the morning,' he said. 'I think you should come home with me, Kate.'

Home. She longed to go home. 'Can't we leave tonight?'

Martin shook his head. 'The roads are too treacherous in this rain. The blacksmith could only do a patch job on the car − it'll have to go into the garage as soon as I get back to Edinburgh.' He looked at her closely. 'Kate, has something happened?'

She whispered, 'I just don't like it here any more, that's all.'

'Has someone hurt you?' His voice was sharp.

'No.' She dug her spoon into her cup and lifted out the skin, and thought that that, at least, was true. It seemed to her that she had hurt herself, by being so stupid as to fall in love with a man who had always been out of her reach.

She managed to steady her voice. 'I don't like the people

here. I preferred Ravenhart House when it was just us, just me and Frazer. I don't much like parties.'

Martin gave a fleeting smile. 'Well, I can sympathize with that.' Then his expression cooled. 'Does Frazer hold many parties?'

'A few.'

'And are they always like this?'

As she looked away, with a sudden feeling of shame, she heard him go on, 'Frazer's friend, Maxwell Gilchrist . . .' and she felt herself stiffen.

'Yes?'

'Do you know him well?'

She was aware of danger. 'Not really.' Not so far from the truth; just now, she didn't think she knew him at all.

'Do you know whether he lives locally?'

'Max's family's from Edinburgh, I think,' she said with studied vagueness.

'Edinburgh . . . you wouldn't happen to know his father's name, would you, Kate?'

She thought for a moment. 'Andrew. Max's father's called Andrew.' She looked at Martin. 'Why?'

'Just curious. I've heard of the family.' Then he said, 'You should get some sleep, Kate. I intend to leave at first light.'

Bess was in the kitchen, helping Mrs Tate make Sunday lunch, when Martin and Kate arrived home. Kate swept Aimée up in her arms and covered her with kisses and then disappeared into her bedroom. Martin explained about his accident and they all trooped outside and inspected the dented bumper, and then Mrs Tate called to say that lunch was ready. Bess sent Eleanor upstairs to fetch Kate, but Eleanor returned shortly, saying that Kate didn't want any lunch. Bess said, 'I'll speak to her,' but Martin put out a warning hand. 'Bess, leave her,' he said, and something in his voice made her drop back into her seat and continue dishing out the vegetables. Throughout the meal her sense of disquiet lingered.

It was after lunch, and Aimée was having her afternoon nap and Eleanor and Rebecca were playing in the garden, when Martin said, 'Bess, I need to talk to you about Frazer.'

'Frazer? He's well, isn't he?'

'Perfectly well.'

They were in the sitting room; Bess poured out coffee. She heard Martin say, 'I don't think Kate should see so much of Frazer.'

She stared at him. 'Why on earth not?'

'I am afraid – I'm afraid he may not be a wholly good influence.'

She put down the coffee pot. 'That's a dreadful thing to say, Martin.'

'And I wouldn't say it without reason.' He sighed. 'Frazer was giving a party when I arrived at the house last night. It was no sedate little affair with sherry and canapés, and it certainly wasn't the sort of party you'd want Kate to attend. There was a great deal of heavy drinking, a lot of horseplay.'

Something inside her turned uneasily. But then she thought, such a fuss about a *party*. It seemed to her unfair of Martin to judge Frazer for enjoying parties just because he himself disliked them. After all, there was nothing wrong with having a good time.

'All young men can be a little wild,' she said defensively. 'Jack was wild. You can hardly expect me to forbid Kate to see her brother simply because he gave a party that got a bit out of hand.'

'I wouldn't dream of suggesting that you forbid Kate to see Frazer. Merely that she sees less of him.'

'Really, Martin, I think you're overreacting.'

In the silence, she heard the girls' shrieks from the garden. Then Martin said, 'Did you know that Maxwell Gilchrist is a friend of Frazer's?'

The name made her freeze, sugar bowl in hand. '*Who?*' she whispered.

'I met him last night.' Martin looked grim. 'He was one of Frazer's guests. I managed to speak to Frazer this morning – I was careful in what I said, of course. But Maxwell is Andrew Gilchrist's son.'

'His *son*,' she echoed. Her heart was hammering against her ribs.

'His youngest son. Maxwell has two elder brothers. Frazer has known Maxwell for more than a year.'

A sudden, frightened thought. '*Kate.*'

Martin sat down beside Bess. 'I have no reason to think that they are any more than casual acquaintances. So there's no harm in it.'

'I don't want *his* son anywhere near my daughter!' The words escaped her, almost a scream; she clamped her hands over her mouth.

'Then either Frazer must be persuaded not to invite Maxwell Gilchrist to Ravenhart, or Kate must see less of Frazer. As I said, I believe that to be the best course of action. There was something in the atmosphere of the house that I disliked. And Kate was upset when I found her. It wasn't a suitable environment for a girl of her age.'

'It's hardly Frazer's fault—'

'He is her elder brother.' Martin's voice was cold. 'He was responsible for her. He should have known that.'

It was as though she had stepped back into a nightmare, a nightmare she had assumed gone for ever, over and done with. The familiar room now seemed strange, pooled with dark shadows, no longer a haven.

She said suddenly, 'What was he like? Was he like *him*?'

'Not to look at, no. And he was perfectly charming. It was an awkward situation, me turning up out of the blue when the party was in full swing, but he tried to smooth it over.' Martin's frown deepened. 'A personable rogue – that would be my estimation of him. He was . . . beguiling.'

'*Beguiling?*'

'A person you might take to, even against your better judgement.' Martin paused. Then he said, 'There is, of course, another point we should consider. Maxwell Gilchrist is not his father. He doesn't live at the family home and he doesn't work for his father, as his elder brothers do. We have no reason to believe him any danger to Kate or Frazer. Should we blame the son for the sins of the father?'

Yes, she thought, *yes, yes*. She said roughly, 'That sort of vileness tarnishes everything it touches,' and stood up.

'Where are you going?'

'To speak to Kate, of course.' Something inside her snapped. She hissed, 'I don't want my children to have anything more to do with him! Frazer must know what sort of family he comes from – neither of them must ever see him again!'

As she left the room, she heard Martin add, a warning note in his voice, 'Frazer is a man, Bess. He may not take kindly to being told how to choose his friends.'

She cried, 'They are my children, Martin!' The door slammed behind her.

When she thought about Frazer and Kate, in Maxwell Gilchrist's company, Bess's blood ran cold. She blamed herself for what had happened. Preoccupied with her younger daughters, she had not kept as close an eye on Kate as she should have. As for Frazer, her reluctance to visit a house she disliked, a house that contained bad memories for her, had meant that she had preferred to see Frazer in Edinburgh rather than at Ravenhart. Which meant in turn that she had been ignorant of Frazer's acquaintance with Maxwell Gilchrist. She must visit Ravenhart more often. She must make sure that Andrew Gilchrist's son had the opportunity neither to hurt Frazer nor to exploit him.

In the end, it was easy enough to make sure that Kate never saw Maxwell Gilchrist again. Kate herself came up with the solution. She had decided to go and stay at Ralph and Pamela's farm for a while, she told Bess; she would take time off work and travel down to Hampshire as soon as possible. Bess saw Kate off from Waverley station with a mixture of relief and sadness.

But her conversation with Frazer seemed to go wrong

from the start. On the train to Pitlochry one Saturday, she worked out everything that she must say to him. Yet what she had intended as gentle maternal advice over the dinner table, a timely warning about wild habits and an unsuitable acquaintance, sounded, even to her own ears, a mixture of nagging and snobbery. The trouble was, of course, that she couldn't tell Frazer *why* she didn't want him to see Maxwell Gilchrist. And anything less than the perfectly unspeakable truth, any hints dropped about the Gilchrist family's greed and corruption, sounded at best an evasion, and at worst spiteful.

Frazer hardly seemed to listen. He simply brushed away everything she said. She found herself floundering, saying to Frazer – and even as she spoke the words she wanted to draw them back – that she wasn't sure whether she wanted to come to Ravenhart if it meant finding herself in the same house as Maxwell Gilchrist. And Frazer looked at her, his blue eyes wide and pained, and said that if that was so then he was very sorry, because he liked her to visit.

It took a second or two to feel the full, sickening force of the impact of his words, and then, understanding that if she forced Frazer to choose between herself and Maxwell Gilchrist, he would choose his friend rather than his mother, she had to pretend that she had swallowed a fishbone and rush out of the room.

At the top of the stairs she paused, clutching the finial with its raven's head. Out of the arrow-shaped window above the front door she could see the glen, and the silver river framed by the looming hills. When, more than a year and a half earlier, Frazer had walked back into her life, she had believed that she could put things right, that she could make everything as it should have been had Cora Ravenhart not taken her son from her. She knew now that she had been mistaken.

Part Four

Kate Fearnley

1937–1961

Chapter Fourteen

Once a week, Kate attended a ballet class in a house in Bedford Gardens in Kensington. Soot-blackened chrysanthemums drooped in pots in the narrow front garden and a tabby cat coiled on the stone steps. In the basement, beads of water gathered on the cracked walls and when Kate changed at the end of class, her clothes were always damp.

Two boys and ten girls attended the class. The girls arrived at Bedford Gardens wearing dresses of fine wool and smart tweed coats; their pink and white complexions, doubled in the mirror by the barre, glowed rose as the hour went on. Their teacher was called Madame Barnova. Madame Barnova always wore an ancient black chiffon evening dress and a pair of faded satin slippers. Her grey hair was tied up in a bun and secured by a black jet comb and there was a dab of rouge on each of her hollow cheeks. Her bony fingers poked and prodded, shoving hips, shoulders and elbows into place. When she was displeased she would scream and stamp her little satin-clad foot. Yet she moved with an airy grace as she demonstrated flowing adagios and elegant enchainements.

It was more than a year since Kate had attended a practice class. Her joints and muscles ached; she seemed to be moving her limbs against something solid and resistant. Her lungs tightened and a stitch burned between her ribs. Glimpsing her reflection in the mirror, seeing her clumsiness and her leaden movements, she felt a mixture of fury and frustration.

Yet, after a while, some of her old facility returned. And when, after weeks of exhausting practice, her body began to obey her and sometimes, just sometimes, to do what she wanted it to, she felt a rush of elation. She was clawing something back, she thought, she was rediscovering her sense of direction.

It came to her only gradually that she would not go home.

In the immediate aftermath of her flight from Scotland, her father's farm had been her refuge, the place where she had been able to lick her wounds. Great events had taken place in the world – the abdication of a king, for love, and the accession of another – and she had remained at the farm.

Staying there for months instead of odd weeks or fortnights, she got to know her brothers better, seemed to separate them out, no longer seeing them as a single boisterous male mass. Tom, at thirteen, was athletic and daring, Henry, a year younger, was quieter, more reflective. Red-haired Archie, the youngest, showed her his collection of carnivorous plants. Peering into the glass case of flytraps and pitcher plants, Kate remembered the sundews that had clustered in the boggy ground beside the path to the hunting lodge, and the tiny black specks of flies caught on their gleaming leaves.

Sometimes she wondered whether, in leaving Scotland, she was running away. She supposed that she was, that she was running from the pain and the obligations of love. Thinking of Frazer made her feel miserable and guilty; thinking of Maxwell seemed to tear her heart in two. Yet she knew that she was heading towards something as well, in a stumbling sort of way. It would have been easy to stay at the farm, which she loved, but she had taken the easy choice before and it had not satisfied. What she had retained from the time she had spent at Ravenhart House was a sense of freedom, of self-discovery. She could not settle back into the comforting blanket of family life and the dependence it entailed.

News from Ravenhart reached her in Frazer's letters. There had been a heavy snowfall and the driveway had been blocked and Frazer hadn't been able to leave the house for three days. The men had started work on the plumbing at last and Mrs McGill had fallen into a hole where the floorboards had been taken up and had sprained her ankle and been off work for a fortnight.

And Maxwell and Naomi had married and Naomi was expecting a child. The afternoon Kate received Frazer's letter telling her that he had evicted Ronald Bain from the gatehouse, she walked for hours through the Hampshire countryside. Copses of leafless elders arched over carpets of moss, and the winter sunlight gleamed weakly on the brown earth turned by the plough. Frazer hadn't put it quite like that in his letter, of course, hadn't used the word *evicted*, but that was what he had done. Kate thought of Ronald Bain, who had belonged to Ravenhart long, long before Frazer had ever seen the house, and she felt a flicker of fear.

Telling her mother that she was not coming home was one of the worst things she had ever had to do. Flurries of telephone calls and letters were followed by Bess threatening to take the next train south and bring Kate back to Scotland herself.

Kate tried again. Sitting in the hallway of the farm one evening, she twisted the telephone wire round her fingers.

Her mother said, 'You can't possibly go and live in London, Kate. You can't possibly live on your own.'

'You did, Mum. You were married and had a child by the time you were my age. You travelled halfway round the world on your own.'

'It wasn't the same at all. I had no choice.'

'This is *my* choice, Mum.'

'Kate, I don't understand. I don't understand why you're doing this.'

A deep breath; there were tears waiting in her own eyes. 'Because I have to. I can't explain.'

'Wait a year, please, darling. Come back home now, and then, if you still want to live in London in a year's time—'

'I want to do this *now*, Mum.' Kate closed her eyes. 'This is what I want. I need to know that I *can* manage on my own.'

A long silence; the telephone wire was tied into a knot.

Then her mother said, 'I'll parcel up a set of sheets and pillowcases and send them down to you. Linen in lodging houses can be so old and damp. And I'll send you some Shetland wool blankets as well. London can be very cold in the winter.' Her mother's voice, filtered by the hundreds of miles that separated them, was distorted by the crackle of the telephone wire and a shiver of tears.

Kate started her new job in February 1937. Peggy Fisher was the director of a small ballet company that performed original works and a few well-chosen classics. Kate was to be Peggy's assistant. The company was based in Pimlico. Kate found a room in a lodging house a few streets away.

Though she was a perfectionist with her dancers, every other area of Peggy Fisher's life was enveloped in chaos. Even her clothing seemed muddled, distrait. Moving from the studio to the theatre, silk scarves would slither from her neck and grips fall unnoticed from her hair. Peggy's office was a nightmare of unanswered letters and unpaid bills; her filing consisted of shoving documents into shoe-boxes and Harrods carrier bags. Kate spent her first week sorting out mounds of paperwork and trying to prevent Peggy putting everything in the wrong place again. Then she answered letters, made sure bills were paid, and persuaded Peggy to dictate thank-you notes to the company's patrons. After a while, Kate began to write to the patrons herself – it was easier than coaxing Peggy to take a few moments from the work she loved, and she thought that she made a better job of it.

She also dealt with the hapless men who were on the sharp end of Peggy's forgetfulness and poor timekeeping. Kate comforted them when they arrived at the studio to take Peggy on a lunch date or to a pre-theatre supper, only to discover that she would be enclosed for hours with the choreographer or the composer, discussing the next project. Kate got to know Peggy's long-suffering men friends by name; sometimes she gave them a cup of tea and a biscuit so at least the poor things had something to eat before returning to their jobs in banks or universities or conservatoires.

She loved her chilly little office at the top of the building, and she loved her room in the lodging house, where she had hung from the picture rail her collection of hats: they lay flat against the walls like oversized, multicoloured poppies. Kate's fellow lodgers were teachers and department store manageresses and secretaries, like herself, all of them female, all unmarried. An air of quietness veiled the house, broken only by murmurings of polite conversation at dinner or by the sound of Miss Barclay, who taught music, practising her scales and arpeggios in the back room.

Kate got to know the other people who worked for Peggy. She drank cocoa after rehearsals with the girls from the corps, and she made friends with one of the seamstresses, who helped her make her own clothes. A dart here, a deft twist of material there, and suddenly a skirt or blouse acquired a particular style.

Billy Marshall was one of Peggy Fisher's dancers. Billy was the same age as Kate; he had bright blue eyes and towcoloured hair. Billy's family were from Manchester; he had run away from home at the age of thirteen and had survived by taking roles in musicals and end-of-the-pier shows and washing up in cafes when the jobs ran out. Kate noticed Billy because of his thin, gawky shape and beaked nose and shabby clothes, and because of his prodigious, half-formed talent. His skinny limbs seemed to lack bone and joint, to bend to any shape.

Like Kate, Billy attended Madame Barnova's class. Once, when Madame's fury was directed at Billy, Kate thought he looked miserable, so afterwards, to cheer him up, she offered to buy him a coffee.

They went to a cafe. Kate said comfortingly, 'She only tells off people she thinks are any good. She doesn't bother with the rest of us.'

'Mrs Barnes can say what she likes. I don't care about her.'

'Mrs Barnes?'

'Julia Barnes. That's her real name.' He sniggered. 'Didn't you know that? You didn't think she was really called Julietta Barnova, did you? I've had much worse than her. Last summer, I did a show on Brighton Pier and the director used to hit us with a stick.' Billy was turning a matchbox over and over on the tabletop. He added carelessly, 'She's a poisonous old cow but she's good for centre work.'

With Billy, Kate went to the theatre and to the ballet, sitting in the cheap seats up in the gods. He was an endless source of gossip, most of it scurrilous. At an after-show party, after a fellow guest had moved out of earshot, he murmured to Kate, 'Fifty if she's a day, but she tells directors she's thirty-nine. Make-up half an inch thick, and I mean *literally*.' Or, of a meek, softly spoken girl from class, 'Of course, she'd sleep with anyone if it meant a decent role. I mean, *anyone*. Stalin, if he'd get her out of the corps de ballet.' Then he would shoot a glance at Kate and say, 'Didn't you know *that*? You *must* have known *that*.'

'Didn't you know *that*?' accompanied by raised brows and an incredulous blue gaze, became the leitmotif of Kate's friendship with Billy. There were, she realised, so many things she didn't know. Sometimes she wondered how she had managed to reach the age of twenty, knowing so little.

'Didn't you know they were lovers?' Billy said, laughter in his eyes, on the occasion she remarked that Freddy and Roman, two dancers from Miss Fisher's company, seemed to be best friends. 'Didn't you know *that*?'

They were in the crush bar at Sadler's Wells, before curtain up. 'But,' she said. 'But—'

'Yes, Kate?'

She blurted out, 'But men can't fall in love with other men,' and he roared with laughter.

'Of course they can. Why shouldn't they? They do all the time. I'm always falling in love. Once a fortnight, at least.' Some of the laughter slipped from his voice. 'Until Alan, that is.'

'Alan?'

Billy pursed his lips and blew out a thin stream of smoke. 'Our gorgeous colonial.'

Kate thought of Alan McKenna, who had recently joined the company from Australia. He had eyes the colour of black treacle and reddish-brown hair that swooped over his brow when he jumped.

Billy studied her curiously. 'You mean to say you haven't fallen for him, Kate? I thought the entire company was in love with Al.' His eyes clouded as he muttered, 'And doesn't he love every minute of it.' He stubbed out his cigarette. 'Freddie and Roman have been together for *years*. They're like an old married couple. They always share a bed on tour. To save money, that's the story. Got to be careful, it's against the law, of course.'

She must have looked utterly bewildered, because he sighed and explained, 'You can go to prison for committing a homosexual act. Think of poor old Oscar Wilde.' He looked at her again, then he raised her hand and kissed her fingertips and said, 'Dear old Kate. So sweet and naive, and the last virgin in Pimlico.'

Walking downstairs from her office one lunchtime, Kate caught sight of a man waiting on the landing outside Peggy's office.

'Oliver? Is that you?' she called. 'Are you waiting for Peggy?'

Oliver Colefax was one of Peggy's friends. Wearing a black overcoat and a crimson scarf, he was leaning against the wall, reading I, *Claudius*. He snapped the book shut, put it in his pocket, straightened, and glanced at his watch.

'We were supposed to meet at one.'

'I'm afraid Peggy's just phoned to say she'll be delayed.'

'Will she be long?'

'A couple of hours at least. I'm awfully sorry.'

He started down the stairs. Then he stopped, turned back

to her and said, 'Have you had lunch, Kate? I've a table booked at Stefano's and it'll only go to waste.'

The thought of a restaurant lunch was too good to resist. 'Thank you,' she said. 'That would be lovely.'

Outside, a strong wind thwacked at Kate's raincoat and blew Oliver's umbrella inside out. The restaurant had pale blue walls and cream-coloured curtains; French windows looked out onto a courtyard garden with terracotta pots and a fountain. They ordered potted shrimps and sole meunière.

When the fish arrived, Oliver Colefax looked at it appreciatively. 'Whenever I try to cook fish it never turns out like this. More like cardboard, in fact.'

'You have to get the pan very hot. And use lots of butter and salt and pepper. And only cook it for a minute or two.'

'Are you a cook as well as a secretary?'

'I learned to cook one summer in France. My stepfather has a house there.'

'Which part of France?'

When she told him, he smiled and said, 'Ah, Champagne country – so lovely and green and gold, don't you think?' Which was exactly how she always thought of it.

'Do you know France well, Oliver?'

'Pretty well. I've travelled there a lot. I'm an antique dealer, you see, and I pick up pieces over there.'

'Do you have a shop?'

'In Portobello Road. We live above it.'

'I love antique shops. I can't ever afford anything, of course, but I like browsing round them.'

A few days later, he sent her a note, asking her to tea

on Sunday. Oliver's shop was bay-windowed, with 'Colefax' painted in green and gold above the door. As Oliver led Kate through the shop to the floor above, Kate's gaze was caught by a chaise longue upholstered in faded pink cretonne, and a huge armoire, like the one in the kitchen of the Lemerciers' farmhouse in France.

In a room upstairs, a little boy of two or three was playing with tin cars on the floor. He had straight dark hair and round dark brown eyes, like Oliver.

'This is my son, Stephen,' said Oliver Colefax. 'Stephen, say hello to Miss Fearnley.'

Stephen showed her his favourite car; Kate and Oliver talked about the shop and France and Portobello market and then Kate played with Stephen while Oliver was making tea. They ate in the kitchen, which was large and airy. Tall French windows led out to a balcony with a filigree iron spiral staircase curving down into a garden thick with trees and shrubs. Stephen sat in a high chair, where he ate egg sandwiches in a slow, exploratory way and mashed jelly in a bowl. 'I'm afraid he's not exactly a tidy eater,' apologized Oliver, 'and there's no hurrying him. I'm convinced he's going to be a scientist when he grows up. He loves taking things apart, having a good look at them.' There was no sign of a Mrs Colefax, and Oliver did not explain her absence.

Kate told Oliver about Peggy's next ballet. 'It's called Elementals. Peggy keeps changing her mind about the costumes. Last week she wanted blacks and reds but now she's decided to have neutrals instead. Pearl – she's a friend of mine, a seamstress – had to bleach out all the black and red dye.'

Oliver was making a second pot of tea when a voice hailed him from the shop below. 'Oliver? Oliver, where are you?'

Oliver looked up. 'We're up here, Margot!' he called. Stephen clapped his hands together, squashing globs of jelly between them.

A tall, thin, brown-haired woman in a dove-grey skirt and jacket came into the room. 'Oliver, darling, you really shouldn't leave the front door open like that. Anyone could come in.' She broke off, catching sight of Kate. If her eyebrows could have risen any more, thought Kate, they would have disappeared off the top of her forehead.

'Aren't you going to introduce me, Oliver?'

'Of course, Margot. This is Kate Fearnley. Kate, this is Margot Stockton, my sister-in-law.'

A pigskin-gloved hand was briefly extended to Kate. Then Margot exclaimed, 'Oh dear, you *have* let Stephen get into a mess, Oliver. There's jelly all over his shirt. You'd better let me take it home for Clarice to launder.'

'There's no need, Margot, I'm sure I can manage to wash a shirt.' Oliver's voice was mild but his expression had, Kate noticed, become rather set.

'I'll take him to the bathroom and clean him up.'

'Margot, please . . .'

But she had already lifted Stephen out of his high chair and was carrying him out of the room and up the stairs. After Margot and Stephen had gone, there was a short silence, and then Oliver said, 'My wife died three years ago, six weeks after giving birth to Stephen.'

Kate stared at him, horrified. 'I'm so sorry, how awful.'

'I probably should have mentioned it before but it's not an easy subject to bring up. Looks as though you're asking for pity or something.' He frowned, glancing up the stairs. 'Margot will just turn up. Not that I mind, but if I'd known I would have warned her.'

Margot came back down to the kitchen, a clean Stephen in her arms. 'He seems rather overtired – too much excitement. Time for bed soon, I think.'

Kate took her cue. 'It's getting late. I'd better go. Thank you so much for the lovely tea, Oliver. May I help with the washing-up?'

'It's quite all right,' said Margot firmly. 'Oliver and I can manage perfectly well.'

Oliver offered to see Kate out. At the door, he said, 'I'm sorry if Margot was rather frosty with you. She still misses Jane terribly – as Stephen and I do, of course. But I hope you'll come to tea again.'

Billy Marshall lived in a room in Ladbroke Grove. His lodgings weren't like Kate's. No one cooked meals or laundered clothes for Billy, who fended for himself, and there seemed to be an extraordinary number of people living in the house. Their quarrels and makings-up were laid bare by the insubstantiality of the building; love and hate seeped with the damp through the thin partition walls.

Every now and then Kate cooked Billy supper on his single gas ring while he talked to her. One evening, he peered in the saucepan. 'What's that?'

'Poule au pot.'

'Such a show-off. Looks like chicken stew to me.'

The couple in the next room were quarrelling; raised voices echoed against the party wall.

'If you heat it up properly,' she said 'it'll keep for supper tomorrow.'

'What a wonderful little wife and mother you'll make one day, Kate.' His voice was acid.

A thud, as something was hurled against the partition wall. Then Billy kissed the back of her neck and said, 'Sorry. Sorry. I don't deserve you, Kate. I can't think why you don't throw the lot over me.'

'What's wrong?'

He ran a hand through his short fair hair, making it stick up in spikes. 'It's been such a bloody awful week.'

'Peggy?'

He shook his head. '*Alan.*'

'Tell me.'

He said first, 'You must be sick to death of me going on about him,' and then, miserably, 'Geraint Baxter took him out to dinner.'

Geraint Baxter was a successful choreographer. Kate said, 'Well, dinner, what's wrong with that?'

'Oh, *Kate*, dinner's never just dinner. Didn't you know *that*?'

She went to sit on the bed beside him. The quarrel in the adjacent room ebbed and rose.

Billy said bitterly, 'He's such a shit. Making up to anyone who might be able to get him a decent role. If I know he's a shit, why don't I hate him?'

She took his hand. His fingernails were bitten little half-moons. 'Because you can't turn it on and off like that. Love, I mean.'

'No. It's a bugger.' He lit a cigarette and lay back on the bed, his head cushioned on his arm. 'Why can't I be a sensible boy and fall in love with you, Kate? We could live in a cottage and you could have my supper on the table when I came home at night.'

'Have you ever fallen in love with a woman?'

'I tried once or twice but I wasn't very good at it.' Billy sighed. 'I can't really blame Al, anyway. It's a tough old business and if you can get your big break by making up to some influential old queen, well, why not?' He blew out a thin stream of smoke. 'I'd probably do exactly the same if I had the chance.'

In Maxwell Gilchrist Bess recognized the enemy. The Gilchrists lived in the gatehouse at the end of the drive. Whenever she walked past the house, she felt a rush of loathing. When Frazer introduced her to Maxwell, she found herself picking out his father's features: the heavy-lidded eyes, the small curve to the corners of the mouth. She was surprised that he did not notice her involuntary shiver of revulsion.

In the months since she had found out about Frazer's friendship with Maxwell Gilchrist, Bess had set about making herself useful to her son. She asked Mrs McGill to let her see the tradesmen's bills, and Mrs McGill, looking shifty, eventually produced a few crumpled scraps of paper. The items listed on the bills didn't seem to correspond to the contents of the larders, and Bess found herself wondering how much of Ravenhart's food and drink found its way to Mrs McGill's many relations in the nearby village.

At breakfast one day, she asked Frazer if she could look at his household accounts.

'My accounts?'

'Your record of your household purchases. Mrs McGill's store book is rather sketchy. And there seem to have been some very large bills – for wine, for instance – and not a great deal left in the cellar to show for it.'

He said vaguely, 'There was a party . . .'

In his study, Frazer opened a drawer. Bess glimpsed a jumble of papers – a garage bill, a receipt from his tailor, a picture postcard with something scribbled on the back of it.

He said, 'I wouldn't say that I exactly kept *records*.'

'You really do need to keep proper accounts for a house of this size, Frazer. My second husband, Kate's father, taught me the value of keeping detailed household accounts. If you like, I could do it for you.'

Bess spent a morning sorting through invoices and receipts. There were a great many unpaid bills – overlooked, she assumed, because of Frazer's confused methods. Letters from his accountant in Edinburgh warned of the need to cash in stocks and shares should Frazer's expenditure remain at its present level. With a sense of increasing disquiet, Bess wondered whether the estate, which relied for its income on rents from the tenant farms, was profitable. Money seemed to pour through Frazer's fingers like sand, money spent on luxuries and on repairs and improvements to the house.

Money spent on Maxwell Gilchrist. Bess found a bill from a garage in Edinburgh. 'A new car, Frazer?' she queried as she studied it. 'But you already have a motor car.'

'It wasn't for me, it was for Max.'

She had to bite back her angry response. 'That's a very expensive present, Frazer.'

'Max needs a car, living here.'

It made her feel cold with fear, to know of Maxwell Gilchrist's constant proximity to her son. She saw what he was doing to Frazer. She saw how he took from Frazer, playing on his good nature to get what he wanted. She saw his worthlessness, his greed, his unscrupulousness and opportunism. Acknowledging how attractive he was, she felt for the first time a wash of relief that Kate was in London, which helped to alleviate her grief at her daughter's distance.

The wedding was a small affair in the parish church. Naomi wore a lilac-coloured two-piece and a picture hat. Her mother, coming into her bedroom, said irritably, 'At least it doesn't show yet. Though everyone will know why you're not wearing white,' and then went off to the church, leaving Naomi staring anxiously at her reflection. Not that *everyone* attended the wedding – Maxwell's side of the church was empty, and even the Jennings' side was distinctly sparse.

Maxwell was very drunk before the ceremony began. Though he made his responses clearly, Naomi could see it in the glitter in his eyes and in the way that, standing at the altar, he would slowly slip from the vertical and then have to right himself every now and then. He got drunker at the wedding breakfast her parents gave after the ceremony, and was gently sarcastic to her father and brothers in a way that made them suspect he was making fun of them without actually being sure of it. Afterwards, they quarrelled, and Naomi spent her wedding night crying into her pillow, but in the morning Maxwell was charming and apologetic and they made love – she never could resist his touch – and afterwards she lay back, satiated, her eyes closed, and thought, I am a married woman. And, I'm going to have a baby, a lovely little baby.

They had a week's honeymoon in Brighton, emerging every now and then from their hotel room to wander through the town, past the fantastic excesses of the Pavilion and rows of dreary boarding houses to the beach, where grey-green waves rustled across the pebbles and her high heels made walking precarious.

Then they travelled back to Scotland, to Edinburgh first, where Maxwell introduced her to his family. It was not until they were inside the Gilchrist family home that Naomi realized that Max hadn't told his father he was getting married.

'Father, this is my wife, Naomi,' Maxwell said, and Naomi saw the shock on Andrew Gilchrist's face, and Maxwell's pleasure in that shock. 'Your wife?' repeated his father.

'I didn't think you'd want to come to the wedding,' Maxwell said airily. 'It was only a small affair.'

'Naomi,' her father-in-law said, 'if you would go to the drawing room for a few moments, Maxwell and I have a few things to discuss.'

The house was solidly built and Naomi, sitting in the drawing room, drinking tea, could hear nothing of the conversation that ensued. She knew, of course, that Max hated his father, and when she thought of the way Andrew

Gilchrist's eyes had raked her body up and down, she too felt a shiver of revulsion.

When he came to join her, Maxwell was white-faced and furious, and they left shortly afterwards. The next day, they travelled to Ravenhart. Naomi adored the gatehouse, which was tiny but sweet, with two reception rooms and a kitchen downstairs and three bedrooms upstairs. There were also the two circular turret rooms that were impossible to furnish but were simply *adorable*. 'Snow White's cottage!' she exclaimed, the first time Maxwell showed her round the house in which she was to begin her married life, and she knew that she was going to be very, very happy there.

Maxwell's sister-in-law, Barbara, gave them a wedding present of a dozen linen sheets, one of the few sensible presents, apart from the house, that they received. Naomi's mother and father gave them a rather stingy cheque, and Simon and Hazel a white porcelain vase that Maxwell, very rudely, said looked like a urinal. Julian and Tessa sent a dinner service so gaudily floral that Naomi shoved it to the back of a cupboard and borrowed some plain white plates from Ravenhart House instead.

She seemed to spend most of the first few months of her marriage in bed, making love or sleeping, or in that languorous, half-dozing state where her dreams would merge with the brush of Maxwell's mouth against the hollow of her neck or the caress of his fingertips on her thigh. She thought that it would be fun to make love in every room in the house, so they did, on both of the spare beds, on the rug in front of the fire, and in the kitchen, the small of her back pressed against the table top. And in the hunting lodge, of course, where they had begun to discover their hunger for each other months ago, the very first day they had met.

A heavy snowfall spread a flat, white covering over the fields and hills. Like royal icing, Naomi thought; you almost wanted to scoop it up and taste its sweetness.

They went for a walk. Snow curled up the sides of walls and buildings and outlined the branches of the trees. Their boots crunched through the drifts and the air was so cold it scorched her face. A blizzard whirled round the summits of the mountains, making them fuzzy and indistinct. The grasses that fringed the burn were encased in ice, and ice froze the still water trapped in the rock pools.

After a while, she began to get fed up with the snow. It was exhausting even to tramp the mile to Ravenhart House. This far north, the sun rose later and set earlier than it did in Surrey, and, as she rarely got up before mid-morning and it became dark around three, it seemed to be night most of the time.

Running her own household for the first time without live-in help bewildered Naomi. There were a great many things she didn't know how to do, such as lighting a coal fire and making a supper dish out of the odds and ends in the pantry. Though there were only two of them, the house got into an awful mess, and the daily help, who lived in the next village, wasn't able to travel because of the snow.

While Maxwell was writing his novel, Naomi played

with Susie, her dog, and read a magazine and tried to sew a nightgown for the baby. She became muddled by the little pieces of winceyette and couldn't work out how they were supposed to fit together, so she made coffee and took a cup up to Maxwell and ran her fingers through his hair, stroking the lobe of his ear with her thumb. He kissed her in a distracted way and then began to type again. Leaving the turret room, she caught sight of herself in the full-length mirror in their bedroom, and with a pang of shock noticed the swell of her stomach, now just visible, and the extra weight on her thighs and haunches. What if he didn't want her any more? What if he became bored with her? Would he still desire her when she was fat and ugly and waddled round the house like a portly old lady?

Then the snow thawed and the sun shone again and Maxwell sold an article to *The Scotsman*, so to celebrate they drove to Edinburgh, where they blew the entire cheque on a night in a hotel and a wonderful meal.

Frazer invited fifty guests to his Hogmanay party. When the bedrooms at Ravenhart House were all full they tucked into sofas and daybeds or rented rooms in cottages in the village. The Lamptons and a couple Maxwell knew from Edinburgh, Alan and Catriona Gibson, stayed at the gatehouse. Catriona was stick-thin and green-eyed, and it came to Naomi, as New Year's Eve went on, that she was attracted to Maxwell. Catriona laughed at his jokes and tossed her hair and crossed her long, slim legs, showing them to their advantage whenever he was in the room. When Catriona patted the sofa for Maxwell to sit next to her, Naomi, who had drunk several glasses of champagne since lunchtime, said, 'No, Max is going to come and sit next to me, aren't you, darling?' Though he did as she asked, she saw the spark of anger in his eyes.

Then they headed up to Ravenhart House for dinner, the six of them squeezing into Charlie's Bentley. Naomi sat on Maxwell's knee; as they started down the drive, he murmured in her ear, 'Don't you think you should lay off the booze a bit, Mimi?' It infuriated her that Maxwell, who had been drinking steadily since lunchtime, should have the gall to criticize her.

At Ravenhart, Frazer sat at the head of the long mahogany table in the dining room. There were five courses and a different wine to accompany each course. After dinner, the women left the men to their port and cigars, and Naomi went to the bathroom to brush out her hair and reapply her lipstick. The alcohol had brought a flush to her cheeks, warming her pale complexion, and she knew that, in spite of her pregnancy, she looked as beautiful as any woman in the room.

The men joined them, and then they danced. Naomi kept an eye on Maxwell, and when Catriona went to speak to him she cut between them, taking his hand, pulling him onto the floor.

'Actually,' he said, 'I don't want to dance.'

'But I do.' She moved her hips, pressing herself against him. 'Dance with me, Max.'

'It's almost midnight. I'm going to give Frazer a hand with the champagne.'

'I want you to dance with me!'

'Dear me.' Enraging her, he smiled. 'Temper, temper.' Then he turned away.

She ran after him and caught hold of his sleeve. 'You'd dance if that woman asked you, I know you would!'

He blinked. 'Which woman?'

'Which woman? You know which woman!'

'No, I don't. Enlighten me.'

'That cow who's been making eyes at you all night,' she said furiously. Several people turned to stare at her.

'Naomi, do shut up, for God's sake.' He sounded weary. 'You're making a fool of yourself.'

'I'm making a fool of myself!' Her voice rose to a shriek. 'What about you? Damn you, Max!'

The band had stopped playing and Frazer was making ready to open the first bottle of champagne. As the guests counted down to midnight, Maxwell dragged Naomi out of the room. Beneath a storm of champagne and the sonorous boom of Ravenhart's great bell, ringing in the year of 1937, he murmured, 'Well, who could blame me if I did look the other way, shackled to a jealous shrew like you?'

They were standing in the hallway. The icy draught from the open front door and the coldness of his words stabbed her.

'Max,' she faltered. 'You don't mean that.'

'Don't I?'

'Max, please.' Her eyes burned with tears. Her defiance dissolved and she whispered, 'I'm sorry, I didn't mean to be a pain.'

He looked down at her dispassionately. 'And you shouldn't drink so much. It can't be good for the baby.'

'No. I won't, I promise.' She put the palm of her hand against his face. 'Kiss me, won't you, Max? For the New Year?'

For a long, awful moment, she thought he was going to refuse. But then he took her in his arms and kissed her, and she felt the strength of his body, crushed against her own, his need responding to hers. And it was only Frazer's voice from behind them, saying, 'Max, they're singing "Auld Lang Syne" and no one knows the bloody words,' that made him draw apart from her.

She wanted him to love her absolutely. Not to look at anyone else, not to think about anyone else. She needed to be loved like that; there was a void at the heart of her that ached to be filled. The first day they had met, they had hardly been able to wait to be alone before they had touched and kissed each other. She had known then that she had found her absolute love.

She loved him more and more as the weeks and months went on. When he was not there, she felt incomplete, her old restlessness threatening to return. Yet though his passion was undiminished, she began to think she saw a slight drifting away, a shifting of his interest, an inequality in their love that frightened her. Why did he not think of her all the time, as she did him? Why could he bear to be away from her, when she hated to be separated from him?

She resented anyone who tried to compete with her for his attention. Any women who dared to flirt with him she saw off smartly. But the person who made most demands on Maxwell's time was a more difficult proposition to deal with. Frazer seemed to think that he had some prior claim over Max. Sometimes the two men spent hours tinkering with the Lagonda or with Max's Lincoln, sometimes Max was out the entire day, fishing or shooting with Frazer. When Frazer called at the lodge, asking whether they fancied a drive to Braemar or Pitlochry, Naomi sensed his lack of warmth towards her, that he included her in the invitation merely out of politeness. She had known for some time that Frazer disliked her – Max might not have noticed, but then there were a great many things Max did not notice, or chose not to notice.

On the table in the hall at Ravenhart House there was a photograph of Maxwell and Frazer and that girl, Kate something, standing outside the old hunting lodge. When she herself was with Frazer and Maxwell, she often felt the outsider, held at a distance by their camaraderie, their rowdy male humour and boundless energy. Had Frazer been nicer to her then she might have felt warmer towards him, but his aloofness had at first surprised her and then it had needled her. She was used to men admiring her. Even if they did not always like her, she had come to expect admiration. She had at first put Frazer's lack of interest down to snobbishness: Frazer Ravenhart, with his castle and estates, looking down on a daughter of the nouveaux riches.

Then, not long after she and Max had married, they called at Ravenhart House one morning. Frazer's mother was visiting. Naomi chatted to Mrs Jago while the men wandered outside. Mrs Jago disappeared to chivvy Mrs McGill to make tea, and Naomi went to find the men. At the doorway, she paused. Frazer and Max were standing on the far side of the courtyard, beside the cars. Frazer's hand rested on Max's shoulder; his golden head was close to Max's dark one. When Max turned to go back to the house, Frazer's hand lingered for a moment or two. Naomi thought of the house, the car. A revelation, pieces falling into place. *So that's where the land lies.*

Now, when she was bored, she sometimes couldn't help teasing Frazer. It was gratifying to see him wriggle. Frazer needed to know that she, Max's wife, had the greater right to his company, and besides, Frazer could be so dreadfully stuffy, so touchy and easy to tease. Sometimes Max took Frazer's part, which made her feel awful, small and unimportant and lost. Although, deep down, she knew that however many cars or houses Frazer might give him, she had something Max wanted far, far more, she still resented the hold Frazer seemed to assume he had over Max. She tucked her secret close to her, knowing that it was dangerous, knowing also that it was a weapon.

The New Year brought bitter weather, snow and frost and harsh, roaring winds that rolled down the mountainsides and hurled themselves against the houses in the glen. Huddled in her fur coat, Naomi picked her way through the soup of icy mud that lay on the paths and roads.

Maxwell had gone to Edinburgh for the day to talk to a publisher. In the evening, Naomi made toast and Marmite and poured herself a drink and had her supper sitting in front of the fire. She tried the radio but found only a thin crackle of interference, so she put on a gramophone record instead and hummed along to the chorus of 'Anything Goes'. Outside, there were no street lamps

414

to relieve the darkness, and the night seemed to press against the windows, squeezing the light out of the small house.

Eventually, she went to bed, taking Susie with her for company. Lying in the darkness, she rested the palm of her hand on her belly. If she kept perfectly still, she could feel the magical, darting, flicker of movement of the baby in her womb. She marvelled that something so perfect should grow inside her, that it should not punish her for the violence that had been done to its predecessor. She knew that she had been given a chance to make up for her mistakes, to try again.

She was on the verge of sleep when she heard the creak, creak, creak of the floorboards. 'Max?' she called out, but there was no reply. She realized that she had not heard the car. She sat up in bed. Susie was asleep, coiled on the eiderdown. There it was again, footsteps. Someone was inside the house. Very quietly, she climbed out of bed and went to the window. Drawing aside the curtain, she looked out. There was no sign of the car.

Before she had come to Ravenhart, she had thought the country quiet, but now she noticed every whisper of branches, every flap of a night hunter's wing. If only Max would come home, she thought; she needed Max to come home. She stood still, shivering and listening.

After a few moments she flung open the bedroom door and went downstairs, her heart pounding. As she flicked on the sitting-room light she saw a bright glare, a shiver of movement, and she heard herself gasp. Beside the dying fire, the rocking chair was moving slightly, as though, a minute or two ago, whoever had been sitting there had sprung up and had quietly walked away.

There was a sound behind her; she screamed. Then she saw Maxwell, in the hallway. She rushed to him.

He embraced her; his skin was cold to the touch. 'What on earth are you doing, Mimi? I thought you'd be asleep hours ago.'

'There was a noise – I thought someone was in the house.'

Unlooping his scarf, he said soothingly, 'Doesn't look like it.'

'I heard footsteps. And the rocking chair was moving!'

'The wind, I should think.' She saw him move from room to room, checking windows and doors. 'Everything's closed up.'

But I heard someone, she was about to say, but then, seeing that he was tired and that he was already unstoppering the Scotch, she pressed her lips together. The wind, and she had mistaken her own heartbeat for footsteps. If she said it to herself often enough, she might believe it.

She put her arms round him as he poured the whisky, resting her head against the broad plane of his back. 'I'm so glad you're home, Max. I don't want you ever to go away again.'

She came to believe that the house was haunted. She looked up the word *poltergeist* in a dictionary: a noisy spirit, it said, which just about summed up the scratchings and tappings that woke her at night, and all the odd little things that seemed to shift and move of their own volition – a smear of ash on the white rug in front of the fire, which she could have sworn wasn't there when she went to bed; Simon and Hazel's porcelain vase, smashed to pieces one morning on the kitchen floor. And the rocking chair, always the rocking chair, swaying to and fro.

She never seemed to hear the noises when Maxwell was in the house. When she pointed out to him the broken vase, he said, 'You'd had one or two last night, Mimi. You probably smashed it yourself and forgot about it. And anyway, it was hideous.' She wondered whether Max was right and she'd knocked the vase over herself, but that evening, alone in the house because Max was with Frazer, she heard the tapping and pattering sounds again and went into the dining room to find the catkins she had picked earlier that day scattered over the hearth, the jam jar in which she had placed them overturned and water running onto the floor. She heard herself scream, 'Why don't you leave me *alone?*' and then she began to cry, and was still crying as she poured herself a drink and sat on the rug in front of the fire, the glass clutched in her hands, staring out through the window at the darkness.

The first time she met Naomi Gilchrist Bess had felt a thrill of hope. Naomi was not the sort of woman who would put up with Ravenhart's isolation for long. Infatuated with her new husband and languid with pregnancy, Naomi seemed content enough, but that would not last. When the baby was born, when she discovered that caring for an infant was a different matter to looking after her wretched lapdog, then, surely, Naomi Gilchrist would head back for the city, her husband and child in tow.

Perhaps discontent had already begun to grow. When the Gilchrists dined at Ravenhart House, Naomi drank and smoked too much. Often, towards the cold, ragged end of the winter, she looked nervous and tired. Bess might have felt sorry for her, pregnant and immured in that isolated little house, had she not suspected that Naomi's unhappiness was the key to Maxwell Gilchrist leaving Ravenhart.

She also noticed Frazer's impatience with Maxwell when he turned up late yet again for dinner, or when, the evening still in full swing, Naomi insisted on returning to the gatehouse. Sometimes Bess heard their raised voices, Frazer's and Maxwell's. She saw that Naomi disliked Frazer, and saw also her clumsy attempts to set Maxwell and Frazer against each other. Though she might have liked to do the same, she did not, sensing the danger in taking that route. Instead, she sympathized with Frazer, taking care never to go too far, to offer comfort rather than criticism. She knew that when the Gilchrists eventually left – because they would leave, she knew they would – she must be there for Frazer, to provide the reassurance that he needed and to fill the gap.

One morning, before she left for Waverley station, Martin asked her, 'Are you going to Ravenhart so often because you love Frazer or because you hate Maxwell Gilchrist?'

His question made her feel uneasy. These days, there was a distance between them.

She brushed her discomfort away. She said harshly, 'Does it matter?'

* * *

Margot's visits were like a cold breeze rushing through Oliver's house. One evening, Kate was cradling Stephen against her as she answered the imperious ring of the doorbell.

Outside, the wind rustled the dead leaves in the gutter and made the ribbons on the brim of Margot's hat shiver. 'Oh, you,' she said, seeing Kate. Then, remembering her manners, 'Is Oliver out, Miss Fearnley?'

'He's gone to the theatre. He'll be back soon. I'm babysitting for him. Would you like to come in, Mrs Stockton?'

Threading efficiently through the dim, shrouded shapes in the shop, Margot said, 'Shouldn't Stephen be in bed?'

'He's a bit cranky tonight. He's woken up a few times.'

In the sitting room, Margot stooped beside Stephen and laid her hand against his pink little face. 'Have you called a doctor?'

'No, I didn't think it was necessary. He hasn't a temperature. I thought perhaps he was coming down with a cold.'

'I think I shall call Dr Radley.' Margot went into the hall. Kate heard the whirr of the telephone dial, then Margot's strong, clipped voice.

As she came back into the room, Margot said, 'Always best to be on the safe side, I believe. Dr Radley has promised to call first thing in the morning. I'll take Stephen now.' She held out her arms for Stephen, who gave a little moan and curled against her chest. Then she muttered, 'I can't think why Oliver didn't ask me . . . I had an engagement but I've told him over and over again that I'll always rearrange.' She focused on Kate. 'Do you often babysit for Oliver, Miss Fearnley?'

'Every now and then.' Feeling that she had to establish her qualifications, Kate added, 'I've three younger brothers and three little sisters, Mrs Stockton. So I do know something about babies.'

Margot gave a polite smile. 'I'm sure. Where did you say Oliver was?'

'At the theatre, with Miss Fisher.'

'Miss Fisher?' Margot's nose wrinkled. 'Oliver didn't mention . . .'

'I work for Peggy Fisher. She directs a dance company.'

'Oh.' Margot looked down at Stephen and her face softened. 'He's fallen asleep. I'll take him upstairs.'

By the time Oliver came home, Margot had left. Telling Oliver about Margot's visit, Kate said, 'She made me feel like a rather incompetent housemaid. It's all right, I don't mind. But I thought I'd better warn you about the doctor.'

'Yes. Oh God.' He flung his coat and hat on the back of a chair. 'I'll go and have a look at him.'

When he returned downstairs, Oliver said, 'He's sound asleep. Seems fine. You don't have to rush off, do you, Kate?' She shook her head. 'A brandy, then.'

'Please.' She liked the way that Oliver's brandy, which he brought back from France, seemed to have lots of tastes, all mingled together.

He poured out two glasses. He said, 'Margot wanted to adopt Stephen, you see.'

She stared at him, shocked. 'Adopt him?'

'Yes. After Jane died. She and Nigel haven't been able to have children, and Jane was Margot's only sister, so when she died . . . The thing was, by then I had come to love him.' Oliver put a glass on the table beside Kate. 'And he seemed to me all that was left of Jane. I daresay Margot felt the same.' He sighed, and ran a hand through his hair. 'I suspect that, in some way, deep down, Margot holds me responsible. If Jane hadn't married me . . . I can't say the same thought didn't cross my mind, back then. So at the time, there was a lot of fuss. The implication was that a man on his own wouldn't be able to look after a baby. And quite often since, I've wondered whether Margot was right.'

'Oliver, how can you think that?'

'Well, I do, sometimes.' She thought he looked tired and worried. 'I feel guilty whenever anything goes wrong, like tonight. Guilty whenever I go out, actually.' He grinned wryly. 'But I realized I was becoming very dull, so that's why I started seeking out adult company again.'

'But Margot doesn't approve?'

'I suspect not.' He sat down on the sofa. 'When Stephen was born, I was pretty ham-fisted to begin with. And then, there were the nannies. I had to hire a nanny because of my work. Margot offered to look after Stephen during the week, but there seemed to me a danger in that – some sort of fudging of lines of demarcation. Anyway, some of the nannies were perfectly competent, but they always ended up leaving for one reason or another. But some were slovenly, and one was unkind – cruel, actually. She used to smack Stephen for making a mess when he was eating. Can you imagine, smacking a two-year-old for his table manners? When I found out, I felt – well, that I'd let him down. I still feel that, whenever I think about it. Anyway, now I manage with Mrs Richards, who lives round the corner and comes in a couple of days a week. And Leo helps in the shop and I've cut down my trips to France. And Margot, of course, is invaluable, I couldn't manage without her. But yes, I sometimes wonder whether Stephen would have been better off with Margot and Nigel. It might have been a more *normal* upbringing. And I wonder whether I was thinking of myself more than of him.'

'But you're his *father*, Oliver!'

'Does blood matter so much, do you think?'

She thought of Frazer. 'If you'd given him to someone else, he might have wondered why. He might have wondered whether it was because you didn't love him.'

Oliver swallowed the remainder of his brandy. 'Poor Margot, she does adore him. Which is why I can never get too annoyed with her for interfering.'

She said slowly, 'Do you think it's possible to love someone too much?'

'I don't know. I hadn't considered. Do you?'

'Perhaps I do. Think of all the ballets, *Swan Lake*, *Giselle*, about love so great, so passionate, you'd die for it.'

'And you don't approve of that?'

'I used to, I used to think all that was so romantic, but I'm not sure I do now. The last time I saw *Giselle*, I found myself thinking, oh, for heaven's sake, don't kill yourself, get a *job* or go away somewhere, or meet someone new.'

He laughed. Then he said gently, 'But love can transform, it can transcend.'

'And it can make people blind to the faults of the person they love.' Again, she thought of Frazer, Frazer with his eyes glazed as he told her that he was giving Mr Bain's house to Maxwell and Naomi. And not caring about the wrongness of what he was doing. *It's my house. I can do what I like with it.*

She said, 'Being in love can make you do things you wouldn't otherwise do. Things you know you shouldn't do. Your mind doesn't seem to belong to you any more. All you can think of is the person. And how can that be a good thing?'

'But if they feel the same, then isn't that what we mean by transcendence – leaving ourselves behind, caring more about someone else than we do about ourselves?'

And she said, 'But if they don't feel the same?'

Chapter Fifteen

At six months pregnant, Naomi's belly was swollen and hard and the infant inside it writhed slowly, like some underwater sea creature. Her breasts were blue-veined and voluptuous, her nipples the colour of cocoa. None of her clothes fitted her; her body seemed to spill from them, soft and white and plentiful. She borrowed Max's shirts and wore them over skirts whose gaping fastenings were held together by safety pins. She worried that Maxwell would no longer want her, looking as she did, and was afraid that he might find someone else. Yet, in bed, his fingertips made tracks over her breasts and traced the dome of her belly, and his expression was for once utterly serious, concentrated, unguarded. And when he was away on business in Edinburgh, he wrote her letters, letters that poked fun at the people he met at political clubs and rallies. In the margins of his letters were cartoons, of the staff of the magazines and news-sheets he sometimes worked for, and once, which made her laugh out loud, of his brothers: Niall, sharp-eyed, his fleshy good looks starting to go to seed; Sandy, stooped, ferrety, glancing suspiciously over his shoulder.

Time seemed to slice in half, day and night. Too often, the nights were bleak with apprehension. She was not a fearful person, risk exhilarated her, made her feel alive, but in the darkness sometimes, listening to the scratchings and the soft, tapping footsteps, her ears strained to hear the creak of the rocking chair and she felt a wash of panic, a dread of something unknown, faceless and malevolent.

She wondered whether pregnancy had made her like this – soft, vulnerable, at the mercy of all the horrible thoughts that seeped inside her head at night. When she confided some of her fears to the doctor, he recommended regular walks and joining the women's church group – 'Company, Mrs Gilchrist, all you need is a bit of company, to take your mind off these morbid thoughts. Lonely little place, this, not good for a woman in your condition.' Because of the way he looked at her as he spoke, she didn't mention the ghosts again. Yet his words stayed with her: *lonely little place, this, not good for a woman in your condition.*

The first time she talked to Maxwell about moving out of the gatehouse, they were in bed. She was lying in his arms, her head on his chest.

'Move out?' he said. 'Why on earth should we do that?'

'It's so quiet here. I never see anyone.'

'You see me. And Frazer.'

'This awful weather. So boring.'

'Then find something to do. Read a book. Go out for a walk. Or you could always tidy up.' The bedroom was scattered with discarded magazines, novels, notepaper and envelopes. Naomi's dressing table was a flurry of powder trails and crumpled tissues and plates smeared with crumbs, and cups in which the dregs of coffee had turned to a hard brown paste. He added, 'And we see plenty of people. There were dozens at the house last weekend.'

'At night. I meant I hate being alone at night.'

She saw the flicker of impatience in his eyes. 'Mimi, this house isn't haunted. It really, really isn't. It isn't even that old, for heaven's sake, and no one's died here as far as I know. And it's a nice house and we're living here rent-free and it simply doesn't make sense to think of moving out. And besides, we can't afford to move.'

'Money,' she said sulkily. 'You're always talking about money, Max.'

'One of us has to. You just spend the bloody stuff.'

A thought occurred to her. 'You could ask your father to lend us some money.'

'No. Never.' His voice was short.

'Why not? He's got plenty of money. Why shouldn't he give some of it to us?'

'Because he would insist that I work for him in return and I won't do that.'

'Just for a year or two.' She was stroking his stomach. 'We could live in Edinburgh. It would be fun to live in Edinburgh. Do it for me, darling.'

'Forget it.' His hand covered hers, stilling it. 'I mean it, Naomi. Never.'

Furious, she slid away from him and put out the lamp, curling up on the far side of the bed, her back to him. Though she waited expectantly for him to touch her, to beg her forgiveness and coax her into turning back to him, he did not, so she ignored him, pretending to be asleep when he offered her a cigarette.

'Suit yourself,' he said. She heard the rasp of a match in the darkness.

When he had given Maxwell the gatehouse, Frazer had seen it as the answer to a problem. Telling Bain that he must move out of his home had been unexpectedly dreadful – the man's fury had been undisguised, had even felt threatening, and Bain had contemptuously refused to take up Frazer's peace offering of continuing to act as Ravenhart's factor.

Frazer comforted himself by reminding himself that Max would be living only a mile from Ravenhart House and everything would go on much as it had before. It hadn't worked out quite as he had hoped, though. Sometimes he didn't see Max for weeks. Max's attention always seemed to be elsewhere – he had a way of wearing himself thin; these days, he looked paper-white, bluish shadows round his eyes.

Towards the end of February, Frazer had a letter from his accountant, Mr Whipple, asking him – no, *requiring* him, Frazer thought, jarred by the tone of the letter – to call at his offices in Edinburgh. Frazer arranged to visit the city at the end of the month.

Mr Whipple was blunt. Placing a sheet of paper covered in figures and graphs in front of Frazer, he said, 'If your earnings and outgoings continue at their present level, Mr Ravenhart, you will be bankrupt in – oh, three or four years, depending on interest rates, I would estimate.'

Bankrupt. Frazer stared at him. 'But the rents — and my grandparents' investments—'

'Lost much of their original value in the slump. And if you recall, over the past six months you have instructed me to liquidate a number of your assets. You have been dipping into your capital for more than a year. As for the rents, they barely cover the necessary repairs to the estate.' Mr Whipple's fat finger stabbed the paper. 'The evidence is there, I'm afraid.'

When he visited his mother that evening, Frazer was unable to hide his shock. After supper, which they ate alone because Martin was out on a call, Frazer paced up and down the drawing room.

'I might lose it,' he said. 'I might lose Ravenhart.' He had to repeat the words over and over to take in the enormity of such a possibility.

Unexpectedly, his mother said, 'Would you mind so much, Frazer?'

'Mind?' he repeated. 'Of course I'd mind.'

'Only . . .' she hesitated, 'sometimes you haven't seemed happy there.'

He said bluntly, 'Sometimes I detest it. But that's not the point. It's my inheritance. What would I be without it? Nothing.' He thumped his fist into his palm. 'Nothing at all.'

'Of course you'd be something,' she said gently. 'You would be *you.* You would be Frazer, my son, my daughters' brother.'

He rubbed his fingertips against his forehead. 'But I wouldn't — I wouldn't *matter.*'

'You would matter to *me*.' She put her hand on his sleeve. 'You would matter to me whatever you were, if you taught in a school or worked in a bank, if you were a dustman or a vagabond. If you were to lose Ravenhart then you would have to start again, that's all. As I myself have done a number of times.'

He stared at her, then his eyes dropped. He muttered, 'I couldn't do that. I couldn't start all over again.'

'It wouldn't be so bad, truly, Frazer. It would be hard at first, but it would get easier.'

'No.' It was inconceivable that he should lose Ravenhart. Whatever reservations he had about the place, it had become a part of him. It was his home, it belonged to him, it was part of his history, and he would let no one take it from him. He felt a sudden iron determination, mixed with excitement as he realized that he had discovered at last what he was meant to do with his life.

'I'm going to keep it,' he said. 'It's mine.'

His mother became brisk and practical. 'Then, if you like, I'll come to the house next weekend and we'll see what savings can be made.'

The following Sunday, they went through the books. Tasks that had once bored him he now found himself taking an interest in. He knew that he must make up for his past neglect. Together they listed the economies that must be made. He must postpone the landscaping of the garden and his scheme to install new bathrooms. He must cut down the bills from the grocer and his wine merchant, and make do with fewer servants, though they were thin on the ground as it was.

One afternoon the following week, he and Maxwell walked to the hunting lodge. Frazer told Max about Mr Whipple's warning. Then he said ruefully, 'So that's it, I'm afraid. No more days of wine and roses. Well, no more champagne or cigars, at least.'

'Bloody hell,' said Max. And then, waving his arms at the vast bowl of the mountains around them, 'But all this is *yours*. You must be able to make money out of it *somehow*.'

Yet he was damned if he could think how. If he put up the rents again the tenant farmers would squeal even louder. Half a dozen of the smaller landholdings were empty, had been empty for years, their few stony acres overgrown with nettles and ragwort. No one wanted to take on such unpromising land; anyone young, strong and ambitious had left for the city years ago.

Many of the great families who had once owned vast tracts of land in Scotland had had to sell up or had been declared bankrupt. You saw the advertisements in *The Scotsman* or *Country Life*, entire territorial empires put to the auctioneer's hammer, their power vanquished, their armies of employees without work, left to fend for themselves. Why should Ravenhart be any different?

Yet he kept his resolve. He would do whatever he must to keep Ravenhart; it had taken the threat of losing it to understand what it meant to him. His gaze drifted to the window, which framed the glen and the distant grey smudge of the hunting lodge. In the dark green patches of forest at the sides of the glen he saw a blur of movement as a group of deer broke from cover.

The deer, he thought. The glen was swarming with deer.

And there were salmon and trout in the river. An idea was beginning to form. He thought of the friends who came to stay at Ravenhart, who liked to fish in the river or hunt game or hike in the hills. And he thought of Ravenhart's many empty bedrooms, and the hunting lodge, that, with Max's help, he could surely make habitable in a month or two. *You must be able to make money out of it somehow*, Max had said, and he was beginning at last to see how he could.

He could rent out the fishing rights and look into how much it would cost to re-establish the grouse moor. People could stay in the house or at the hunting lodge. Paying guests at Ravenhart House . . . Could he stand it? Strangers in his house – but it wouldn't be his house much longer if he didn't steel himself to make some changes.

Family life had always been something Maxwell had tried to escape from – he had invariably had his bolt-holes: a cupboard under the stairs, the clump of trees at the bottom of the Charlotte Square garden, and later, as soon as he had grown up, a stranger's bed, or that attic room which existed only in his imagination, with its desk and chair and neat rows of books.

Nothing in the gatehouse was neat. If he made it so, Naomi only seemed to have to pass through a room for it to be scattered with dirty crockery, every table and shelf covered with pots of nail polish and cold cream, combs and tissues, magazines and knitting patterns. If he remarked on the untidiness she complained that they should hire a maid. She couldn't seem to see that, even if such a crea-ture could be found in this wilderness, they hadn't enough money to pay a maid, had barely enough money to pay for the Welsh rarebits and omelettes they lived on, the only dishes Naomi could be bothered to cook. Maxwell didn't mind the monotony of their diet, he had never bothered much about food, but after a while the pale runniness of the omelettes and the sour smell of the cheese nauseated him. He seemed to have a headache most of the time. He knew that it was probably the drink, and that he – both of them – should stop drinking. But Naomi's demands – for his undivided attention, for clothes and treats and to leave the gatehouse – needed to be blurred, deadened by alcohol.

And he couldn't finish the book. Three-quarters of the way through, he seemed to have hit the buffers, come across some sort of invisible stopping point, the strands of the plot flung out wide and unjoined, the characters lacking any conviction. If he managed to type a few pages, reading them through he saw that they were thin and flat, and chucked them in the bin. Lately, he had found himself avoiding his novel, doing anything but work on it, almost frightened by it, as though its incompleteness was a reproachful judgement. He wrote a flurry of articles for journals – he needed the money, for Naomi, for the baby – but Frazer's remark (*you'll never finish it, you never stick anything out*) rang in his ears, echoing his father's old estimate of him. A sponger, a good-for-nothing. He had believed he didn't mind, had even courted his father's displeasure, using it as a weapon, but lately something had begun to rankle.

He often thought that he could have found his way through the barrier if only he had had the time and peace to think things through. But he never did. Sometimes Naomi insisted they go to Edinburgh for the weekend, and sometimes they travelled to London, where they stayed with her louche, wealthy friends, and went to parties where, with the rising of the sun, the guests finally drifted away, slipping crumpled into black cabs or melting arm in arm into the orange-grey mist.

At Ravenhart, the peace he had once found there had, since his marriage, evaporated. When Naomi's friends or relations visited, the house was busy and noisy, his sanctuary in the turret taken up with their bags and coats, his presence demanded, insisted on. Sometimes he fudged up an excuse and drove to Edinburgh, where he would sit in his favourite cafes and pubs and meet old friends.

He might have left Naomi, called it a day, tried to make her understand that it was never going to work, if only it had not been for the baby. Sometimes the thought of the baby terrified him – what sort of father would he be, with only the pattern of his own father to follow? But at other times, thinking of the child filled him with an unexpected excitement and delight: the great adventure of bringing a new human being into the world, the possibility of creating a better family to replace the sham of a family he had left behind. He had begun to see that you did not have to repeat the same mistakes over and over. His child would give him a chance to start again, to prove himself.

Once or twice recently he had ended up in bed with Jenny Watts, his old flame from the Two Magpies. He felt a murmur of guilt, knowing that he hadn't kept his marriage vows for as long as six months. But in the smoky, paint-fumed peace of Jenny's studio, while Jenny worked silently at her easel, something whirred and clicked into place, and the book began to free itself, and he was able to write again, curled in a corner of Jenny's threadbare sofa, a cigarette in one hand, a cup of black coffee within reach of the other. Jenny listened, paintbrush in hand, when he talked about the baby, his tangled feelings for it, his mixture of optimism and dread and exhilaration.

And then there was Frazer. From Frazer, too, Maxwell sensed unfulfilled expectations, a running out of patience. It was as if, in giving him the gatehouse, some sort of invisible balance had been tipped. He had taken too much, far more than he was able to repay. They were not equals any more; all the weight of obligation had shifted to his side, all the moral high ground to Frazer's. Their once easy friendship had become burdened by indebtedness. Frazer had always possessed a touch of arrogance; lately, it seemed to Maxwell that Frazer's condescension had become tinged with resentment. Frazer seemed to believe that he, Maxwell, owed him something, that some kind of compensation was required from him – his time, his attention, his ability to amuse, which was stretched thin these days and only really came to life when he was fuelled by drink.

More and more often, he felt trapped between them. He, who distrusted love, now found himself pulled apart by it. He wondered whether what he felt for Naomi, that fierce desire that was mixed sometimes with exasperation and sometimes with tenderness, was love. Waking in the morning, he would watch her sleep, and see the rise and fall of her breast, and the way that, sleeping, she seemed younger, more defenceless. Yet his fondness evaporated as the day went on. In company, he could feel her watching him, feel the heat of her jealous gaze. Speak to or even glance at another woman, and she could be viperish and irrational, given to making scenes, capable of resorting to anything to secure his undivided attention. Something in Naomi enjoyed conflict, courted it, manipulated it. *Takes one to know one*, he thought.

At weekends, Kate went with Pearl, the seamstress, to the Hammersmith Palais. Boys with slicked-back hair and five-shilling suits asked them to dance. There was the glitter of lights and the smell of cigarettes and cheap perfume. The beat of the music pulsed through the walls and floor, seeping into Kate's limbs.

She went home for a long weekend. Her mother was busy, restless, on edge. After supper, Martin went to his study to work on his book. Once, when it was very late and she couldn't sleep, Kate went downstairs to make herself cocoa and saw the thin bright sliver of light beneath Martin's study door. She thought that the book, with its dark crannogs and souterrains, was where Martin hid himself when he didn't feel in tune with the world.

She never stayed at home long; it made her feel unsettled, as if she was being dragged back into a life she had grown out of. There was the initial joy of seeing her mother and Martin and her sisters, and the pleasure of her familiar room and her own bed, but quite soon she began to feel reduced and diminished, a child again. And eventually there was the relief of being back on the train, her face pressed against the window as she waved to her family, who became smaller and smaller as the engine pulled out of the station, while her delight in returning to London was mixed with a sense of loss at the parting and guilt at the hopeless jumble of her feelings.

Back in London, babysitting for Oliver, she lifted Stephen out of his bed when he cried and cuddled him, breathing in his warm infant smell of sleep and milk and talcum powder. His cheek, against hers, was as soft as velvet. She remembered how Rebecca's sooty black lashes curved, making half-moons against her skin, and how, when Aimée had been a newborn baby, she had fed her a bottle and little milky bubbles had gathered at the puckered corners of her mouth.

'When I'm away from them I miss them,' she said exasperatedly to Oliver one evening. 'And when I'm with them I seem to feel annoyed with them a lot the time.'

'Ah, family life, Kate,' said Oliver wryly, 'family life.'

Oliver's wife, Jane, had been a concert pianist. The first time Oliver had seen Jane she had been playing Chopin at the Wigmore Hall. In the portrait of her on the grand piano in Oliver's drawing room, her long, tranquil face was framed by straight, soft hair pinned back with a diamond clip. In another photograph Jane was standing in the garden at the foot of the spiral staircase, wearing a maternity smock and clutching in her hands a bunch of flowers. Kate thought she looked wistful, slightly apprehensive, as though she had suspected even then the price she would be required to pay for love.

*　*　*

So sweet and naive, and the only virgin in Pimlico. Billy's words rankled. She didn't want to be sweet and naive any more. Sweet and naive, she had fallen in love with Maxwell Gilchrist and it had taken her far, far too long to understand that he had only kissed her because he would have kissed any passably presentable girl who had let him. *Didn't you know that?* But she hadn't known anything, anything at all. Ignorance wasn't bliss, ignorance humiliated you, left you unguarded.

Boys took her to the cinema and bought her suppers in cafes. Though none of them touched her heart, she grew fond of some and kissed them and held their hands. In an attic room on the Embankment, she lost her virginity. She was nervous as she let her lover take off her clothes, nervous that she would not come up to scratch, that he would somehow be disappointed. Mist blurred the uncurtained windows and the gas fire sputtered as he kissed her breasts, her navel, her belly.

Afterwards, he lit two cigarettes and gave one to her and they smoked companionably in the mess of sheets and blankets. She thought that this was the part she liked best, her body curled against someone else's as the ships hooted their foghorns on the misty river. She felt a certain triumph, having crossed from being a girl to a woman, having got it over and done with.

Kate saw in the newspapers the photographs of Guernica, the Basque town in northern Spain bombed by the German Condor Legion. Her gaze spanned the bleak snapshots of ruined buildings, pausing at the tangles of brick, cloth and debris from which something – a spar of wood? A human limb? – jutted at an angle.

She was drinking coffee and eating toast with Billy late one night when she said, 'Do you think wicked people always get their own way? Do you think that evil's always stronger than good?'

Billy looked at her and yawned, and said, 'Blimey, Kate, I've no idea, no idea at all. What a question. Couldn't we talk about something a bit more, a bit more . . . *fun?*' Then he rubbed his eyes and added gloomily, 'Knowing my luck, Hitler'll pick his moment just as I get my first solo. My first break, and wham, everything blown to pieces.'

She asked Oliver the same question. She had cooked Sunday lunch in Oliver's flat. After the roast lamb, Stephen had banana custard and Kate and Oliver devoured a tarte aux noix that Oliver had brought back with him from France. Cutting the tart, Oliver said, 'Stronger? In what way?'

'Wicked people have nothing to hold them back. They do whatever they want. Good people are always thinking, what if I do this, what if I do that, then something awful might happen.'

'But there comes a point,' said Oliver slowly, 'when they stop thinking that. When they feel that they have nothing left to lose.'

Kate looked up at him. 'If there is a war, what will you do?'

Oliver was spooning a piece of banana into Stephen's mouth. 'I'm not sure. I may not have much choice – none of us may have any choice. I shall send Stephen to the country, though. If London is bombed . . .'

Sunlight filtered through the leaves of the wisteria beside the French windows, making shifting dappled shapes on the kitchen floor. Kate thought how odd it was, how vile, that they could be sitting in Oliver's kitchen, eating tarte aux noix and talking of war. There was the scent of flowers and the taste of walnuts and the thought that in a few months or years, death could rain down from that pure blue sky.

Oliver said, 'And you, Kate? What would you do?'

'I'd join one of the women's services.' Her statement took her by surprise; she had never put it in words before, the need she felt to align herself against tyranny.

'Good for you.' He put Stephen's bowl in the sink. Then he said, 'I should miss you.'

'And I'd miss you, Oliver. And Stephen.'

He was leaning against the sink, his hands dug into his jacket pockets, looking at her. 'I'd miss all of my friends, of course, but I think I'd miss you most of all, Kate.'

Turning aside, she went to stand at the top of the spiral staircase. She heard herself say, her voice thin and glassy, 'Such a gorgeous day. Why don't we have our coffee outside?'

They were sitting in the garden when Margot arrived in a whirl of Lentheric Tweed, blue-green feathers sticking spikily from her hat.

'Just thought I'd pop by on my way home.' She scooped Stephen off the grass and kissed him. 'Now, why aren't you having your afternoon nap, young man? Surely he should be having his nap, Oliver?'

'I don't think he needs one, these days. He just sits in his bed and talks to himself, and he might as well do that here.'

'He looks a little overtired.'

'He's three,' said Oliver firmly. 'He's not a baby any more, Margot, he's a little boy.'

'Yes.' Margot looked suddenly stricken. 'So awful to think that Jane never—' She turned away, blowing her nose.

Oliver put his arm round Margot, and Kate went back upstairs to the flat and gathered up her things. She was walking out through the shop when Margot, looking blotchy, caught up with her. 'Can I give you a lift, Miss Fearnley? Where are you heading?'

'Pimlico. That's very kind of you, Mrs Stockton, but there's no need.'

'It's quite all right, it's on my way.' Outside, Margot peered through the front passenger window of her car, to where a terrier slept, curled up on a folded coat. 'You don't mind sitting in the back, do you, Miss Fearnley? Tommy is so bad-tempered if he's woken up.'

Margot drove with a crashing of gears and a stabbing of the accelerator, darting precipitately out of junctions and swerving rapidly round corners. Every now and then, raising her voice above the sound of the engine, she flung remarks over her shoulder to Kate.

'Oliver does a terrific job with Stephen, don't you think? So hard for him at first – sterling task – never easy bringing up a child on one's own, especially for a man.'

Kate said, 'Stephen's a lovely little boy.'

'Isn't he? And so advanced for his age. I'm sure he's going to be musical, like Jane.' Margot pulled out of a junction into an invisible gap in the traffic. There was a screech of brakes; a horn sounded. 'This friend of Oliver's, Miss Fisher . . .'

'Peggy?'

'Have they known each other long, do you know?'

'Six months or so, I think.'

'Oh.' The single syllable was loaded with disapproval and suspicion. 'Oliver didn't say . . . How did they meet?'

'Peggy wanted to borrow some antique furniture for a set. Someone recommended Oliver's shop. Peggy took Oliver to dinner to say thank you.' Taking pity on Margot, Kate added, 'Peggy has lots of men friends. But ballet's the only thing she really cares about.'

A sharp jab of the horn and the cyclist in front of them lurched and wobbled. Margot said, 'No one will ever be able to take Jane's place, of course. They were so much in love. Oliver adored Jane from the moment he saw her. She was one of a kind – beautiful and talented and gentle. You don't meet many such people in the course of a lifetime.'

Kate looked out at the people hurrying along the pavement.

Margot raised her voice again. 'I did wonder whether he would find someone else, when Stephen was very tiny.'

Kate echoed, 'Someone else?'

'A widow, perhaps. It would have been a marriage of convenience, of course, because Oliver will never love any woman except Jane. But I suppose he couldn't bear to think of another woman living in Jane's house, taking care of Jane's child. It would have been too painful for him.'

She was warning her off, Kate realized. Margot was warning her off Oliver. She felt a sudden urge to giggle, which she stifled by biting her lip. Margot was afraid that she was in love with Oliver, who must be ten years older than she was, and who lived in amiable chaos, and whom

441

she liked enormously while finding even the idea of being in love with him completely ridiculous. There's not the smallest chance of me being in love with Oliver, she wanted to say. He's not the sort of man I fall in love with.

Her private amusement lasted until Margot dropped her off outside her lodgings and she let herself into her room. Then she sat down on her bed, her gaze drifting round her possessions: the books, the family photographs, the collection of hats, the pot plant on the window sill. She thought of the day that Naomi Jennings had first come to Ravenhart. She remembered her own wild elation, waking that morning, her mouth bruised, her skin alive, tingling with the memory of Maxwell Gilchrist's touch. And how, walking from the hunting lodge to the house, the colours of the burn and moorland had contained a particular vividness, and how the air that surrounded her had seemed to resonate, its chemistry altered by the events of the previous night. And how, after Maxwell and Naomi had met, with whatever mutual flash of lightning that encounter had entailed, she had continued to deceive herself, to tell herself there was hope where no hope had ever existed, to long for a man who had never loved her and never would.

Covering her face with her hands she felt the tears seep through her fingers. Not much of a love affair – a handshake at a railway station, a step in the dark across a starlit rooftop, a few kisses. Such a small thing, but why did it wound so, why did it have the power to alter her into something she had not chosen to be?

She knew that there wasn't the smallest chance that she would fall in love with Oliver Colefax, just as there wasn't the smallest chance that she would fall in love with any of the boys she met through the theatre or at the Hammersmith Palais. She seemed incapable of love, of passion, seemed to have lost the capacity for it, and wasn't at all sure that she would ever discover it again.

A month before the baby was due, Maxwell drove Naomi to Edinburgh, where they bought a Moses basket and a pram and sheets and blankets and clothes. He was touched by the pleasure Naomi took in picking out the tiny white clothes; it showed him a side of her he hadn't seen before.

Everything was going well. Laden with carrier bags, they had tea at Jenners. They were to stay the night with Niall and Barbara. When they arrived at the house that evening, Maxwell saw his father, standing by the drawing-room fire. Barbara must have seen him recoil, because she steered him into a side room and, putting a large tumbler of whisky in his hands, said, 'I didn't know he was coming, honestly. He just turned up and Niall asked him to stay to dinner.' She peered at him. 'I'm awfully sorry, Max. Can you bear it?'

Because he was fond of Barbara, he made himself smile and say, 'I lived with the old bastard for eighteen years, I'm sure I can cope for a few hours.'

Oddly, his father seemed in an unusually amenable frame of mind, praising the food and failing to criticize Niall's choice of wine. When Naomi, who was sitting next to Andrew Gilchrist, proudly listed the newspapers and journals that had bought Maxwell's articles, his father said only, 'I'm pleased to hear you're making a decent living, Maxwell.'

And though Maxwell studied the sentence for sarcasm, he couldn't find any.

Then Naomi sighed and said, 'Well, we get along, but we'd love to be able to move to Edinburgh,' and he felt himself tense.

'Edinburgh?' His father shifted his bulk on his chair, and scooped more pudding from the serving dish. 'Why not? I've got an empty flat, as it happens. You can have it, if you like.'

Naomi's face brightened.

Maxwell said quickly, 'It's all right, Father, we're happy where we are.'

'But Max—'

'Leave it, Mimi.'

Her mouth opened, then shut again. Barbara began to talk about her daughters; Maxwell, glancing at Naomi, saw her angry, resentful expression.

Later, in their bedroom, Naomi wrenched the silk flowers from her hair. 'I can't believe you said that!'

Maxwell was lying on the bed, fully dressed. 'Said what?'

'About the flat. Your father was going to give us a flat.'

She was fumbling with the fastening of her necklace; he rose and unclasped it for her. 'My father never *gives* anything. There's always a price to pay. If you'd known him longer you'd understand that.'

She swung round to him, her eyes blazing. 'I don't care! Anything to get out of that awful hole! How can you be so unkind? Making me live in a place that's haunted!'

He said wearily, 'Christ, not that again.' And then, with a huge effort, 'If you really want to move away from

Ravenhart, then I'll find a way of doing it. But not with his help. Please, Naomi.'

He bent and kissed the slope of her neck, but she pushed him away. He felt his temper fraying; he went to the door.

'Where are you going?'

'Out,' he said shortly. 'I'm not in the mood for this.'

'Don't you dare walk out on me!' Her voice rose in a shriek as he shut the door behind him. He heard something thump against the back of the door – a shoe, her jar of cold cream.

Driving north the following day, she was unspeaking, as taut as a coiled spring. Back at the gatehouse, she had poured herself a drink before he finished unloading the bags. He said, 'The poor little devil's going to come into the world with a hangover.'

'Shut up, Max,' she hissed at him. 'Shut up, shut up, shut up!'

He went upstairs to the turret room. Writing was like squeezing tears out of stone. He rested his head on his folded arms, and then, without expecting to, fell asleep.

He was woken by the sound of the car engine. Looking out of the window he glimpsed Naomi, at the wheel, reversing the Lincoln into the drive. He ran outside, calling out to her, but the car did not pause as it headed through the gates.

It was almost dark, and it had been raining heavily. The roads were a slippery mixture of mud and rain. Back inside the house, he saw the bottle of gin on the table. He stood for a moment, feeling cold inside, seized by a premonition of disaster, and then he grabbed his coat and a torch and headed out through the gates. The rain had thinned to a drizzle and he peered through the murk as he jogged along the verge. She was a lousy driver even when she was sober, erratic and too fond of speed, and he couldn't remember whether she had put on the headlamps. In his mind's eye, he saw her involved in a head-on collision, or skidding on the narrow, twisting roads, the car concertinaed against a rock face.

Rounding a corner, he saw the Lincoln. It lay across the road, the front wheels jammed into a grassy bank. He began to run.

He yanked open the driver's door and Naomi half fell against him. 'Max . . .' she said. She was shaking and she sounded dazed.

He hauled her out of the car. She hadn't even put her coat on. For some reason that made him even angrier. He yelled, 'You stupid, stupid bitch! What the hell did you think you were doing?'

'I was getting away from you, Max! I hate you!' Her fists drummed against his chest.

'You could have killed yourself!'

'I don't care, I'd rather be dead. You don't love me . . .'

The words blurred and distorted, and she began to cry, breathless sobs interspersed with loud, high-pitched, despairing screams. He stared at her, appalled, and then he put his arms round her and stroked her wet hair. After what seemed like an age, he felt her relax and lean against him, the weight of the child between them, her sobs coming further apart now, her shaking less violent. Eventually, he made her stand to the side of the road, his coat wrapped round her shoulders, while he rolled the car, whose bonnet was staved in, onto the verge. Then they walked back to the gatehouse.

It had all seemed so easy, so feasible, when Frazer had first thought of it. Drawing up lists of what needed to be done – the important stuff at the top of the list, such as having the bedroom chimneys swept so that the house didn't catch fire and his guests didn't actually die of pneumonia – had been satisfying. Frazer intended to open Ravenhart for business in the late summer, in time for the shooting season. He must have money coming in as soon as possible; the estate needed to start earning cash instead of devouring it.

Putting his plans into practice, though, proved more difficult than he had anticipated. Finding reliable builders, painters and decorators was a frustrating and long-drawn-out task. Everyone he spoke to in the village seemed to be mysteriously otherwise engaged. He had to go to Pitlochry to find a chimney sweep, to Braemar to find a seamstress to help his mother repair the moth-eaten curtains.

Maxwell was supposed to be helping him finish the hunting lodge. But Max, too, was infuriatingly unreliable. Once – it seemed a long time ago – he had tolerated Max's poor timekeeping, had found it endearing, almost. Yet a bit of hard work seemed little enough to ask, especially considering everything he had done for Max. The trouble with Max, Frazer thought, was that he preferred to take rather than to give. Understanding that at last made him feel raw and humiliated.

The hunting lodge was almost habitable. They had

repaired the roof the previous summer; Frazer himself had fixed the chimney so that it drew properly at last. The stone flags on the ground floor were in reasonable condition, and he had succeeded, through paying considerably over the odds, in persuading a glazier to haul his tools and materials along the burn-side path so that he could replace the windows.

Maxwell had promised to help him replace the floorboards on the upper storey of the house. Single-handed, it would be a pig of a job. On the day they were to start work on the floor, Frazer turned up early at the lodge. Maxwell hadn't arrived yet, so he began on his own. Though he kept peering out of the window at the path and the hills, there was no sign of Max. Midday came, and still Max had not appeared, and Frazer began, as he lugged planks up the narrow, winding staircase, to feel an impotent rage.

As the afternoon lengthened he must have been tiring, because his concentration slipped and he struck his thumb with the hammer. Dizzy with pain, he closed his eyes. When he opened them again, he saw that the nail was already darkening.

Stumbling downstairs, he had a sudden sharp, sweet memory of the times they had spent here, himself and Kate and Maxwell, and he felt a stab of misery and regret. He missed Kate, who had been sweet and easygoing, and whose place had been taken by Naomi, with her whining demands and her unpleasant, suggestive way of looking at him.

He walked back to the house, where Phemie, her brown eyes full of sympathy, bandaged his thumb. He took a couple of aspirins and discovered that he was out of cigarettes, so he drove to the village.

As he came out of the shop, he saw Maxwell, on the other side of the road. He looked pleased with himself, Frazer thought furiously. Catching sight of him, Max waved and ambled across the road to him.

Frazer said, 'What the hell happened to you?' and Max's expression altered, becoming wary.

'What's wrong? Have I forgotten something?'

'You were supposed to be helping me at the lodge.'

'Oh.' Maxwell produced his familiar charming smile. 'Sorry. Slipped my mind.' Then he frowned. 'Frazer . . .'

'What?'

'Could you give me a lift back to the gatehouse? It's just that the car's in the garage and this bloody weather . . .'

Frazer hissed, 'Sometimes, I could kill you!' and Max, looking alarmed, took a step back.

'It doesn't matter. I'll walk.'

Maxwell headed off into the rain. Frazer swore, and then he noticed Ronald Bain, standing just a few feet away from him, watching. 'Enjoying the show, are you?' Frazer snarled at him before he walked back to the car.

Maxwell said, 'Bloody awful day out there.'

Naomi, turning to look at him as he came into the gatehouse kitchen, said, 'I suppose you think that's my fault, too.'

He took a deep breath as he peeled off his wet coat. First Frazer and now Naomi. That morning, he had reached the end of his novel. He had felt a glow of elation and relief.

He said lightly, 'Hardly. Unless you have influence with the gods.'

She was standing at the sink, peeling potatoes. 'I meant, because of the car. Where have you been?'

'I walked to the village. I phoned the garage.'

'Oh. Have they fixed it?'

'Not yet. They've had to send for a part from Glasgow.'

She looked dismayed. She asked, 'Did you see anyone in the village?'

The whisky bottle was on the table; he poured himself a measure. 'Only Frazer.'

The knife paused and a length of potato peel dropped into the water. She said, 'Aren't you going to give me a drink, Max?'

He saw the empty glass on the window sill, and the way that the swell of her belly meant she had to stand away from the sink. As she moved the pan of potatoes to the stove, water sloshed onto the floor. He said, 'I thought you said you were going to cut down.'

'I have. I haven't had a thing all week. But I felt so miserable this afternoon, all on my own in this horrible house in this horrible weather.' She shoved the glass under his nose. Her voice dropped, and became soft, purring, menacing. 'Come on, Max, give me a drink. You're not going to say no, are you? I didn't think you ever said no. Drink . . . ciggies . . . sex . . .'

He poured her a drink. She raised her glass in a toast. 'Bottoms up.' Then she drained the glass and leaned back against the sink, her eyes closed. 'That's better.' She held out her glass again. 'Another one, darling.'

'I don't think—'

'I want another one!' She seized the bottle and upended it into the glass. He made to leave the room, but as he reached the door, she whispered, 'Don't go,' and he paused, his back to her. 'Please, Max.'

He turned to look at her. There were dark thumbprints round her eye sockets and her skin looked colourless, drained. He shrugged. 'Are you sure you don't want me to go? I seem only to annoy you.'

'I'm sorry.' There were tears in her eyes and she pressed her teeth into her lower lip. She wailed, 'I wanted to make you a lovely dinner, Max. But I always seem to get it wrong!' She held out her arms to him. 'Please, darling, give me a hug.'

In her embrace, he remembered why, meeting her for the first time in the courtyard of Ravenhart House, he had felt such a powerful attraction to her. Her velvety skin and rich, dark hair, and the way she moved, felt and smelt of sex. Even now, at almost eight months pregnant, wearing a grubby apron over her clothes and with whisky on her breath, he still wanted her.

They kissed for a while and then, drawing back from him, she said excitedly, 'Why don't we go to London, Max? We could stay with Tessa and Julian. It's ages since we've been to London. We could go tomorrow.'

He shook his head. 'Not tomorrow – maybe in a week or so. I have to type out the last part of the book and I said I'd help Frazer with the hunting lodge.'

'*Frazer.*' Her lower lip stuck out. 'I need to go away now, Max, not in a week's time. I don't see why I should have to wait because of Frazer.'

She sounded petulant, like a small child that has been crossed. He felt a surge of irritation, and said coldly, 'Don't you? Perhaps it's because we wouldn't have a roof over our heads if it weren't for Frazer. For God's sake, Naomi, I'm only asking you to wait a week.'

She took a bowl of eggs from the pantry; he watched her crack them. The snap of the shell on the rim, the blob of yolk and albumen sliding into the earthenware dish with fragments of shell. Her movements were clumsy and blurred and he thought she looked ill. He damped down his impatience and made another effort. 'Why don't you sit down, have a break? I'll make you some tea. You look tired.'

Without warning, she hurled the bowl at him. He ducked, a reflex action, and it smashed onto the floor tiles beside him, spraying a star shape of yellow slime. 'Tired?' she screamed. 'You mean ugly, don't you? Poor old Naomi, fat and ugly! No wonder you can't stand being with me!'

'No.' He knew he shouldn't say it, and knew also that he would. 'It's not how you look that makes me long to get away from you. It's how you behave.'

'Me? You're criticizing my behaviour?' She lurched across the floor towards him, careless of the fragments of pottery and shell and the glutinous strands of egg. Her eyes had become narrowed and knowing and her voice dropped. 'You've got a nerve. What about you, Max? Some of the things you do aren't exactly in the boy scouts' manual, are they? What about your friend Frazer, for instance? What about dear old Frazer?'

'Shut up, Naomi.' He took a step back from her.

'Oh, poor baby.' She pouted, the words dripping feigned

452

sympathy and venom. 'Don't you want to talk about him, Max? What's wrong? Do you think I don't know about him? Do you think I don't know why he hates me? Shall I tell you why? It's because I took you away from him. Poor old Frazer's jealous, isn't he? He's the reason you won't leave this awful house, he's the reason—'

'I said, shut up!'

'Why? Didn't you know, Max?' Her smile was crowing, triumphant. 'Didn't you know your best friend has the hots for you?'

His fists clenched, then he pushed past her and flung open the door. Outside, it was still raining. He took a deep breath of cool air as he fumbled in his pocket for his cigarettes. Silence for a while, and an immense relief as her taunting voice stopped. Then she called out his name. At first, he ignored her, but, hearing a new timbre to her voice, he glanced back and saw that she was sitting at the table, hunched, her hand clutched protectively over her belly.

She looked up at him. 'I've got a pain, Max.'

He wondered whether she was putting it on, whether this was just another ploy to grab his attention. 'A pain?'

'What if it's the baby?' she whispered. 'What if something's wrong with the baby?'

She sounded frightened; the remaining colour had drained from her face. His anger dissolved and was replaced by fear. He went back into the kitchen. 'You're probably just tired. You shouldn't get so upset. If you had a rest—'

'Yes.' She grabbed his words like a lifeline. 'That's it, I need a rest.'

In their room, she lay motionless on the bed as he tucked the eiderdown over her. Her dark, alarmed gaze followed him round the bedroom. He heard her say, 'I couldn't bear anything to happen to the baby.'

'I'll fetch Dr Macbean. Just to make sure.'

'Don't go.' Her hand reached for his; mechanically, he took it. 'Those things I said . . . I'm sorry. I shouldn't have.' Her voice was scarcely audible, as if she was too tired to speak. 'I don't know why I say things like that. I know I shouldn't, but something makes me. I think it's because I'm so afraid of losing you.'

'Hush.' He smoothed back her tangled hair. 'It doesn't matter.'

She closed her eyes. She said nothing for a while, and he thought she had fallen asleep, but then she murmured, 'It's this place. I've got to get away from it, Max. I've got to.'

A storm battered the glen over the next two days. When, on the third day, it eased, Frazer left the house after breakfast, reminding Phemie that his mother would be arriving that afternoon.

Iron-grey clouds drifted around the summits of the hills as he made his way to the hunting lodge. The water in the burn was high, lapping over the stepping stones; looking down, the stones seemed to Frazer to shiver slightly as he placed his feet.

As he reached the far bank of the river, he caught sight of the broken windowpane beside the door of the hunting lodge. He thought at first that a stray branch, blown by the wind, must have smashed it, but then, as his gaze swept over the windows of the upper storey, he saw that they, too, were broken. Circling the lodge, he discovered that not a single intact sheet of glass remained. In his absence, someone had come out to the lodge and had staved in every pane.

He found a cardboard box and began to gather up the shards strewn across the floorboards – now wet from the rainstorm – he had nailed down only a few days earlier. When the box was full, he walked up the path by the burn to the pool with the waterfall. Standing on one of the rocks that fringed the pool, he upended the box over the deepest part of the pool, where the glass could do no harm. The splinters of glass danced in the water, their facets glinting in the weak sunlight, and then the deep water took them, and they were gone.

Two days earlier, Dr Macbean, after examining Naomi, had taken Maxwell aside. 'I've listened to the baby's heartbeat and it seems fine,' he said, and Maxwell had felt an intense relief. Then the doctor had paused for a moment before adding, 'But your wife seems very overwrought, Mr Gilchrist. I'm afraid that she's rather highly strung. Of course, pregnancy can make women prone to strange fancies and I'm sure she'll be as right as rain after the child is born, but I think you need to keep an eye on her, never-theless. Perhaps her mother could come to stay with her. With Mrs Gilchrist's temperament it might be better if she didn't spend too much time on her own.'

As he showed the doctor out of the house, Maxwell had

said flatly, 'My wife doesn't get on with her mother. But I'll think of something.'

He had two choices, he thought: to run away, or to stay with Naomi and try to make a proper go of it. The trouble with running away was that you had to run to somewhere, and then all the difficulties, of people and money and career and choices, were liable to start all over again. And besides, there was the baby. Some things couldn't easily be unpicked.

But to stay with Naomi would involve a number of compromises. He would have to find a means to support himself and his wife and child. No more living from hand to mouth, no more grim lodging houses or strangers' beds. No more dependence on the generosity of friends. Somehow, he would have to fashion himself into a reasonably conventional member of society. He wasn't absolutely certain that he could.

And they would have to leave Ravenhart. If he insisted they stayed here, their marriage would be doomed to failure. They quarrelled because Naomi drank; she drank because she was unhappy, and part of her unhappiness was her dislike of the house.

And besides, her outburst the other day had made their leaving Ravenhart inevitable. She had said things that made it impossible for him to stay here. He had always known, at some level, that Frazer's liking for him was more than that of common friendship. He had known men like Frazer at school, men with a tenderness for their own sex. The outrage that many people felt about such things had always bewildered him. His own moral compass never seemed to quite match others'. He sought out new experiences, even when they frightened him, and though sex was great fun and he missed it enormously if for some reason he didn't have it, he had never found it hugely meaningful. As for love, it was hard enough to find that at all without questioning the exact nature of it.

But he knew that most people didn't think as he did, and that Naomi's understanding of Frazer's nature would lie uneasily between them, to be unearthed whenever she was jealous or angry. When she was drinking, she was rash and indifferent to who her audience might be, capable of seizing any weapon that came to hand and digging it in as deep as possible. He didn't care to have that hanging over him. He didn't care to have to worry about what she might do. It made him feel trapped.

When he told her that they were to move out of the gatehouse she flung her arms round him and cried. The next day, he hired a car from the garage and, from the village, telephoned Naomi's sister-in-law, Tessa. Tessa was only too happy for Naomi to come to London and stay with her. 'I'll make sure she doesn't rush about,' she reassured him. 'I'll insist she has a proper rest.' Maxwell arranged to drive Naomi to Edinburgh the following day, where he would put her on the overnight train to London. Tessa would meet her at Euston, he explained to her, and he would join her in a week, after he had finished typing up the book and had sorted things out with Frazer. 'Only a week,' he reminded Naomi, as he said goodbye to her at Waverley station. 'That's all. Then I'll come and fetch you, I promise.'

The next morning, he walked to the hunting lodge. Taking the path across the moorland, Maxwell's gaze took in the great mass of the hills, towering above him, and the yellow and blue and white flowers that starred the grassland in the valley. The river was high, swirling over the stepping stones. He paused for a moment, halfway across, enjoying the sensation of being perched in the centre of the torrent. At the hunting lodge he noticed that all the windows were broken, which was strange, and noticed also how much work Frazer had done to the place since he had last been there. The only signs of Frazer's presence were a mackintosh, slung over the banisters, and a canvas bag with a thermos and a hip flask inside it. When he went outside and called out Frazer's name, the sound echoed hollowly against the hills.

He set off up the path by the burn. Mud clung stickily to the soles of his shoes as he made his way up the hill. The fronds of leaves and ferns sprayed him with drops of rain. He could hear the splash of the waterfall, growing louder, and the chime of drops of water trailing from the boulders into the rock pools. He pushed through a final curtain of branches and saw Frazer, sitting by the pool.

Frazer had had to walk up to the pool half a dozen times to get rid of all the broken glass. After the last box was emptied, he sat down on a rock and gazed at the water. The hostility he had sensed at Ravenhart from the first day he had arrived here had today been made overt. Every one of the people in this godforsaken valley, he suspected, hated him and wished him ill.

Out of the corner of his eye he saw a flicker of movement. Looking up, he saw Maxwell. Frazer stood up. 'Come to help, have you?' he said bitterly. 'Better late than never, I suppose.'

Max said, 'I need to talk to you, Frazer.'

'Fire away, then.'

'Naomi and I have decided to leave.'

'Leave?' Frazer repeated. He couldn't think what Max was talking about. 'What do you mean, *leave?*'

'Leave Ravenhart. We're going back to Edinburgh.'

The shock was like a physical blow. 'You can't.'

Maxwell blinked, and said, 'Sorry?'

'I said, you can't. Not after all I've done for you.'

Maxwell's eyes widened. In the gently sarcastic tone that Frazer recognized was a sign that he was angry, he said, 'Well, it's really just a question of walking away.'

The silence was filled by the trickle of the water. Frazer saw Max's gaze drop, heard him take a deep breath. Then Max said, in a more friendly voice, 'The thing is, Frazer, I've got to go. Naomi doesn't like it here. And it's making her ill, which isn't good for the baby. The other day, Naomi thought that there was something wrong – something wrong with the baby. Well, there wasn't, it's fine, thank God, but I realized—' he broke off; Frazer thought he looked puzzled. 'You wouldn't think you could love something that didn't really exist yet, would you?'

Listening to him, Frazer felt a mixture of misery and rage. He searched for the words that would convince Maxwell to stay, but before he could speak, Max said, 'I've finished the book at last. I know you thought I'd never make it to the end, but I have. So now I have to go and hawk it round the publishing houses. And if no one wants it, then I need to find a job.'

'A job?' said Frazer scornfully. 'You?'

'Someone I know at *The Scotsman* said they might be able to find a post for me. I'd have to begin at the bottom, births, marriages and deaths, I expect, but it would be a start.'

'But you can't just *go*, Max . . .' Frazer hated the pleading note that had come into his voice. 'It's almost summer. Naomi'll be happier when the weather's better. She loved it here last summer.' He put his hand on Max's shoulder. 'So did you.'

'I know.' Max's gaze ran round the pool; he smiled, as if remembering. 'I'll miss all this.'

'Then stay.'

'Frazer, I can't. I just can't.' Max moved away; Frazer's hand slid from his shoulder. 'We've made up our minds.'

We, our. Frazer imagined Max and Naomi plotting, planning, laughing at him behind his back. They'd taken him for a ride, he realized, the pair of them, and now they intended to walk away without a backward glance and leave him stranded in this wilderness on his own. He said furiously, 'The house, the car, the money I've given you – does none of that count for anything?'

Max's features had become set and hard. 'I'll pay it all back.'

'The hell you will. When have you ever paid me a penny back?'

'I didn't realize,' said Max silkily, 'that you were counting.'

Frazer's anger almost choked him. Max was walking

round the edge of the pool; then, turning back to Frazer, he said, 'Hell, I didn't come here to quarrel with you, Frazer. But we have to leave. You must see that.'

'What you mean is, now the money's run out, you might as well go.'

Maxwell gave a hiss of exasperation. 'If that's how you choose to see it.'

'Well, push off, then,' Frazer said bitterly. 'I don't doubt you'll soon find someone else with a bit of cash to spare. You use people, don't you, Max? You get what you want and then you're off and no one can see you for dust.'

'And you, Frazer?' Maxwell was frowning. 'Tell me, what do you want from me?'

Something in Max's expression made Frazer falter. His clenched fists dropped to his sides, and he felt an immense grief, an awareness that a part of his life, which had from time to time contained a sharp, fierce happiness, was coming to an end.

He said stiffly, 'I don't want anything from you. Not now.'

'That's fine, then. So we're quits.'

A silence, then Frazer said slowly, 'I suppose you worked it out that first time we met, in the pub.'

'What do you mean?'

'I saw how you looked when I showed you the photo of the castle.' Frazer's voice was unsteady, but the words came out rolling and fluent. 'You like to pretend you don't care about money, don't you, Max? But it simply isn't true. You'd love to have your own place, servants, cars, wouldn't you? You're as fond of the comforts of life as the next man, and you haven't too many scruples about how you go about getting them. So long as you don't have to work for them, that is.'

'That's not true.'

'Isn't it? Are you sure?' He chose his words like weapons, selecting those that would hurt the most. 'Why don't you try and see yourself for what you really are? The things you claim to despise in your father – his greed, his corruption – they're in you as well, aren't they, Max?'

Max had whitened. 'Don't be ridiculous.'

Frazer shook his head. 'You're just the same as him. Why else did you come to Ravenhart? I know why. Because you wanted some of what I'd got.'

Max's eyes were frozen sea-green pools. He said, 'I came here because it was fun. And it was fun. At first.' Then he walked away.

It was fun, at first. Something inside Frazer broke, and his roar of anguish, as he hurled himself towards Maxwell, echoed against the mountainside.

Chapter Sixteen

L ate August, and by the end of the afternoon the heat lay solid and heavy in the London streets. As she hauled her suitcase from Victoria station to her lodgings, Kate's shoulders ached. She would have tea and toast and a bath, she thought, and then she must mend some stockings or she wouldn't have any to wear for work on Monday morning.

As she fitted her key to the lock, she saw out of the corner of her eye a woman emerging from the park on the other side of the road. A voice called out, 'Kate Fearnley!' and then, to Kate's surprise, Naomi Gilchrist dashed out between the cars and bicycles.

'May I have a word with you? I've been trying to speak to you for weeks.'

'We've been away on tour.'

'Yes, your landlady told me.'

'How are you, Naomi? And Maxwell?'

'It's Max I came to talk to you about.'

A moment's disorientation, and then Kate asked, 'Won't you come in?'

Inside, the rooms seemed shabby and unfamiliar; she felt as if she had been away far longer than six weeks. They sat in the parlour. Kate fetched a tray of tea and biscuits. Miss Logan, who taught at a girls' school, sat on the other side of the room, reading Rosamond Lehmann. A glass door was open to the garden; outside, in the bright afternoon sunlight, a Russian vine trailed from a peeling white pergola and a ginger cat padded across the lawn.

Naomi Gilchrist said, 'So sorry to have just turned up like this. Do you mind if I smoke? I called a fortnight ago but you were away. Sugar, no milk, please. I had to speak to you, Kate.' Her great brown eyes, which had been darting round the room, settled at last on Kate. She said, 'I thought you might know where Maxwell was.'

Kate put down the teapot. 'Isn't he with you?'

'No. That's the thing. And I know that you were friends. I've been talking to all his friends. But no one's seen him. Do you know where he is?'

'I'm afraid not. I haven't seen Maxwell since the night you became engaged.'

'Oh.' Naomi sighed. 'A letter? A telephone call?'

Kate shook her head. A flick of the page as Miss Logan read her book; a bee drifted through the open door and then floated back into the garden.

Kate asked, 'How long is it since you've heard from him?'

'Three months.'

She tried to disguise her shock. *Three months.* 'And you've no idea where—'

'No.' A short laugh. 'Max didn't leave a forwarding address. I was in town with my sister-in-law in May. Max was supposed to come and join me there. He stayed behind at the gatehouse to finish his novel and then we were going to travel back to Edinburgh together. When he didn't turn up, I was annoyed, but I didn't worry too much at first. Max isn't a punctual person. But I kept waiting for him and he still didn't come, and I began to think . . .' she broke off, crushing the stub of her cigarette into a saucer. 'We don't have a telephone at the gatehouse, and I thought perhaps he just wasn't answering my letters. He writes lovely letters – they always make me laugh, and he draws little pictures in the margins – but sometimes he doesn't write at all. I wanted to go back to Ravenhart to find him but they wouldn't let me, because of the baby. I wasn't very well – I had to go into a nursing home and rest. I'm sure I was ill because I was so worried about Max. Morven was fine in the end, thank goodness, but it was rather a frightening time.'

'Morven?'

'My daughter. Max chose the name. It's beautiful, isn't it?' Naomi's expression softened. 'She's with my sister-in-law. I have to get back to her soon, she misses me when I'm not there.' Naomi spooned more sugar into her tea. Then she said, 'If Max meant to leave me, have you any idea where he might go?'

It was painful to imagine what it had cost Naomi to ask the question. There was the temptation to brush it aside, to make some comforting response, but the desperation in Naomi Gilchrist's eyes made Kate say, 'I'm afraid I don't know. I'm so sorry.'

'His friends – he has so many friends. I've tried to speak to all of them but perhaps I've missed some.'

'There were the people who came to the parties at Ravenhart, of course. And there was a girl in Edinburgh, an artist – I can't remember her name.'

'Jenny Watts? I spoke to her. She told me she hasn't seen him for months. Of course, you never know whether people are telling the truth, do you?'

Kate said slowly, 'I suppose Max might have gone to Spain.'

'Spain?'

'He admired the people who'd gone to fight with the International Brigades. I remember that he wrote an article about it.'

Naomi foraged through a capacious handbag. A powder compact, a pair of gloves and a baby's dummy spilled into her lap. She blew her nose on an embroidered handker-chief then opened her cigarette case and offered it to Kate.

'No thanks.'

The lighter snapped. 'I'll kill him if he has. Fighting someone else's war. Just when I need him.' Naomi drew on her cigarette. 'I keep thinking – I keep thinking he'll turn up. The door will open and I'll look up, and there he'll be. And he'll have some ridiculous excuse, and I'll yell at him and we'll quarrel and then we'll make up and every-thing will be all right.' Tears glittered in Naomi's eyes. Her voice lowered to a whisper. 'We had a dreadful quarrel, you see, just before I went to London. I said things . . . mean things. I'm afraid he's had enough of me. I'm afraid he never intended to come to London.'

Kate said, to fill in the ensuing silence, 'Frazer knows Max best. Doesn't he have any idea where he is?'

Naomi shook her head. 'He hasn't a clue. We never really hit it off, Frazer and I, but, since Max disappeared, he's been very decent. But he hasn't been able to help. I think he misses Max too.'

'How are you managing?' Kate asked hesitantly. 'It must be very hard, with the baby.'

'Oh, we're fine, we're both fine. My father-in-law's been helping me out with money and Frazer's let me stay in the gatehouse. I have to be there, you see, for when Max comes home.'

Naomi left shortly afterwards. Later, lying in the bath, Kate let her limbs drift in perfumed water as she thought of Maxwell and Frazer. She remembered picnics at the hunting lodge, and the roof terrace at Ravenhart House, looking up at the stars. It seemed a long time ago, in another world.

She wondered whether she still missed Maxwell. Testing the thought was like pressing a thumb against a cut finger. It hardly hurt at all. She had covered it up well. Thinking about it, she wasn't all that surprised that Maxwell had gone. He had always had an air of impermanence about him.

She ducked beneath the surface of the water. When she re-emerged, her hair was plastered to her face like river-weed. Her mind drifted to the events of the past six weeks, to the succession of seaside towns and train journeys and boarding houses and theatres of peeling gilt and faded plush. She thought of fine, golden sand trickling through her fingers and the pull and the rush of the sea as she waded in the shallows, and the moving pattern of the sunlight on the waves, shifting beneath the sky.

In January 1938, when she turned twenty-one, Kate bought a flat with the money her father had put in trust for her. The flat was in South Kensington, and she decorated it herself, papering the walls and painting the woodwork. She bought a second-hand camera and took pictures of Peggy's dancers as they rehearsed, and had a photographer friend make large prints, which she framed and hung on the walls. In the kitchen, she arranged the French cookware she had bought when visiting Martin's house in France.

In March, her mother came to stay for a weekend. Kate thought she looked tired and worried.

Cooking supper, they talked. 'Eleanor's in a hockey team,' Bess told her. 'She's terribly proud – apparently it's a great honour. And Becky's in the school play. I'm making her a beggar maid's costume. Shall I do those onions for you?'

'Please. And Aimée?'

'She doesn't *grow* – I give her cod liver oil and orange juice every day but she's still so tiny. I suppose she could go to nursery when she's three, but she's no trouble, it seems more sensible to keep her at home.'

'Mum?'

There were tears trailing down Bess's cheeks. She dabbed at them with a handkerchief. 'These wretched onions . . .'

'I'll do them. They never make me cry. Are you worried about Aimée?'

'Not about *Aimée*. About Frazer.'

'How is he?'

'I don't know.' Bess put down the knife; she looked suddenly hopeless. Then she said, 'He seems to have gone away.'

There was a bottle of wine open for the coq au vin. Kate poured some into a glass and slid it across the table to her mother, saying, 'It's rotgut, I'm afraid, but it'll do. Has Frazer gone back to Paris? He sent me a postcard the last time.'

'I don't mean for a holiday.' A deep breath; Bess blew her nose. 'I'm afraid that he's left Ravenhart for good.'

Kate stared at her mother. 'Mum?'

There was a deep sadness in her mother's eyes. She said softly, 'Yes, I'm sure he has.'

'Where has he gone?'

'I don't know.'

'But didn't he tell you?'

'Nothing. He hasn't told me anything.' Bess looked exhausted; she sat down. 'I write to him every day. But then, a few weeks ago, he stopped answering my letters. He's been travelling a great deal recently, as you know, so at first I thought that he'd gone to the continent again. But then I had a letter from his solicitor.'

'What sort of letter?'

'Frazer has signed a document, putting the estate in my care,' her mother said dully. She took a deep breath. 'If Frazer doesn't return within five years, then Ravenhart is mine.'

Kate stared at her mother, shocked. 'But why? Why would he do that?'

'I don't know.'

'He must have said *something*.'

'Nothing, nothing at all. He just seems to have . . . gone.'

Kate remembered the day that Frazer had come into their lives. A knock on the door and there he had been, the brother she had never seen before. He had brought a magic with him, an enchantment, and since then nothing had ever been quite the same again. Was it possible that he had disappeared as abruptly as he had entered their lives?

Her mother said, 'Martin and I went up to the house, but it was closed up. The servants had been sent away, though Phemie still comes in once a week to clean.'

'Naomi might know. Did you ask her?'

'I spoke to Mrs Gilchrist, yes. But she didn't know anything at all. She hadn't even realized that Frazer had gone away.' Bess was twisting her wedding ring round her finger. 'But she told me that Frazer has given her the gatehouse. It's hers now, she owns it. She can sell it, rent it out, do what she likes with it.'

'Did she ever hear from Maxwell?'

Her mother rose and fetched a punnet of mushrooms from the larder and began to peel them. 'I don't think so.'

'So strange, both of them . . .' Kate had a sudden idea. 'Perhaps Frazer's gone wherever Maxwell went.'

The knife dropped to the table; Bess's eyes, focused on Kate, were wide and dark. 'No. No, of course he hasn't.'

'They were great friends, Mum,' said Kate gently.

'Wherever Frazer is, I'm sure he's not with Maxwell Gilchrist.'

Bess sounded angry, so Kate changed the subject. 'Frazer had money worries, didn't he?'

'The estate's outgoings have exceeded its income for some time.' Bess took a pan out of the cupboard. 'I went to see Mr Daintree, Frazer's solicitor – I thought he might have some idea. But he didn't know anything either. Apparently he tried to ask Frazer what his intentions were, but Frazer refused to tell him.'

'I expect he was just being sensible. I expect he's gone abroad for a while and he wanted to make sure that the estate was in safe hands while he was away.'

'Yes.' A forced smile. 'I'm sure you're right, Kate.'

'He'll be back in a few months. Frazer knows how to look after himself. He'll be fine.'

'Yes, of course.'

They worked for a while in silence. Then Bess said suddenly, 'Oh Kate, I keep thinking, what if I never see him again? How could he do it? How could he leave me all over again?'

If she could have pinpointed a time when the political began to overwhelm the personal in all their lives, then that time, Kate thought later, was in the autumn of 1938. Events earlier that same year – Hitler's march into Austria, to be welcomed by cheering crowds who showered his army with flowers and kisses, and the retreat of the Republican army in war-torn Spain – had the power to chill, to frighten. But if she tried hard enough, she could put all that to the back of her mind as she danced to 'I've Got You Under My Skin', or stood in the wings of the theatre and witnessed that nightly transformation from the ordinary to the magical as Peggy's dancers made their entrance onto the stage.

Then, in September 1938, Hitler threatened to invade Czechoslovakia unless Germany was permitted to take over the German-speaking Sudetenland. Britain and Germany teetered on the edge of war. Trenches were dug in London parks and air-raid sirens were tested. Kate saw her own fear mirrored in the eyes of strangers on the tube and fellow customers in the shops. Loud noises made her jump; when an aeroplane flew over the city, she no longer saw it as a symbol of freedom, of escape, but as something dark and threatening. There was a stillness in the air; they waited for something unfathomable.

At the end of the month, Britain's Prime Minister, Neville Chamberlain, and France's Édouard Daladier returned from Munich with an agreement that Hitler be permitted to enter the Sudetenland so long as the remainder of Czechoslovakia was spared. The initial relief that war had been averted gave way to a growing shame that a small, democratic country had been meekly permitted to be butchered by a larger, tyrannical one. Munich was closely followed by the horror of Kristallnacht, when German Jews were murdered by the Nazis and their synagogues and schools destroyed. After that, Kate couldn't block out the darkness any more. With the flick of a switch, night might fall, and all that was precious could be taken away from her.

In March 1939, Hitler reneged on the Munich Agreement and a Nazi dictatorship was established in the remaining, indefensible remnant of Czechoslovakia. At the end of same month, the Republicans abandoned the fight in Spain and the Fascist General Franco's grip on the country was complete. Men and women who had fought in the International Brigades had already returned to the countries of their birth. Kate wondered whether Maxwell Gilchrist was among them.

There came a point, she discovered during those tense, unreal months, when you could no longer reach for the retreat of dance or music. The Kindertransporte had already begun to bring thousands of Jewish refugee children from Germany and Austria to the safety of Britain. Kate became involved with the refugee organization, baking cakes for the children's tea when they arrived in London, exhausted and traumatized after their long journeys across Europe. Sometimes she took children back to her flat when arrangements for their care had fallen through, and looked after them until more permanent foster parents could be found. She got to know these little scraps of flotsam and jetsam who had washed up on foreign shores, far from their homes and families. She comforted them when they had nightmares, she read them stories and brushed their hair and held them when they cried. She tried to provide a small place of safety in lives that had been fractured. More and more, she found herself aware of the fragility of everything, aware, too, that the impermanence of life gave it a sharp, fierce brightness. You did not love so intensely if you were not afraid of losing.

After the declaration of war in September, she felt at first a mixture of anger and grief. And yet, and yet . . . Walking through London that day, she had never felt so alive, so certain of what it was that she valued.

The following month, she gave in her notice to Peggy Fisher and joined the WAAF.

At first, the outbreak of war changed little. The winter of 1939/40 passed without the air raids that everyone had feared. Though the British Expeditionary Force left for the continent, France, Holland and Belgium remained, for the moment, untouched, and Bess allowed herself to relax a little. Perhaps this war would not be a repetition of the last. Perhaps men would not die in their millions in the trenches, trodden into the mud of Flanders.

Still, she dug the roses out of the garden and planted vegetables instead. Some lessons always stayed with you, and she would not risk her family going hungry. Aimée helped her, dropping a seed into each hollow in the soil, her face solemn. Bess told herself that she had not sent Aimée to nursery school because Aimée was delicate. But she knew that that was not quite the truth. She needed company, she needed a house filled with chatter and laughter, and not silence. She dreaded silence. When there was silence, she thought, and she remembered.

In April 1940, the uneasy calm came to an end as Germany occupied Denmark and invaded Norway. On 10 May, German troops attacked Holland, Belgium and Luxembourg; on the same day, Winston Churchill replaced Neville Chamberlain as Prime Minister. The battle for France began, ending within a fortnight with bitter defeat for the French and British armies, closely followed by the mixture of humiliation and glory that was the Dunkirk evacuation. On 14 June, the German army entered Paris. Listening to the radio, Bess felt both horror and anguish; in all the senseless destruction of the Great War, Paris, at least, had remained free.

In the early summer of 1940, Kate was posted to Tangmere Fighter Command base. Her day-to-day work was much the same as it had been in peacetime – typing and filing and answering the telephone – but at least here, she thought, there seemed more of a point to it.

Tangmere was in Sussex, at the tip of the South Downs. The base had a dreamy, rural atmosphere; red creeper smothered the mess, and at the nearby seaside town of Bosham, you could sit on the balcony at the Old Ship and watch the sun set over the Channel.

It was at the Old Ship that she met Hugh Willoughby. A few days after her arrival at Tangmere, a WAAF friend, Sally Vincent, drove her to the pub. The bar was crowded, every one of the men inside it, it seemed, in air-force blue. Sally caught sight of her boyfriend and disappeared into the heaving, noisy mass; Kate, after weighing things up for a few moments, remained outside.

A voice said, 'Bit of a squash, isn't it?' and she turned and saw a young man in RAF uniform, leaning against the wall, smoking.

'Rather.'

'I hate crowds.' He offered Kate a cigarette. 'That's what I like about flying. It's so nice and peaceful up there.' His gaze flicked to the Channel. 'Not that it will be much longer, I don't suppose. I'm Hugh Willoughby, by the way.'

She looked at him properly, and saw a straight-nosed, Grecian profile, curly chestnut hair and hazel eyes, and a warm smile. She took his hand. 'Kate Fearnley.'

'I haven't seen you here before.'

'I've only just been posted to Tangmere.' She looked out to where the dying sun glittered on the sea. 'It's glorious, isn't it?'

'Looks nice enough.' He shivered. 'I'd hate to go into the drink, though. Knew a chap who did at the place where I was stationed before. His Spitfire went into a dive and he couldn't get it out of it in time.'

'How awful,' she said.

'Where are you from, Kate?'

'Edinburgh.'

'Scots, then.'

'My father's Scots, but my mother's a mixture of Anglo-Indian and Irish. And I can speak French.'

'Go on, then.'

She said the first thing that came into her head, a verse of a folk song. '*Le fils du Roi s'en va chassant, avec son beau fusil d'argent.*'

He seemed to concentrate hard; then he said, 'I was always pretty clueless at languages. What does it mean?'

'Oh, it's about a handsome prince going hunting.' She was glad of the deepening twilight; she knew that she was blushing. 'What about you?' she asked. 'Where do you come from?'

'Just over there.' He waved a hand in a vaguely easterly

direction. 'I'm English through and through. My family live near Chichester. All the Willoughby men go into the Navy – they were terribly put out when I joined the RAF. My father died a year ago but my mother's still in the old house. I drop over to see Ma as often as I can. You should come along sometime – she cooks the most terrific Sunday lunches.'

Kate told him about her father and Pamela, in Hampshire, and about her mother and Martin and her brothers and sisters; Hugh told her about his school days and about his decision to join the RAF. 'I always knew I wanted to fly,' he said. 'I can't think of anything better, can you? I tried to get them to take me when I was seventeen, but they wouldn't, so I had another go a year later. I was so happy when they said yes, I had to go and have a celebratory drink. By the time I got back to school I was plastered.' He smiled. 'I've had a marvellous time these past few years, flying.' He glanced into the open door of the pub. 'I say, it seems to have thinned down a bit. Can I buy you a drink, Kate?'

They huddled in a dim corner of the pub, glasses in hand. Hugh looked at her closely; this time, she did not blush. He said, 'That thing you said – the French thing. Teach me to say it, would you?'

Falling in love with Hugh Willoughby wasn't like falling in love with Maxwell Gilchrist. For one thing, knowing Maxwell had been like trying to understand a rather confusing book; Hugh was easy, she almost seemed to know him already, and besides, they had so much in common. They both disliked crowds, and they both enjoyed walking in the countryside. Neither of them was very keen on swimming; Hugh preferred the air to water and promised to wangle her a flight as soon as he could. They liked the same novels and films and songs – 'These Foolish Things' was their favourite song, and they sang it at the top of their voices, cycling through winding Sussex lanes – and their favourite colour was blue, and their favourite meal was sausage and egg and chips.

For another thing, they were always aware of the shortness of time. At Ravenhart, time had seemed to stretch out ahead of her, lazy and languid, there for the taking. But after the fall of France, she knew that every moment was precious. She wanted to scoop it up, to hold and preserve it somehow, so that she never forgot a moment of the best bits: the day they drove to Hugh's family home, and she met his mother, Dorothy; the party in Tangmere Cottage, to celebrate a pilot's twenty-first birthday, when they danced till dawn; and the spill of pink and cream May blossom in the hedgerows the first time she and Hugh kissed, lying in a cornfield, the chalky earth below them and a sapphire sky, dotted with larks, above.

But enemy forces were gathering in France in preparation for the invasion of England, and soon the storm broke. On 12 August, the Luftwaffe bombed radar stations along the Kent coast. Shortly afterwards, airfields at Lympne, Hawkinge and Manston were attacked. Over two hundred aircraft filled the sky over the Isle of Wight, black, buzzing gnats that cast a shadow over the Channel.

A few days later, it was Tangmere's turn. The tranquil atmosphere of the airfield was shattered when Stukas dived on the base, flattening the officers' mess, workshops, stores and hangars. Emerging from the wreckage, Kate swallowed down her shock and fear, brushed the brick dust off her uniform, tucked her hair behind her ears, and set to work, helping to make the base operational again. Ten of the ground staff had been killed; two Hurricanes, defending the airfield, had been shot down. When, later that day, Hugh's plane landed, she was waiting for him in the shelter of the trees. He took her in his arms and crushed her against him, kissing her over and over again.

Each day, she woke with the knowledge that by night-fall she might have lost him. Cycling along the country lanes, she paused and looked up at the sky. No skylarks now; instead, drawn on the wash of blue were the whorls and arcs of white tracer fire. Looking up, she shaded her eyes with her hand. Was that tiny black dot in the sky his plane? Was that Hugh who twisted and turned, caught in a ball of fire before plunging into the sea?

Martin was in London, working as a surgeon in an army hospital. At his insistence, Bess remained in Edinburgh with the children, safe from the bombs that nightly blitzed London. Visiting Martin that winter, she wore her red cashmere coat. He had bought her the coat fourteen years ago; she remembered standing in the sitting room of his house in France and unwrapping the box that contained it. Now Martin's house was once more under German occupation. With a shiver of fear, she wondered once again what had happened to the Lemerciers and to all their friends and neighbours in France.

As for Martin, she saw in his exhaustion and silence what it had cost him to return to an occupation that, in a previous war, had begun to sicken him. Constantly, her thoughts turned to her family. To Kate, in Sussex, and to Eleanor, Rebecca and Aimée, who, on the weekends she was able to visit Martin, stayed with Izzy and Davey. And to Frazer, adrift, lost once more.

War separated, war pulled you apart. She had once believed that she could protect her family with the strength of her own will; recently, she had lost that conviction. War might yet prove a more powerful enemy than either Cora Ravenhart or Andrew Gilchrist had been.

Hugh had his first weekend off in months in October. He and Kate drove up to London, where they had supper, and then danced at a nightclub. Sometime around three in the morning, they walked back to their hotel through the intense darkness of the blacked-out city. The jagged shapes of the blitzed buildings jutted from the ground like inky icebergs.

When the air-raid siren sounded, they took shelter in a tube station along with hundreds of others. They were sitting on the platform, holding hands, when Hugh asked her to marry him. Kate felt such a surge of joy in her heart that it was hard to remember to breathe in the hot, dusty air. When they embraced, she was aware of the scratchy fabric of his uniform jacket, and his mouth, hard against hers, and the way his fingertips pressed into the back of her neck as he kissed her, as if he wanted to squeeze her into him, to make her a part of him.

*　　*　　*

Now there were ghosts. In the late spring of 1941, the bus dropped Bess at the gatehouse; as she walked along the drive and saw the curtain of trees part to reveal Ravenhart House, her heart seemed to still and pause for a moment before resuming its steady beat.

Already, barbed wire had been strung round the perimeter of the garden. As she let herself into the house, she thought she saw a movement in the darkness – a figure running down the stairs, perhaps, or a hand pulling back a curtain to let in the light. But there was no one, only the wind swirling dry, copper-coloured leaves into the hallway, and she waited for the disappointment to ebb away as she walked through rooms containing nothing but silence and emptiness.

Yet her ghosts walked with her as she opened drawers and ran her gaze over furniture and paintings, checking for any valuables that must be taken away before Ravenhart was requisitioned by the army the following month. The house still smelt of beeswax and cobwebs, as it had done when she had first come here, in Sheldon Ravenhart's time. Phemie called once a fortnight or so, to dust and air the principal rooms, but even Phemie's faithful service could not keep at bay the effects of time and neglect. Bess had checked on the house every few months or so since Frazer had left it, visits that had become ever more difficult as the war had lengthened, as the rationing of fuel made every journey a challenge, an expedition.

She kept her coat on, the fur collar turned up against the cold as she walked from room to room. She had been cold, she thought, ever since she had first come to England, so long ago. Inside dark rooms, furniture, covered in dust sheets, loomed, and her thoughts drifted back to the months that had preceded Frazer's disappearance. During that time, Frazer had abandoned his schemes for the house and estate and had stayed away from Ravenhart as much as possible, visiting London and Paris. She had seen him only on his occasional visits to Edinburgh. In their moments of privacy, there had been a bond, a closeness between them.

Yet she must not think of Frazer. Never look back, she had promised herself; she must think of the present, not the past. Of Kate, now married and living with Hugh's mother, and expecting a baby towards the end of the year. She must think of the grandchild she would soon have, and she must think of her little girls, Eleanor, Rebecca and Aimée, so dear, so perfect.

Opening the curtains in one of the turret rooms, Bess saw the flurry of snow that blanched the slopes of the mountains. Her gaze drifted to the hunting lodge, in the confluence between the two rivers. *Perhaps Frazer has gone wherever Maxwell went*, Kate had said to her. Remembering, she dug her fingernails into her palms.

More corridors, more stairs. She had to steel herself to enter Frazer's bedroom. In this room, the furniture was uncovered and free of dust. Phemie kept it clean and tidy. Bess set to work methodically, checking drawers and cupboards for any valuables that Frazer might have left behind. But after a while, an intense weariness overcame her, and she sat down on the edge of the bed, one of Frazer's sweaters clutched in her hands, holding it to her cheek, just as she had once treasured the knitted baby jacket she had brought with her from India to England.

Remembering Frazer as a baby was almost too much to bear. A newborn infant, in her arms, as she lay exhausted in bed after a long labour. A golden-haired little boy, laughing as the dappled sunlight filtered through the leaves in a garden in Simla. By the time she had seen him again, in 1935, he had changed: Cora Ravenhart had changed him. Ravenhart House had altered him further. Just then, she hated the house. Let the army despoil it, let the ivy smother and strangle it, she thought savagely. She swept her keepsakes into a bag and walked out, longing only to return home.

Yet, at the gatehouse, she paused. A small girl was playing in the garden. Muffled in coat and gloves, she was treading circles in the snow. Black curls sprang from beneath her blue bonnet. Bess watched her for a moment, and then she walked on.

Kate's son was born three days after the Japanese bombed Pearl Harbor. They called him Sam, after Hugh's father. He was a big, healthy baby, born in the front bedroom of Dorothy Willoughby's home, where Hugh himself had been born twenty-four years earlier. Afterwards, Kate lay in bed, watching Sam in his cradle, and seeing how his tiny dimpled hands wandered aimlessly, and how his gaze flickered, seeming to pause every now and then whenever he caught sight of her. When she put her finger into his palm, his hand curled round it.

Dorothy Willoughby's house was large and rambling,

perched on the edge of rolling countryside, three miles from Chichester. Dorothy had taken in three evacuees at the time of the London Blitz, brothers from the East End of London, who all had tow-coloured hair and bright blue eyes and whose knees and elbows always seemed to be covered with scratches and scabs. When German planes flew overhead, Dorothy, Kate, Sam, Alfie, Eddy and George hid beneath the oak kitchen table. Dorothy tapped the timber with her fist. 'It's supposed to have come from one of the ships that fought the French at the Battle of the Nile. I don't suppose it did for a moment, but it's as strong as steel and it'll keep us all safe.'

Kate spent her days looking after Sam and the evacuees and helping Dorothy in the house and garden. In the evenings, she listened to the radio and wrote letters to her family and to Oliver and Billy. Oliver was working at the Admiralty; he visited Stephen, who was with Margot in Margot and Nigel's country house in Wiltshire, as often as he could. Billy was touring military bases with ENSA – 'Such dreary lodgings, Kate, worse than Peggy's tours, and not all of our audience appreciate ballet . . .'

The immediate threat of invasion over, Hugh's squadron was now patrolling the Channel and escorting bombers to occupied France. Kate began to notice a certain careless-ness in him, a flippancy, as though the loss of so many friends and the endurance of so much danger had erased his capacity for deep emotion. She knew that the pitch at which he had been forced to live for more than eighteen months had left him hollowed and burnt-out. He was no longer the man who had bawled songs at the top of his voice, cycling through the Sussex Downs, no longer the man who had learned by heart a verse of a French song in a noisy pub. Hugh's concentration had become fitful and fragile. He fell asleep doing *The Times* crossword or while turning the page of a novel. He dozed in cinemas and at concert halls, and sometimes, in bed, his hand stilled as he caressed her breast, and his head became heavy against hers. Hearing his deep, regular breathing, she lay motionless, unwilling to wake him, knowing that, when he did sleep, he slept badly, waking frequently during the night.

Once, she woke to see him silhouetted against the window. She said his name, and he turned.

'Sorry. I didn't mean to wake you, darling.'

'What time is it?'

'Almost four.'

She patted the pillow. 'Come back to bed, Hugh.'

He shook his head. 'Can't sleep.'

'I'll make us some tea.'

She went downstairs to the kitchen and made two cups of tea. 'I've put a little whisky in it,' she said, handing him a cup. 'It'll help you sleep. I put some in mine as well, so if Sam wakes for a feed, he'll get drunk.'

'Thanks.'

'What is it?' she asked gently. 'What's up?'

'Oh, nothing much.'

'*Hugh.*'

'Go back to bed, darling, you're getting cold.'

She climbed back beneath the blankets and eiderdown. After a silence, he said, 'It's just that sometimes I can't seem to see the point of it any more. All those sorties over the

Channel just to chuck a few bombs on some poor blighters below. Half the people we polish off must be French, I should think.' He put the cup on the window sill. 'When it was just us and them, in the air, it seemed cleaner, somehow. More of a fair fight.' Then he gave a quick smile, and said, 'Oh well, what the hell. I suppose we have to bomb them to stop them bombing us. What a game, eh, Kate?'

A few days later, she was returning to Dorothy's house from the village shop. It was February, and a sharp wind battered the snowdrops on the verges. She was wheeling Sam in his pram; he was hungry and he had begun to grizzle, impatient for his feed. As she reached Dorothy's house, Kate saw the car parked on the gravel courtyard. She recognized the Morgan; it belonged to Hugh's commanding officer.

She paused, her fingers twisting round the pram handle. Sam was crying properly now, stretching out his body, his face scarlet. She picked him out of the pram and held him against her, patting his back. 'Poor old Sam. Poor old thing.'

She wanted to remain outside, to put off the moment of going into the house for as long as possible. To put off the moment of knowing, because so long as she didn't know, she wouldn't have to think how she would live without Hugh.

But Sam was cold and hungry, and sometime – this minute or the next or the next – she would have to learn to begin again. She caught a glimpse through the sitting-room window of Dorothy's face, pale against the glass, and then she wheeled the pram into the porch.

*　　*　　*

In the May of 1942, Martin had a fortnight's leave and came home to Edinburgh. He looked drained and tired, and he slept much of the first week, emerging every now and then to eat or to play with the girls.

Returning from posting a letter one afternoon, Bess heard her daughters' raised voices as she came back to the house.

'Give it to me!' Rebecca was yelling. 'I want it!'

Eleanor, who was several inches taller than Rebecca, waved her paintbox in the air, out of her sister's reach. 'Go away, you silly little girl. It's mine. Daddy bought it for *me*.'

'It's mine! I want it! I want to paint a picture for Mummy.'

'Then find your own paintbox. You're not having mine.'

'I hate you!'

The paintbox clasped to her chest, Eleanor ran upstairs. Rebecca gave a howl of frustration. Aimée looked at her, wide-eyed. '*Becky*.' Rebecca gave her younger sister a hard shove and Aimée sat down suddenly, bouncing the back of her head against the coat stand. A moment's open-mouthed shock, and then she began to wail.

Martin had emerged from his study. 'Rebecca. Go to your room.'

'Daddy—'

'I said, go to your room.'

Rebecca plodded upstairs, sobbing. Bess scooped up Aimée and rubbed the bruise on the back of her head. Then she made tea and bathed the girls and put them to bed. Downstairs, her gaze ran over the litter of toys and children's books, the pile of mending on a chair, and the abandoned half-eaten biscuit on the sill.

She sat down with a sigh. 'Rebecca can be so appalling.

I don't know what to do with her sometimes. I even find myself wondering whether we should send her to boarding school.'

'Nonsense.' Martin handed her a glass. 'It's cooking sherry, I'm afraid – it seems to be all we have left. When I remember the bottles of Scotch grateful patients used to give me . . .' He smiled. 'Rebecca's just a little wilful, that's all. Takes after her mother.'

She sipped the sherry. 'Poor Martin. Often I think you would have been happier left with your pots and your old bones.'

'Happier? I doubt it. Duller, certainly.'

She said cautiously, 'You don't sometimes hanker after all that? After the freedom you used to have?'

'Me? No.' His gaze came to rest on her. 'Do you, Bess?'

She began to gather up the scattered toys and clothes. 'Not at all.'

'It surprises me how often I hear people speaking of domestic life in such disparaging terms. As though all this wasn't an adventure, too. As though bringing a child into the world isn't, perhaps, the greatest adventure there is. No, I wouldn't change any of this, not one little bit.' He paused. From upstairs, he could hear his daughters' voices, laughing now. Then he said, 'But you, Bess . . . lately I've wondered.'

Her arms were full of cardigans and sandals. 'Wondered what, Martin?'

'Whether you were entirely happy.'

'Of course I'm happy.' Yet her voice seemed brittle and hollow, like a glass vessel.

'I suppose I've always known that I might not be enough for you.'

She stared at him. 'Martin, that's not true.'

'It's crossed my mind, you see, more than once, that perhaps the children have made up for a marriage you hadn't particularly sought out.' She saw the sadness in his eyes. 'You are the sort of woman men dream about, Bess, beautiful, passionate and responsive. I've sometimes thought that your deepest feelings have always been for your children. I know you didn't intend to marry again. And after all, you had little choice but to marry me. And I've always wondered whether part of the reason you agreed to have me was so that you could have another son.'

'How can you believe that?'

'Is it so irrational? You were prepared to risk your life for a son.'

Her gaze dropped. She thought of Frazer and of Michael; just then it seemed to her that her sons had brought her only grief.

'No, Martin. You're wrong.' She sat down again, the clothes bundled on her lap. She said slowly, 'I used to long for a son, yes. But that was then, and this is now. I love my daughters. They are enough for me. And if I haven't seemed perfectly happy, then, of course, there's the war. I worry about the children – about Kate, of course. Since poor Hugh died, I worry about her, all on her own.'

'She has Dorothy,' he reminded her. 'And Sam. And I know that Ralph and Pamela visit whenever they can.'

She sighed. 'If only she lived nearer.'

He came to sit beside her. 'And you worry about Frazer, too, don't you?'

She looked away. 'I try not to.'

He took her hand. 'Wherever he is, it's unlikely that he'll have been able to avoid involvement with the war. He will have fought, or, if he was in France at the time of the occupation, he may have been interned as an enemy alien. In either case, he'll be mentioned in records. After the war's over, I'll help you look for him, if you like. And the Red Cross may be able to help, of course.'

'No,' she said. Now, she made herself meet his eyes. 'Not this time. This time he's chosen to go. So I won't look for him.' Her voice faltered; the room blurred with her tears. 'I won't look for him,' she repeated softly. 'Frazer had his reasons for leaving. But I'll look after Ravenhart for him so that if he does come back, there'll be a home for him. And if he comes home . . .' She pressed her lips together, unable to say more.

Martin said gently, 'You did your best for him.'

'I failed him, Martin! His flaws, his weaknesses, they were my fault!'

'No.' His voice was firm. 'Frazer was an adult. He was responsible for his own life.'

'But I'm his *mother*.'

He began to gather together the papers scattered on the table. 'That first time you came with me to France,' he said. 'Do you remember?'

Her head shot up. 'Martin, please—'

'When I went back to Scotland after taking you and Kate to France, I sought out Andrew Gilchrist.'

She flinched, hearing his name.

Martin said, 'I managed to get him on his own one night. Gilchrist was very drunk, and I hit him. Twice. I wanted to kill him, actually.'

'You never told me.'

'No.' He frowned. 'Perhaps I was ashamed. Though I don't regret it. Looking back, I can't see that I could have done differently.'

She whispered, 'Why are you telling me this?'

He put the papers in a drawer. His back was to her as he spoke; she could not see his face. 'Each of us has parts of ourselves that we keep from everyone else – including ourselves, perhaps. If we think we know ourselves completely, then maybe that's only because we haven't been tested.'

There was a silence. When he looked round, his expression had altered. He said lightly, 'Let's go out tomorrow, Bess. The five of us – a picnic, perhaps. Wear the children out.'

'Martin, it's freezing, there was hail this afternoon.' Yet she rose and crossed the room to him, and he took her in his arms.

'I love you, Bess,' he said. 'Never doubt that I love you.'

'Still?' Her voice trembled; she put her hand up to her hair. 'Even though I'm growing old?'

'Are you? I hadn't noticed.' She heard him sigh softly. 'Bess, I love you more than life itself.'

She rested her forehead against his chest. 'Will you always love me, Martin?'

'Always.'

'Whatever I do, whatever I am?'

'I couldn't help but do so.'

She stood back from him, looking at him, learning him by heart for when he went away again. 'My children are a part of me,' she said. 'They came from my body, and they will always be a part of me. Yet they haven't always brought me joy. But you have, Martin. If I were to lose you, I would survive, and I would carry on, but the joy would have gone from my life.'

After Hugh's death, Kate remained at Dorothy's house. It was a strange time, she thought later, characterized by a jarring mixture of emotions – despair at losing Hugh, and delight in her baby son. At night, her dreams were of falling – tumbling from cliffs, from high buildings, and once, from the flat roof on top of Ravenhart House. Waking, she wept for Hugh, who had died when his plane had plunged into the sea that he had feared so much.

Yet she picked up the pieces and started again. She had to, for Sam's sake. There were feeds to give and nappies to change, and later, as Sam grew older, clothes to mend and meals to cook. After the war ended, and when Sam was old enough to start school, she trained to be a teacher. Though she had her widow's pension, there was still that need for independence, to manage on her own. In the holidays, Kate took Sam to stay with her father and Pamela at the farm, or they travelled to Edinburgh.

It pleased her that Sam took after Hugh. Tall for his age, Sam's curling hair was the colour of conkers and his eyes were a warm honey-brown. She could see Hugh in him, in his sunny nature, his quickness of mind, and his unstinting affection. She did her best to fill the yawning gap of a father in Sam's life, and tried to do the things that Hugh would have done, had he lived. She played cricket with her son in the park, and, visiting Les Trois Cheminées two years after the end of the war, she conquered her fear of the water and taught Sam to swim in the river. Martin's house had been requisitioned by German officers during the war. The apple trees in the orchard had been cut down – for firewood, presumably. The old house showed the scars of occupation and neglect, its paintwork scratched and its furniture and floors scuffed.

Martin had decided to sell Les Trois Cheminées. 'Bess and I own three rather large houses between us,' he said to Kate one day, as they walked through the woods, 'which is quite ridiculous. And Bess won't sell Ravenhart. I don't think she thinks of it as truly hers to sell – I'm afraid she still believes that Frazer may return.'

'Do you think he will, Martin?'

Martin shook his head. 'I can't help thinking that if he intended to, he would have made contact by now. If he is alive, then he seems to have hidden himself very thoroughly.' His stick thwacked the nettles and brambles in the undergrowth. 'Anyway, I thought I should sell up. Perhaps I might buy a small flat in Le Touquet instead – so much easier to travel to. And you and Sam could use it for holidays, of course, Kate.'

In the years that followed, Kate helped Sam with his homework, nursed him through mumps and measles and a broken arm and appendicitis, and tried to take an interest in his hobbies – go-karting and roller-skating and Airfix model kits of the aeroplanes his father had once flown. In the summer of 1951, they both attended Rebecca's wedding to Stuart Renfrew, a wealthy businessman who owned a string of estate agencies in London and Edinburgh. Stuart was twenty-nine, ten years older than Rebecca, and both Bess and Martin had tried to persuade her to wait until she was twenty-one before marrying. But Rebecca was insistent. She would marry Stuart, she declared, with or without her parents' permission. Eventually, after a great deal of argument, Rebecca got her way.

There was a grand wedding, with Rebecca looking exquisite and triumphant in white lace over tussore silk. *It's mine, I want it*, had been Rebecca's cry throughout her childhood, and, in marrying Stuart, Rebecca now surely had everything she could desire: houses in Belgravia and Edinburgh, a flat in the south of France, and a little sports car all of her own. Yet it seemed to Kate, watching Rebecca dart round London or return from France, her skin toasted gold by the Mediterranean sun, that she was still not content. In contrast, Eleanor, who had trained as a doctor after the war, was in her element.

Kate moved back to London after Dorothy died, when Sam was fourteen. She bought a house in Chelsea, and quit teaching for child psychotherapy, studying Freud and Jung and Melanie Klein. She found a good school for Sam and, having lost contact with Oliver for a while after the war, was delighted to discover that he had returned, with Stephen, to the antique shop in Portobello Road. Coming back to London, she was aware of a pleasure in the gathering up of old threads, as, once more, she started again.

By the end of the war, the army had left the Ravenhart estate. In the late forties, large houses throughout the country changed hands or were willed to the National Trust or simply fell into disrepair because their owners could no longer afford to maintain them. Though she sold hundreds of acres of Ravenhart land, Bess baulked at selling the house itself and the wide strip of land that bound it to the hunting lodge and the pool. There was always the hope, which she had never abandoned, that Frazer would come home.

In the early fifties, she let the house to a removals firm, who used it to store items of furniture. Every six months or so she travelled to Perthshire, to check on the Ravenhart estate, staying for a day or two in the few rooms in the house that remained private, and which loyal Phemie kept in good order. Sometimes she caught sight of Naomi's daughter, Morven, walking through the estate. Always, lying awake at night, she remembered Frazer, sitting at the head of the long mahogany table, or standing by the fireplace in the great hall.

By the mid-fifties, all her daughters had left home. Aimée was the last to leave. Rather to Bess's surprise, Aimée had acquired, as she grew up, a strange and powerful beauty. At eighteen, she became a fashion model. An overnight success, she travelled to Paris and to Rome, was feted and photographed, and her high cheekbones and pointed face, with its cloud of white-blonde hair and huge grey eyes, stared out from the front covers of *Vogue* and *Vanity Fair*. As for Eleanor, she had discovered a focus for her passions at last. Armed with her medical degree, Eleanor travelled to India in 1955, and fell in love with it, and remained there, working in a hospital in Calcutta.

Bess missed her daughters dreadfully. It was hard to accept that such an important part of her life was over, finished with. Yet she began to take pleasure in being alone with Martin. They had never had the house to themselves; there had been children since the very first day of their marriage.

Martin retired in 1956; the following summer they toured Scotland for six weeks, visiting castles and prehistoric sites, exploring beaches and mountains, staying in hotels and bed and breakfast establishments. It was a fine day when they sailed from Ullapool on the west coast of Scotland to the Isle of Lewis. The sea was calm, and the sun had a sheen like shot silk. They stood side by side on the deck of the boat, watching as the island appeared on the horizon. In Stornoway, they booked into a small hotel and spent the rest of the day exploring the town. The next morning they drove to Callanish. The standing stones burst from the ground like a petrified forest, black against the moorland and sea. The site was wild and remote, perched on the edge of the Atlantic Ocean, a survivor of storms and tempests, and, in the evening, hand in hand, they watched the sun set through the standing stones.

Martin's health began to fail the following year. He succumbed to a succession of minor ailments, colds and coughs and low fevers, and he lost weight. The slow decline in the energy and enthusiasm that had always characterized him worried Bess, and she tried to persuade him to go for a check-up, but he refused, brushing off her anxieties, telling her that he only needed some sun. They went to Le Touquet for a fortnight in June, and he seemed to rally, sitting on the balcony of their flat, looking out to the beach and the sea.

Then, in October, he went out for the day, to visit Edin's Hall in the Borders. There was a rainstorm while he was exploring the site and he became soaked. He drove home in damp clothes and was exhausted and feverish by the time he reached Edinburgh. The following morning, the doctor visited and prescribed penicillin.

Martin seemed to be recovering, but then, two days later, in the early hours of the morning, he suffered a massive heart attack. The stretch of time that followed, waiting for the doctor, was unspeakable. Bess sat beside her husband's body, his hand in hers. A few days later, Charlie Campbell, Martin's former colleague during the twenties, came to see her. After offering his condolences, Charlie told Bess that Martin had visited him earlier that year to ask for a second opinion. Martin had diagnosed himself as suffering from lung cancer, and Charlie had confirmed the diagnosis. Charlie added, 'If it's any comfort at all, it's better that he died this way. Pneumonia's a kinder death, Bess, quicker and kinder.'

If I were to lose you, I would survive, and I would carry on, but the joy would have gone from my life, she had once told Martin. Each day she endured after his death bore out her prediction. She discovered that you didn't get over the loss of a much-loved husband. The best you could hope for was to become used to it, to realize that his absence was permanent and was not, as your instincts told you, a temporary void, to be resolved at any moment by a door opening and a familiar voice calling out. Martin's shadow lived on in every part of their home: the sitting room, the basement rooms that had once been the dispensary and surgery, and, of course, the bedroom, where, waking at night, she would reach out an arm, and her fingers would claw at the emptiness of sheet and pillow. Sometimes she thought she heard his voice; she would seem to catch the end of a sentence, an echo, and she would whirl round, staring into the darkness.

Yet she did not flee from this house that was laden with memories, as she had done after Michael had died. Her memories had a sharp edge – how those mundane domestic artefacts had the power to hurt! The cup in which she had always brought him his morning coffee, and his watch and glasses, which she could neither bear to look at nor throw away. But they comforted as well. She remembered Martin speaking once to her about his great love, archaeology. 'Some people think my fascination with grave sites is morbid,' he had said. 'They can't seem to understand that I find them so unendurably touching, those evidences of past lives. Not the great treasures, the gold and the jewels, but the ordinary things – the bead necklaces, the knives and pots and pans. Those little things that were valued and loved.'

She, too, discovered the power of little things. Though she would not make the house into a shrine, Bess cherished Martin's belongings, dusting his books and keeping his piano tuned. Kate helped her with the worst task, sorting through Martin's wardrobe and study, throwing away old, worn clothes and papers of no interest to anyone else, and finding good homes for any useful items. And she set herself the task of gathering his notes on the prehistory of Scotland into some sort of order, with a view to their eventual publication, privately if necessary. It was a mammoth task, as the volume had grown and expanded over the decades, filling half a dozen box files. She taught herself to use Martin's typewriter; she felt close to him, sitting at his desk, deciphering his handwriting and poring over notes and diagrams.

Though her daughters tried to persuade her to sell the big, empty house, she refused to do so. 'It's too soon,' she murmured, to silence them. 'And there would be so much to do. Perhaps later.' These days, she avoided conflict, discussion. Conversation tired her. Visiting her daughters, she would find herself longing after a day or two to return to the silence of her home. Even Eleanor's letters from India, with their admonitions to remember to eat properly and not to stint on heating the permanently draughty house, she read once, and then put aside with a fond smile. She seemed to have lost the ability, she often thought, to feel very much other than grief. Only Kate's son, Sam, with his teenage gangliness and awkward affection, had a way of touching her unexpectedly, so that sometimes, when she was with him, she had to blink away her tears.

All that, and her constant awareness of the utter pointlessness of the remaining portion of her life, she kept to herself, of course. She had always been a private person, had nurtured her secrets for years. She had endured loss and grief so many times in her life that she should be practised at it, she told herself.

In the house in the Old Town, Martin's shadow kept her company. She made herself cook and eat and mend her clothes, knowing that, if she didn't, her daughters would worry about her. She joined a music society, for the company, and she kept in touch with her friends – Izzy and Davey, and Charlie Campbell, and Iona, in Ireland.

A few things pierced the fog. Her worries about her daughters. Her memories of the immense happiness that her marriage had given her.

And the announcement in *The Scotsman*, in April 1961, of the death of Andrew Gilchrist.

Part Five

Morven Gilchrist

Spring 1961

Chapter Seventeen

The funeral was miserable, as all funerals are, even when no one has much cared for the person who has died. It rained. Looking round the churchyard, Morven thought that they resembled a gathering of wet, black crows.

Afterwards, they went back to the Charlotte Square house. Uncle Niall and Aunt Barbara had been living in Charlotte Square for the past eight months, looking after Grandfather since he had had his stroke. He had refused to go into a nursing home. When Morven and her mother had visited, one side of Andrew Gilchrist's face had drooped like molten wax, and he had called Morven Maxwell, which was disconcerting, to say the least – wrong person, wrong sex, wrong time by more than two decades. Now, Uncle Niall owned the house, and, even before Grandfather's death, it had begun to change. Heavy swagged velvet curtains had been replaced with modern florals and stripes; the kitchen had been stylishly refitted with Formica worktops. 'Not the faintest hope of finding a decent daily if she has to work with a washing machine and stove left over from the Ark,' Aunt Barbara had pointed out to Morven and her mother, 'and besides, it gives me something to take my mind off – well, you know.' She had looked up, towards the room where Grandfather was dying, very slowly.

After the tension of the funeral, a lightened, almost festive air seemed to settle over the high-ceilinged rooms. Whisky was poured down throats, and a cold collation served in the dining room. You had to hand it to Uncle Niall, he didn't stint his guests. There was caviar like spoon-fuls of shiny red ant's eggs, and cold salmon, ham and salads. Not like Uncle Sandy, the younger Gilchrist brother, who measured out drinks in teaspoons and counted the biscuits you took with your coffee. Over the years, Niall had grown outwards, becoming red and shiny and bulbous, like a balloon. Only a certain flintiness in his small, dark eyes belied his jolly, avuncular appearance. In contrast, Sandy was gaunt, his skin starting to sag in loose folds, his reddish hair paling and thinning, as though something inside him that had never had much life anyway had begun to shrink to a small, hard nut.

In the presence of the Gilchrist family, friends and colleagues, the house seemed to come alive again, shaking itself awake after the long hiatus of Andrew Gilchrist's illness. The afternoon lengthened. In Grandfather's study, the uncles plotted and schemed and talked of money; not far away, small boys raced Dinky cars on the shiny marble hallway. In the kitchen, the daily help, Mrs Black, washed up while Barbara cut up cake into slices and the two women talked of children and grandchildren. At four o'clock, sandwiches and fruit cake were distributed. Barbara thrust a plate of sausage rolls into Morven's hands and sent her to the drawing room to make her offering to the mourners.

The women, resplendent in black skirts and jackets or white-collared black dresses, set off with pearls and little black velvet hats, monopolized the comfortable seats by the hearth. A fire burned in the grate; Barbara's elder daughter, Pat, who was in her late twenties, had surreptitiously slid off her high heels and was warming her toes. Avril's daughter, June, was cradling a red-faced baby, which was wrapped up in cardigans and shawls like a caterpillar in a cocoon.

Avril caught sight of Morven. 'Sausage rolls! Too fatty for me, I'm afraid.'

'Perhaps just one. They look so delicious.' Pat, who was cheerful and well-covered, like her mother, helped herself.

Avril's eyes raked Morven up and down. 'You're looking very svelte, Morven. How are you, dear?'

'Very well, thank you, Aunt Avril.'

'And how is your mother? She seems in high spirits.'

Morven's mother, easily spotted by the large scarlet silk flower worn like a banner on her black hat, was standing by the piano, surrounded by half a dozen of Grandfather's business cronies. Her sudden roar of laughter, as rich and pungent as 25-year-old malt, pealed across the room.

'Mum's very well, too.'

'Is she still up in – I can never remember the name of the place.'

'Ravenhart, Aunt Avril. Yes, she's been back there for about a year.'

Aunt Avril lit a cigarette. 'It must be terribly quiet for a girl like you, Morven.'

'I'm living in London just now.'

'*London?*' Avril's thin eyebrows rose. 'Goodness me, what a long way to go! Isn't Edinburgh good enough for you?'

'I just wanted a change.'

Pat asked, 'What are you doing now?'

'I'm working in Selfridges, on the Elizabeth Arden counter. So if you're ever in London and fancy a new lipstick . . .'

'And have you found a young man yet, dear?' Avril gave a quick glance over Morven's shoulder, as if an eligible male might be perched there, preening himself like a parrot.

'No, Aunt Avril,' said Morven calmly.

'Mustn't leave it too late!' A wag of the finger and an arch smile. 'How old are you? Now, let me see – Naomi and Maxwell were married in November of nineteen thirty-six, and you were born . . .'

'In June the following year,' said Morven, as you perfectly well know, you old witch, she thought. 'I'm twenty-three.'

'Twenty-three! I was married and expecting June by the time I was twenty-four. And look at Pat – three lovely boys already.' Avril settled back in her seat, satisfied at having made her point. 'How *are* Clive's tonsils, Pat dear?'

The conversation drifted into a discussion of children's ailments. Morven moved to where Niall and Barbara's younger daughter, Frannie, her husband, Calum, and Andy, who was Avril and Sandy's son, perched on the window seat.

Calum spied the sausage rolls, said, 'My favourite, yum,' and took three.

Frannie said, 'We're wondering how soon we dare slip out to the pub.'

Andy peered round the room. 'Crowd has to thin down a little more, I'd say.'

Morven waved the plate under their noses. 'Do eat them, please.'

'Couldn't possibly, I'm afraid, darling. Mum's shovelled so much food down our throats I'm fit to bust.' Frannie shifted up the window seat to make a place for Morven. 'How's things?'

'Fine. Absolutely fine.' Another shriek of laughter from her mother; across the room, the red silk flower bobbed.

'You must pop in on us tomorrow morning for a coffee, Morven, before you head home. If you can stand the chaos, that is.' A wail: they turned to see a very small girl making her way towards them, tears mingling with the chocolate smeared over her face. Frannie said, rather exasperatedly, 'Oh, why are children so different to what you think they're going to be? I suppose it's a trick of nature – we'd stop having them if we knew the truth. Ruthie, Ruthie, whatever's the matter, honey?'

Calum picked up his daughter; Frannie extracted tissues from her handbag and wiped Ruth's face. She murmured, 'Is one allowed to say what a relief it is that it's over?'

'The funeral?'

'Of course. But Grandfather, too. Such a blessing all that's finished with. So grim.'

'Fran,' said Andy.

'Oh, come on, Andy, you couldn't stand him either.' She shrugged. 'We were all terrified of him, weren't we? I wonder if anyone ever actually *liked* him?'

Andy gave a bark of laughter. 'Our grandmother, presumably, at some point.'

'I don't know about that. Mum once told me that Grandfather was absolutely ghastly to her.'

They talked for a while longer and then the group broke up, Andy summoned by his mother, Frannie in search of her other daughter. In the cool sanctuary of a corridor, Morven ate a sausage roll and thought about the events of the last week – the phone call to the Bayswater boarding house where she lived, when her mother had told her of Grandfather's death, and her train journey, two days ago, to Edinburgh. It was hard to believe, even now, that Grandfather was gone. Before his illness, he had seemed such a massive and unyielding figure, as weighty and impermeable as a chunk of the Grampians. *We were all terrified of him, weren't we?* Not true, thought Morven. She had not been afraid of Andrew Gilchrist, and neither had her mother. Her mother had hardly troubled to hide her loathing for Grandfather. It would not have surprised Morven if she had refused to attend the funeral. Her mother had decided to go, Morven guessed, more out of fondness for Barbara, Frannie and Pat than because of any regard for Grandfather. And, of course, she always enjoyed a party.

Leaning her back against the cool marble edging of a niche, Morven told herself that she would be back in London on Monday. Yet Aunt Avril's voice, falsely solicitous, echoed in her ears, unsettling her. *And how is your mother?* She wondered whether Aunt Avril set out to provoke, or whether it just happened. A bit of both, she concluded. The ostentatious reminding of her listeners that Morven had been born only seven months after her parents' marriage seemed as much out of habit as born of any particular desire to wound. Or perhaps Avril had never got over the shock of discovering that someone in the Gilchrist family had given in to the demands of passion. Impossible to imagine Avril, who in her late forties had already begun to look withered, ever doing likewise. And anyway, Avril had a point, because how *was* her mother? Brittle, fragile and ominously high-spirited, acknowledged Morven. Which wasn't promising.

Morven had for a long time thought of her mother's drinking as a circle. There was the crisis, which was followed by the tearful resolution never to touch alcohol again, coupled with a great deal of shame and regret. And then, during the period of abstention, the boredom and loneliness that were a consequence of not drinking. And eventually, after weeks or months, impatience and anger with the boredom and loneliness, and the rediscovery that they could be banished by just one little drink. Which, sometimes slowly and at other times with alarming speed, eventually developed into a full-scale binge. And then, sooner or later, something dreadful would happen – her mother would fall downstairs or have her heart broken by some utterly appalling man – and at that point someone, most often Auntie Tessa, or Raymond at the pub, would phone, and Morven would dash up to Scotland and find her mother stranded on the sofa with a sprained ankle or in the depths of an inert, tear-stained depression. Morven would clean up the house while her mother wept and hated herself and apologized for wrecking her daughter's life, and, in due course, everything would calm down and Naomi would insist that she was fine and promise never to touch another drop. And then Morven would leave Ravenhart once more, to find another job, another bed-sitting room.

Perhaps that was why she wasn't married yet, she mused, with a brood of babies, like Pat and Frannie and June. Because of her mother. There always came a point when her mother had to be explained to a boyfriend, and that point was often when she had to race back unexpectedly to Ravenhart. She had tried evasion, and had sensed that they thought she was making excuses, that she was giving them the brush-off. Once, to a man she had thought herself in love with, she had told the truth. She had seen disgust in his eyes; she had not made the same mistake again. However much her mother might drive her wild with frustration, however deeply she might sometimes resent her demands, she hated anyone else to criticize her. It was easier not to bother, easier to keep men at arm's length – a trip to the cinema, a dinner, an evening in a smoky little Soho pub.

But she was too honest with herself to blame her current lack of boyfriend, fiancé or husband on her mother. Men so often seemed as disappointing as the April weather. They were unreliable or they were complacent or they slipped too easily into expecting a woman to look after them – and she, who had known how to tidy a kitchen and make a cup of tea almost since infancy, had had more than her fair share of that. Away from home and her mother, the height of her culinary ambitions were beans on toast or a cheese and pickle sandwich.

Or did she still expect to meet the man who was capable of sweeping her off her feet, the man who inspired her to love at first glance? *I loved your father the first time I saw him,* her mother had often told her. Did she compare her suitors with the father she had never known, and find them wanting? An uncomfortable thought, especially as she had for a long time distrusted her mother's version of her courtship and marriage. Perfect love, Morven couldn't help thinking, would not have been ended by her father walking off to who knows where. Not that she would ever have voiced such cynicism to her mother; Morven sensed that her mother's idealized view of the past held her together, like the skeins of a net. Destroy that, and she might fall apart completely.

A very small fire engine struck her on the ankle. Morven propelled it back down to corridor towards Pat's boys. Then, abandoning the sausage rolls in the niche, she wandered down the corridor.

Through the open door of Grandfather's study, her uncles' voices issued.

'We'll sell up Harvards.' Niall was speaking. Harvards was a Gilchrist-owned restaurant in Princes Street.

'If anyone'll buy it. Place is losing money hand over fist.' Uncle Sandy's voice, somewhat slurred.

'Should have got rid of it long ago,' said Niall, with a touch of asperity. 'Thank God we haven't got him breathing down our necks any more. Father rather lost the plot, this past couple of years.'

'Father's been letting things slip for far longer than that. He was never the same after Maxwell.'

'Maxwell? It was that bloody Voyle.'

Sandy shook his head. Then he said ruminatively, 'When you remember how he was with Maxwell, you wouldn't have thought he would have minded.'

In the doorway, Morven said, 'What do you mean, Uncle Sandy?'

The brothers looked up, squinting at her. Though they were dissimilar in appearance, they shared mannerisms, turns of phrase.

Sandy said, 'Mind him running off.'

She came into the room. The air was acrid with cigar smoke. 'No, I meant, how was Grandfather with my father?'

'Oh, sweetness and light, Morven,' said Niall with a snort of laughter. 'Sweetness and light, same as he was with all of us.'

Sandy knocked back the remainder of his drink. Then his small, pale eyes settled on Morven, and he said viciously, 'He beat him black and blue often enough.'

'Sandy!'

Morven made sure not to let her shock show on her face. 'Grandfather used to hit my father?'

Niall gave a little laugh and said, 'All water under the bridge now.'

'He used the belt on all of us, of course, but Maxwell got it most.' Sandy sloshed more whisky into his glass. 'Thank God. Maxwell was a lightning rod. We needed him to deflect the heat from us.'

Niall shrugged. 'He was a violent man, our father, and Maxwell had a way of bringing out the worst in him.'

'And most of the time he deserved it. I don't doubt your mother paints him as an angel, but he wasn't, you know. There wasn't much that Maxwell wouldn't do.' Sandy's bland, small-featured face had taken on an ugly twist. 'He had a way of looking for trouble – I think he enjoyed it, enjoyed the attention. He was chucked out of more than one school and he was always stirring up things at home.'

Niall put his hand on his brother's shoulder. 'Shut up, Sandy, she's only a kid.'

Sandy shook off Niall's hand, stood up clumsily, went to the window, and peered out. 'Bloody rain.' He drew on his cigar. Then he said, 'Father liked him best, though.'

'Tommy rot.'

'Yes, he did. I always knew he did.'

'Too much to drink, Sandy, dear fellow,' said Niall bracingly. 'You're getting addled. We should go out, get some air.'

Morven said, 'Who's Voyle?'

The two men turned to look at her. Niall crushed his cigar stub in an ashtray. 'Simon Voyle's an inglorious and best-forgotten chapter in the house of Gilchrist. He used to be my father's assistant. A couple of years before the war, he dished the dirt, spilled the beans.' He explained, 'Some of your grandfather's business dealings weren't exactly above board, if you know what I mean, Morven. All squeaky clean now, of course. Voyle had been storing the evidence away for years, dribs and drabs he could use against Father – letters and records of financial transactions,

513

that sort of thing. Father got away with it – good lawyers and not enough that could be pinned down – but it damaged him.'

Sandy pressed the palm of his hand against the window, as if he could wipe away the rain. Condensation trickled down the glass. 'Put paid to Father's chances of preferment, didn't it, though? He always fancied himself Lord Provost.'

'Anyway,' Niall blew out smoke between pursed lips and his hard dark eyes settled on Morven, 'it's common knowledge. Old scandal. The war broke out six months or so after the trial ended and people had something else to talk about.'

Sandy said suddenly, 'But you're wrong, Niall. It was Maxwell buggering off that hurt Father, not Voyle. If Father had been himself, he could have dealt with a poisonous little rat like Voyle.' His voice dropped, becoming low and brooding. 'Father might have acted as though he hated Maxwell, but he loved him. Oh yes, he loved him. Maxwell was the only person ever to hurt Father.' There was a sour amusement in his eyes. 'Wouldn't he have loved to have known that?' With a wild gesture, he raised his glass. 'To Maxwell, wherever you are.'

Barbara and Niall saw off the last of the mourners. Then Niall whistled for the dog and he and Sandy headed out for the pub.

Barbara gave a heartfelt sigh of relief. Despite Mrs Black's sterling efforts that afternoon, cups, plates and glasses still littered tables and mantelpieces. But at least the house was hers again – properly hers, with her father-in-law gone. Pleasurably, she thought of all the things she would do to the place, the rooms to be decorated, the garden to be overhauled. She would start tomorrow morning by clearing out the old man's wardrobe. She had not realized until this moment how deeply she longed to eradicate every trace of Andrew Gilchrist.

She began to stack plates – people always ate so much at funerals, only weddings were worse, because they seemed to go on so much longer. But then, suddenly aware that she hadn't seen Naomi for a while, which was a worry, she put the plates down and went upstairs. Morven was washing up in the kitchen – nice girl, Morven, thought Barbara. In spite of there being something ethereal about her appearance, that wavy dark hair, those sea-green eyes – Maxwell's eyes – she had a down-to-earth, practical nature. Which was just as well, thought Barbara grimly, with Naomi for a mother.

Barbara tapped on Naomi's bedroom door. 'Naomi, dear, I'm making a cup of tea. Would you like one?' There was no answer, so she pushed open the door. Naomi was standing at the window, looking out, silhouetted by the silvery-grey late afternoon light. Barbara felt a stab of envy. It didn't seem fair that Naomi had kept her figure so well, especially when she didn't exactly stint herself and seemed to eat and drink (especially drink) whatever she liked, whereas she herself only had to look at a chocolate biscuit to put on pounds.

Naomi's hat, of which some of the staider mourners had muttered their disapproval, lay discarded on the bed, its scarlet flower drooping. Barbara knew why Naomi had worn that hat – because she saw Andrew Gilchrist's death as a cause for celebration, not regret. Naomi was incapable of hiding her feelings. Her emotions were uncovered, naked for all to see.

Barbara coughed and said, 'Naomi?' and Naomi turned to look at her. Tears had gouged channels through her make-up; her mascara and eyeliner had run, giving her a clownish look.

She whispered, 'I thought he might come!'

Barbara, bewildered, said, 'Who? Who did you think might come?'

'Max,' said Naomi. 'I thought he might come home, now that his father's dead!' And she began to cry again. She looked destroyed, thought Barbara as she put her arms round her, and not in the least bit enviable at all.

These days, the house in the Old Town seemed very quiet. When Bess cooked, the scrape of the spoon on the saucepan and the rasp of the knife as she peeled seemed abnormally loud.

She was making an apple pie to take to Izzy Kirkpatrick. Izzy had twisted her ankle and was laid up, and Davey even burned toast, so Bess had promised to bring round supper. As she weighed out flour and butter, she felt a touch of irritation, mainly directed at her daughters. Oh why, she thought, couldn't they ever be *settled*? When they had been younger, she had been so certain that one day, each of her girls would lead the sort of sensible, well-ordered life that she herself had always meant to lead but had so signally failed to do. Kate, Eleanor, Rebecca and Aimée would all have interesting occupations or careers, and all, of course, would be happily married, with children of their own. It wasn't much to ask, was it?

Instead, her daughters' lives, with their extremes of complexity or austerity, and their tendencies to chaos, exasperated her. She had tried her best to give them a secure, conventional upbringing, hadn't she? They hadn't been hauled the length and breadth of India, or left to fend for themselves while still in their teens, as she herself had. Yet they seemed to understand neither the shortness of life nor the cold, impersonal cruelty of time.

Her four beautiful daughters lived separate lives, seeing each other infrequently and squabbling on the occasions when they were together. Yet they must love each other, she needed them to love each other, because who else would they have to turn to, when she, like Martin, was gone? To make matters worse, they had produced, so far, only one child between them. And though Bess adored Sam, and though he was everything she could have wished for in her grandson, one grandchild seemed disappointing, thin pickings. She had had six children, yet she had only one grandchild. And it was not as if they were girls any more, not as if one could smile affectionately and say to oneself, give them time. Kate was now forty-four, older than Bess had been when she had given birth to Aimée, her last child. Hugh's death had been a tragedy, of course, but Bess had always treasured the hope that eventually Kate might love someone else, might find happiness again. Yet she had not. When, in October, Sam went to Oxford, Kate would be alone.

And then there was Eleanor. Eleanor's passion for India

hadn't, as Bess had hoped, extended to some fellow doctor working in the Calcutta hospital, and neither had her work among the barefoot children of the subcontinent implanted in her a need to have children of her own – quite the opposite, in fact. 'There are far too many children anyway, Mum,' Eleanor had announced, when, years ago, Bess had first brought up the subject, 'and the world can't feed them, so why produce any more?' Adding, 'If it was up to me I wouldn't allow anyone to have more than two children.' Bess had managed to stop herself pointing out that if that rule had applied to herself, then Eleanor and her sisters would never have been born.

As for Aimée, she seemed to prefer *donkeys* to children. A year ago, at the age of twenty-five, Aimée had abruptly left modelling, had turned her back on the glamour and the parties and the money without the least appearance of regret, and had used her savings to buy a farmhouse in Cornwall. She had then proceeded to populate it with donkeys rescued from dire circumstances throughout the country. 'Donkeys!' cried Eleanor, disgustedly. 'When thousands of children die of hunger every day!' But Bess, visiting Aimée in Cornwall, had seen that she loved her donkeys, had seen also her steady stream of visitors, friends from Edinburgh and London, men who gazed at Aimée with the same bewitched expression that Aimée directed at her donkeys. Bess had said nothing, but mourned the waste of it, the utter waste of it.

But then Aimée had always followed her own path, smiling with a peculiar sweetness at those who offered advice, and then disregarding them completely. 'I can't believe she's mine!' Bess had more than once cried despairingly to Martin. 'They must have mixed her up in the hospital!'

Bess had never doubted for one moment that Rebecca was hers. Rebecca was wilful and manipulative and hungry for life, and hadn't an ounce of Martin in her. Rebecca was *her* child, black-haired and blue-eyed, as like her in looks as in character. Which was why, Bess supposed, she could not condemn Rebecca as perhaps she should have done, why she could not harden her heart against her.

Rebecca, bright, self-centred, indolent, discontented Rebecca, had one outstanding talent: for making men fall in love with her. In the third year of her marriage to Stuart, Rebecca had become pregnant, but had lost the baby at the end of the fourth month. The miscarriage had cut deeper than Rebecca cared to acknowledge, Bess suspected, and afterwards Rebecca had been harder, wilder, and had embarked upon a series of affairs, culminating in the one that had eventually led to her divorce from Stuart and subsequently to her second marriage to Jared Cooper.

Jared was fine-featured, with silky black hair and smouldering dark brown eyes. He was also a poet. Rebecca had abandoned her palaces for a three-roomed flat in Ladbroke Grove, her Chanel gowns for blue jeans and black turtleneck sweaters. Bess had dared to hope that Rebecca, in marrying for love this time, had satisfied her hungry soul at last. Yet the marriage was stormy, crowded with dramatic partings and equally dramatic reconciliations.

Rolling out the pastry, Bess's thoughts drifted to her other problem: Ravenhart House. Two months ago, the removal company to which she had rented the house for more than ten years had gone into liquidation. None of her daughters had the least interest in Ravenhart, none of them ever visited it. Every now and then Kate promised to, but in the end always cancelled her visit because she was too busy. Rebecca, who craved modernity and glamour, had no interest in an old, unfashionable Scottish mansion. Eleanor and Aimée had made their homes far away from Perthshire. So she must do *something* with the house. She must find another use for it or she must sell it. It was too great a drain on her resources to be allowed to stand empty. She must make some sort of a decision or the estate would remain a burden to her daughters after she died.

Yet she dithered, uncertain what to do, and was annoyed with herself for dithering. She had too many memories, she supposed, too much love and hate and sorrow bound up in Ravenhart to simply dispose of the house. And there was, of course, that last, small kernel of hope that Frazer would come home again.

She would go to Ravenhart the following week, she resolved. She needed to check that the last of the furniture that belonged to the removal company had been taken away, and perhaps, at Ravenhart itself, she might be able to make up her mind.

The telephone rang. Bess brushed her floury hands on her apron and went to answer it.

'Mum,' said Kate's voice, 'you've got to come. Rebecca's left Jared.'

* * *

The gatehouse, when Morven and Naomi returned to it late the afternoon after the funeral, had a dusty, crumpled appearance. Naomi fussed over her dog, Lulu, then said, 'I might have a bit of a lie-down,' and disappeared upstairs.

After inspecting empty kitchen cupboards, Morven drove to the village shop and bought milk, bread, eggs and bacon and fruit and veg, household soap and Vim. Back home, she parked her mother's Hillman Minx outside the gate-house. Opening the boot, she paused, looking down the glen to where Ravenhart House was hidden by trees and hills.

There was a feeling of anticipation in the pit of her stomach, the same feeling she always had when she was soon to see the house after being away for a long time. Since she had been a child, she had thought of Ravenhart House as her own private domain. As a little girl, the deserted house, with its pinnacles and gables, had seemed to her stolen from a fairy tale. Tomorrow, she said to herself as she lifted the shopping bags out of the boot. I'll go there tomorrow.

Then a sound, from not far away, made her glance up. A man had turned the corner of the footpath from Ravenhart House and was heading towards the gates. His dark blond hair was uncovered and he was wearing boots and hiking gear. Morven noticed that he walked with a limp. She called out a greeting as he passed her, and he glanced at her very briefly, gave the smallest of nods, and then walked on.

Friendly type, she thought wryly – city-bred, most likely, and didn't believe in acknowledging those he hadn't been formally introduced to. She went into the gatehouse. There was a note on the kitchen table from her mother: *Gone to see Moira, back soon, Mum.*

After Naomi had spent a couple of hours with Moira, who ran a shop that sold knitting wool and sewing things, she popped into the Half Moon. The Half Moon was a decent-sized pub with a few rooms for guests upstairs; Naomi had known its proprietor, Raymond Erskine, for several years.

Raymond wasn't behind the bar tonight, which was a shame, because she was fond of Ray and could have done with a chat. The new lad, a nice-looking boy called Fergus, was serving drinks. Perhaps it was just as well, Naomi told herself as she ordered a Bloody Mary and sat down at the bar, because Raymond might have fussed.

She needed to cheer herself up, and she deserved to have a good time after the ordeal of Andrew Gilchrist's funeral. The cocktail made her feel chirpier. She ordered another and let her gaze wander round the room. She was wearing her camel wool skirt and a cream cashmere jersey beneath her mink-collared coat – it might only be a poxy little Highland village, but she had always believed in making an effort. Raymond did breakfasts and bar snacks; Naomi wondered whether she should ask Fergus to knock her up a cold beef sandwich, but she wasn't really all that hungry. A couple of drinks and a few cigarettes and someone to talk to, someone who wasn't a Gilchrist, someone who was fun and would take her mind off things – that would do the trick.

With an experienced eye, Naomi surveyed the customers sitting at the tables in the saloon bar. There was a sprinkling of men from the larger local businesses and farms, as well as guests of the Half Moon, hikers and anglers and salesmen stopping off for a night on a trip to the north. Naomi's glance paused at a man sitting by himself, drinking a beer and reading a book. Fair hair, broad shoulders beneath his khaki jersey, nice mouth, thought Naomi approvingly. Younger than her, but then she was good for her age. Naomi crossed and uncrossed her nylon-stockinged legs; he looked up briefly and then went back to his book. Miserable beggar, she thought, and let her gaze roam on, catching the eye of one of the salesmen, who rose and came to the bar and offered to buy her a drink. Only her third, and she had been so good for such a long time. So long as she could still count them, she must be fine, mustn't she, she thought with a bubble of laughter.

The salesman's name was Kevin and he came from Belfast; he sold linen to hotels and restaurants, he told her, good quality linen at half the price you'd pay in the shops. 'I bet some of my bedsheets have seen a thing or two,' he said roguishly.

Naomi fluttered her eyelashes and put her hand on his arm and said, 'I don't know what you mean, Kevin.' She offered him a cigarette and took one herself, and as he lit hers she leaned across to him; she saw his gaze fall to the deep V of her sweater, and she smiled to herself.

At nine o'clock Raymond came into the bar. 'Ray, darling,' she said, and embraced him. Then she kissed Kevin, so that he would not feel jealous. She felt beautiful and happy; everything she did and said seemed to come out just right. She had almost forgotten how good a few drinks made her feel.

She fumbled in her handbag for her purse. 'What will you have, boys?'

Kevin said, 'A Scotch,' but Ray reached over and clasped her purse and put it back in her bag.

'I'm making coffee. Blue Mountain.'

Naomi pouted. 'I want a drink, Ray.'

'Coffee,' he said firmly. 'And I want to talk to you about the restaurant.'

'The lady said she'd like a drink,' began Kevin, and Ray, who was ex-army and built like one of the tanks he had commanded, turned to look at him.

'I should push off now, if I were you, sonny.'

Kevin seemed to consider for a moment, and then drifted away, looking sulky.

'Ray,' said Naomi reprovingly.

He smiled at her. 'You know I make good coffee.'

Ray disappeared into the kitchen. Naomi took the opportunity to wheedle a double vodka from the barman, drinking it quickly so that Ray would not scold her. Or not *scold*, Ray never scolded; instead, he had a way of looking disappointed and unhappy, which was worse. Ray had had a bit of a problem with alcohol himself at one time. He had become a publican, he had told her, because he needed to look his devil in the eyes. That way, it couldn't sneak up behind him. Not that she had a *problem*, Naomi told herself, scooping up the last of the vodka with a fingertip and shoving the glass out of sight as Ray came back into the barroom. She could give up any time she wanted to – hadn't she proved that over and over again?

Ray came back with the coffee, sat down beside her and

showed her the plans his architect had drawn up for the restaurant. His talk of supporting walls and knocking through floated over her, and she thought happily how fond she was of him. He had asked her to marry him a couple of times and had been nice enough not to be offended by her refusal. Ray was comfortably off, about to expand his business, and he was good in bed. Naomi had been tempted. She had refused him, she supposed, because her brief marriage to her deceitful, adulterous, untrustworthy bastard of a husband had put her off the institution forever.

While Ray nipped out to put on a new barrel of beer, Naomi poured a slug of brandy into her coffee from the hip flask in her handbag. The brandy made her feel warm and relaxed. Ray came back. Slipping off a shoe, she ran the tips of her toes down his calf. She would go to bed with him tonight, she decided; she was sick of sleeping on her own. Morven wouldn't mind, Morven had made it perfectly clear that she preferred her own company. Morven—

The door to the barroom opened, and Naomi looked up and saw Morven, standing in the doorway. It was almost as though her thoughts had conjured her daughter up. A quick reproachful glance at Ray, who made an apologetic gesture, and then Naomi called out, 'Darling!' and waved and slid off the bar stool and lurched across the room to greet her daughter. She had forgotten that she was still holding her cup of coffee; brown liquid splashed on the floor. Stumbling between the tables, she tripped over a rucksack and found herself in the arms of the fair-haired man.

Coffee dripped onto the pages of his book. 'Sorry. So sorry, darling,' she purred, in her low, throaty voice, and scrubbed at the book with her sleeve.

Morven said, 'Come on, Mum, we're going home,' and took her bag and coat from Ray, and steered her into the car.

A few days later, while her mother was asleep on the sofa, Morven walked to Ravenhart House. Walking down the drive, the scent of pine and grass and the sound of the river, rushing not far away between its fringes of silver birch, drove away some of her frustration. At the hump-backed bridge, she rested her elbows on the parapet, looking out to the mountains. Something in the way they rose up into the sky always lifted her heart. Further down the road, pine trees crowded to the edge of the verge, and, for a few moments, as she walked beneath their branches, there was darkness, and her footsteps were silenced by the bed of needles.

As the trees thinned, she saw the house. Blank, black windows stared out at her, and lichen blossomed on the stone portico that framed the front door. A stillness had fallen over the house and garden; it was hard to imagine that anyone had ever lived there.

Morven walked round to the side of the house, to the little door that, the first time she had discovered it, had been almost completely concealed beneath tendrils of ivy. She had been eleven years old when she had first gone inside Ravenhart House. Before, she had been content to roam the garden, with its weed-choked pathways and mossy stone urns and drifts of roses smothering overgrown flowerbeds. The ivy-covered door had been unlocked. Opening it, and venturing into the house, she had discovered rooms stacked with huge, old-fashioned tables and wardrobes and chests of drawers. In the years that followed, she had got to know the house, and she had been bewitched by its magic. Sometimes she had closed her eyes tightly, concentrating fiercely, half convinced that when she opened them the rooms would be bright and warm and filled with people.

The house had been a place of solace for her throughout her childhood. When, every other year or so, Naomi had declared herself sick of living in the sticks and they had decamped to London or to Edinburgh, it had been the house that Morven had missed. Ravenhart had been one of the few constants in her life. Homes, schools, and her mother's boyfriends had changed with the seasons. Ravenhart House had provided a respite from all that. Each time she had explored the house, she had made new discoveries – a room at the end of a long, dark passageway, a door in a panelled wall. A cupboard full of tin helmets and water bottles, left over from the war, and rows of shallow wooden shelves, their glass lids framing the fragile brown butterflies pinioned inside. Inside a wardrobe in an upstairs room, she had unearthed neat stacks of men's shirts, wrapped in tissue paper. The cotton had been fine and silky and had smelt of lavender.

Since her last visit, several snakes of ivy had clawed their way across the door. Morven tore them aside, raised the latch and went inside. The door led into a maze of pantries and larders and low passageways. A beetle scurried across a stone sink, and she ran her fingertips over a marble worktop and it felt as cold as ice.

Narrow corridors branched into wider ones, and she found herself in the heart of the house. Looking into a room, she saw to her surprise that much of the furniture that had been stored in the house for years had gone. Working her way through the house, she discovered that most of the tea chests and many of the wardrobes, tables and chairs had been taken away. What furniture remained presumably belonged to Ravenhart House itself.

The clearing of the rooms had its advantages. Drawers and cupboards, unobtainable before, were now revealed to her. In a cupboard built into the panelling, she discovered boxes of photographs. Sepia Victorian children glowered in sailor suits and white dresses. Formal groups of family and servants posed on manicured lawns. A black-hatted woman wearing a dark, severe dress stood beside a plump baby in a pram.

She picked up another photograph. Her father smiled up at her. The snapshot captured the laughter in his eyes. He was wearing a white shirt and light-coloured trousers and he was standing in front of a small stone house, backed by mountains. He looked, she thought, much the same age as she was now.

Phrases from the afternoon of the funeral drifted through her mind. *He beat him black and blue . . . there wasn't much Maxwell wouldn't do . . . some of your grandfather's business dealings weren't exactly above board . . .* Her father was standing between a man and a girl. The man was fair-haired, and the girl was most definitely not Naomi. This girl was light-haired and slight. She wore shorts and a shirt knotted round her waist; she, too, was smiling and looked happy.

It was growing dark. Morven shoved the photographs back into the cardboard boxes, all except the snapshot of her father and his friends, which she put in her pocket. Then she left the house.

Walking away, she looked back just once. The dying sunlight caught the panes of glass in the windows and, for a moment, there was a flare of light, and it seemed as though the building was illuminated from within, its fires burning and its lamps lit. Then the pine trees closed over her, and Ravenhart House was lost in the curve of the road.

At the gatehouse, she saw that the Hillman, which had been parked outside, had gone. The gatehouse had been left unlocked, the kitchen door swinging open. There was no sign of her mother, but inside, on the table, was an empty bottle of gin.

Morven phoned Moira, at the knitting shop, and Pamela, at the village store. Then Raymond at the pub, but Raymond's new barman, Fergus, told her that Ray had gone to Perth that day and wouldn't be back till late. And no, Mrs Gilchrist hadn't been in the pub that evening. She phoned every other friend and acquaintance of her mother she could think of, and then she thought of calling the police but decided against it and instead made herself a cup of tea but poured half of it down the sink because she felt too sick to drink it. She walked to the gates and jogged a short distance up and down the road, and saw nothing but the way the night was closing in and the tightness of the sharp bends in the road, and the proximity of rock and marsh and ditch. Her mother wasn't the steadiest driver at the best of times; it always took a certain resolution of spirit to get into a car with her. Drunk, she was a menace.

Morven went back into the house and started Vimming grimy cupboards again, her ears straining constantly for the sound of a car. She blamed herself; she shouldn't have gone to Ravenhart, she should have recognized the all-too-familiar signs: the squalid state of the house, her mother's lurches of mood and wild behaviour.

It was almost ten o'clock when she heard the screech of wheels, closely followed by a clang so loud it seemed to shake the gatehouse. Running outside, her heart seemed to have jammed in her throat and her legs felt leaden, as though she was trying to move through a swamp. By the light from the gatehouse window she saw her mother's car skewed across the entrance to the driveway, its bonnet embedded in Ravenhart's iron gates. A little further up the road, and at an odd angle to the verge, was a Land Rover. Someone had climbed out of the Land Rover and was hurrying to the gates. Morven recognized the fair-haired hiker from the pub by his limp.

Inside the Hillman, her mother lay slumped over the steering wheel, her eyes closed.

'Mum,' Morven whispered. 'Mum.'

A voice from behind her said, 'She was coming round the corner too fast, she nearly drove into me.'

Morven reached out to shake her mother's shoulder.

'Don't move her,' he warned. 'She may have broken something. Is there a pulse?'

She put her fingertips against her mother's neck. 'Yes,' she said, and felt weak with relief.

Naomi was wearing only a skirt and short-sleeved sweater. The fair-haired man took off his parka and put it over her. 'Have you a phone? You'd better call an ambulance.'

Morven ran back into the house to phone the ambulance. She was allowed to travel in the back of the ambulance to the cottage hospital in Pitlochry. By then, her mother had begun to come round, to murmur and weep while Morven held her hand and tried to soothe her. At the hospital, they wheeled Naomi away on a trolley and Morven sat for ages on a metal chair in a corridor as starched nurses walked up and down, and she seemed to see, over and over again, her mother slumped over the wheel of the car. The sounds of purposeful footsteps in the wards and the traffic on the road outside lessened as the night drew on. Eventually, Raymond arrived at the hospital and gave her a hug and said reassuring things, though she could hear the worry in his voice, and then a white-coated doctor with bags of tiredness under his eyes appeared and told her that her mother had several broken ribs and mild concussion and that she was now sleeping soundly so they might as well go home.

Raymond drove her back to the gatehouse and she let herself in, and the gin bottle was still on the table and the Vim beside the cupboard. It was one o'clock in the morning.

Kate took the opportunity to escape while her mother was talking to Rebecca. Outside, it was a clear, bright day; she could feel spring in the air. She went first to Greek Street in Soho, where, in a small but excellent delicatessen, she bought olives, Brie, a jar of artichokes and a bottle of Merlot wine. Then her eye was caught by a vast wheel of a tart, displayed on the counter. Breathing in the scents of walnuts and cream and toffee, she found herself transported back to the past. Once, a very long time ago, she had cooked roast lamb in Oliver's kitchen, and afterwards they had eaten the tarte aux noix he had brought back from France.

Kate bought a large slice of tart and left the shop. It occurred to her that she might be able to find a birthday present for her friend, Ursula, in Portobello Road. Ursula was well off and had unerring taste, and was difficult to find presents for, and Oliver would be just the person to help.

Hurrying to the tube station, Kate caught a glimpse of herself in a shop window and saw a middle-aged woman in a raincoat and knee-length skirt, laden with shopping bags, her hair flying out of whatever style she had half-heartedly tried to contain it in that morning. Quite often now, she discovered white hairs among the auburn; she always pulled them out, in spite of her mother's dire warnings that, if she did so, three more would sprout in their place.

On the train, she picked walnuts off the tart and read the Iris Murdoch she had stuffed into her bag before leaving the house. She had to have a book to read on the underground; she disliked the tube train, with its hurtling darkness.

In Portobello Road, the sign above Oliver's shop wasn't

green and gold any more; instead, 'Colefax and Son', painted in black letters on a pinky-brown background, proudly proclaimed Stephen's entrance into the same profession as his father. Kate peered into the shop window, her gaze drifting past the chaises longues and writing desks to the man standing at the far end of the shop. When she caught his eye, she waved madly.

'Kate,' Oliver said, opening the door. 'What a lovely surprise.' He kissed her.

'I had a Proustian moment,' she explained, after he had put the Closed sign on the front door of the shop and they had gone up to the flat. 'A madeleine moment, only it was tarte aux noix. I thought of you, Oliver.' She extracted a paper bag from her shopping. 'Do have some, it's only slightly nibbled.' She smiled. 'I don't suppose you remember.'

Oliver was making coffee. He slid the tart onto a plate and cut it in two. 'Of course I remember. I brought it home from France. We ate the lot.'

Kate looked down at her figure. 'I wouldn't dare do that now. My hips . . .'

'Nonsense, you're as beautiful as ever.'

She said, 'Such a flatterer, Oliver,' but she felt pleased. 'How are you?'

'I'm very well.'

'And Stephen?'

'He's away at the moment, visiting a house sale in the north of England.' Oliver looked proud. 'He has an eye for the business, a real flair. I don't know how I managed without him. And how's Sam?'

Kate said, with equal pride, 'He's very well. And so delighted at having passed his Oxford entrance.'

Oliver put a tiny turquoise cup and saucer in front of her. Kate asked tentatively, 'And Margot? How is she?' Margot had been diagnosed as suffering from cancer the previous year.

Oliver looked miserable. 'Nigel phoned a couple of hours ago. She's back in hospital, I'm afraid. She seems to have taken a turn for the worse.'

'Oh Oliver, I'm so sorry. Poor Margot. Poor Nigel.' She squeezed his hand.

'She's always been *there*, such a strength. And she's always adored Stephen. It's so important for a child, don't you think, to be adored?'

Not only for a child, she thought.

He asked, 'And you, Kate? How are you?'

Kate groaned. 'My sister's driving me mad.'

'Rebecca?'

'Of course. Who else? She's left Jared. Her second husband, Oliver, her *second*, and she's only twenty-nine! She's staying with me. If she's in my house much longer I'll need psychotherapy more than my patients. My mother's come down to try and persuade her to go back to Jared, but she hasn't had much success so far.' Kate fell gloomily silent. Jared, also, had tried to coax Rebecca into returning to him. When he called, their arguments echoed through the small Chelsea house; their brief but passionate reconciliations were equally clamorous.

She added, 'The only silver lining is that I suppose it's given Mum something to do. She still misses Martin so much.'

'How long were they married?'

'Almost thirty-three years. It must be terribly hard, after so long.' Was it worse to be widowed, she had sometimes found herself wondering, after thirty-three years of marriage, or after less than eighteen months? Did the accumulation of memories make it better or worse?

She left half an hour later, a tiny blue and gold Meissen jug that Oliver had picked out for Ursula in her bag, and a promise given that they meet up for supper soon.

Travelling home on the tube, waiting for the District Line train, she found herself remembering the evening that Hugh had proposed to her, down here in the inky darkness. She recalled her joy, which had seemed to blot out both the people around them and the battle that raged in the skies overhead. Sometimes recently she had wondered whether she was still capable of such intensity of emotion – with Sam, of course, but apart from when she was with Sam, she seemed to feel much of the time a vague discontent, a fleeting longing for which she could not pinpoint an object. She should ignore it, she told herself briskly. So ridiculous to feel that there was something missing when she had a lovely home, an interesting career and a wonderful son. It was nothing more than her age, her hormones, and the tendency we all have to romanticize the past.

At Mulberry Walk, Kate knocked on the door of her next-door neighbour, a widow in her eighties, to give her the small gift of Bourbon biscuits she had bought at the delicatessen and to chat for a few moments. Then she let herself into her house. She went into the kitchen to put away her purchases. Her mother was washing up and Rebecca was painting her toenails, and Sam, all six foot one of him, was lolling against the fridge, wolfing down the cake she had made earlier that day and talking to her through a mouthful of crumbs. She put her arms round him and hugged him, and he said, 'Oh Mum,' but hugged her back, and she felt happy again.

A wakeful, dream-haunted night; at half past six Morven got up and made herself a cup of tea. At eight, she phoned the hospital, and was told that her mother's condition was satisfactory, whatever that meant, and that visiting hour was between three and four in the afternoon. Then she phoned the garage to arrange for the car to be towed away. She'd have to let Mrs Jago know about the damaged gate, she realized, and she supposed she might as well finish cleaning the kitchen, but they were almost out of Vim, so she walked to the village instead. A soft rain was falling; she put up her face to the sky, letting it cool her aching head.

Inside the general store, Phemie Drummond was at the head of the queue, laboriously reading out the items on her mother's shopping list. Phemie was wearing, as always, a man's tweed jacket tied up with an old leather belt. She was short and fat and the layers of frayed cardigans and sweaters beneath the jacket made her as round as a ball. Her greying hair, with its jagged fringe, was topped with a bottle-green beret. The sour, musty scent of unaired clothes always accompanied Phemie. She left the shop, but the mustiness lingered.

Standing in the queue, Morven had a moment's blankness – what had she come here for? – and she thrust her hands into her jacket pocket, searching for her shopping list, but instead brought out the photograph she had found at Ravenhart House the previous afternoon.

The queue shortened. Catching sight of Morven, Pamela asked after her mother. Morven gave a quick, truncated version of the accident, and sensed the ears of the people in the queue behind her pricking up. Pamela murmured shock and sympathy and then scurried around, fetching Morven's messages. As she was paying for them, Morven showed the snapshot to Pamela. Pointing to the unknown man and girl, she asked, 'You wouldn't happen to know who they are, would you, Pamela?'

Pamela fetched her reading glasses and peered. Morven said, 'It must have been taken a long time ago. In the mid-thirties, I should think.'

'I could ask my mother, if you like,' began Pamela, but then a voice at Morven's shoulder interrupted.

'That's Frazer Ravenhart and the lassie's his sister.'

Morven turned to look at the old man who had spoken. He was dressed in tweeds. His head was covered by a cloth cap and his skin was brick-red and leathery. He said curtly, 'Matches,' and slapped a few coins down on the counter. Then, as he turned to go, he shot Morven a look of such venom that it made her go cold inside, and said, 'Couple of nancy boys, the pair of them. I knew their sort. Ravenhart was well rid of them.'

He left the shop. Pamela gazed after him, open-mouthed, and then she managed to say, 'He's an old misery, Ronald Bain. You don't want to take any notice of him, dear. Going a bit soft in the head, I'd say.'

Morven put the photograph back in her pocket and left the shop. Halfway back to the gatehouse, she passed the Carterhaugh cottage. Carterhaugh Farm was owned by the Nairns, who rented out the cottage, a single-storey bothy, to hikers and holidaymakers. She noticed that a Land Rover was parked outside the cottage. The mountain soared up behind the building and the vehicle, capturing them both in shadow.

Chapter Eighteen

In her bed in the women's surgical ward, Naomi was recovering slowly. There was a bandage round her forehead, and she moved cautiously, fearful of disturbing the pain in her ribs.

On her way home from visiting her mother, Morven called at the Carterhaugh cottage. The Land Rover was still parked outside. When the fair-haired man opened the front door to her, she said, 'I'm sorry to bother you, but I brought you this.' She took his parka out of her rucksack. 'You left it in my mother's car the other night. I thought you might need it.'

'Thanks.' He took the jacket. 'How is your mother?'

'Much better. She's coming home tomorrow morning.'

'Good, that's good.' He held out his hand to her. 'I'm Patrick Roper, by the way.'

'Morven Gilchrist.'

Surprising her, he said, 'Would you like a coffee?'

'Coffee?'

'Yes, you know, stuff you drink. Or people chuck over you in pubs. I've just made some.'

'My mother didn't mean to do that.'

'I daresay. She probably didn't mean to run me off the road the other night, either.'

She said stiffly, 'If there's any damage to your car, we'll pay for it, of course.'

'I'm not worried about a few dents in the car. The dent to my pride was a bit more painful, but I'm a forgiving soul.'

'I don't see—'

'Your mother, taking the mickey in the pub the other night.' She must have looked blank, because he explained, 'My leg. Your mother was limping. I have a limp, and I thought – well, I thought she was having a laugh.'

Morven had a sudden vivid memory of Naomi, lurching unsteadily across the barroom of the Half Moon. She felt herself flush. 'Mum wouldn't – she'd lost one of her shoes, that's all. Honestly, I'm sure she wouldn't . . .' She looked away. 'Oh God.'

'Och, it doesn't matter. I was probably being overly touchy. The leg's a nuisance and I'm sick of it, to be honest.' When he smiled, his face lightened. 'Take pity on a lonely old crock and have coffee with me and I'll consider us quits.'

She heard herself murmur an assent. She followed him into the cottage. The walls of the bothy were more than a foot thick, and the windows were so small the room seemed to strain to gather up the dim light.

She asked, 'How did you hurt your leg?'

'I was shot,' he said briefly.

Morven, who had been expecting a motor accident or a fall down a rock face, said, 'Good grief.'

He went into the kitchen to fetch another mug. When he came back, she said, 'And?'

'And what?'

'Well, you can't just leave it like that. Shot. What happened?'

'I work as a private investigator,' he explained as he poured the coffee. 'I was in the army – the military police – till a couple of years ago. I travelled a lot, mostly in the Far East. When I left the forces, I couldn't face a nine-to-five job, so I thought I'd run my own show. Anyway, I was hired to look into the disappearance of some cases of cigarettes from a warehouse in Glasgow. A steady drip-drip rather than one big haul – easier to conceal, you see. Anyway, to cut a long story short, the cigarettes were one end of a chain that ended up in Marseilles. And someone found me poking my nose in where I wasn't wanted, and they didn't appreciate it.' He handed Morven a mug.

She said, 'So why are you here?'

'To convalesce – to try and get back into shape. I thought I'd do a bit of walking, climb a few hills. I'm convinced that when I manage to get to the top of Ben Liath, I'll be better, and I'll be able to get back to work. But I keep getting halfway up and the wretched leg starts to give out on me and I have to stagger back down.'

She wondered whether the severe expression she had previously noticed had been caused by pain, rather than by a disapproving nature, as she had earlier assumed. She watched him as he opened a packet of biscuits. He was of average height, in his late twenties, she guessed. His accent was Glaswegian. Nice thick brown and gold hair to go with his blue-grey eyes; and he was broad-shouldered and strong-looking, she noticed approvingly.

He said, 'By the way, is the house yours, Morven? The big house?'

'Ravenhart House? No. A lady called Mrs Jago owns it. She lives in Edinburgh. I go there for a walk sometimes, when I come home.'

'You don't live at the gatehouse, then?'

'My mother lives there. I live in London. Well,' a pang of regret, 'I *did* live in London.'

'You're not going back?'

'My mother's going to need someone with her for the next few weeks, at least,' she said flatly. 'My employers won't keep my job open for me. They never do.'

'I'm sorry. Can't your father help out?'

'My father's dead — at least, I assume he is.'

He frowned. 'You *assume?*'

'I don't know for certain. He disappeared before I was born. But he's been gone so long, almost twenty-four years, and no one's seen or heard of him, so I'm sure he must be dead.'

He must have caught her offhand tone of voice, because he said, 'Don't you *want* to know?'

'I never knew my father and he never knew me, so it's not as though I was ever fond of him.' She stirred sugar into her coffee. 'To tell the truth, sometimes I've hated him. He's been gone for almost a quarter of a century, but he still dominates our lives. My mother still loves him, after all this time. But I refuse to be obsessed with him, like she is. *He's* the reason why we never manage to move away from here. And *he's* the reason why . . .' she paused, then she ploughed doggedly on, 'why Mum drinks.'

'So what happened?'

'I don't know in detail. Only the bare bones.'

'But your mother—'

'I don't talk to my mother about him. I don't want to upset her.'

'Avoiding the subject hasn't exactly solved the problem, has it?' At her glare, he raised his hands, palms up, saying, 'OK, OK. I'll shut up.'

But she found herself taking the photograph she had discovered at Ravenhart House out of her pocket and showing it to him. 'That's my father,' she said, pointing to the dark-haired figure. 'About a month before I was born, my mother went to stay with my aunt in London. My father was supposed to join her sometime later. He never turned up. Of course, it's obvious what happened, I worked it out long ago. My father had to marry my mother because she was pregnant. He never wanted to marry her and he never wanted to have a child. And eventually, I suppose, he just couldn't face it, so he ran off.' She looked up at him. 'So you could say that he left because of me.'

Patrick studied the photograph. 'Who are the others?'

'That's Frazer Ravenhart.' Morven pointed to the other man. 'He owned Ravenhart House before Mrs Jago – Mrs Jago's his mother. And that's Frazer's sister.'

'Do either of them have any theories?'

'I've no idea. Frazer disappeared too.'

'You're kidding.'

'It's true. Vanished into thin air.'

'At the same time?'

'No. Later. I'm not sure how much later – six months, maybe a year. It's one of those local scandals that was a great mystery donkey's years ago and people still mention it now and again. There's not that much to talk about round here, I suppose. It's funny, though, isn't it? Both of them just . . . disappearing.'

'Funny? Is that what you'd call it?' He looked thoughtful. 'Where was this taken?'

'I'm not sure. I have an idea, though. There's a tumble-down building a mile or so behind Ravenhart House. I think it might be there.' She put the photograph back in her pocket. 'I'd better head off,' she said. 'I need to get things ready for my mother coming home. Thanks for the coffee, Patrick.'

As she left the house, she asked, 'Which route did you take up Ben Liath?'

When he told her, she shook her head. 'I know an easier way. I'll show you sometime, if you like.'

'I might just take you up on that.'

She looked back once as she was walking down the track and saw that he was still standing in the doorway. She heard him call out to her, 'And people don't just disappear, Morven! They don't just vanish into thin air!'

Patrick's words stayed with her as she walked back to the gatehouse. It was a fine day, so, after leaving the shopping she had picked up in Pitlochry in the kitchen, she headed down the drive. Instead of turning off to Ravenhart House, however, she took the footpath that skirted the side of it, leading down through the glen. Her spirits rose, seeing the starring of spring flowers in the fields, and she breathed in the sharp, heady fresh air.

Eventually, looking ahead, she saw the small stone building captured between the two rivers. She took the photograph out of her pocket. She realized that her instinct had been correct, that it was the house in the photograph, the house in front of which her father and Frazer Ravenhart and Frazer's sister had once stood, smiling in the summer sun.

She crossed the large, flat rocks that bordered the burn, and stood at the water's edge. The burn was high after the recent rains; some way beneath the surface of the water, stepping stones shimmered. In the years since the photograph had been taken, the hunting lodge had been battered by time and neglect and the Scottish weather. The roof had caved in and the chimney stack had crumbled; fallen stones lay in the long grass.

The sun was sinking towards the horizon. Morven walked back along the path. As she passed Ravenhart House, she caught a flicker of movement out of the corner of her eye. Shading her eyes from the sun, she looked across the forecourt.

Someone was standing at the foot of the steps that led into the portico. There was a car, a Ford Zephyr, parked on the gravel. Its owner was tall and young, and his hair seemed as brightly gold as the rays of sunlight that pierced the barrier of fir trees.

Morven called out, 'Can I help you?' and he spun round.

'I don't know. Can you?' His voice had a colonial twang – Australian, she thought, or perhaps New Zealand.

As he walked towards her, she asked, 'Are you lost?'

'I don't think so.' His smile broadened.

She saw a tanned, startlingly handsome face and eyes of azure blue. Those eyes captured and held hers as he said, 'To tell the truth, I think I've just come home.'

'Home?' she echoed.

He said, 'My name's Adam Ravenhart. What's yours?'

Kate had invited Ursula to supper to celebrate her birthday. Rebecca had gone out with a friend, and Sam was at the cinema with his girlfriend, Jill. As Kate served the pudding, Ursula said, 'How heavenly, tarte tatin, my favourite. You're spoiling me, Kate.'

'I like to cook, you know that. And soon there won't be anyone to cook for.' The sentence, with its tinge of self-pity, escaped before she could stop it.

'You should find a man, Kate, I've told you before.' Ursula poured cream on her tart.

'How can you do that?'

Ursula looked up. 'What, darling?'

'Eat all that cream and stay so thin.'

Ursula smoothed her fine, grey wool dress over her slender hips. 'I haven't eaten a thing all day, just tea and a cocktail at six. That's what I do if I'm going out to dinner.'

Kate asked, 'How's Bernard?'

Ursula smiled. 'He thinks we'll be able to have a weekend soon. Nancy is going to stay with her mother.'

Ursula had for the past ten years been the mistress of a

wealthy married businessman. Kate sometimes found herself rather envious of Ursula's state. It seemed to her that Ursula's long-term, adulterous love affair had many of the advantages of marriage, without the disadvantages. Someone to dine with, without the day in, day out need for breakfast, lunch, supper. Someone to love, without the socks to wash.

Ursula said, 'We might go to the Lake District. Bernard could whizz up on Friday afternoon and I'll go the day before so that I can be waiting for him.'

'In your black negligée,' said Kate, rather tartly.

'Powder blue,' said Ursula, eyeing Kate. 'Classier, you see. Kate, what's wrong?'

Kate sighed. 'Nothing really.'

'Is it because of Sam? You'll miss him awfully when he goes to university, won't you?'

'Yes. I can't imagine it, actually, Sam not being around.' To her horror, Kate realized that she could have cried, so she added quickly, 'It's not for ages, though. And anyway, I have my friends.'

'And your sisters,' said Ursula meaningfully. 'How's Rebecca? You must tell me the latest instalment, darling.'

'She's still here,' said Kate exasperatedly. 'And she makes such a mess and she eats everything – she's worse than Sam. Mum did her best but Becky wouldn't listen – she never does – and Mum gave up eventually. She's gone back to Edinburgh now. Becky won't even tell us why she's so annoyed with Jared.'

'It's probably nothing much,' said Ursula. 'Men do these things, don't they? They say the wrong thing or they don't turn up when they say they will and half the time they don't even realize they've upset us. Bernard promised me he'd be free tonight, for my birthday, but in the end Nancy needed him for something and he couldn't make it. A few years ago I'd have made a scene, but now . . .' She shrugged.

'Don't you *mind*? Don't you mind sharing him?'

'Of course I do. I mind a great deal. But Nancy is his wife, so she has the greater claim. I've had to accept that. And besides, there's the *excitement*. Knowing that I *might* see him.' Ursula smiled fondly. 'Sometimes, when he has to work late, he drops in on the way home, just for half an hour. I never know whether he'll be able to come or not, so I'm always ready, always wearing something nice, just in case. And often he can't make it, but when he does, when the doorbell rings, well, goodness me, it's worth it, the waiting and the absences.' She glanced at Kate. 'You know what I mean. You must have felt like that with Hugh.'

'Oh yes.' And because it had been wartime, there had been that added particular sharpness of not knowing, much of the time, whether he would survive the day.

They had known each other for years, she and Ursula; had known they would be great friends from the first day they had met. Every now and then Ursula tried, with little success, to organize her. She did so now.

'Kate, you must find a man. There's no excuse now that Sam's leaving home.' Ursula put up a hand to stave off Kate's arguments. 'He doesn't have to be the great love of your life, I'm not suggesting that, just someone to go to dinner with and to carry your bags when you go shopping. And to feel excited about when you're waiting for him.'

'It's not so easy at my age,' began Kate feebly.

'Nonsense. You should buy a couple of new oufits and I'll book you in with Antoine to get your hair done properly. In fact,' Ursula took a small diary out of her bag, 'I'll make an appointment for you tomorrow, to thank you for cooking me this gorgeous dinner.'

'Ursula—'

'I insist. Now, Kate, there must be *someone*.' Ursula's eyes narrowed. 'Paul. How about Paul? He's been unattached for years.'

Paul Kendall was the brother of a mutual friend. 'Bristly moustache,' Kate reminded Ursula. 'And I believe he collects stamps.'

'Oh dear. We'll cross him off, then.' Ursula brightened. 'What about that lovely man, what was his name?'

'Who?'

'The antique shop.'

'Oh, *Oliver*,' said Kate, dismissively. 'No, Ursula.'

'Why not? Do you still see him?'

'Well, yes, quite often.'

'I'm sure he's madly in love with you.'

'Nonsense,' said Kate roundly. 'Oliver and I are just friends.'

'Kate, men don't hang around for years unless they're in love with you. If they spend time with a woman, then it's because they want to be with that woman.'

The telephone rang, sparing Kate from having to think of a response. She went into the hall. When she came back, Ursula looked up at her and said, 'Goodness, Kate, are you all right? That wasn't bad news, I hope. You look like you've seen a ghost.'

549

Kate felt rather shaky. She sat down. 'I think I have,' she said. 'Or at least my mother has.' She had to take a gulp of wine before she could explain to Ursula. 'Do you remember me telling you about my brother, Frazer, who disappeared?'

Ursula's eyes widened. 'He hasn't turned up, has he? How *romantic*.'

Kate said, 'Not Frazer. Someone who claims to be his son. Adam.'

It had been Naomi Gilchrist who phoned Bess to tell her about Adam Ravenhart. Bess had then calmly explained to Naomi that she was travelling north to Ravenhart that morning and would call at the gatehouse in the afternoon – she should be there by half past three, she estimated, providing the train was punctual.

Leaving the house, her calm persisted. Naomi drank too much; drunks, Bess knew, sometimes hallucinated. Or she herself had imagined the call, just as she sometimes imagined she heard Martin's voice, fancies born of longing and loneliness.

On the train north, she thought about Rebecca. She had been unable to persuade Rebecca to return to Jared. Bess had then suggested that Rebecca come back to Edinburgh with her, but Rebecca had refused. During her stay in London, Bess had been to see Jared, in the Ladbroke Grove flat. 'You have to stand up to her,' Bess had tried to point out to him. 'If something comes too easily to her then she doesn't think she wants it. You should let her stew in her own juice for a while. Make her think that you've forgotten her. Then she'll come running.'

Jared had looked horrified. 'I couldn't do that.' He had pressed his clenched fist against his heart in a dramatic gesture. 'I adore her, you see.'

Bess, stifling a groan of impatience, had said firmly, 'Jared, you must trust me in this,' and had kissed him goodbye and caught the train back to Edinburgh.

A taxi met her at Pitlochry station. Travelling through the hills, some of her serenity seemed to evaporate. Ravenhart had always had a capacity for the unexpected, had always been a place where dreams could take shape or be destroyed.

The taxi dropped her off at the gatehouse but carried her luggage on to Ravenhart House, where Phemie would be waiting. Morven Gilchrist let her into the gatehouse and offered her tea. Naomi was sitting on the sofa, smoking. She looked ill, Bess thought, and there was a large plaster on her forehead. She was enquiring after Naomi's health when there was the skirl of car wheels on the drive outside, followed by a knock on the door.

She made herself study Adam Ravenhart as they were introduced, searching for Frazer in him, matching up memory to the man who stood in front of her. He had Frazer's height and colouring and regular features, as well as his eagerness to please. His voice, with its strong Australian accent, filled the small room. It seemed to her that he also possessed something that Frazer had lacked, though she could not pinpoint what it was. She asked him questions and found out what she most needed to know. Then, after a short time, she rose from her seat. She couldn't think clearly, not with this ghost, this doppelgänger, and not with

Morven, so disconcertingly like her father, present. Not knowing all that she now knew. She felt nervous and desperately upset, and she couldn't let herself believe, not yet.

She refused Adam's offer of a lift to the house, telling him that she preferred to walk, inviting him to call on her the following morning. Yet the walk, after her long journey, tired her, and she was thankful to reach the house.

Phemie had lit the fire in the great hall. As Bess took off her coat and hat, Phemie hovered behind her. The words burst out, 'Is it true, Mrs Jago? Is it true that Mr Frazer's son's come to Ravenhart?'

'Perhaps,' she murmured. 'Perhaps.'

'And Mr Frazer?' Phemie was twisting her hands together.

'If what that boy tells us is true, Frazer is dead, I'm afraid, Phemie. He died of tuberculosis about a year ago.' There was a tremor in her voice as she spoke. The tears in Phemie's eyes matched the ones that ached in her own. She took Phemie's hands, stilling them, and said quietly, 'If Adam really is Frazer's then he married and had a child. A good life, Phemie, and we must be thankful for that.' A better life than I feared he might have, she added silently to herself.

Phemie nodded mutely, then shuffled off to the kitchen to fetch Bess's supper. But, sitting in front of the fire, the bowl of soup and the plate of sandwiches on a table drawn up beside her, Bess found that she could not eat at all, and watched the shake of her hand as she put down the spoon. She felt exhausted almost beyond endurance. She thought of Frazer, dying so far away from his home, so very far from his family, and her heart seemed to tear in two. She would phone Kate tonight, she thought. She needed to hear her daughter's voice. And talking to Kate might make it seem more real.

Adam called at the house at ten o'clock the next morning. Taking something from his pocket, he said diffidently, 'I don't know whether you remember this.' Looking down, Bess saw, nestling in his palm, a ring.

A gold signet ring bearing the insignia of the raven and the heart. Frazer's ring. She pressed her knuckles against her mouth.

He said softly, 'I'm sorry, I didn't mean to startle you. Are you all right? Can I get you something? A glass of water?'

She shook her head. The last of her doubts evaporated. In the great hall, with the sunlight pouring in diamonds through the mullioned windows, he might have been Frazer, tall and strong and handsome, returned from the void. An emotion that since Martin's death had grown rusty with disuse, stirred: joy.

She put up a hand to touch his face. Her fingertips drifted against his skin. Only touch quelled her fear that she might blink, and he would disappear, melting back into the wilderness.

'Adam,' she whispered. 'Oh, Adam, my dear. You don't know what this means to me.'

He possessed other tokens, other remnants of Frazer's life: Frazer's Patek Philippe gold watch, scratched and dented after all these years, and a photograph of Ravenhart House, creased after much folding, its corners dog-eared. Bess looked down at the photograph, remembering where she had first seen it, in Cora Ravenhart's Simla bungalow.

She asked Adam to tell her everything all over again. His life with Frazer, how they had wandered together through the vast red heart of Australia, moving from town to town, looking for work. It sounded a hand-to-mouth sort of existence, but then she, too, had once had to live on her wits, and she found herself surprised and relieved that Frazer had been able to adapt to such a different life.

'We were a team,' Adam told her. 'We never had much money, but you don't need money to be happy, do you? We turned our hands to anything – a couple of months at a farm in the shearing season, a week or two helping out in a garage or workshop. There's always work if you want it, if you're not too choosy and you don't mind getting your hands dirty. I'm not saying our bellies weren't empty sometimes. When times were hard, there wasn't always enough for the both of us to eat. But Dad never let me go hungry. He always made sure I had food in my mouth, even if it meant taking it out of his.' He looked up at her; she found herself caught in his unblinking blue gaze. 'Sometimes I feel bad about that. Sometimes I wonder if that, well, if that was what made him fall ill, him giving me his grub.'

'You mustn't think about that, Adam. It was what Frazer chose to do. Any father would have done the same.' She took his hand, which was hard and calloused, the hand of man who has had to work for his living. She said, 'And now that we've found each other, you won't ever have to go hungry again.'

His mother had died a few days after he had been born, he told her. She had been called Emily. A nice name. If he ever had a daughter he would call her Emily.

She said, 'Please would you tell me how Frazer died, Adam. If it's not too painful for you.'

He took a deep breath. 'Dad had a cough. A real bad cough – he'd had it for months. He wouldn't go and see anyone about it – said it was nothing. Then we were travelling and he was taken bad one night, coughing and coughing, coughing up blood. I fetched the doc and bought him medicine and stuff, but it was too late.'

He turned away from her, staring out through the high windows that looked out over the courtyard. 'I nursed him for three days. I held his hand while he died. Buried him in a nice little churchyard in the outback. Before he died, he said I should come here, to Scotland. He told me I had relatives here, that I had an inheritance.' When he looked round she saw that his face was wet with tears. 'Is that true? Have I an inheritance?'

'Frazer left me the estate when he went away.' She dug her fingernails into her palms to keep her own tears at bay. 'I've been thinking of selling it. I've no use for it any more, and none of my daughters care for it.'

'Sell it?' he repeated.

'I need to sort my affairs out, you see, Adam. At my age, you don't know how much longer you have left.'

'You mustn't talk like that, not when I've only just found you.'

'Adam, my dear, I'm almost sixty-seven,' she said gently. But there was something else she needed to know. It took all her courage to form the words. 'Adam, did your father ever tell you why he left Ravenhart?'

There was a pause before he answered her. She felt his

gaze resting on her, and her heart pounded painfully in her chest. Then he said, 'Not really. He had money worries, he said,' and a long, slow breath left her like a sigh.

She showed him the house, pointing out to him Frazer's favourite rooms. 'We would never have eaten in the kitchen, then,' she told him. 'The kitchen was for the servants. Frazer always dined here, in the dining room.' The long mahogany table was now covered with a dust sheet, but in her mind's eye she saw it as it had been almost a quarter of a century ago, with the candelabra and crystals glittering like stars. 'Frazer liked to do things properly,' she said. 'He believed in keeping up standards.'

In Frazer's study, she opened the desk and took out his Mont Blanc fountain pen. She watched Adam unscrew the cap and examine the gold nib. 'So strange,' he said, 'to think that *he* used it.' When he put down the pen, she placed it back in his hand.

'Keep it, Adam,' she said. 'It's yours now.'

He told her that he was staying at the Half Moon, adding, 'I won't hang on there for more than another couple of nights. My fare over here used up most of my funds.'

'What will you do?'

'Oh, I'll sleep in the car,' he said cheerfully. 'No worries. I'm used to roughing it. Or I might head off somewhere else, take a look round the country.'

She could not lose him so soon. 'You must come and stay here with me, Adam,' she said firmly. 'I'll have Phemie air Frazer's room for you.'

When he began to protest she cut him off. 'You're a Ravenhart, Adam,' she said. She enjoyed saying the words; she felt a swell of pride and delight in reminding Adam that he belonged to her family. 'Of course you must stay here. If you'd like to, that is.'

His smile widened. 'I can't think of anything I'd like better.'

She saw that his shirt collar was frayed at the tips, and his shoes, though well polished, were scuffed. She opened her handbag and took twenty pounds out of her purse. 'Here, take this, it'll help tide you over.'

'Aw, Grandmother.'

The title moved her so much she could not speak. She folded his fingers round the notes.

As he walked out into the courtyard, he turned and waved to her, and she marvelled that someone so young and beautiful and new should come into her life now, so late. Another grandson, when she had almost resigned herself to only ever having one. The return of hope, of optimism, of a future.

Over supper in an Italian restaurant in Dean Street, Kate told Oliver about Adam Ravenhart. 'I'm so worried,' she said. 'My mother doesn't seem to have questioned for a moment whether he is who he says he is. She's letting him live at the house, for heaven's sake. So there's just her and this *stranger*.' Oliver poured her another glass of red wine. 'Of course, I know *why*,' she added, with a sigh. 'She's lost so much, over the years, poor Mum. This *Adam*,' she said the name spitefully, 'must seem like a godsend, Frazer come back from the dead, miraculously young again. She seems completely taken in by him. I'm terrified she'll do something stupid. Or that he'll just break her heart all over again when she finds out that he's lying.'

'There's always the possibility,' suggested Oliver, 'that he may not be an impostor. That he could be your brother's son.'

'No.' Kate shook her head.

'Why not? How long ago did Frazer leave Scotland?'

'Twenty-three years. And this man claims to be twenty-one, almost twenty-two. I checked all that out.'

'So, theoretically, he could be your nephew.'

'He isn't. I'm sure of it.'

'How can you be, Kate?'

She said bluntly, 'Because Frazer would never have married. He would never have fathered a son. He wasn't interested in women, not at all. All the time I knew him I never once saw him kiss a girl or even look at a girl.'

'Did your mother know that?'

'No.' Kate sighed again. 'When my brother was living at Ravenhart, Mum always assumed he'd eventually marry and have a family. And even afterwards, when I realized that Frazer was incapable of that, I could never somehow bring myself to tell her the truth.' She looked up at Oliver. 'Mum was born in Queen Victoria's reign, for heaven's sake. It would never even have crossed her mind that her son might be homosexual, and she wouldn't have believed me if I'd told her.'

Oliver said slowly, 'Your brother could have changed, perhaps.'

Kate said thoughtfully, 'Some people are attracted to both sexes, I believe. I think perhaps Maxwell was a little like that. But not Frazer.'

'Maxwell?'

'Maxwell Gilchrist was a friend of Frazer's.' The waiter came to clear their plates away; after he had gone, she said, 'Max was my first love.'

'Ah. I always wondered whether there had been someone.'

'It was because of Max that I came to London.' She smiled. 'So I suppose it was because of Max that I met you, Oliver.'

He touched her hand. 'Then I'm very glad you met him.' He sat back in his chair. 'You look different tonight, Kate.'

Her fingers flew self-consciously to her hair, brushing against the unfamiliarly short, feathery waves. 'Ursula insisted I went to her hairdresser,' she explained. 'He pretends to be French but he's really from Bermondsey and he cut off *yards*.'

'It suits you. When I saw you this evening it made me remember the first time we had lunch together. You were wearing a green coat and your hair was all blown about by the wind.'

His eyes, which were that wonderful blackish-brown, the colour, she always thought, of treacle toffee and Marmite, met hers. There was an odd sort of electricity in the air. Too many unexpected events, she thought, they seemed to have peeled away a layer of her skin. Into her mind came the recollection of Ursula saying, *I'm sure he's madly in love with you*, and she felt suddenly confused. What if, by some extraordinary chance, Ursula was right? Both she and Oliver shared a diffidence, a lack of resilience where love was concerned. They had both lost people they loved early in life; had that made them cautious, wary of involvement?

The waiter returned with the pudding menu and she grabbed at it like a lifeline. Fumbling in her bag for her reading glasses, Kate heard herself gabble, 'Zabaglione, how marvellous. I never can be bothered to make it – too many leftover egg whites.'

Oliver said, 'If you think this chap might be a fake, what will you do?'

'Oh,' Kate said exasperatedly, taking off her glasses, 'I suppose I shall have to go to Scotland.'

The entire village was talking about Adam Ravenhart. He was the sole topic of conversation in the post office, the pub, and the general store. Morven caught the tail ends of the gossip, which faded in her presence, and the whispered names, Frazer's and her father's.

One morning, needing to talk to Mrs Jago about the gates, she walked to Ravenhart House.

Adam Ravenhart opened the door to her. He smiled. 'Hi there.'

'Is Mrs Jago in?'

He had driven Mrs Jago to Pitlochry that morning, he told her; he would collect her later. He asked Morven indoors, and she found herself standing inside the hall, where light poured from the high windows onto the tiled floor. With Adam Ravenhart's arrival, the house had come alive. Dust sheets had been removed from furniture, floors swept and mantelpieces polished.

He said, 'Lovely old place, isn't it? I've been exploring. Can I show you what I've found?'

'I don't want to trouble you.'

'No trouble. Come on, Morven. It'll take your breath away, I promise.'

She followed him up the stairs. 'You ever been to Australia?' he asked, as he went ahead of her.

'I'm afraid not. I've never travelled further than London. It must have been rather a shock for you, coming to Scotland – so different. And all those relatives you've never seen before.'

'I'm longing to meet them.' She saw how he paused at the top of the stairs, one hand balanced on the wooden head of the raven on the finial. 'All my aunts. I daresay they'll be rushing up here to see me.' He grinned, showing white teeth. 'You and me, Morven, we're two sides of the same penny, have you thought of that?'

'What do you mean?'

'I've come back here after years and years. And then there's you, waiting all this time for your father.'

I've come back. He spoke as if it was he who had gone away, she thought, and not Frazer Ravenhart. As though he was taking on Frazer Ravenhart's persona. She said calmly, 'I'm not waiting for my father. He's dead, I'm sure of it.'

A shutting out of light as they headed down a dark corridor. She heard him laugh out loud. 'Don't you just love this place, Morven?' he called back to her. 'Don't you just love it?'

The corridor twisted and turned; a narrow staircase led up to the next floor. The upper reaches of the house were bathed in gothic gloom. Phemie's broom had not yet reached these rooms and corridors, where spiders had slung grey, drifting webs around the cornices and a felting of dust dulled mantelpieces and window sills.

'Should have brought a torch,' muttered Adam. Candles stood in grimy sconces; he took one out and flicked his cigarette lighter. The flame illuminated hefty fireplaces and wide floorboards scattered with faded rugs and old, unfashionable furniture. Slices of light intruded between closed curtains, making pale stripes on the walls and floor. In a tarnished mirror, she glimpsed herself, and saw him come up close behind her, casting a shadow over her.

Another staircase, and she was in the attics among cobwebbed heaps of Edwardian clutter. 'Can't think why they kept all this rubbish.' Adam nudged a heap of old curtains with his toe. 'When this place is mine, I'll get rid of the lot.'

Then he opened a low door in the wainscotting and stooped and slipped through. *When this place is mine.* The words echoed against the bare wooden walls.

She followed him, and found herself in a part of the house she had never explored before, inside a dark, musty-smelling room. There were no windows and she could no longer see Adam. This room seemed colder than the rest of the house. She shivered. 'Where are you?' she whispered, and her voice seemed to die, flat and lost in the emptiness. There was no reply. She called out, 'Adam, don't fool around. Where are you?'

Then there was a grating noise, and a square of light opened up above her, Adam's laughing face contained in it, and she realized that she was in one of the uppermost attics, and that he must be standing on the roof.

A ladder led up to the trapdoor. Several of the treads had rotted through. He stretched down a hand and lifted her through. She found herself on a flat section of roof edged with a low balustrade. Above her, the sky was a cloudless, perfect blue. Mountains soared around them, green and grey and purple, streaked with silver where streams cascaded down the slopes.

He said, 'What do you think?'

'It's beautiful.' And it was. Her gaze followed the circle of the hills.

'My dad told me about this place,' he said. 'I've been searching for it for ages. Those attics are like a ruddy maze.'

A cool breeze rippled her hair and the sun cast inky shadows. He said, 'My dad and your dad, they used to come up here and drink champagne,' and she imagined them, the two young men in the photograph, passing a bottle of champagne between them.

Adam went to stand at the edge of the roof. 'That's what I'm going to do the day I inherit Ravenhart,' he said. 'I'm going to bring a bottle of champagne up here and drink the lot.' When he looked back at her, Morven saw that his eyes were wild with elation. He said, 'The old girl's leaving it all to me. That's why she's gone to Pitlochry this morning, to see her solicitor. She's changing her will. When she dies, all this will be mine.' He held out his hands to her. 'Come here.' When she did not move, he said, 'What's wrong? Are you afraid of heights?'

'Of course not.' She went to stand beside him. The

ground swung giddily as she peered over the edge of the balustrade.

He brushed aside a lock of hair that had blown across her face. 'You're like Ravenhart, aren't you, Morven?' he said softly. 'I thought that the first time I saw you. Beautiful and wild, just the same as this place.'

She found herself staring at him, seeing him clearly in the strong sunlight. Frazer Ravenhart's son must be almost two years younger than her. Yet there was a golden glitter of stubble across his jaw and his skin was deeply tanned and weatherbeaten.

His eyes narrowed to slits of sapphire blue. 'What is it?'

'You have lines. Little lines round your eyes.'

'It's the sun. In Australia, it can burn you to a crisp.'

And then, without warning, his arms were round her and his hands were sliding beneath the cotton of her blouse, and his mouth was hard against her own. She sensed the nearness of the precipice, only inches away, and was disoriented, unable to remember where the parapet was, afraid that if she pulled away from him she would find herself falling through the empty air.

'Adam – stop it –' The momentary dizziness passed; she pushed him away. 'I told you to stop,' she said sharply.

There was the sound of a car in the courtyard below; she saw him glance over the precipice. A quick exhalation of breath as his grasp slackened. There were small beads of sweat on his upper lip; he wiped the back of his hand across his mouth. 'The old girl must have got a taxi,' he muttered. 'Better go and meet her, hadn't I?'

* * *

Two days later Kate arrived at Pitlochry station. She hauled her bags off the train and onto the platform. She had taken too much luggage, she suspected, but one never knew what weather to expect at this time of year. Perhaps she should have driven, but then she would have had to find somewhere to stay overnight and this whole wretched expedition would have taken longer. Of course it had been she, Kate thought resentfully, who had had to rearrange half a dozen appointments to dash hundreds of miles. Eleanor was too far away and Aimée couldn't leave her donkeys, and as for Rebecca, well, one never expected anything useful of Rebecca. Even so, she needed to sort things out quickly because she couldn't afford to take more than a few days off work – many of the children who were her patients were emotionally fragile and needed to know that she could be depended on. It was how you built up trust.

And then she stopped suddenly, her broodings forgotten, as the train pulled away and she caught sight of the bridge. This was where she had first seen Maxwell, when he had leaned over the bridge and waved. She felt jarred, as if she had choked and someone had walloped her hard on the back, and it was a few moments before she was able to pick up her bags and walk on.

An hour later, at the house, what bothered Kate most was that this impostor, this cuckoo in the nest, was wearing Frazer's clothes. Tweed jackets and cashmere jerseys that she hadn't seen for decades, lovingly preserved by Phemie, presumably, in tissue paper and mothballs, now fitted perfectly across Adam Ravenhart's broad shoulders.

When she spoke to her mother about it, she said complacently, 'Yes, isn't it marvellous to find a use for them at last. They've been sitting in a cupboard for years, going to waste.' Her mother seemed elated; her entire aspect, which had, since Martin's death, been robbed of her usual exuberance, had brightened.

Over supper, Kate studied Adam. There was a resemblance to Frazer, she could not deny it, but to her it seemed no more than the superficialities of build and colouring. She asked him questions about his upbringing and background and he answered easily enough, and when he couldn't answer he said merely, 'Dad never talked about that,' which was, of course, impossible to dispute. Though his demeanour was friendly and relaxed, once or twice Kate caught him looking at her with a knowing look in his eye. He knows I don't believe him, she thought. Her mother, chattering happily, was oblivious to the currents that ran across the supper table, but then her mother looked at her children through rose-coloured spectacles, which was why, when they did not behave as she wanted them to, she was always taken by surprise.

Though Kate went to bed expecting her worries to keep her awake, she dropped off immediately. In the morning, waking in the turret bedroom that had always been her favourite, she stretched luxuriously and saw how the sunlight streamed through the gaps in the curtains. Motes of dust danced in the beams of light; she put up a hand as if to grasp them. Though she had intended to get up early, she lay in bed, dipping every now and then into a dream-filled sleep. When, eventually, she rose, she took a long bath; she could feel her skin breathing a sigh of pleasure as she soaked in Ravenhart's soft, peaty brown water.

She had intended to speak to her mother over breakfast, but Adam appeared, offering an outing to Balmoral, and her mother rushed off to fetch her coat. Tossing his car keys from one hand to another, he said, 'Won't you join us, Kate?' but she declined, saying that she had letters to write.

Yet, looking out of the window, she saw that it was such a glorious day that it would be wrong to stay indoors. After she had helped Phemie clear up, Kate went outside. Her feet seemed automatically to veer to the path that ran parallel to the burn, towards the hunting lodge. After a while, she broke off from the path, climbing up the mountainside, taking in deep lungfuls of air that seemed to taste of spring and sun. Overhead, the sky was the colour of bluebells and the peaks were pearled with the pockets of snow that still lay in the shadowed corries.

Her legs ached as the incline steepened; she was dreadfully out of shape, she scolded herself – once, she would have run along this path. Climbing higher, she caught sight of the hunting lodge, and she flopped onto the grass, her arms wrapped round her knees, staring at it.

A line from a poem had been rattling through her head since she had woken up that morning. *So we'll go no more a-roving, so late into the night.* What was the rest of the stanza? *Though the heart be still as loving, and the moon be still as bright.* Was her heart as loving as it had been when she was nineteen, when she had fallen for Maxwell Gilchrist? Or had she

567

hardened it, glazing it over with a layer of lacquer so that no one could touch her?

Bringing up Sam on her own, she had taught herself to be efficient and hardworking, because she had had to. Yet now she was coming to the end of it all. Looking back, she felt as though she had spent the past two decades running, without time to think or to take breath. She seemed to have been caught in the eye of a whirlwind, and now the whirlwind was dumping her down, and when she looked at herself she saw that her hair was greying and her hips were spreading and there was a worry line between her eyebrows. During the chinks in her life between work and Sam, she had tried to be a good neighbour, friend, daughter and sister. But how often, since Hugh had died, had she let anyone close to her?

She was no longer the girl who had fallen in love at first glance. She had learned to protect herself, to stand back, so that she could not be hurt. The price she had paid for her survival had been a measure of loneliness, and an ache, now, for the wild elation she had once felt here, at Ravenhart. A kiss, a smile, the touch of a hand, these were things that had changed her for ever.

Kate rose. There were things she must do. She must return to the house before Adam came back. And she must visit Naomi and Morven. That much she owed to Maxwell's memory. She would tell Morven what had taken her so many years to fully understand, that Max had trusted no one but himself, and that a lack of trust was a common legacy of an abusive childhood. That what Max and Frazer had had in common had been their difficult upbringings, Frazer's scarred by separation from his mother, Max's scarred by violence. That Max had learned to be different things to different people, that there had been no middle ground with him, and that he had inspired love and hate in equal measure.

And she would tell Morven that Max had been funny and affectionate and handsome and generous and kind, and that, had she known him, she would have loved him.

Looking down at herself, she saw that fragments of grass and petal clung to her. The warm sun beat on her head; she felt as though something was beginning to melt. She wished she had worn something different today, a brightly coloured shirt instead of a sensible crew-necked jumper; a ribbon to tie through her hair.

Kate went to Bess's room the night before she was due to return to London. Bess said, 'Such a shame you have to go back to London so soon, darling.'

'I wish I didn't.' Kate sat down on the bed. 'I don't like to think of you alone in the house with him.'

'Adam's my grandson,' Bess said patiently. 'He's a Ravenhart. Of course he must stay here.'

'What if he isn't, Mum?' Kate's eyes were troubled. 'What if it's all a story? What if he saw his opportunity and decided to take a chance?'

'He has Frazer's ring.' Bess took off her diamond earrings. 'And his watch and the photograph of the house. And he knows so much about Ravenhart. And about Frazer.'

'That doesn't necessarily mean anything.'

Bess put the earrings in their red velvet case. 'Why should he lie?'

'For the same reason that people often lie,' said Kate bluntly. 'For money.'

The jewellery case snapped shut. Bess turned to look at her daughter. 'You think I'm being foolish, don't you, Kate?'

'You *want* him to be Frazer's son, Mum. Don't you think that might have distorted your judgement?'

Bess said softly, 'And if it has? I have tried so hard not to think about Frazer. I've tried so hard not to dwell on what happened. Do you think I don't know how longing and love can warp, can bias? But you can't expect me to forget him. He was my son.'

'Mum.' Kate squeezed her mother's hand. 'Of course I don't think you should forget him. I loved Frazer too, remember. And if it was Sam—' She broke off. Then she said, 'I'm only asking you to be careful.'

'I know, darling. And I appreciate your concern.'

'I just don't see how you can possibly be certain that Adam is Frazer's son.'

'I learnt long ago that certainty is something of a luxury, an illusion even,' said Bess calmly.

'But then—'

'If you always waited until you were absolutely certain then you would never do anything.' Bess took the pins out of her hair. 'I married three times, Kate,' she said, turning to look at her daughter. 'I wasn't sure that I was making the right choice any of those times.' Kate started to speak but Bess interrupted. 'It's the truth. Jack was adorable, of course – any young woman would have fallen in love with

570

him. But I didn't know him when we married. As for your father, I should never have married him. Ralph's a good man — too good for me, perhaps — but we weren't suited and I realized that very quickly.'

'Martin,' said Kate. 'You were sure about Martin, weren't you, Mum?'

'Not when I married him.' Bess remembered Martin's proposal of marriage, on a rainy evening in Princes Street. 'I wasn't sure at all. To be honest, I was afraid that we were utterly unsuited. It was only after we'd been together for some time that I realized that he was the love of my life.' She stroked Kate's hair. 'But I don't regret anything. I had a wonderful two years with Jack. As for Ralph, he gave me Michael and he gave me you. You can't go through life never doing anything till you're absolutely certain, Kate. You'd have a very dull time if you did.'

In the morning, Kate finished her packing. Pairing up stockings, she glanced out of the window. Adam was walking through the gardens. He was surveying his domain, she thought, marking out his territory.

She put her camera into her handbag and went downstairs for breakfast. Adam had offered to drive her to Pitlochry. After breakfast, she took her case out to the car, and then she waited for her mother and Adam to come out of the house. 'Smile,' she called out, and they looked up, and she pressed the camera shutter. She saw the flicker of anger in Adam's eyes, and the pleasure in her mother's.

On the way to Pitlochry, he drove very fast, gunning the engine of the Zephyr as they headed into the tight bends.

They didn't speak at all, and she kept the camera safe in her bag, on her lap.

At Pitlochry station, unloading her case from the boot, he spoke at last. 'You don't like me, do you, Kate?'

She took the case from him. 'I neither like nor dislike you.' She made herself meet his eyes, and recognized the touch of mockery in them. 'But know this, Adam — I love my mother and I'll do whatever I can to protect her.' Hearing the train, she walked onto the platform.

The weather broke, drumming in steel-grey rods, turning the grass into a swamp, the paths into a muddy soup. In the village, Morven heard someone call out her name as she emerged from the shop.

Patrick Roper was on the far pavement. She crossed the road to him.

'Can I give you a lift?'

She accepted gratefully. He opened the door of the Land Rover. 'Be back in a couple of minutes,' he told her. She climbed inside, leaning out to squeeze water from the sleeves of her anorak into the gutter.

Patrick returned to the Land Rover with a loaf of bread and a newspaper which he flung into the back. He started up the engine. 'I was thinking of having another go at Ben Liath,' he said.

'Not today. It's too wet. In a few days' time, perhaps, when it's dried out. There's some patches of scree — they can be treacherous after a rainstorm.'

They drove out of the village. She liked watching him drive: the swell of his forearms with their glint of golden hairs, the practised expertise with which he steered the vehicle over the potholes and ruts. Careful, Morven, she warned herself. You know nothing about him. He might have a girlfriend, or even a wife and child. He might have all sorts of dreadful hobbies and habits, or he might be boring as hell.

Though she thought not. She said, 'When you told me the other day that people don't just vanish, what did you mean?'

He frowned. 'I do a lot of missing persons. And most of them turn up in a week or two. Some take a bit longer, but the vast majority do come back. They don't tend to simply disappear, like your father and Frazer Ravenhart.'

She put up a hand to wipe the condensation from the windscreen. 'Kate Willoughby − Frazer's sister, the girl in the photograph − came to see me a few days ago.'

In the lowest-lying part of the road, where the rain had gathered, the Land Rover's wheels sent up curls of water. She could see the interest in Patrick's eyes. She went on, 'Kate talked to me about my father. She knew him quite well.' She paused, remembering their conversation. 'She made me think of him differently. He's never seemed quite real to me before. But he sounded . . . well, good fun . . . warm-hearted . . . and he didn't have an easy time of it. I knew some of that already − my uncles told me how awful Grandfather was to him. But apart from Aunt Barbara, not many people have ever said anything *nice* about my father before.'

'Your mother?'

She frowned. 'Sometimes she loves him. But sometimes

she hates him because she's convinced he walked out on her.' She shrugged. 'And then at other times she's sure he had an accident – fell down a crevasse, or drowned in a loch, something like that.'

'Bodies tend to be found after accidents.' He glanced at her. 'Just a thought, that's all.'

'If he didn't run away and he didn't have an accident, what happened to him?'

He braked as they neared the gatehouse. 'As I said, the majority of missing persons turn up again. Of the ones who don't, most are suicides. Is it possible that your father killed himself?'

She looked out through the rain, to the broken gates and to the distant fringe of trees that hid Ravenhart House. She thought of Uncle Sandy, at the funeral. *There wasn't anything Maxwell wouldn't do.* But Kate Willoughby had said Max was a survivor. A bit of a chancer, perhaps, but a survivor.

'It's always been so hard to pin my father down. He seems to have inspired such extremes of emotion in people. Some of them loved him, and some of them hated him.' Kate, she thought, had fitted into the first category, Uncle Sandy, perhaps, into the second. 'But I've no reason to think he might have killed himself. No one has ever suggested anything like that.'

Patrick climbed out of the Land Rover and walked round to open the passenger door for her. 'I'll give you a hand in with your shopping.' He swung her rucksack onto his shoulder.

She said, 'If he didn't do a bunk and it wasn't an accident or suicide, what then?'

He paused, looking down at her. He looked troubled.
'Well, there's one other possibility.'

'What's that?'

'Murder,' he said.

Chapter Nineteen

The first time she noticed there was money missing from her purse, Bess thought she must have made a mistake. Perhaps this was what it was like to grow old, to lose track of the ordinary, day-to-day things, to become confused and then frightened by your confusion.

After it happened a second and a third time, however, she was sure. Decades ago, Ralph had taught her to be careful with money, to keep receipts and to make a note of the cash she withdrew from the bank. Concentrating hard, she studied the receipts, added and subtracted.

Someone was taking money from her purse. Only two people had the opportunity: Phemie and Adam. She trusted Phemie absolutely, so that left Adam. She wondered whether she should speak to him, whether she should reassure him that if he needed more money he had only to ask her. But something held her back, a sudden glimpse of her own vulnerability, perhaps. She had never before felt so conscious of her age, her increasing frailty. She wished that Kate were still here. She wished, with a great ache in her heart, that Martin, her lover and her protector, was still alive.

Did Adam steal from her because he was afraid of the poverty that had marked his earlier years, a poverty that she herself had once endured, and that always left a scar? Or did he steal because he despised her?

He had changed since he had first come to Ravenhart. He had a swagger, now, as he walked round the house and estate. He wore Frazer's clothes and wrote with Frazer's pen. He took drinks and cigarettes from the cabinet without asking her permission. His voice echoed in Ravenhart's panelled hallway, calling for Phemie to fetch his coat or to bring him food. There was a confident, greedy, hungry look in his eyes.

She found herself watching him. Who are you? she wondered. Are you Frazer's son? Or have I made a terrible mistake?

In London, Kate rescheduled her appointments and whisked through the house, cleaning up the worst of the mess and replacing the food that Sam and Rebecca had eaten. She wished there was a telephone at Ravenhart House; since there was not, she wrote each day to her mother.

Rebecca, who had been away when Kate returned to London, came back to the house one evening. In the kitchen, Kate brandished a bottle of wine. 'Drink, Becky?'

Rebecca shook her head. 'I'm starving, though. I'd love a sandwich.'

Kate peered into the fridge. 'There's some ham. And gherkins.'

'Oh yes, please. Lots of gherkins.'

Rebecca looked awful, Kate thought, pale and drained and slightly grubby-looking. Her thin wrists poked from her black jumper, her dark hair was clipped back in a rather messy ponytail, and she was picking at a hangnail.

'How's Mum?' she asked. 'What was that man like?'

'Mum's fine.' Kate cut bread. 'And Adam's loathsome, simply loathsome.'

'Does he look like Frazer?'

'I suppose so, in a way. But he's not like Frazer. It's hard to explain. It's like – Oliver once showed me a real sketch by Turner and a fake. I couldn't have said how they were different, but I could see that one was counterfeit.'

Rebecca was doodling on Kate's shopping list. 'I can't remember Frazer at all. Eleanor can, just.'

Kate sighed. 'I can see why you might be convinced by him if you wanted to be. Which Mum does, unfortunately. And I'm horribly afraid that she's given him money. She hasn't said, but I suspect she has.'

'Why didn't you ask her?'

'I couldn't. He was always around, and anyway, it would have been cruel.' Kate paused, knife in hand. 'Mum was happier than I've seen her since Martin died. I don't know what to do – I'm so worried.' She put the sandwich in front of her sister.

'Eleanor will think of something,' said Rebecca.

'Eleanor?'

'She's coming over.'

'From India?'

'Well, yes,' said Rebecca, through a mouthful of sandwich.

'Of course. Aimée sent her a telegram.' Catching Kate's surprised look, she added, rather heatedly, 'You're not the only one who's worried about Mum, you know. Aimée phoned while you were away. One of her boyfriends is going to look after the donkeys and she's driving up tomorrow. She can pick up Eleanor from London Airport. She's flying, lucky thing.'

Kate felt a rush of relief at the news that Eleanor, who was by far her most sensible sister, was coming home. She sat down beside Rebecca. 'I did do *something*,' she confided. 'A couple of things, actually. I searched his room.'

Rebecca's eyes widened. 'Adam's room? Kate, how *brave*. What if he'd seen you?'

'I was very careful. Actually, it was terrifying, I kept imagining footsteps in the corridor. But I thought there might be something to tell us who he really was.'

'His passport?'

'I couldn't find it. No driving licence or chequebook, either. But I did take a photograph of him, the day I left. I thought it might be useful. He hated me taking it.'

'Do you think we should tell the police?'

'Tell them what?' Kate's anxiety returned. 'He hasn't done anything. All he's done is to stay with Mum and eat her food. And I don't want to upset her. I don't want to make her feel stupid and humiliated.' Kate topped up her wine glass. 'Are you sure you won't . . . ?'

'No thanks. I don't feel like it at the moment.'

Something in Rebecca's tone made Kate looked at her closely. 'Becky?'

Rebecca bit her lip. 'I'm pregnant, actually. I went to see the doctor this afternoon.'

A pause to gather her thoughts, then Kate said, 'But that's wonderful, isn't it?'

'I suppose so. I haven't told the others yet.'

'Jared's pleased, isn't he?'

'I don't know. I haven't told him.' Rebecca's voice was small.

'Why on earth not?'

'I was afraid, when I first realized. I thought if I spoke about it then something dreadful might happen.'

'Oh, Becky.'

Rebecca was chewing at the hangnail once more. 'And then – we never talked about babies, you know.'

Kate found it hard to imagine Rebecca and Jared talking about anything sensible at all. 'But that doesn't mean,' she pointed out, 'that he doesn't want them. You want this baby, don't you?'

'Oh yes. So much. But what if it goes wrong again? I don't think I could bear it.' Rebecca looked frightened; Kate felt a pang of sympathy for her.

'You were just unlucky the last time. There's no reason why everything shouldn't be fine.' Kate patted Rebecca's hand. 'But you must speak to Jared.'

Rebecca picked at the remains of the sandwich, putting the gherkins in little heaps. 'I do love him, you know. I never really loved Stuart – I thought I did at the time, but then I realized I didn't. But I do love Jared.'

'But, then, Becky, why did you leave him?'

Rebecca stared at her, wide-eyed. 'You see, sometimes

I'm so horrible to him. I don't even know why, half the time. After Dad died, I was so miserable for ages, and when I'm miserable I tend to, well, I can be a bit mean.' She drew in her breath; Kate could see that she was trying not to cry. 'And then, when I thought I might be pregnant . . . I was trying to see whether he'd put up with me, so that I could tell whether he really loves me. And then it all got a bit out of hand. He didn't say the right things. You'd think a poet would say the right things, wouldn't you? And I said dreadful things, and then we had an awful quarrel and . . .' She was weeping openly now; she wiped her nose with the back of her hand. 'Lots of men tell me they're in love with me,' a sniff, 'but most of them only say it because they want to go to bed with me.' She looked up at Kate. 'Don't you find that?'

Well, no, thought Kate. 'You have to talk to Jared,' she said firmly.

'I can't.'

'Of course you can. Tell him what you feel, the same as you've told me. That's all you have to do.' She became brisk. 'And now eat up your sandwich, Becky. You're looking far too thin and you must keep up your strength.'

He seemed to have spread through the house like a mist, blurring her judgement. He had opened the most distant rooms in the house. Bess glimpsed him, sometimes, yanking dust sheets from furniture and flinging open curtains, going through cupboards and drawers. He left his mark on the rooms – a discarded coffee cup here, a jacket hanging over a chair back there, books pulled from the shelves and scattered over tables and window sills. In the mornings, he walked for miles through the estate, always taking the path that led through the glen to the hunting lodge. She felt his delight in taking ownership of Ravenhart, and saw how he preened himself, and how he liked to look out of the windows to the hills, an expression of concentration on his face.

There's no fool like an old fool. The saying came unbidden into her mind. Had Adam somehow come across those remnants of Frazer – the ring, the watch, the snapshot – and wondered what profit he might make of them? Arriving in Britain and discovering the estate was owned by a frail old lady, had he seen his opportunity? Had he laughed to himself, realizing he could use her gullibility, her credulousness, her blind, aching love for her long-lost son?

Often, she was able to brush the doubts away. Frazer had had his faults, after all; Frazer, too, had been arrogant and vain. So had Jack and Cora Ravenhart. Vanity and arrogance ran like a seam of fool's gold through the Ravenhart line, so why should Adam not share the same defects of character? Wandering through the Australian bush, what chance had he to learn the niceties of behaviour? You could make too much of the loss of a few pounds from a purse.

Dressing for dinner one evening, she discovered that her diamond earrings were missing. Her blue diamonds that Jack had bought her almost fifty years ago. Her heart pounded as she opened drawer after drawer, searching for the small red velvet box. She went downstairs to dinner, feeling old and unsteady and frightened. Though she kissed Adam in greeting, inside her something shivered.

Phemie had served the first course when Bess said, 'I can't seem to find my earrings, Adam.'

He looked up. 'Earrings?'

'My blue diamonds. They are rather valuable. I can't find them anywhere.'

'Are you sure?'

'I'm perfectly sure.'

He frowned. 'Phemie—'

'Phemie wouldn't have touched them. She's worked for the family for decades. I trust her completely.'

'Then I expect you've put them in the wrong place.'

She whispered, 'I don't think so.'

'Don't you? Perhaps you should think more carefully.' Reaching across the table, he put his hand over hers. His hand was large and strong and it seemed to swallow up her own. 'You've put them in the wrong place,' he said softly. 'Or you left them in your house in Edinburgh. You must be getting forgetful. Don't you think that's what's happened?'

She heard herself murmur, 'Yes, Adam, I'm sure you're right.'

Two o'clock on Friday afternoon was Kate's time for seeing Jacqueline. Jacqueline was thirteen years old, a deeply disturbed child whose profound unhappiness had been discovered when, at her day school, she had simply stopped speaking. Every now and then, Jacqueline managed to say a few words to Kate; today, however, she was silent, her eyes evading Kate's as she twisted the end of her plait round a finger.

After Jacqueline had left, Kate phoned Oliver.

'How was Scotland?' he asked.

'A bit hopeless, really.' Briefly, she told him about Adam.

When she had finished, there was a pause, and he said, 'I'm sure you did your best, Kate.'

'Oliver, is something wrong?'

'Margot died yesterday.'

'Oh, Oliver. I'm so sorry.'

'I've spent the day helping poor old Nigel with all the arrangements. Bloody depressing.'

'I'll come round,' she said. 'I'll be as quick as I can.'

She put the phone down, found the bottle of whisky she had bought in Scotland for Oliver, and stuffed it in her bag. Then she scribbled a note for Sam and Rebecca and left it on the kitchen table.

The 'Closed' sign was up on the shop door when she arrived. Kate went inside and hurried upstairs to the flat. Oliver opened the door; she kissed him and gave him the parcel.

'This might come in handy.'

He unwrapped the bottle of whisky. 'Thank you, Kate.' He poured two measures. 'To Margot,' he said, and they raised their glasses in a toast.

She asked gently, 'Was it awful?'

'Pretty awful. Though mercifully quick at the end, thank God. And Stephen managed to get there in time and she still knew him, so that was a blessing.'

'He'll miss her, won't he?'

'Enormously. I've sent him off to see Philippa. She'll cheer him up.' Philippa was Stephen's fiancée. Oliver looked down at his glass. 'Poor Margot, the one thing she really wanted, a child, she never had. Such rotten luck.'

'She and Stephen were close, though, weren't they?'

'Yes, of course. But it can't have been the same.'

'Margot had Nigel and her dogs and all her committees. I don't think she was unhappy.' Kate smiled. 'I always thought of Margot as like a stiff breeze. So honest and frank and not at all the sort of person you could ignore.'

'Good grief, certainly not. Margot was a brick. She'd do anything for you and the stiff upper lip rarely faltered. I rather suspect her kind are passing.'

Kate drank her whisky, remembering. 'I was terrified of her when I was younger.'

'Really?' He looked amused. 'Why?'

'She was quite a bit older than me and so much more sophisticated. And she always seemed so sure of herself.'

'She used to tell me how to bring up Stephen. It was because she loved him so much, of course.'

Kate remembered sitting in the back of Margot's car, Margot crashing the gears and passers-by hurrying along the pavements. She said, 'I never told you, did I, Oliver, that Margot once warned me off you.'

'Warned you off?' He looked startled.

'I think she thought I had designs on you.'

'Good Lord. I had no idea.'

'Mind you, I suspect she thought that any woman who spoke to you had designs on you.'

'Ironic, isn't it? I don't suppose they ever did. At least, not the women I cared about.'

'Goodness, Oliver,' she said lightly. 'You sound as if there were *dozens*.'

He shook his head. 'Only one, ever.'

A silence, filled by the rumble of the traffic outside. She should go home, Kate thought; Eleanor and Aimée would have reached London by now.

But instead she said, 'This one woman . . . did you ever tell her?'

'I tried to several times. But I could see she wasn't interested.' Oliver was fiddling with the top of the whisky bottle. 'And, since then, I've often thought that perhaps I've, um, missed my turn, as it were. You get out of practice at all that, don't you, when you have a child. You concentrate all your energies on protecting them, teaching them to survive. And then suddenly you look up and you see that they've grown up, and you – well, you're fifty and you've gone grey.' His gaze moved slowly over her. 'Not you, of course, Kate. You're just the same. As beautiful as the day I met you.'

All her sisters and Sam, she thought, and she hadn't even decided what to cook for tea. With a feeling of something like panic, she rose, and heard herself say, 'I'd better go – almost the entire family's staying with me tonight.' Then she grabbed her bag and kissed Oliver on the cheek.

Outside, as she headed for Ladbroke Grove tube station, her thoughts were scattered and disjointed, as though she was seeing fragments in a kaleidoscope: Oliver and her mother and Adam Ravenhart and Rebecca's baby, and her sisters. It was too much. Why couldn't things just stay the same?

You can't go through life never doing anything till you're absolutely certain, Kate, her mother had said. *You'd have a very dull time if you did.*

She remembered that, years ago, her father had once told her that Michael had been the dominant twin. That he had led while she had followed. That he had been reckless and she cautious, that they had been mirrored halves of the same whole.

She had reached the entrance to the tube station. She stared at the dark maw as it swallowed people up and shovelled them into the depths of the earth. Then she turned on her heel and ran all the way back to Portobello Road, weaving in and out of the rush-hour crowds, panting for breath as she hammered on the front door of Oliver's flat until he opened it.

Two hours later, travelling home, she got on the wrong train and found herself heading off to the City, and had to unpick herself, and wait, crushed on a platform with bowler-hatted businessmen, at Edgware Road for a Circle Line train. She looked down at herself, suddenly afraid of wrongly buttoned clothes and smeared lipstick. She and Oliver had gone to bed, and it had been glorious, pleasurable and exciting as well as somehow like coming home. When eventually she had looked at her watch, she had yelped and scrambled into her clothes, lingering only for him to kiss her one last time before she dashed out of the house. She might be pregnant, like Rebecca, she thought suddenly, as a train arrived and she pushed, with a dozen others, into a carriage. It wasn't likely, at her age, but it wasn't completely impossible. Well, if she was, then so be it, she thought; she and Oliver would have the most lovely baby, and she felt such an upswelling of joy at the events of the afternoon that she laughed out loud and the people standing near her moved fractionally away, looking uneasy.

When she left the train at Sloane Square, her heart seemed to have lightened; she could cope with anything, she thought: her mother, her sisters, even Adam Ravenhart.

As she let herself into her house, she heard raised voices. Eleanor's first. 'You can't possibly have the spare room to yourself, Rebecca. It's ridiculous. I've said that you can have the bed – I'm happy to sleep on the floor.'

Then Rebecca. 'You know I can't sleep if there's someone else in the room.'

Eleanor snorted. 'How on earth have you managed married life, then?'

'That's different, you know that's different.'

Aimée, seeing Kate in the doorway, said, '*Darling*,' and went to hug her. 'You look so well.' She turned to her sisters. 'Doesn't Kate look well?'

'Blooming.' Eleanor gave Kate a kiss.

'And you both look marvellous,' said Kate. Eleanor, who was tall and tanned and lean, was wearing cream-coloured trousers and a white shirt and her long brown hair was tied back with a turquoise chiffon scarf. Aimée was elegant in grey linen Capri pants and a pink short-sleeved silk top.

Rebecca said, rather tremulously, 'I was trying to explain that I've been in your spare room for weeks, Kate.'

'Oh, for heaven's sake, grow up, Rebecca,' said Eleanor crossly. 'You can't expect Aimée and me to squash up on Kate's sofa just because you want a room to yourself. You're always so selfish.'

'It doesn't matter,' said Aimée. 'Rebecca can stay in the

spare room and you can have the sofa, Eleanor. If that's all right with you, Kate.'

'Of course it is. But what about you?'

'Oh, I'll stay with a friend. We'll only be here for a night or two anyway. I think that Eleanor and I should drive up to Scotland as soon as possible. Don't you agree?'

Kate didn't reply because she was remembering Oliver telling her that he loved her, Oliver kissing her and then unbuttoning her blouse. They hadn't even managed to get *inside* the bed, they had been in such a rush; now, it seemed extraordinary to think they had waited so long.

'Kate?' said Aimée.

'Oh. Yes. Supper.' Kate opened the fridge and stared blankly inside it.

'Don't worry, we'll go out.' Aimée perched on the table, swinging her long legs. 'I know some lovely places.'

Kate struggled to gather her thoughts. She took an envelope out of a drawer and showed her sisters the photograph she had collected from the developers earlier that day.

'That's him,' she said. 'That's Adam Ravenhart.'

Aimée squinted. 'He's a handsome devil.'

'Poor Mum.'

'Do you think he looks like Frazer, Eleanor?'

Eleanor frowned. 'I'm not sure. If only we could find out who he really is.'

'He's Australian, isn't he?' Rebecca put the photograph in her handbag. 'I'll go to Earls Court. To Kangaroo Valley. *Someone* must know him.'

* * *

More and more often, Bess kept to her room, where she sat at her desk, trying to write letters, her pen frozen on the paper, a dark blot growing from its nib.

Once, from the upstairs gallery, she saw him taunting Phemie. 'I like your hat, Phemie,' he crowed. 'It suits you. D'you think it'd suit me?'

He had taken Phemie's bottle-green beret and was holding it high. Phemie jumped up and down on her fat little legs, arms outstretched, trying to reach it.

'Take it,' Adam said suddenly, throwing it to the far corner of the hall. 'I don't want it. It smells.'

Phemie grabbed her hat and then scurried out of the front door. Her footsteps faded as she ran across the gravel forecourt.

At night, it was Adam's footsteps that Bess heard, pacing along the corridors. In the darkness, listening, she thought she would phone her daughters from the gatehouse the next day and ask them to come to her. But each morning, by the time dawn seeped through her bedroom window, she had changed her mind. Her girls had their own lives, their own problems, and she should not trouble them with hers. And besides, if there was danger here – and she sensed that there was – she did not want them in this house. Ravenhart had its malign history, after all, and she valued her own life less than theirs.

Perhaps she would leave Ravenhart. Pack her bags and head back to Edinburgh, to the house where she still felt Martin's presence, the house she had always loved. Forget Ravenhart, which had brought her so much unhappiness. What did it matter? It would solve a problem, wouldn't it, to let this man, who might or might not be Frazer's son, have the house.

There was the rub. She had to know. If he was Frazer's son, then she must love him whatever his failings, for Frazer's sake. And if he was not, then there were questions she must have answers to. If Adam was an impostor, then how had Frazer's possessions come into his hands? Had he known Frazer? Had they been friends, companions, the older man and this beautiful young boy? Had Frazer given Adam the ring, the photograph and the watch? Or had Adam stolen them from him, as he had stolen her earrings? And, if so, what had happened to Frazer? Might he still be alive?

What did Adam want, why had he come here? He had come for Ravenhart, of course, for the dream of power and wealth that went with the house and land. That dream had seduced Frazer, and it had, for a while, bewitched Maxwell Gilchrist. Even Kate had fallen under the spell of the house. Only she, Bess, had never desired it.

The thought came to her in the small hours of the night that she could use Adam's lust for Ravenhart to discover the truth. A test: which did he long for, the house, or the family of which he claimed to be a part? In the darkness, the moonlight cast its cold metallic gleam on her room, and she watched and waited.

The weather improved, and Naomi mended. The cut on her forehead had faded to a pinkish bruise, and she moved more easily as her broken ribs healed.

Raymond had invited Naomi to lunch at the Half Moon,

and Morven decided that she would find out whether Patrick would like to climb Ben Liath that day. She walked to the Carterhaugh cottage, but Patrick was out, so she scribbled a note on a scrap of paper, suggesting that he call at the gatehouse the following morning, and pushed it through his letterbox.

By the time she returned to the gatehouse, the postman had called, and there was a large envelope waiting on the table in the hall. It was from Barbara Gilchrist. Barbara's accompanying letter said, *I found this among your grandfather's things. It seemed wrong to throw it away without letting you see it, Morven, and I thought it best not to send it directly to Naomi in case it upset her. I leave it to you to decide what to do with it.*

Barbara had sent a copy of a report, about twenty pages in length, written by a private detective by the name of Bellamy. Mr Bellamy had been hired by Andrew Gilchrist to investigate the disappearance of his son, Maxwell. The report was dated January 1938. Morven flicked through the pages. Then a sentence caught her eye.

When making my enquiries I was careful, as instructed, not to refer to the bad feeling between my client and Mrs Jago.

Morven stared at it, blinked then stared again. She read the sentence twice, just to make sure. Then her mother called out to her and she stuffed the envelope into the cutlery drawer, and was unable to look at it again until late in the evening.

Yet it haunted her throughout the day. Two families, Frazer's and her own, the Ravenharts and the Gilchrists. Her father and Frazer Ravenhart had been great friends. Up until today, she had believed that to be the only connection between them. Yet Mr Bellamy's report implied that her grandfather, Andrew Gilchrist, and Frazer's mother, Bess Jago, had known each other long before Frazer and Maxwell met. And that they had disliked each other.

Patrick had said, *There's one other possibility: murder.*

Who had hated her father enough to kill him? Ronald Bain, perhaps. Ronald Bain, Mr Bellamy had pointed out, had had a motive, his resentment at having lost the gate-house. Bain had owned a shotgun, and, as factor of the Ravenhart estate, he would have known the land intimately, known all the sink holes and bogs and patches of earth where you would be able to dig deep enough to hide anything you might not want to be found.

Who else? The Gilchrist family, of course. Uncle Sandy had been jealous of his younger brother. And Niall had no great liking for him. Maxwell had had scars on his back from where his father had beaten him, Kate Willoughby had told her. Maxwell had been afraid of his father, had had his nature shaped by his father. Morven thought of her grandfather's lack of human warmth, and his coldness to his sons, who had always tried to please him, and the streak of cruelty that Andrew Gilchrist had barely troubled to hide.

And then there was Frazer. Mr Bellamy's questioning of Frazer Ravenhart occupied several pages of the report. Frazer, who had been her father's friend. Frazer, who had given Maxwell and Naomi Mr Bain's home. Frazer, who had also disappeared, only months after Mr Bellamy had interviewed him.

* * *

593

Eleanor and Aimée left the house early that morning to drive to Scotland. Kate was working, so Rebecca decided to head for Earls Court. In the tube, Rebecca spent a few enjoyable moments picturing Eleanor's look of admiration if she, Rebecca, managed to discover Adam Ravenhart's true identity. Eleanor, who always considered herself the brainiest Jago sister, would be forced to admit how clever she, Rebecca, was.

Reaching Earls Court, she went first to the Overseas Visitors Club hostel. She had once had an Australian boyfriend called Jim, who had had wild red hair and had been at least a foot taller than her. He had pointed out the club to her, explaining that it was where recent arrivals from the Commonwealth stayed when they first came to Britain. Inside the club, Rebecca showed the photograph Kate had taken of Adam Ravenhart to the staff and residents. No one recognized him, so she left the hostel and continued along Earls Court Road.

It was midday, and the pubs had opened. In dark, gloomy bars, she was assailed by foreign accents. Australians wearing brightly coloured shirts offered her drinks and cigarettes. Tall South Africans and Rhodesians showed her snapshots of their fathers' farms. Rebecca found herself wondering whether she should have married a farmer. She imagined herself in khaki shorts and a white shirt, riding across the whatever-it-was-called. *Veldt*, that was it.

But she had always hated horses, had loathed the afternoons she had been forced to spend as a child in freezing cold fields, watching Eleanor ride her pony. So typical of Eleanor to have pleased Mum by loving riding and Dad by being good at science. Rebecca hadn't been much good at anything at school apart from art. But she had had to do *something*. So when Stuart had come into her life it had been, as much as anything, an enormous relief. She had enjoyed being engaged to Stuart, had enjoyed her friends' envy of her sapphire engagement ring. And she had adored her wedding day, when everyone had admired her in her glorious dress.

It had been later that things had begun to go wrong, when she had discovered that Stuart was – there was no other word for it – *boring*. Though she had tried to keep herself busy, dashing between Cannes and London and Edinburgh, an emptiness had seemed to open out around her. And then there had been the baby. Rebecca tried not to think of the pain and messiness of losing her baby, and how miserable and useless she had felt afterwards. And after that, there had been her various lovers, though she hadn't, looking back, enjoyed them all that much.

A green sports car hurtled down the road. Red roses smothered the railings and Rebecca breathed in their scent. On the day that she and Jared had moved into the Ladbroke Grove flat, Jared had brought her red roses, dozens and dozens of them, so that the rooms had been perfumed with them and fallen petals had dotted the lino like rubies. He had stolen them from front gardens, Rebecca guessed; she had imagined her lithe, dark Jared leaping over walls and darting around bushes, gathering blooms in his long, thin hands.

A girl in a tobacconist peered at the photograph, and said, 'No. Never seen him before. Sorry, love.' Rebecca began to feel tired and hungry and rather fed up. Perhaps Adam Ravenhart had never come to London. Perhaps hoping to find someone who recognized him in all the millions of people in London had been a silly idea. Perhaps Adam really was Frazer's son – though Kate didn't think so, and Rebecca had always respected Kate's opinion.

Crossing Kensington High Street, Rebecca found herself in Melbury Road. In a small cafe squeezed between a barber's and a secretarial agency, she ordered sausage, egg, chips and beans. Apart from the mornings, when she felt dreadful, she seemed to be permanently ravenous. As the espresso machine hissed, she showed the snapshot to the waitress, more out of habit than because of any vestige of hope. The girl glanced at it briefly before turning away.

Rebecca sat down at a corner table. She hadn't seen Jared for weeks. He hadn't called, hadn't phoned. Recently, she had begun to feel frightened. Perhaps he had forgotten her. Perhaps he didn't care about her.

Yet the previous evening she had met a friend who had told her that Jared was now working for a publisher in Golden Square. It had crossed her mind that he was doing it for her. One of her complaints had been the awfulness of their basement flat, which was so damp that snails slithered into the kitchen. Jared hadn't seemed to notice, which Rebecca had found infuriating – how could even Jared fail to notice a snail? Although it had been lovely being married to a poet, and she had adored being a beatnik at first, she was beginning to feel tired of scratchy black pullovers and not being able to afford ever to go to a decent restaurant.

And babies, Rebecca feared, cost a lot of money. You couldn't live on love and air when you had a baby.

She knew that Kate was right and that she must tell Jared about the baby. It was just that she was afraid to. Would he still love her, pale and nauseated in the mornings? Would he love her in six months' time, when she was fat and tired? It was the thought of losing his love that frightened her, the utter desert of a life without love.

Oh, grow up, Rebecca: Eleanor's voice echoed in her ears. If Jared had compromised his principles and got a job, then she must, in turn, find the courage to talk to him. She would go and see him that evening, she resolved. She would apologize for being so moody, and she would tell him about the baby.

The waitress brought over her lunch. The sausages gleamed enticingly; Rebecca felt her stomach rumble.

Then the girl said, 'That photo, can I take another look at it?'

Rebecca handed it to her. The waitress frowned. 'I'm not sure. He didn't look so smart then. But I *think* it's him.'

Phemie didn't come to the house that morning. In the kitchen, cutting bread, nervous because Adam was standing a few paces away from her, Bess's hand slipped.

A bead of blood blotted the loaf; she put her finger to her mouth.

'Clumsy,' said Adam.

She went upstairs to find a plaster. In the early hours of the morning, she had packed her bags. After she left this house today she knew that she would never come back.

597

She walked out of the bedroom. Standing on the raised gallery overlooking the hall, she watched him. He was silhouetted in the doorway; the sunlight streaming through the open door made a halo of his fair hair. She felt an ache of regret.

She said clearly, 'You're not Frazer's son, are you?' and he spun round, looking up to her.

'I know you're not,' she said. 'Frazer was always kind, you see. And so was Jack. But you are not.'

He came into the hall, his hands in his pockets. His swagger had gone; he looked wary. He gave a little laugh. 'Feeling a bit crook this morning. Must have eaten something. Makes me bad-tempered. Why don't we go out for a walk, you and I, Grandmother, and start the day again?'

'Don't call me that.' She shook her head. 'Now, when I look at you, I can't think how I was ever taken in.'

His laugh was uneasy. 'Frazer wasn't so bloody perfect, you know.'

'True, he wasn't. I had to learn that. But he was capable of love, and I suspect that you are not.'

His clenched fist struck his open palm. 'You shouldn't say things like that. You should think a bit before you say things like that.'

His long shadow darkened the tiles on the hall floor. She said, 'I don't believe you are Frazer's son, Adam. But you knew him, didn't you?'

A measuring pause, and then something in him seemed to relax, and he smiled and said, 'Oh, I knew him all right.'

'You were . . . friends?'

'*He* thought we were friends.'

'Where?' she whispered. 'When?'

'Eight months or so ago. In some hellhole in the Northern Territories.'

'And he told you about Ravenhart?'

'He liked to shoot his mouth off, did Frazer. Specially after a drink or two. He was partial to a drink or two – or nine or ten, if he had the money. Partial to a pretty face as well. I didn't believe him at first, I thought he was just another old soak telling tall tales. But I had nothing better to do, so I hung around. They called him the Duke, the other blokes in the pub. Because of all his nonsense about castles.'

He was climbing the stairs as he spoke; she remained where she was, on the gallery, her hand resting on the banister. She said, 'Tell me how he was.'

'Oh, like any old alkie who's had too much booze and too long in the sun.' He leaned against the finial at the top of the stairs, his eyes on her. 'He was boring, boring as hell, if you must know. Droning on about how he owned a great chunk of Scotland. As I said, I thought he was lying till he showed me the ring and the photo.'

Her mouth was dry; she licked her lips. 'So you stole them from him?'

He shook his head. 'Not then. I needed to know a bit more, didn't I? What good would a poxy old ring do me? It'd get me a few dollars at most. No, I wanted more than that. And I knew the old fool would give me whatever I asked for so long as I was nice to him.'

She was cold inside. She whispered, 'What did you do?'

'He liked to lord it over me, make out he was better

than me. Told me he'd had such a fine time, doing this and that, travelling all over the place – he went round Africa and the Far East, he said, before he ended up in Australia. And he boasted – God, he boasted – about the jobs he'd had, the places he'd lived, and the people he'd known. He said there wasn't anything he hadn't done, wasn't a country he hadn't seen.' Adam laughed again, though his eyes remained the opaque blue of the thickest ice. 'He thought I admired him, he actually thought I *admired* him. I played up to it, of course. But he got on my nerves. All that talk. And the coughing. Cough, cough, cough, all bloody night. So I squeezed everything I could out of the stupid old bastard till he was telling me the same old stories over and over again and I couldn't stand it any more.'

She had to suppress a shudder. She said again, 'What did you do to him?'

'I killed him.'

She closed her eyes tightly, shutting out the light pouring through the window, and the smile on his face. She heard him say, mockingly, 'Oh, don't look like that. I hardly had to touch the poor old sod. Just put my hand over his face while he slept. He had so many holes in his lungs the air wouldn't stay inside. You can think of it as an act of mercy if you like.'

Frazer, she thought, *my poor Frazer*. When she could speak again, she said, 'I want you to go. I'm going to collect my things, and by the time I come back you will have left this house. I shall change my will, of course. You will not have my son's house. You will not take his place.'

She walked away from him.

* * *

When making my enquiries I was careful, as instructed, not to refer to the bad feeling between my client and Mrs Jago. The sentence nagged at Morven, keeping her awake at night. Andrew Gilchrist had forbidden Mr Bellamy to interview Mrs Jago. Why? What did it mean? What possible connection could there have been between her grandfather and Mrs Jago?

The next day was warm, the warmest so far that summer. The sky was a blank wash of blue; by mid-morning the heat was gathering in the small rooms of the gatehouse. Morven packed her jacket and a thermos into her rucksack and told her mother that she was going to Ravenhart House. If Patrick turned up at the gatehouse before she came back, she explained to Naomi, he should head down the drive and meet her halfway. 'Have a lovely time with Raymond,' Morven said, kissing her mother before she left the house.

In her room, Bess put on her coat. Her fingers fumbled with the buttons; catching sight of her reflection in the mirror, she glimpsed the horror in her eyes. She was shaking; she sat down on the bed. Frazer was gone, this time for ever. He had died, far from his home and his family, at the hand of a man who had exploited and despised him.

She had to drag her suitcase down the corridor; she no longer had the strength to lift it. Turning a corner, she saw that Adam was standing where she had left him, at the top of the stairs. She cried out, 'I told you to leave!'

'So you did.' His expression had altered, the wariness gone, the preening swagger returned. 'The thing is, we haven't finished talking.'

'I have nothing more to say to you, Adam.' She gave him a contemptuous glance. 'If Adam's your name.'

'Oh, it is. Adam Ravenhart. I like that.'

'No,' she said coldly. 'Never.'

He moved a few steps towards her; she found herself shrinking back. She would have to abandon the suitcase, she thought; she would ask Phemie to send it on to her.

'Maybe you want to think more carefully, Mrs Jago.' His voice was low and menacing. 'Frazer and me, we were together quite a while. He told me *everything*, and I mean *everything*.'

She froze, standing on the gallery. A new fear, one she had not previously considered. But she made herself say, 'I asked you to leave, Adam. You should be thankful that I'm giving you the opportunity. If you don't go, then I shall send for the police.'

'Oh, I shouldn't do that.'

Frazer, she thought sadly, oh, Frazer. How much of yourself did you give to this beautiful, evil creature? It took all her courage to walk on, to pass him. When the hem of her coat brushed against him, she flinched.

She heard him say, 'Frazer told me what a wonderful mother you were, Mrs Jago. How you'd do anything for him. Anything at all.'

She was standing a few feet away from him, at the top of the stairs. Now she was certain. The secret delight in his voice told her everything.

But she said calmly, 'What do you want, Adam?'

'You know what I want. You won't go to the police, because if you do I'll tell them what you and your precious

Frazer did. And you won't change your will, either. You'll leave Ravenhart to me, just like you said you would.'

'I meant what I said. Never.'

Because what, after all, had she left to lose? She turned to face him. 'You won't have the house, Adam. I don't care who finds out about Maxwell Gilchrist now. The two people I wanted to protect have gone. My husband is dead. And I have lost Frazer, too. So you may share my secrets with whomever you wish. I almost wish you would. In a way, it would be a relief.'

She put a foot on the stairs. Briefly, she looked back at him. 'As for me, I did what I did for Frazer. I did it because I loved him. But I don't expect you'd understand that.'

She started down the stairs. A second's silence, and then she heard him move. A footstep, a hand on the small of her back, a sudden pressure, and, in the split second before she fell, the knowledge of utter defeat. This monster would have Ravenhart. Frazer's killer would have Ravenhart.

A last, desperate grab for the banister, but she failed to reach it. Then she was falling, falling. Just before the darkness became complete, she thought she heard them, the monkeys at Hanuman's shrine, running, endlessly running, through the pines and the deodars.

Adam Ravenhart's Ford Zephyr was parked in the courtyard and the front door of the house was open when Morven arrived at Ravenhart House. From the doorway, she called out Mrs Jago's and Phemie's names.

When there was no reply she took a step into the hall. She saw the dark shape at the foot of the stairs. She thought at first that someone had dropped a coat on the tiles, but then, looking again, she ran forward.

'Leave her,' a voice said.

'Adam.' She whirled round.

He grabbed her arm. 'I said, leave her.'

'Is she dead?'

There was blood on Mrs Jago's face; his foot nudged the cloth of her coat. He said, 'You can't do anything for her anyway.'

'Oh God,' she whispered.

His eyes, as he looked at her, were intent. 'She was going to take the house from me. I couldn't let her do that. You have to see that.'

Her gaze rose to the long sweep of stairs.

'Let me go. Let me get help.'

'No.' A quick shake of the head.

He was mad, she thought, quite mad. 'Adam, please let me go. We have to call an ambulance for Mrs Jago.'

His eyes flicked to the body on the floor. He muttered, 'I didn't mean this to happen. It wasn't supposed to happen.'

'I believe you, Adam. If you let me go, we can sort it out.' Her voice coaxed, cajoled.

'She doesn't matter.' He frowned, then tugged her arm, pulling her towards the door. 'There's something I want to show you.'

'Adam, please.'

'You have to come with me.'

He steered her out of the door, into the courtyard. His hand gripped her arm like a vice.

'Where are we going?'

'To the hunting lodge,' he said.

The hunting lodge. She remembered the photograph of her father, Frazer Ravenhart and Kate.

And she remembered Patrick. Patrick would come to Ravenhart House as soon as he discovered that she was not at the gatehouse. Get Adam out of the way, and Patrick would be able to fetch help for Mrs Jago.

'All right,' she said. 'The hunting lodge.'

They were heading along the path by the burn, and Adam was walking behind her, when he said, 'I know what happened to your father.'

Sweat on her brow and on the back of her neck and a jarring to the pit of her stomach. 'I don't believe you.'

'It's true. I'll tell you.'

'Liar,' she hissed. 'Everything you say is a lie. Your name, your age, everything you claim Frazer Ravenhart told you – it's all a lie.'

The heel of his hand struck her hard between the shoulder blades and she stumbled. 'Don't call me a liar. I hate it when people say that. Frazer killed your father. Frazer killed him, and his mother helped him hide the body.'

The sun hurt her eyes; her back felt bruised where he had struck her. She said stubbornly, 'I don't believe you.'

'You should, you know, because he told me. It's the gospel truth. I'll prove it to you, if you like.'

They reached the place where the stepping stones crossed the burn to the hunting lodge. 'Not there,' he said. 'I've changed my mind.' He grabbed her arm again, hauling her along a path that snaked indistinctly up the hillside.

Fragments of quartz, captured in the rock, glittered like diamonds. The boulders were tumbled together, as if a giant had cast them down the mountainside. Where the path narrowed, it was clogged with brambles, ferns and nettles. He took a knife from his pocket; she saw the sun glint on the blade. Then he pushed ahead of her, hacking at the undergrowth.

They headed into a copse of silver birch and rowan where branches arched overhead, temporarily shutting out the sun. Ferns drooped from crevices in the rocks, and the sound of rushing water became louder and louder, until it seemed to fill the air.

Beads of sweat formed on her forehead. They climbed higher, towards the sound of the water. *I know what happened to your father. Frazer killed him.* There was a dark V of sweat on the back of Adam's shirt, and a smile on his face as, every now and then, he looked over his shoulder at her. Once, pausing for breath, she asked, 'Who are you?' and he shook his head.

'It doesn't matter. I'm Adam Ravenhart now.'

Her heart pounded; she was afraid it would choke her. At last, ahead, she saw a narrow aperture between two boulders. A flash of sunlight, caught between the stones, and she squeezed her eyes shut, the shape of the two great sentinel stones imprinted on her vision. Another shove, and she was stumbling through the gap between the boulders, and ahead of her was a wide, circular pool, bordered with rocks that had been smoothed to globes and ovals by the running water. A waterfall plunged from the rock cliff high overhead, scooping out the great stone basin, and spreading ripples through the pool. At one end of the pool, the rock forced the water into a narrow channel, so that it descended in a series of cascades and pools down the hillside to the glen below.

When she walked to the edge of the pool and looked down, she saw how the shapes hidden inside it shifted and blurred, far below the surface, in the blackish-gold depths. She knelt down, splashing water over her face and arms.

From behind her, she heard him say, 'It was here, somewhere. I've been trying to find the exact place.'

She stood up. In spite of the heat, she was shivering. 'Tell me what happened.'

'They had a fight by the pool. Maxwell hit his head when he fell in the water.'

Spray from the waterfall dripped in grey circles on the stones. 'So it was an accident?'

'*He* said so.' Adam was pacing across the stones. He frowned. 'But why hide the body if it was an accident?'

She pressed her wet hands against her face. In her mind's eye she saw them, the men in the photograph, golden-haired Frazer and dark Maxwell. Rays of sunlight glittered on the water, and her head ached – the long climb, her sleepless night.

'Why? Why did they fight?'

'I dunno.' A turn of the head; he smiled at her. 'I've been trying to find him, Morven. I wanted to do that for you.'

Her stomach coiled; she felt sick. 'Find him?'

He crouched on his haunches beside the pool, and dipped an arm in. 'I never knew my father. Always wished I had. Thought it was like a piece of me was missing, a piece other people had. Always thought I'd been dealt a rough hand. I was brought up in an orphanage. I ran away when I was twelve – I couldn't stand it.'

The force of the water had dug deep beneath an over-hanging rock; reaching under it, Adam scooped out stones and gravel. 'I did this and that. Worked on cattle stations, travelled about. You don't need much money if you know how to look after yourself. But I always wanted something better – a nice place, money in my pocket. People looking at me as if I was something.' He looked up at her. 'Frazer buried him beneath an overhang. That's what he told me. Silly old fool – he boasted about it at first. Then he got all blubbering and weepy. I hated his snivelling and moaning.'

She whispered, 'Frazer buried my father here?'

He looked round the rock amphitheatre. Then he smacked his wet hands together. 'Not a bad place to end up, is it? Frazer put him in the bottom of a pool, he said, weighted down with stones. I told you, I've been trying to find him.'

A wave of nausea; she had to sit down on a stone. He was shovelling debris from the water. She watched, with sickened fascination, as he hurled out stones the size of tea plates, which gleamed in the sunlight, and pieces of detritus, dragged down the mountainside by rainwater.

Then he kicked off his shoes and slid into the pool, ducking beneath the overhang. A twist and a squirm, and he slid underwater, hidden by the sandstone roof. 'It's cold,' she heard him call out to her when he came up for air. 'And bloody deep.' Pushing a hank of wet hair out of his face, he dived again.

A tin can, branches and clumps of vegetation now lay

wet and shining on the rock. She should run, now, while she had the chance. Yet she seemed rooted to the ground, as though she was part of the stone on which she sat, watching, hypnotized, as he bobbed beneath the surface of the water. What horrors would the pool give up? A skull, with empty, eyeless sockets? A bone, polished white by time?

A bird swooped low over the water. Adam dived again, and she shut her eyes tightly. Her father had sat here, perhaps. Her father had dived into that pool, his body slicing cleanly through the surface of the water. Did his ghost linger here, in this place? Did a spark of him survive, loving and protective, watching over his only child?

There was a splash as Adam re-emerged. When he shook his head, droplets of water sprayed onto the stones. 'Nothing,' he said.

She stood up. She thought of the knife, the ease with which he could hurt her. But she said, 'I'm going back to the house.'

'You don't owe her anything,' he shouted. 'You can say it was an accident. If you back me up, no one'll ever know the difference.'

You don't owe her anything. And he was right, of course, she owed Mrs Jago nothing. All those years her mother had waited for a man who would never come home. All those years that she, Morven, had lived with the belief that her father had chosen not to know her. Yet it hadn't been like that at all. He hadn't run away; it had not been *he* who had committed the act of betrayal.

Adam was climbing out of the pool. 'You know I'm

right, Morven.' Water dripped from his clothes and his bare soles made dark footprints on the stone, and he was smiling. 'I'll make you a deal. You keep quiet about the old girl and you can share the house with me.'

'Share it?'

'You'd like that, wouldn't you? You love Ravenhart, I know you do – I saw it in your eyes. Marry me, and you can have it.'

A croak of laughter escaped from her throat; she saw the flicker of rage cross his features.

'Don't laugh at me, Morven. I hate it when people laugh at me.' He gripped her arms again and she swayed on the stones; the edge of the largest pool was only a few feet away.

But she said softly, 'Do you think that I would choose to live a lie? Do you think that Ravenhart is worth that to me, to live with a man I could never love, and a house that shouldn't be mine? I would hate you both, Adam, you and Ravenhart.' Her gaze drifted to the black, glittering water. 'And hatred wears you away, haven't you learned that? There would be no more left of me than there is of my father.'

And then the distant chime of a bell reverberated against the rocks, over and over again. In the fringe of trees up the mountainside, crows circled, black rags against the blue sky, startled by the sound.

Adam's hands slackened. 'That noise . . .'

'It's the Ravenhart bell,' she whispered. 'Patrick's found Mrs Jago.'

His eyes were glazed. 'Patrick?'

'He'll look for me, Adam. He knew I was going to

Ravenhart. He'll come and find me. And I'll tell him *everything*.'

His gaze flicked to the pool, and she felt a shiver of fear. But she said calmly, 'It won't work, Adam. All those sudden deaths, all those disappearances. No one would believe it. Patrick certainly wouldn't. He'd nose around, he'd ask questions. He wouldn't let it go till he found out who you really were.'

A silence, then his arms fell to his sides. He gave a sudden wide, charming smile. 'Clever girl, aren't you, Morven?' His eyes rose to the rock cliff above them, and he said slowly, 'You could be right. Maybe I should cut my losses.'

The bell still boomed, echoing round the glen. She said softly, 'If I were you, Adam, I'd make a run for it. That's your best chance. Run away. You've done it before, haven't you? Go on, run away now, before they come for you.'

She was holding her breath. As he turned away from her, she let it out slowly. He was making for the fallen rocks to one side of the pool. As he reached them, he looked back and smiled wryly, and said, 'Shame. It was fun while it lasted. Me, lord of the glen. I liked that. Still, I'll find something else. People believe what they want to believe, don't they? Which is fine by me.'

Then, in one quick, darting movement, he scrambled up the rocks and, reaching the cliff edge, was swallowed up by the darkness beneath the fir trees.

Chapter Twenty

There was a comfort in being incarcerated in hospital, your care handed over to kind, efficient strangers, no decisions to make, nothing to do but eat and sleep and submit to being poked and prodded. She had a broken collarbone and ankle, and was bruised from head to toe, bruises that faded from red to purple to green as the days went on. Her head ached badly, and for the first few days they wouldn't let her sit up. Drifting on painkillers, she slept most of the time. And she dreamed, and she remembered.

She was in Simla, dancing at the Viceroy's ball. She was in a London hotel, dining with Dempster Harris. She was in Edinburgh, walking down Princes Street, and the snow was whirling amber-yellow round the gas lamps.

And she was at Callanish, with Martin, and the sun was sinking behind the standing stones as he kissed her. Now, in her dreams, she could see the sea pinks and the marram grass, and she could hear the murmur of the sea. There was the taste of salt in the air, and the warm sun on her head. And Martin's arms were round her, and she could feel the beat of his heart and the warmth of his skin, and she felt her own heart lift and fly, freed from all grief and sorrow.

Eleanor and Aimée were her first visitors. It had been Eleanor, Bess suspected, who had insisted she have the privacy of her own room, instead of a public ward. Eleanor had an iron will.

Eleanor told her what had happened. How Patrick Roper, looking for Morven, had gone to the house and found her, Bess, lying unconscious at the bottom of the stairs. And how he had rung Ravenhart's great bell to summon help.

'Raymond – you remember, Mum, the publican at the Half Moon – was on his way anyway,' said Eleanor. 'Rebecca had found out who Adam Ravenhart really was, so Kate phoned Naomi to ask her to warn you. And Naomi phoned Raymond and they drove to the house.' Eleanor gave her mother a swift, professional glance. 'Just as well, you had a nasty knock on the head. It's a good thing you were found so quickly.'

She said, 'I feel so foolish.'

Aimée squeezed her hand. 'You shouldn't do. He was a practised conman. And a thief.'

'He stole my diamonds.'

'He could have taken a great deal more from you, Mum. You were lucky.'

Her mouth was dry; she took a sip of water. 'Who was he?'

'His name was Adam Collins. At least, that's the name

he was using in London. He was working in a cafe in Melbury Road for a while – he spun them some hard-luck story about being robbed on the voyage to England and they let him sleep in a room behind the cafe. Until he made off with the contents of the till and various other valuables, that is. Of course his car was stolen too.'

Bess shivered. 'Have they caught him?'

Eleanor shook her head. 'Not yet. He disappeared, took off over the hills.'

She imagined Adam running away, running until he found another bolt-hole, another fool to be taken in by his charm, his good looks. Soon, he would have taken on another life, soon he would have become another person.

Eleanor added, 'Morven was the last person to see him.'

'Morven?'

Eleanor looked puzzled. 'Adam made her go with him to a place in the glen, a place with a pool and a waterfall. Do you know it, Mum?'

She murmured, 'Yes, I know it.'

Before her daughters left, she said, 'I have to speak to Naomi Gilchrist. Would you ask her to come and see me, please, Eleanor?'

Bess said, 'I want to tell you what happened. I want to tell you about the day that Maxwell died.'

Naomi was wearing a pink jacket and a black linen skirt. She was leaning against the sill, smoking, tapping her ash out of the open window, her face pale, wary.

'I had arranged to visit Frazer that day,' said Bess. 'When he didn't turn up to meet me in Pitlochry, I was surprised

– he was usually so punctilious about that sort of thing. So I took a taxi to Ravenhart. When I arrived at the house, Phemie told me that he had gone to the hunting lodge. It was a fine day, so I decided to walk there. When I reached the lodge, I saw that Frazer was sitting on the front step. I called out to him, but he didn't reply. I got closer to him and I saw that his clothes were soaking wet. I suppose that's when I began to feel uneasy. He was shivering, and his shoes were unlaced. I asked him whether he'd fallen into the river. And he told me – he told me that he had killed Maxwell.'

She recalled every word of their exchange. You did not forget those moments when your life turned on a pivot, never to be the same again. *I've killed him*, he said, and she tried to comfort him. *Don't be silly, Frazer – what on earth are you talking about?* As though she were speaking to a naughty child. And then he said again, in that same monotone, with that same dullness of eye, *I've killed Maxwell*, and she had found herself glancing into the lodge and then to the grass-land that surrounded it, searching for Maxwell Gilchrist.

'I thought at first that he was ill. I thought he had a fever. I tried to persuade him to come back to the house. Then he told me what had happened, and I began to believe him. That he and Maxwell had had a fight, and that Maxwell had slipped and hit his head and fallen into the pool.'

Speaking of it for the first time, she still felt the same sick sensation that had almost overcome her that day, the same dreadful anticipation of all the events that must grow from this one, rolling out before them, the fog and the darkness falling once more across her life.

'Frazer took me up to the pool. Maxwell was lying on the stones. Even then, I hoped he might be mistaken. That Maxwell might be unconscious, not dead. I think Frazer shared the same hope. He had put his coat over Maxwell, he said, to keep him warm. He had tried to make him drink some whisky. But when he removed the coat and I saw him, I knew there was no hope.'

Black curls adhering to white skin, and a smear of blood pasting the rock. In a flash of memory she had seen the hills above Simla and had heard the sound of horses' hooves and laughter, and her own voice crying out, *No, Jack!* And she had seen herself stumbling down the hillside to where her husband lay among the ferns and saplings, his head at an unnatural angle.

'His neck was broken, you see. I'm sorry, Naomi. I'm so sorry.'

The rasp of a match as Naomi lit another cigarette. 'Why?' Her voice trembled. 'Why did they fight?'

'Maxwell had told Frazer that he was leaving Ravenhart. Frazer tried to persuade him not to go, but Maxwell wouldn't change his mind. Then Maxwell said something – I don't know what – and Frazer lost his temper and hit him.'

Naomi's back was to her, and she was staring out of the window. A moment's silence, then she said, 'Max could be cutting. He had a way with words. He knew how to hurt, if he chose to.' She turned round. Her great, dark eyes glittered with tears. 'But it was an accident?'

'Yes. Maxwell slipped on the wet stones beside the pool. He lost his balance and fell into the water. When he didn't come up, Frazer thought at first that he was trying to frighten him. Then he dived into the pool. Maxwell was in the deepest part, at the bottom. Frazer dragged him out and tried to revive him, but . . . I suppose he must have hit his head on a stone.' She looked up to Naomi. 'Maxwell's death was an accident, a terrible accident. Frazer never meant to kill him. I suspect that he spent the rest of his life regretting it.'

Naomi's face was anguished. 'But if it was an accident, why hide it? Why not go to the police? At least then I'd have known!'

'I tried to persuade him. But he begged me not to.' Bess remembered putting her arms round Frazer and stroking his wet hair. She remembered the weight of Frazer's head on her shoulder, the warmth of his face against hers. No stiffness, no resistance. A month, a week, a day before, to hold her son like that would have given her such joy.

She said, 'He was afraid, you see. His factor, Mr Bain, had heard him threaten Maxwell only a few days before. Frazer knew that Bain hated him and he was afraid that Bain's evidence would go against him in a court of law. So he made me promise not to tell anyone. Then he hid Maxwell's body in a pool beneath an overhang, and he buried it under stones.'

The worst memory: Frazer carrying Maxwell's body to the pool. The dead weight of him, in Frazer's arms, the nightmarish loll of his head, and the agony on Frazer's face as he tipped his friend's body into the water.

'But how could you?' Naomi's voice was a taut, agonized,

whisper. 'To leave me like that, not knowing, never knowing what had happened to him?'

'Yes.' The word was a sigh. She, more than most, had known the void to which they had condemned Naomi Gilchrist: the waiting, the endless waiting, for someone who would never return.

She made herself meet Naomi's eyes. 'How well did you know your father-in-law?'

'Andrew?' Naomi blinked. 'Well enough.'

'Did you like him?'

'Not at all. He was a horrible man. But I don't understand. I don't understand what Andrew has to do with this.'

There was another event that she recalled with perfect clarity. How some memories seemed to imprint themselves permanently on the retina, as clearly delineated as images on film.

'After the Great War, I left my second husband, Kate's father, and went to live in Edinburgh. It was hard, on my own, but I managed, and it was better than an unhappy marriage. I worked in a nightclub to earn some extra money. I met Andrew Gilchrist at the nightclub. He wanted me to become his mistress, but I refused. He didn't like that. So he took what he wanted by force.'

The cigarette, halfway to Naomi's lips, stilled. 'You mean he raped you?'

'Yes. In my house. Kate was asleep in the next room.'

Playing cards scattered on the floor and the rip of fabric as he tore at her clothes. Her mouth tasted sour.

A longer silence, and then Naomi said, 'I used to hate visiting Andrew. I was his daughter-in-law, and yet he looked

618

at me as though he wanted to undress me. What did you do?'

'Nothing. What could I do? I told Martin, only Martin. I knew that no one else would believe me. And I felt ashamed.' She pressed her lips together; then she whispered, 'Why do we torment ourselves, wondering whether we were to blame? Why do we think that if we hadn't worn that dress or said those words or smiled that smile . . .'

She had to take a moment or two to compose herself. 'Many years afterwards, Frazer met Maxwell. I don't know how they met, or where. I didn't realize they knew each other till quite a long time later. Frazer and I weren't close – we had been separated for most of his childhood. He was brought up by his grandmother, in India. When he was twenty-one, his grandmother died and we were reunited. When I found out that Maxwell Gilchrist was a friend of his, I was horrified. I tried to separate them, but he wouldn't listen to me. And I couldn't tell him why, of course – that would have been impossible. And then, that day, when Maxwell died . . . Andrew Gilchrist knew that I hated him. Would he have accepted that his son's death had been an accident? I didn't think so. He would have wanted revenge. He was a vengeful man, incapable of forgiveness. I had already learned that to my cost, and he would have persecuted Frazer, or worse. I am still convinced of that. So I agreed to do as Frazer asked me. I agreed, because I believed it was the only way to save my son's life.'

Naomi left the window sill and went to where she had left her handbag on a chair. She took out a handkerchief and dabbed her face. 'When Max didn't turn up,' she said slowly, 'I wasn't worried at first. I thought it was just typical Max. He was always a poor timekeeper. You never knew whether or not he'd appear. On my wedding day, I was biting my nails, because I wasn't sure whether he'd make it. But then, after a couple of weeks had gone by, I became afraid – afraid that he'd met someone. He wasn't a faithful man, you see. But when I eventually went back to the gate-house, it was as though he'd just stepped out for a moment. Coffee cups in the sink, paper in his typewriter. I asked around, but no one had seen him. Then I went to the police. They asked me all sorts of questions. Did Max have many friends – I knew they meant female friends. Was our marriage happy, did Max have any money troubles? I'm afraid I lost my temper with them. They promised to make enquiries, but I could see they weren't interested. So I spoke to Andrew. I couldn't think what else to do, and I knew he'd do something. Max was his possession, you see, like that ghastly house, and he'd never have let one of his possessions slip out of his grasp. Never. Never.'

After Naomi had gone, Bess lay back on the pillows and closed her eyes. She remembered her train journey back to Edinburgh, the day after Maxwell Gilchrist's death. She had stared out of the window and had seen not hills and towns, but the pool and the waterfall and the burn, with its deep, dark overhangs. She had thought of what they had done, she and Frazer, and of what would stem from it. Andrew Gilchrist would wait for his son, as she had once waited for hers. He would suffer as she had suffered. Yet Andrew Gilchrist's wait would never end.

But there had been no triumph in taking her vengeance at last, only an intense weariness, mixed with fear and disillusion. She had seen clearly that the Frazer she had treasured during their years of separation was not the actual Frazer. Though he might resemble Jack physically, Frazer lacked Jack's courage and fire. Where Jack had been a leader, Frazer preferred to follow; where Jack had been forthright, Frazer was evasive and self-deceiving, his temper unpredictable. Frazer would not have been susceptible to Maxwell Gilchrist's bad influence had he not had weaknesses of his own.

Maxwell Gilchrist had looked forlorn and pitiable lying on the stones. She hadn't been able to hate him any more, and had instead felt only a sharp regret that someone so young should lose his life in such a fashion.

She knew where the blame truly lay. Cora Ravenhart had kept Frazer close to her side, limiting his contact with the outside world. She had spoiled him, as she had once spoiled Jack. An over-indulged only grandson, the pampered boy-child, Frazer had never been thwarted and had not acquired the strength to fight his own battles. Cora had left him fatally defenceless, his initiative sapped, and with an inflated sense of his own worth.

Yet, back then, sitting in the carriage, she had also acknowledged that she, surely, bore the greatest responsibility. She had mourned the person Frazer might have been – should have been – had events turned out differently, had Jack lived, had she not been so foolish as to trust Cora Ravenhart. Over and over again she had relived the events of the day at the pool, clawing at her choices, tearing them apart.

She had thought of Naomi Gilchrist. In Naomi's impulsive greed for life she had seen an echo of her own younger self. Because of what she and Frazer had done, a child would be born without a father, and a wife would long for her husband to return, never knowing whether he was alive or dead. Just then, she had longed to turn the clock back. Her thoughts had raced – perhaps it was not too late to go to the police, perhaps a way might be found to placate Andrew Gilchrist . . .

A moment's reflection and she had known that the die was cast. Concealment implied guilt; delaying telling the authorities had in itself incriminated Frazer. The choice she had made was fixed, inviolable and could not be reversed.

Frazer had begged her not to tell anyone what had happened, he had implored her not to tell Martin. Returning to her home that evening, she had wondered what shadow she had brought with her to the house which had for ten years been her haven, her sanctuary. How could she put a smile on her face and pretend that nothing had happened? How could she adopt a facade tomorrow and the next day and the day after that, and for all the endless days that must follow?

Yet she had done so. She had known a moment's longing – could she confide in Martin? Could she share her fear and regret with the one person she trusted absolutely, the one person she knew would never let her down?

Yet sharing a secret meant handing on a burden. No matter how much she might long to share this burden, she must not. She had always known that Martin possessed an innate goodness that she herself, perhaps, lacked. She could not ask Martin, who was sworn to preserve life, to help her conceal a death.

So she had kept her secret, and had kept it well. Many, she knew, would question whether you could love and keep such a secret. Yet she had loved intensely, the more so, perhaps, for knowing the fragility of love, the ease with which it might be taken away from her. Would he have forgiven her, had he known? That was not, she thought, the point. In protecting Frazer, she had been forced to choose between conscience and love. She could not have asked Martin to make the same choice: it would have broken him.

Naomi said to Raymond, 'I suppose I ought to hate her.'

They were in Raymond's sitting room at the Half Moon. There was coffee and biscuits on the table, and, in the distance, the hum of conversation from the bar.

He said, 'But you don't?' and she frowned.

'Funny, isn't it, the one time I'd be perfectly justified in screaming and making a scene, yet I don't seem to want to.' She dunked a biscuit in her coffee. 'Max and Frazer – you just knew that it was the sort of thing that would end in tears. Max took from Frazer and in the end I suppose he didn't want to give anything back. And that must have hurt Frazer terribly. Frazer would have done anything for Max, you see, Ray, anything at all, and it must have been dreadful to have that thrown back in his face.' She gave a small, sad smile. 'I felt like killing him sometimes. I always knew he didn't love me as much as I loved him. It's hard to live with that.'

He said, 'Yes,' and she looked up at him.

'I've been thinking a lot since I spoke to Mrs Jago. I've been a fool, haven't I? Pining for the past, making out Max and I had a perfect love when half the time we fought like cat and dog. And the worst of it is that I've been a bad mother to Morven.'

'Nonsense, Naomi. That's rubbish.'

'It's true, I know it is. I've made it more difficult for her. Bad enough that she never had a father without her having to act as nursemaid to me.'

He said, 'But it hasn't always been bad, has it, you and Morven?'

'Of course not.' She smiled, remembering. 'When she was little, we had such fun.'

She delved into her handbag for a tissue. A comb, a chiffon scarf and a powder compact spilled onto her lap. Raymond handed her his handkerchief and put his arm round her as she blew her nose. Then she said, 'I think Mrs Jago's expecting me to go to the police. The poor old thing – how awful to have that hanging over you all these years.'

'Will you? Will you go to the police?'

Naomi sighed. 'I meant to, straight after she told me. But then I thought – what would be the point? I believed her when she told me it was an accident, you see. Frazer loved Max. I don't believe he would have intended to hurt him.' She had screwed the handkerchief into a damp ball. She looked up at Ray. 'Do you think it would be very wrong to leave him there, at the pool? Just – don't do anything, let things be? I talked to Morven about it. She says that it's up to me. Max wasn't religious, and really, what would there be left of him by now? And he used to love the pool. I remember us having such happy times there. And I'd hate to think of them trampling all over it, spoiling it, digging and searching for him.' A last sniff; she pressed her lips together. 'I think that I'd rather imagine him up there, in such a beautiful, peaceful place, where he was young and happy. Better than a heap of bones in some church he never cared for.'

'I think Morven's right.' He kissed her. 'It's up to you.'

'I thought I could take some flowers to the pool.'

'Good idea. I'll come with you, if you like.'

'Darling Ray.' She squeezed his hand. 'I can't think why you put up with me.'

'Oh,' he said seriously, 'because you're beautiful and you're fun and you make me laugh. And because I've loved you for years.'

She smiled, and pressed his hand against her face. Then he said, 'What will you do now?'

'Leave the gatehouse, I think. I need a new start.'

'Where will you go?'

'I don't know. I haven't thought.'

'What about here?'

'Ray—'

'I've worked it all out. You can manage the restaurant. Front of house – you can welcome our guests when they come in, make them feel relaxed. You'd be good at it.'

'But, Ray,' she said, and shot a glance in the direction of the bar. 'Such a sweet idea, but, you know . . . so close. My problem . . .'

'We'll beat it,' he said firmly. 'You and I, together. Two

heads are always better than one, and I know what it's like more than most. And both of us know that if you're determined to have a drink then you'll cross a hundred miles of desert to get it. So what difference will it make to have the bar next door?'

She whispered, 'But what if I fail, what if I *slip*?'

'Then we'll try again. No fuss, no recriminations, I promise.'

She looked down at her hands. 'The thing is, I always end up hating myself when I don't drink. I feel so dull.' She gave a little laugh. 'I even bore myself.'

'Well, you don't bore me,' said Raymond firmly. He took her hands in his. 'I'm not saying it'll be easy. But I know you'll give it your best shot. You've never lacked courage, Naomi. That's something I've always admired about you.'

'Dear Ray.' Her voice trembled; she stroked his face. 'Manage your restaurant – I don't know . . .'

'And marry me, of course.' In spite of his bulk, he had gone down on one knee in front of her.

There was the impulse to laugh or to cry, but instead she said, 'Yes, Ray. If you like.'

Had he known? Had Martin guessed some of what had happened? Had her refusal to search for Frazer after the war told him that she had known the reason for her son's departure, at least?

She would never know for certain. But he had vowed to love her whatever happened, whatever she did, and she treasured that memory. As for Frazer, how had he filled the years between Maxwell Gilchrist's death and his own? In the months that had followed his disappearance, she had been afraid that, unable to live with what he had done, he had killed himself. The gift that Adam had unwittingly given her was that of knowing that he had not, that he had survived for almost a quarter of a century. Adam had also told her that Frazer had travelled, had seen the world. *He'd had such a fine time, doing this and that, travelling all over the place. He said there wasn't anything he hadn't done, wasn't a country he hadn't seen.* She treasured that, too, the thought that Frazer had taken pleasure in his wanderings, and that he had found, perhaps, some peace of mind and happiness.

Slowly, she was learning to forgive herself. How young she had been, she thought – only a year older than Kate's Sam – when Cora Ravenhart had tricked her into leaving India without her son. So young, so powerless, so unable to protect what she had loved most in the world.

Eleanor came to see her again. She sat down beside the bed. 'Loads of family news, Mum. Rebecca's back with Jared and she's expecting a baby. And Kate's getting married, to that man with the antique shop. Oliver something.' Then she said hesitantly, 'I'm afraid you'll have to wait for rather a long time to hear that sort of news from me, Mum. I don't think marriage and babies will ever be for me.'

'It doesn't matter, darling.' She took Eleanor's hand. 'I'm delighted for Kate and Rebecca, of course I am, but I'm so proud of you as well. And so would your father have been.'

Eleanor smiled. 'When you're better, Mum, you must come and visit me in India.'

She ached everywhere; walking to the bathroom exhausted her. 'I couldn't possibly, Eleanor.'

'Why not? You've always wanted to go back to India, haven't you, Mum?'

'Yes, but darling—'

'Then come. You can fly. It doesn't take long.'

'Darling, I'm getting far too old.'

'Then you shouldn't keep putting it off,' said Eleanor firmly. 'I want you to come to India. I want you to see what I do.'

Bess stroked her daughter's face. 'Dear Eleanor. I can't possibly come to India, I'm afraid. It's out of the question.'

Morven and Patrick were climbing Ben Liath. When Morven looked down, the streams were threads of silver, sewn through the green velvet slopes.

They paused to get their breath. The wind tugged at their clothes. She asked, 'Did you read the report?'

'Our friend Mr Bellamy? Yes.'

'He was always suspicious of Frazer, wasn't he?'

'He was right in that. Of course, Andrew Gilchrist forbidding him to interview Mrs Jago must have hindered his investigation. Gilchrist fobbed him off with some story about them having had a disagreement, years before. Obviously, he didn't want Bellamy to know about the rape.'

Morven remembered her conversation with her uncles at Andrew Gilchrist's funeral. 'Bellamy would have been looking into Maxwell's disappearance at much the same time as Simon Voyle, Grandfather's assistant, had begun to spread rumours about him. Perhaps he had begun to get worried that his past was catching up with him, and that all these skeletons in his closet might have an effect on his social standing.' She shaded her eyes, looking down into the valley. 'Of course, Mrs Jago would never have told Mr Bellamy what Grandfather did to her. Until she spoke to my mother last week, she'd kept it secret from everyone except her husband. But Grandfather couldn't be sure of that.'

They hauled their rucksacks onto their backs and started up the hill again. Patrick said, 'Bellamy was a bit sloppy in some ways. He should have spent more time talking to the servants. Bain waved a shotgun at him, which scared him off – though he did manage to work out that Bain was probably the person who had tried to scare your mother out of the gatehouse. I assume Bain had kept a key and he used it every now and then to nip in and make the odd noise in the night. But Bellamy hardly bothered talking to the maid, Phemie – he wrote her off as being of limited intelligence, of little use to him. Yet Phemie knew – Phemie was the one person, apart from Mrs Jago, of course, who knew that both Frazer and Maxwell had gone to the hunting lodge that day, and that only Frazer had returned.'

'Why didn't she say anything?'

'She was protecting Frazer. She was a loyal servant. Actually, I think that she loved him. Remember how lovingly she looked after Frazer's room and clothes, after he'd gone.' Patrick looked ahead. 'Is that really the summit, or is my heart going to sink again when I discover another slope behind it?'

'It's really the summit.'

One last steep climb – his limp wasn't bad at all, she thought. She heard him say, 'Your father's novel – the report referred to it several times. Have you any idea what happened to it?'

'I asked Mum about it. She'd kept it all these years. She showed it to me last night. It's a bit singed round the edges – she tried to burn it once, and then she changed her mind.'

'Are you going to read it?'

She nodded. 'I've already started. It's as though I'm hearing his voice.' She paused, then she said hesitantly, 'There was something else in the report, something rather marvellous. Mr Bellamy interviewed a girl called Jenny Watts, who was a friend of my father's. She told him that my father was looking forward to the birth of his baby – that he was looking forward to *me*.'

He smiled at her. 'Well, of course he was. How could he do otherwise?'

He took her hand as they climbed the last few yards. On the summit, she beamed at him. 'Congratulations. You've made it, Patrick.'

They looked out to where the mountains rose like waves, one behind the other, green and grey and misty blue. She said, 'I suppose there's nothing to keep you here now. I suppose you'll go back to Glasgow.'

'Soon.'

'Your family and friends must have missed you. Your girlfriend . . .' Her glance slid to him.

He shook his head. 'No girlfriend. Not at the moment. And you, Morven? Will you go back to London?'

'I don't know. Perhaps.'

'What about your job?'

She shook her head. 'They've taken on someone else. And selling perfume to rich old ladies isn't really what I want to do with my life.'

'What do you want to do, then?'

'I don't know. I've never had the chance to find out. Something that's fun and interesting and exciting.'

'Does it have to be in London?'

'Not necessarily. I went to London because it was far away from home. I felt free there. But with Mum marrying Raymond, I can go anywhere now.'

A flicker of delight as she said it: *I can go anywhere now.* Then she told him, 'I had a letter from Mrs Jago yesterday. She offered to leave me Ravenhart House.' She shrugged. 'I thought about it, but in the end I said no. It would be too much of a tie, too much of a burden. I don't want that any more. All those secrets . . .' She looked up at him. 'I'm afraid we've burdened you with our secrets, Patrick. My father . . .'

His eyes met hers. 'Oh, I'm good at keeping secrets. You don't need to worry about me.'

'Mum and I talked about it. If the truth about what happened to my father ever does come out, then we'll say that Frazer acted alone. The only person who can contradict that — apart from Mrs Jago herself, of course — is Adam, and he's hardly likely to want to talk to the police. When you think what Grandfather did to Mrs Jago . . .' Her voice faded away. Then she took a deep breath and said, 'Anyway, she's going to sell the estate.'

'So, what now?'

She smiled. 'Now we go downhill, I'm afraid, Patrick.'

His hands rested on her waist. 'In a minute. There's a few things I wanted to say to you.'

A rush of excitement; something sang in the air.

'Do you like Glasgow?'

She couldn't stop smiling. 'Glasgow's not bad. But what would I do there, Patrick?'

'You could work for me. The business is growing – I could teach you the ropes. What do you think?'

'Sounds fantastic.'

He ran a fingertip gently down the side of her face. 'So long as you don't think there'd be a conflict of interests.' He drew her to him with a jangle of zips, a rustle of nylon anorak. His mouth brushed against hers. 'We'd have to get that straight from the start.'

Postscript – three months later

At Heathrow Airport, waiting for her flight, Bess remembered the last time she had undertaken this journey. The sea voyage across the Indian Ocean, through the Red Sea and the Suez Canal, into the Mediterranean. The intense heat of Port Said and the cooler air as they sailed through the Straits of Gibraltar and around the coast of Spain. Docking in Southampton, and the train journey to London and the cab ride to her father's hotel. She remembered how she had peered out of the window of the cab, straining to see through the mist, straining to see the country that would be her home for almost fifty years.

The voyage had taken weeks. This time, she would reach Calcutta late the following day, flying via Cairo and Karachi. Eleanor would meet her at the airport, and she would stay at Eleanor's house for a few days while she recovered from the journey. Then, Eleanor had planned to take three weeks' holiday so that they could tour the country together.

Her flight was called; she picked up her case. Queueing to have her ticket checked, she felt a rush of excitement.

She walked out of the terminal building. She could already feel the soft air of India, and smell the heat and the spices. It would be, she thought, like going home.

She crossed the tarmac to the plane.